SILENT VOWS

A DARK, MAFIA ROMANCE

BONDS OF BETRAYAL

AJME WILLIAMS

Copyright © 2025 by Ajme Williams

All rights reserved.

No part of this book may be reproduced in any form or by any electronic or mechanical means, including information storage and retrieval systems, without written permission from the author, except for the use of brief quotations in a book review.

This is a work of fiction. Names, characters, businesses, places, events and incidents are either the products of authors imagination or used in a fictitious manner. Any resemblance to actual persons, living or dead, or actual events is purely coincidental. The following story contains mature themes, strong language and sexual situations. It is intended for mature readers only.

All characters are 18+ years of age and all sexual acts are consensual.

ABOUT THE AUTHOR

Ajme Williams writes emotional, angsty contemporary romance. All her books can be enjoyed as full length, standalone romances and are FREE to read in Kindle Unlimited.

Bonds of Betrayal (this series)
Silent Vows | Forbidden Vengeance

Mafia Lords of Sin
Tangled Loyalties | Savage Devotion | Bulletproof Baby | Cursed Confessions | Borrowed Bride

Dynasty of Deception
Merciless King | Ice Princess | Lost Prince | Stolen Queen | Triplets for the Mafia Prince | The Godfather's Christmas Twins

Shadows of Redemption
Soldier of Death | Queen of Misfortune | Prince of Darkness | Angel of Mercy

The Why Choose Haremland
Protecting Their Princess | Protecting Her Secret | Unwrapping their Christmas Present | Cupid Strikes... 3 Times | Their Easter Bunny | SEAL Daddies Next Door | Naughty Lessons | See Me After Class | Blurred Lines | Nanny for the Firefighters | Snowy Secrets

High Stakes
Bet On It | A Friendly Wager | Triple or Nothing | Press Your Luck

Heart of Hope
Our Last Chance | An Irish Affair | So Wrong | Imperfect Love | Eight Long Years | Friends to Lovers | The One and Only | Best Friend's Brother | Maybe It's Fate | Gone Too Far | Christmas with Brother's Best Friend | Fighting for US | Against All Odds | Hoping to Score | Thankful for Us | The Vegas Bluff | 365 Days | Meant to Be | Mile High

Baby | Silver Fox's Secret Baby | Snowed In with Best Friend's Dad | Secret Triplets for Christmas | Off-Limits Daddy

Billionaire Secrets
Twin Secrets | Just A Sham | Let's Start Over | The Baby Contract | Too Complicated

Dominant Bosses
His Rules | His Desires | His Needs | His Punishments | His Secret

Strong Brothers
Say Yes to Love | Giving In to Love | Wrong to Love You | Hate to Love You

Fake Marriage
Accidental Love | Accidental Baby | Accidental Affair | Accidental Meeting

Irresistible Billionaires
Admit You Miss Me | Admit You Love Me | Admit You Want Me | Admit You Need Me

Check out Ajme's full Amazon catalogue here.

Join her VIP NL here.

DESCRIPTION

FORCED TO WED: A grieving mafia princess trapped in a deadly alliance...with the one man she swore she could never have.

She's my best friend's daughter.
Barely twenty-two.
Sacred. Forbidden. *Mine.*

She never dreamed she'd wear my ring, share my name, warm my bed...
But with her father's blood still fresh on the streets and vultures circling, I'm the devil she knows.

What began as duty ignites into an obsession I can't control.

Because when I look at Bella now, I don't see Giovanni's innocent little girl.
I see the woman who could bring me to my knees.

As she claws her way to power at my side, I'm losing the battle to resist her.

The walls I built from my first wife's betrayal are falling,
And the secrets in my past could get us both killed.

With my baby growing inside her,
And my brother plotting our destruction,
I'll paint this city red.
Because I'll slaughter anyone who tries to take what's mine.

"You were never just a duty, Bella. You were always meant to be my salvation."

1

BELLA

I step back from my canvas, tilting my head to study the interplay of shadow and light. The late afternoon sun streams through the tall industrial windows of Columbia's art studio, catching the paint flecks on my hands and turning them into constellations against my skin. My thesis exhibition piece is finally starting to speak—a moody interpretation of the New York skyline that Professor Martinez says shows promise, but needs more emotion, more raw truth beneath the surface.

Paint-splattered easels crowd the space around me, their wooden frames worn smooth by generations of aspiring artists. The scent of linseed oil and turpentine hangs heavy in the air, mingling with the earthy smell of clay from the sculpture studio next door.

This is my sanctuary, the one place where I can truly be myself—or at least, the self I want to be.

I study my canvas critically. The skyline emerges from a background of deep blues and purples, the buildings more suggestion than reality. There's something missing, though. Some truth I'm not quite brave enough to paint. The shadows need to be darker, more threatening.

Like the ones that have always lurked at the edges of my world, no matter how hard I try to paint them away.

"You need to push harder," Professor Martinez had said during our last critique. "Find the emotion you're afraid to show."

I almost laughed. How do you explain that your father is one of New York's most feared Mafia dons? That the careful, controlled life I've built—art student by day, dutiful daughter by night—is just another kind of canvas, one where I paint myself normal? That maybe the reason I'm drawn to cityscapes is because they let me control the chaos, decide which shadows to highlight and which to hide?

My phone buzzes again—the third time in ten minutes. I ignore it, focusing instead on mixing the perfect shade of midnight blue. The color reminds me of my father's study late at night, when the deals are made that we never talk about over breakfast.

The phone starts ringing again. The sound echoes through the empty studio, making me jump. A drop of blue paint splatters onto my white sneaker as I glance at the screen. My mother's name flashes urgently, and something in my gut twists. She never calls this many times unless ...

"Bella?" Her voice is shrill, stripped of its usual affected sophistication. "Where have you been? I've been trying to reach you for—"

"I'm working on my thesis piece," I cut in, already annoyed. God, Mom knows how to get under my skin so easily. "You know how important—"

"It's your father." The words slice through my irritation. "There's been ... there's been an accident. You need to come to Mount Sinai right now."

The paintbrush slips from my fingers, clattering to the floor. "What kind of accident?"

"Just come. Quickly." She hangs up before I can ask more questions.

My hands shake as I shove supplies into my bag, not bothering to clean up properly. Paint water spills across the table, turquoise blue bleeding into crimson red. I should clean it up—good materials aren't cheap on a student budget—but I can't bring myself to care.

All I can think about is my father—Giovanni Russo, the man who's always been invincible in my eyes, even though I know what he does for a living.

What our whole family is involved in.

The taxi ride to the hospital is twenty minutes of pure torture. Every red light feels like an eternity as my mind spins through possibilities. I've spent my life pretending the whispered conversations and late-night meetings were normal business dealings, but I know better. Maybe it was a rival family. Maybe someone finally decided to make a move. Maybe—

I throw money at the driver and practically run through the emergency room doors. The antiseptic smell hits me first, then the fluorescent lights that make everything look sickly and unreal. The waiting room is a patchwork of misery—worried families huddled in uncomfortable chairs, nurses rushing past with purposeful strides, the quiet beeping of machines that means someone somewhere is still alive.

I spot them immediately—my uncle Carmine, speaking in hushed tones with Matteo DeLuca, my father's best friend and one of the most dangerous men in New York. Carmine looks out of place in his expensive Italian suit, his balding head shining under the harsh lights. But it's Matteo who commands attention.

At thirty-eight, he cuts an imposing figure in his perfectly tailored black suit, his broad shoulders tense as he nods at whatever Carmine is saying. Silver threads at his temples only add to his authority. When he turns and sees me, his steel-blue eyes lock onto mine with an intensity that makes my breath catch. I've always felt like prey when he looks at me like that, even though he's supposedly on our side.

"Isabella," he says, my full name rolling off his tongue like a prayer or a curse—I'm never quite sure which with him. There's something in his eyes, something heavy and significant that makes my heart stutter.

Before he can say more, my mother appears, mascara streaking down her carefully made-up face. At forty-five, Cher Russo is still stunning, all sleek blonde hair and elegant bones. But now her perfect facade is cracking, her designer dress wrinkled as if she's been hugging herself.

"He's gone, *bella mia*." She pulls me into an embrace that smells of Chanel No. 5 and despair. "Your father ... he didn't make it."

The world tilts sideways. I feel strong hands steady me—Matteo's —but I jerk away from his touch. Through the roaring in my ears, I catch fragments of conversation: "shooting" ... "rival family" ... "protection needed." My mother is wailing now, a perfect performance of grief that seems more practiced than genuine. Uncle Carmine's eyes gleam with something that looks disturbingly like opportunity.

"We need to discuss arrangements," Carmine is saying, but Matteo cuts him off with a sharp gesture.

"Not now," he growls, and for a moment, I see why men fear him. His gaze returns to me, softer but no less intense. "Go say goodbye to your father, Isabella. I'll handle everything else."

As I walk numbly toward the hospital room where my father's body lies, I catch snippets of a heated conversation behind me. Matteo's deep voice rumbles, "I made a promise to Giovanni ..."

Followed by Carmine's oily response, "Then you know what needs to be done."

I pause at the doorway, my hand trembling on the handle. Through the small window, I can see the still form under the white sheet, and reality crashes over me. This isn't one of my paintings where I can control the shadows, where I can choose what to reveal and what to hide. My father is dead. My carefully constructed world of art school and normal life has just shattered.

Inside the room, the machines are silent. The sheet covers him completely, but I can still see the strong line of his jaw, the hands that used to lift me onto his shoulders when I was little. The hands that probably killed people. The hands that definitely ordered deaths. But also, the hands that held mine steady the first time he taught me to paint, telling me that art was my escape, my way to be something different than what we are.

My legs give out and I sink into the chair beside his bed. Just yesterday morning, he was at the breakfast table, drinking his espresso and reading the paper like always. He asked about my thesis exhibition, his dark eyes crinkling at the corners when he smiled. "Show them who you really are, *bella mia*," he said, squeezing my hand. "Art is the purest truth we have."

Was he trying to tell me goodbye? Did he know something was coming?

I reach for his hand under the sheet but stop myself. I don't want to feel the coldness, I don't want that to be my last memory of him. Instead, I remember him warm and alive—teaching me to mix colors when I was five, steadying me on my first bicycle, wiping away tears after my first heartbreak. Always strong. Always there.

"Papa," I whisper, my voice breaking. "Papa, *please*."

The grief hits me like a physical blow, and suddenly I can't breathe. My chest feels too tight, each breath a struggle. The fluorescent lights are too bright, too harsh, turning everything into a grotesque still life—the white sheet, the gray walls, the chrome railings of the hospital bed. My artist's eye tries to break it down into shapes and shadows, a futile attempt to make sense of the senseless.

A sob tears from my throat, raw and primal. I press my fist against my mouth to stifle it, but it's like trying to hold back the ocean. Years of careful control shatter as the tears come, hot and endless. I cry for the father I knew—the one who sat through every school art show, who taught me to see beauty in shadows.

And I cry for the father I didn't know—the one who ruled New York's underworld, who had enemies dangerous enough to put him here.

Memories flood back, taking on new meaning. The way he always checked the cars before we got in them. The armed men who followed us at a discrete distance when we went shopping. The nights he came home late, tension lined in his shoulders, but he always stopped to kiss my forehead and ask about my latest painting.

He tried so hard to give me a normal life, to let me live in the light while he handled the darkness. But the darkness found us anyway.

"I should have listened more," I whisper, gripping the edge of his bed until my knuckles turn white. "Should have let you teach me about your world instead of hiding in mine. Should have told you I loved you this morning instead of rushing off to the studio."

My tears fall onto the white sheet, creating small dark circles. Like paint on canvas, I think hysterically. Like the drops of midnight blue that fell on my sneaker just an hour ago when my whole world was still intact.

"I'm so sorry, Papa," I whisper. "I should have been here. I should have ..."

But I don't know how to finish that sentence. Should have *what*? Accepted the world he tried to protect me from? Paid more attention to the danger instead of hiding in my art?

The door opens behind me, and I know without turning that it's Matteo. His presence fills the room like smoke, dangerous and impossible to ignore. I try to wipe away my tears, to rebuild my composure, but it's like trying to rebuild a sandcastle after the tide has already come in.

"Your father would want you to be strong now," he says quietly.

A hollow laugh escapes me. "Strong? I'm an art student. I paint pretty pictures. I'm not ... I was never ..." The words tangle in my throat.

"You're Giovanni Russo's daughter," Matteo says, his voice gentle but firm. "You're stronger than you know."

I don't know if I believe him. Instead, I look at my father's body one last time, trying to burn every detail into my memory. The proud line of his nose beneath the sheet. The way his presence fills the room even in death. The last time I painted him, it was a Father's Day gift—a portrait of him in his study, reading glasses perched on his nose, warm lamplight softening his features. I made him look kind, approachable.

Now I wonder if I ever really saw him at all.

His voice echoes in my head: *Remember who you are, bella mia. You're an artist, yes, but you're also my daughter. And in our world, that means something whether you want it to or not.*

"Come," Matteo says gently, and this time when his hand touches my shoulder, I don't pull away. "There are things we need to discuss."

I press a kiss to my father's sheet-covered forehead, my tears falling freely now. "*Ti amo*, Papa," I whisper. "*Perdonami.*" I love you. Forgive me.

As I follow him out of the room, I can feel the weight of eyes on us—Carmine's calculating gaze, my mother's tearful stare, and the curious glances of the hospital staff who probably think we're just another grieving family. If only they knew what was really happening.

If only I knew.

But one thing is becoming terrifyingly clear—the safe, separate life I've built for myself was always just an illusion. A pretty picture I painted to hide the truth. And now that illusion is shattering, leaving me with nothing but shadows and the weight of all the things my father never told me. All the things I was too afraid to learn.

My heart feels like a canvas slashed to pieces, and I don't know how to repair it. All I know is that my father's world is coming for me, whether I'm ready or not.

2

MATTEO

The scotch burns going down, but I welcome the pain. Twenty-four hours since Giovanni's death, and the weight of unspoken promises sits heavy on my shoulders like a burial shroud. From behind my mahogany desk, I stare at the Manhattan skyline through bulletproof glass, watching my city glitter like broken glass in the darkness.

The crystal tumbler in my hand is my third of the night—or maybe my fourth. I've lost count, though I never lose control.

Control. It's what separates men like me from common thugs. It's what's kept me alive for fifteen years as the head of this business, what's built the DeLuca empire into what it is today. But watching my best friend die in that hospital bed, seeing the light fade from his eyes while I could do nothing ... well, some things you can't control.

The ice in my glass clinks as my hand tightens. I shouldn't have let him go alone to that meeting. I knew something was wrong—the way he insisted on meeting the fucking Calabreses without backup, how he'd been making arrangements these past few weeks. Like he knew what was coming.

"Another report, Boss." Antonio materializes from the shadows of my office, silent as always. My most trusted captain places a manila folder on the desk, his lined face grim. "Surveillance footage confirms it was the Calabrese family."

My jaw clenches until I taste copper. I'd warned Gio about this three fucking weeks ago, laid out the intelligence showing the Calabreses were making moves. But he'd been stubborn, convinced he could handle them alone. "I've dealt with their kind before," he'd said, waving away my concerns.

Now he's dead, and his daughter ...

Christ. Isabella.

The image of her in the hospital haunts me—all wild dark hair and devastated hazel eyes, looking so much like her mother had twenty-plus years ago, before Cher turned into the society-obsessed harpy she is now.

But where Cher's beauty was always calculated, Isabella's hits like a punch to the gut. Raw. Real. Dangerous in a way she doesn't even understand.

"What's our exposure?" My voice is granite, betraying none of the turmoil beneath. A lifetime of practice makes it easy to hide the way my hands want to shake, the way grief and rage war in my chest.

"They're making moves on all the Russo territory. Without Giovanni ..." Antonio hesitates, choosing his words carefully. "Carmine's already fielding offers for alliances. Some families think the Russos are vulnerable now."

"They are." I stand, walking to the window. My reflection stares back at me—at thirty-eight, I'm in my prime, silver threading through my dark hair at the temples only adding to my authority. The same authority that had failed to save my best friend. "And Isabella's safety?"

The slight shift in Antonio's stance tells me everything before he opens his mouth. "There's been chatter." He clears his throat. "Johnny Calabrese ... he's been asking questions about her. Some say he plans to force a marriage, secure the Russo assets that way."

The crystal tumbler shatters in my grip, shards embedding in my palm. Blood drips onto my imported carpet, but I barely feel it. The rage I've been suppressing all day roars to life at the thought of

Johnny Calabrese anywhere near Isabella. The man is a sadist, known for breaking his toys—two dead wives in five years, both ruled "accidents."

A marriage to him would be Isabella's death sentence.

My phone buzzes. A text from Carmine.

We need to discuss Isabella's future. The vultures are circling.

Blood trickles down my wrist as my hand clenches. The last conversation I had with Gio plays in my mind like a film I can't stop watching. We'd been sharing cigars on the terrace of the DeLuca compound just days ago—the kind of quiet moment rare in our violent world. The sweet notes of aged Cuban tobacco had mingled with the autumn air, our glasses of thirty-year-old Macallan catching the setting sun.

Gio had seemed ... calm. Like a man who'd made his peace with what was coming.

"If anything happens to me, Matteo," he'd said, staring into the gathering darkness, "protect her. Isabella ... she's everything good I ever did in this life. Don't let our world destroy that."

"You know I will," I'd promised, not knowing how soon I'd have to make good on those words.

Not knowing how much that promise would cost us both.

Antonio clears his throat, drawing me back to the present. He gestures to my bleeding hand, but I wave him off. Physical pain is easier to deal with than the weight of failure crushing my chest.

A soft knock interrupts my dark thoughts. "Mr. DeLuca?" My assistant peers in, her professional mask slipping slightly at the sight of the blood. "The funeral home is ready for you to review the arrangements. And ... Miss Russo is here."

My head snaps up. "Isabella?" Her name tastes different on my tongue now—heavier, more significant. "Send her in."

I quickly wrap a handkerchief around my bleeding hand, straightening my tie as the door opens. The moment Isabella steps in, the air changes. My carefully constructed world of dark woods, leather, and power shifts on its axis.

The fluorescent lights from the hallway illuminate her for a moment in the doorway, and Christ help me, she takes my breath away.

She's traded her paint-splattered clothes for a simple black dress that makes her pale skin glow like porcelain in the dim light of my office. Her dark hair falls in waves past her shoulders—so like Gio's in color but with her mother's wild curl. Everything about her is a study in contradictions: the artistic soul subdued by mourning, the girl becoming a woman before my eyes, the innocence wrapped in unconscious sensuality that makes my blood burn with shame.

I've watched her grow up, keeping my distance, protecting her from our world without letting her know she needed protection. But somehow that little girl with scraped knees and paint-stained fingers has become this woman who makes my heart race like I'm some goddamn teenager instead of the most feared man in New York.

She looks lost in my massive office, like a dove that's wandered into a hawk's nest. The space around her is all dark wood and leather, weapons disguised as decoration, power masquerading as taste.

There's only one photo in the room—a group shot of the DeLuca men. My father, Giuseppe DeLuca stands central, imperious, one hand on my shoulder. God, I couldn't have been more than fourteen there. I keep the frame turned slightly away from my desk, but I notice her artist's eye cataloging it along with everything else.

I wonder what she sees—the calculating display of wealth and influence, or the emptiness beneath it all? Does she notice how my father's hand on my shoulder looks less like pride and more like possession?

There's steel in her spine as she meets my gaze, and for a moment, I see Gio in the set of her jaw, the quiet strength she probably doesn't even know she possesses. It makes my chest ache with something dangerously close to tenderness. Her hazel eyes, though red-rimmed from crying, still flash with that inner fire that draws me like a moth to flame.

"Mr. DeLuca," she says formally, my body betraying me as she moves closer—heart pounding, muscles tensing like I'm bracing for a fight. But the only battle here is with myself.

She perches on the edge of one of my leather chairs, her posture perfect thanks to years of her mother's training. The dress rides up slightly, and she tugs it down revealing a small artist's callus on her thumb where she holds her brushes. Such a delicate thing, that small imperfection.

Such a dangerous thing, how much I notice it.

"My mother said you're handling the funeral arrangements." Her voice is husky from crying, and it does things to me that will surely damn my soul. Gio would kill me if he could see inside my head right now.

"Your father would have wanted—" I begin, but she cuts me off.

"My father would have wanted to see me graduate in the spring." Her voice cracks slightly, and the sound hits me harder than any bullet ever has. "He would have wanted to walk me down the aisle someday. He would have wanted to grow old and spoil his grandchildren. But what he wanted doesn't matter anymore, does it?"

The accusation in her tone is a blade between my ribs. She's right —I failed to protect her father. My best friend died because I wasn't fast enough, wasn't smart enough, didn't see the betrayal coming until it was too late.

But I won't fail to protect her. Even if it means making her hate me.

Looking at her now, I see flashes of the past like photographs: her sixth birthday party, where she showed everyone her first "real" painting; her high school graduation, where I watched from the back row because Giovanni thought my presence would draw too much attention; last month's art show that I attended in secret, proud of her talent even as I worried about her vulnerability in our world.

The sun has fully set now, casting my office in shadows. A strand of her hair falls across her face, and my hands itch to brush it back. Instead, I clench my fist, letting the pain from the glass cuts ground me. I'm almost twice her age. Her father's best friend.

The man about to destroy her carefully constructed world of art and innocence.

My phone buzzes again. Another message from Carmine.

Johnny Calabrese is making his move tonight. Time's up.

The rage that fills me at the thought of Johnny touching her surprises even me with its intensity. I've killed men for less than the thoughts I know he's having about her. The protectiveness I feel goes far beyond my promise to Gio, and that's another sin to add to my growing list.

She's almost half my age. My best friend's daughter. The one pure thing in our corrupt world.

I look at Isabella, *really* look at her. So young and fierce and unknowing of the dangers closing in around her. Paint still stains her fingers—midnight blue, like the bruises that will mark her skin if Johnny gets his hands on her. She has no idea what men like him do to beautiful things, no concept of the violence waiting to swallow her whole.

But God help me, I can't stop my treacherous mind from noticing how she's changed. The slight tattoo peeking out from her shoulder —when did she get that? The way she tucks her hair behind her ear when she's nervous, exposing the graceful line of her neck. The shadow of her lashes against her cheeks when she looks down, trying to hide her tears.

I've spent years protecting her from afar, making sure she never knew how many threats I eliminated before they got near her. Like her father, I wanted to preserve her innocence, her ability to create beauty in a world full of ugliness.

She shifts in her seat, and a hint of jasmine reaches me—her signature scent, the one she's worn since she was eighteen. I remember when she first started wearing it, how it softened her edges and highlighted her transition from girl to woman. How it made me start seeing her differently, much as I tried not to.

In that moment, I make my decision. I think of my promise to Gio, of Johnny Calabrese's sadistic reputation, of the vultures circling the Russo empire.

I'm about to change everything for her. About to drag her from her world of light and color into my shadows. The thought makes me sick, but not as sick as the alternative.

Isabella might hate me for what I'm about to do, but she'll be alive to hate me.

Better she hate me than end up another one of Johnny's broken women.

"Sit down, Isabella," I say softly, my tone making it clear it's not a request as I sit down at my desk. "There's something we need to discuss about your father's last wishes."

The sun has fully set now, casting my office in shadows. In the darkness, I can almost pretend I don't see the fear that flickers across her face, the way her hands tremble slightly as she takes the seat across from me. I've spent years protecting her from our world, just as Gio wanted. But now, to keep her safe, I'll have to drag her right into the heart of it.

God forgive me for what I'm about to do.

3

BELLA

The words echo in my head like a death knell: "Your father arranged our marriage before his death."

I stare at Matteo across his massive desk, waiting for the punchline, for any sign that this is some twisted joke. The Manhattan skyline behind him blurs as tears threaten to fall, but I refuse to cry. Not here. Not in front of him. Not in this office that screams old money and violence, with its dark woods and subtle hints of weapons displayed as art.

My stomach churns. Less than forty-eight hours ago, I was in my studio mixing colors for my thesis piece. Now I'm here, being told I have to marry my father's best friend. Matteo DeLuca. The boogeyman of New York's underworld.

"That's impossible," I manage, proud that my voice doesn't shake. "My father would never—"

"Your father," Matteo interrupts, his deep voice gentle but firm, "knew exactly what would happen if he died. The vultures are already circling, Isabella. Without protection, you'll be forced to marry someone far worse than me."

A hysterical laugh bubbles up in my throat. Memories flash through my mind—Matteo at family dinners when I was young, his presence always making the room feel darker, more dangerous. The way other men would go quiet when he entered a room. The whispers about what he did to the last family that crossed him.

"Worse than you?" The words come out sharp as broken glass. "You're my father's best friend. You're sixteen years older than me. You're—" I cut myself off, but we both know what I was about to say.

You're a killer.

My fingers twitch for a paintbrush, for the comfort of canvas and color. Art has always been my escape from this world—the violence, the power plays, the constant undercurrent of threat. In my studio, I could pretend to be normal. Could paint beauty instead of darkness.

Now even that's being taken from me.

Matteo rises from his chair, and I fight the urge to step back. Even in my heels, he towers over me. He moves around the desk with a predator's grace, stopping close enough that I can smell his expensive cologne mixed with the lingering scent of scotch. My heart pounds traitorously. I've always been aware of him, even when I didn't want to be. Even when I was painting, I would sometimes catch myself thinking about the way he moved, the intensity in his eyes, the—

No. I shut that thought down hard. This is insane. This is *wrong*.

"I'm also the only one who can keep you alive," he says quietly. "Johnny Calabrese has already put in a bid for your hand. Do you know what he does to his wives, Isabella?"

The blood drains from my face. Everyone in this world knows about Johnny Calabrese's last wife, who "accidentally" fell down a flight of stairs. And the one before that, who "tragically" overdosed. I've seen him at family functions, the way he looks at women like they're toys to be broken.

"This is insane," I whisper, more to myself than to him. "I'm supposed to be preparing for my thesis exhibition. I'm supposed to be graduating in the spring. I'm supposed to—"

"You're supposed to be alive," Matteo cuts in, his voice hardening. "Everything else is secondary."

A knock at the door makes me jump. Carmine enters without waiting for permission, his oily smile making my skin crawl. My uncle has always watched me with calculating eyes, waiting for his chance. I see it clearly now—with my father dead and me married off, who else could take over the Russo family but him?

"Ah, good. You must be telling her about the arrangements."

"Get out," Matteo growls, and something in his tone makes even Carmine take a step back.

"Of course, of course. But remember, we need an answer tonight. The Calabrese family won't wait forever." The door clicks shut behind him.

I want to scream. Carmine has always resented me, I realize. The artist daughter who should have been a son. Who should have wanted to take over the family business. He can have it all—the territory, the power, the blood money. I never wanted any of it. I wanted galleries and paint-stained fingers and a normal life where I didn't have to watch every shadow.

I wrap my arms around myself, suddenly cold despite the warmth of the office. My entire world is imploding, again, and I can't seem to catch my breath. Matteo watches me with those intense eyes that have always seen too much. Even when I was younger, trying so hard to avoid this world, I was aware of his gaze.

The way he would watch me at functions, how he always seemed to know where I was, what I was doing.

I used to think it was just him being a friend to my father. But there were moments, especially in the last few years, when I caught him looking at me differently. Like now, with that mix of guilt and hunger that makes my stomach flip.

"When?" I manage to ask, hating how breathless I sound.

"Three days," Matteo answers. "After the funeral. It needs to be done quickly to ensure your safety and maintain control of the territory."

"Territory?" My voice rises. "Is that all this is about? Real estate and power?"

Something flashes in his eyes—pain, maybe, or guilt—but it's gone so quickly I might have imagined it. I've spent years studying his expressions, though I'd never admit it. The slight tightening around his eyes when he's angry, the barely perceptible softening of his mouth when he's pleased.

"This is about keeping a promise to your father," he corrects. "About protecting you."

"By forcing me to marry you?" The tears I've been holding back finally spill over. "Some protection."

Matteo reaches out, his hand hovering near my face as if to wipe away my tears, but I jerk back. The gesture is too intimate, too close to the dreams I've guiltily pushed away. Dreams where those hands, capable of such violence, touch me with surprising gentleness. Dreams I hate myself for having.

He lets his hand fall, and for a moment, I see something like regret cross his features. "The choice is yours, Isabella," he says quietly. "But understand this—if you refuse, I won't be able to stop what comes next. Johnny Calabrese will claim you, and your father's empire will fall into the hands of the man who ordered his death."

The accusation hangs in the air between us. My legs give out, and I sink into the leather chair behind me. "The Calabrese family ... they killed my father?"

Matteo's silence is answer enough. I close my eyes, remembering my father's laugh, his proud smile when he visited my art studio last month, his promise to be at my graduation. All of it gone, because of this world I've tried so hard to escape.

And now here I am, being offered a choice that's not really a choice at all. Marry Matteo DeLuca—the man who both terrifies and fascinates me, who I've spent years trying not to think about, trying not to notice how he fills a room with his presence. The man who makes me feel like prey and protected all at once. The man who's sixteen years my senior and was my father's best friend.

Or marry Johnny Calabrese and end up another tragic accident.

My artist's mind betrays me, sketching out the contrasts. Matteo's controlled power versus Johnny's sadistic impulses. The way Matteo's eyes follow me with that mixture of guilt and want, versus the way Johnny looks at women like they're toys to be broken. The memories of Matteo always being there, a shadow of protection in my peripheral vision, versus the stories of Johnny's wives and their "accidents."

When I open my eyes again, they're dry. "I want conditions," I say, my voice stronger than I feel. This may be a cage, but I'll be damned if I don't set some of the terms of my imprisonment.

Matteo's dark eyebrow rises slightly, surprise and something like respect flickering across his face. "Name them."

"I finish my degree. I keep my art studio. I maintain my own bank account." I take a deep breath. "And this marriage is in name only. We may have to live together, but we won't ... we won't ..."

"Share a bed?" His voice is low, dangerous. He leans down, bracing his hands on the arms of my chair, caging me in. "Don't make conditions you don't fully understand, little girl. This marriage will be real in every way. Anything less would raise suspicions."

My body betrays me immediately. Heat floods my cheeks and spreads lower, my heart hammering so hard I'm sure he can hear it. This close, his cologne wraps around me—something expensive and masculine that makes my head spin. I can see the flecks of gray in his blue eyes, the slight stubble on his jaw, the tiny scar above his right eyebrow. My artist's eye catalogs these details against my will, already knowing how I would paint him—in oils, all dark colors and sharp edges, danger barely contained by the expensive suit.

Share his bed. The words echo in my mind, bringing unwanted images with them.

No. I feel sick at my own thoughts, disgusted by the way my body responds to his proximity. He's my father's best friend. A killer. The very embodiment of the world I've tried to escape.

And now I'll be his wife. The thought hits me like a physical blow. Everything I've worked for, every dream I've had of a normal life—gone. Instead of gallery openings and art shows, my life will be endless charity galas and family functions. I'll be expected to smile prettily on his arm, to play the perfect Mafia wife like my mother does. The thought of becoming like her—empty eyes behind designer clothes, drowning her misery in pills and cocktails—makes bile rise in my throat.

Will I be forced to give up my art entirely? Will my studio become just another room in his mansion, my paints gathering dust while I learn to navigate the politics of our world? And children ... God, he'll expect children. Heirs to his empire. The idea of bringing innocent lives into this makes me want to scream.

"Do we have a deal?" he asks softly, his breath warm against my face.

I think of my father, of Johnny Calabrese, of the life I wanted versus the life I'm being forced to take. Of my mother, who traded her soul for security and designer dresses. Of Carmine, who will use my marriage to consolidate his power. Of Matteo, who has always been both protection and darkness, safety and danger.

I'll be trapped in a gilded cage, expected to be the perfect wife to one of the most dangerous men in New York. No more late nights in my studio, no more freedom to come and go as I please. Everything will be controlled, monitored, arranged. My entire existence reduced to being an ornament on Matteo DeLuca's arm.

And at night ... at night I'll have to share his bed. My skin prickles with goosebumps at the thought, and I hate myself for the shiver that runs through me. It's not entirely fear, and that terrifies me more than anything. How can my body react this way to someone who represents everything I've tried to run from?

Finally, I meet his gaze squarely.

"Yes," I whisper, and with that single word, seal my fate.

4

MATTEO

The predawn hours find me in my private gym, punishing a heavy bag with precise, brutal strikes. Each hit echoes through the empty space, matching the rhythm of accusations in my head. *Monster. Predator. Betrayer.*

Sweat drips down my bare chest as I work through the rage that's been building since Isabella left my office. Her whispered "yes" haunts me, along with the look of defeat in her eyes—like I'd personally extinguished some vital light within her.

The bag absorbs another series of combinations. Left hook. Right cross. Uppercut. Each impact sends shockwaves through my wrapped hands, but the pain does nothing to quiet my mind. I've spent years protecting her from afar, watching her bloom into an artist, keeping the darkness of our world from touching her innocent soul.

Now I've become the very thing she needs protection from.

The irony would be amusing if it wasn't so fucking tragic.

Blood seeps through the wraps—I've split my knuckles again. Good. Physical pain is easier to handle than the memory of Isabella's face when I told her about the marriage. The way she'd looked at me, like I was something monstrous.

She wasn't wrong.

The gym door opens, and Antonio enters, tablet in hand. At fifty-five, my consigliere moves with the same deadly grace he had when I took over the family fifteen years ago. His silver hair and grandfatherly appearance mask one of the sharpest tactical minds in New York. "Boss, we've got updates."

I deliver one final punch that sends the bag swinging violently on its chain. "Report," I order, unwrapping my hands. The white gauze is stained crimson—a fitting metaphor for what I'm about to do to Isabella's life.

"The Calabrese family isn't happy about the engagement announcement. Johnny's already making threats." Antonio swipes through his tablet. "We've increased security around Miss Russo's apartment and studio. Father Romano has been arranged for both ceremonies—funeral and wedding. And ..." He hesitates.

"What?"

"Miss Russo's mother is at the front gate. She's ... quite insistent about seeing you."

"This fucking early?" I curse in Italian. Of course Cher would show up now, probably to negotiate her cut of this arrangement. "Send her to my office. I'll shower first."

Thirty minutes later, I'm dressed in one of my signature black suits, my hair still damp as I enter my office to find Cher Russo pacing the floor in designer heels. At forty-five, she's still stunning—all sleek blonde hair and elegant bones.

But where Isabella's beauty is natural, unconscious, her mother's is a weapon, carefully honed and deployed. They share the same pale skin and delicate features, but there's a hardness to Cher that Isabella hasn't developed. Yet.

"How dare you?" she hisses, whirling to face me, her face the perfect mask of motherly rage. "My husband isn't even cold in his grave, and you're forcing my daughter into marriage?"

"Sit down, Cher," I say coldly, already sick of her shit. "We both know you're not here out of maternal concern."

The mask immediately drops as she takes a seat, crossing her legs elegantly. Even in mourning, she's perfectly coiffed, not a platinum hair out of place. Her black Chanel dress probably cost more than most people make in a month. "Fine. Let's discuss numbers."

"Your monthly allowance will continue. Isabella's trust fund remains untouched." I sit behind my desk, already tired of this conversation. "That's nonnegotiable."

"And my position in society?"

What a piece of fucking work she is. Instead of being concerned about her daughter's well-being, she's more focused on whether she will be invited to the next society ball.

"Will be secured by your daughter's marriage to me." My tone turns dangerous. "But understand this, Cher—if you do anything to upset Isabella during this transition, both your allowance and your social standing will disappear. Permanently."

The threat isn't lost on her. She stands, smoothing her designer dress. Her eyes drift to the turned photo on my desk, and her lips curve into a knowing smile.

"Your father Giuseppe always knew how to handle delicate situations," she says with calculated casualness. "Especially involving young girls."

Something dark flashes across my face before I can hide it. "My father isn't relevant to this conversation."

"No?" Cher's smile widens. "He was so ... *invested* in your marriage to Sophia." A pause. "Just remember, Matteo—she's not Sophia. Your first wife, may she rest in peace, was such a perfect DeLuca donna. Such a *tragic* loss."

The name hits me like a physical blow. My hand tightens on the desk, the wood creaking under my grip. "Get out."

Once she's gone, I remain at my desk, my hands shaking with the effort not to destroy something. Sophia. Even after ten years, the name is a blade between my ribs. Cher knows exactly what she's doing, invoking her memory now. Trying to provoke me, to make me doubt myself. To make me remember what happens to the women I try to protect.

I force myself to breathe, to push back the memories of blood-stained emeralds and broken promises. Isabella isn't Sophia. She's stronger, fiercer, more alive. But the fear claws at my gut anyway—fear that history will repeat itself, that I'll fail her just as catastrophically.

Needing reassurance, I pull up the security feed on my laptop. Isabella's in her studio, probably seeking refuge in her art. She looks small surrounded by her canvases, but there's determination in every brush stroke as she works on what appears to be a new piece. The colors are darker than her usual palette—all blacks and deep blues, sharp edges where she usually favors soft lines. She's working through her trauma the only way she knows how.

My chest tightens watching her. Even through the grainy security footage, I can see the tension in her shoulders, the way she attacks the canvas like it's personally wronged her. She's wearing one of her oversized painting shirts, dark hair piled messily on top of her head, completely unaware of how beautiful she is.

How vulnerable.

My phone buzzes with a message from Carmine.

Meeting tonight. The other families want assurances about the transition of power.

Another buzz, this one from my head of security.

Johnny Calabrese spotted near Miss Russo's studio building.

Final buzz, from an unknown number.

You can't protect her like you couldn't protect Sophia.

The laptop screen cracks under my grip, spiderwebbing out from where my fingers press too hard. Rage and fear war in my chest, making it hard to breathe. They're coming at us from all sides—the Calabrese family, the other dons, whoever sent that anonymous message.

And Isabella sits in her studio, painting her darkness, completely unaware of how many shadows are gathering around her.

I pick up my phone, forcing my voice to remain steady. "Antonio, send a car for Isabella. Bring her to the compound immediately." A pause, remembering Johnny's proximity to her studio. "And if Johnny Calabrese comes within fifty feet of her, kill him."

My feet carry me to the private safe almost unconsciously. The combination is muscle memory—Sophia's birthday, because I'm a masochist apparently.

Inside, beside stacks of cash and important documents, sits a small velvet box. Even after a decade, I still hesitate before touching it.

The ring had been my grandmother's—a flawless emerald surrounded by diamonds. A symbol of DeLuca power, passed down through generations. I'd given it to Sophia once, watching her eyes light up as I slid it onto her finger. Those same eyes had been empty and lifeless when they found her body, her blood staining the stone a darker shade of green.

I've had it cleaned and reset, but sometimes I swear I can still see the stains. Still feel the sticky warmth of her blood as I cradled her broken body. The emerald gleams up at me now, innocent as a serpent in the garden.

Will it bring the same curse to Isabella's finger?

My office door crashes open, interrupting my dark thoughts. Bianca storms in, my seventeen-year-old daughter radiating fury in designer jeans and a cropped leather jacket. She's so much my daughter it hurts sometimes—the same black hair, the same blue-gray eyes, the same inability to hide her emotions.

"Tell me it's not true," she demands, her voice cracking. "Tell me you're not marrying Bella *Russo*."

"Bianca—"

"She's barely older than me!" The hurt in her voice is like knives in my gut. "What is she—twenty-two? Are you serious right now? You bitched me out for talking to a college freshman at Juliana's party, but you can marry one?"

"That's different—"

"How?" She paces the office like a caged animal. "How is it different? Because it's about power? Because you need to control the Russo territory now that Giovanni's dead?"

"Watch your tone." My warning comes out sharper than intended as my temper frays. "You don't understand the complexities of—"

"Oh, I understand perfectly." Her laugh is bitter, cutting. "I understand that less than two days after her father dies, you're forcing some girl nearly my age to marry you. Real classy, Dad. Really living up to the DeLuca name there."

"This isn't about—"

"Does she know about Mom?" The question hits like a bullet and Bianca knows it. Her eyes gleam at the hit. "Does she know what happened to her? Or are you going to keep Bella in the dark like you keep everyone else?"

"Enough!" My voice thunders through the office, making even my fierce daughter step back. The guilt is immediate—I hate using my "don" voice on her. More quietly, I add, "What's done is done. Isabella will be your stepmother, and you will treat her with respect."

"My *stepmother*?" Now she's shouting, all pretense of control gone. "She's only five years older than me, Dad! We are literally part of the same generation! But sure, let's pretend this is normal. Let's pretend you're not just using her like you use everyone else."

"I said that's enough." My voice drops low, dangerous. Bianca is crossing the line and I will not tolerate it. "You have no idea what I've done to keep this family safe. What I'm still doing."

"Family?" Her voice cracks on the word, her eyes flashing with hurt and fury. "Is that what we're calling it? Because from where I'm standing, you're just repeating history. Another young wife, another power play—"

"Your mother made her choices," I cut in, my control hanging by a thread. Speaking of Sophia still feels like swallowing glass, even after all these years. "Isabella's situation is different."

Bianca scoffs, crossing her arms over her chest and glaring at me. "Right. Because this time you're forcing her into it." Her words drip with venom. "At least Mom loved you. I'm not stupid. Bella's probably terrified of you. But I guess that doesn't matter as long as you get your precious territory, right?"

The accusation hits like a physical blow. Because she's right—Isabella is afraid of me. But fear might keep her alive when love couldn't save Sophia.

"This discussion is over." I move around the desk, trying to bridge the distance between us. "I know this is difficult—"

"Difficult?" She backs away from my attempt to touch her shoulder. "You're turning our lives upside down for some girl who has probably never been to our house. Who probably doesn't even know I exist beyond being "Matteo's daughter." And now what—we're supposed to play happy family while the whole city watches?"

"Everything I do is for this family. For you."

"No." Her eyes are pure ice now, so like her mother's it hurts to look at them. "Everything *you* do is for power. For control. And Bella's just your newest victim."

She slams out of the office before I can respond, leaving me alone with the ring box and my demons. The truth in her accusations burns worse than any bullet wound. Because she's right—I am using Isabella. The fact that it's to protect her doesn't make it any less of a manipulation.

Outside my window, storm clouds gather over Manhattan, transforming the morning sun into an apocalyptic gloom. Lightning flickers in the distance, promising violence. The city I've spent my life controlling looks alien now, threatening. Every shadow could hide an enemy. Every glittering window could conceal a sniper's scope. In three days, I'll bury my best friend and marry his daughter, and nothing will ever be the same.

The ring box feels heavy in my hand, weighted with history and blood. The emerald catches what little light remains, throwing green fire across my desk. Sophia wore this ring for years before she died. Now it will grace Isabella's finger—marking her as both protected and condemned.

I think of how young she looked in her studio this morning, paint on her fingers, darkness flowing from her brush. So much talent. So much life. Everything Sophia was, and everything she wasn't. Where Sophia was delicate, Isabella is steel beneath silk. Where Sophia accepted our world, Isabella fights it with every breath. And where Sophia once loved me, Isabella …

Christ. I have no right to think about Isabella that way. No right to notice how her eyes flash when she's angry, how her hands move when she talks about art, how she fills a room with light just by existing. She's Gio's daughter. A responsibility.

But she's also the woman who's haunted my dreams for longer than I care to admit.

Thunder cracks overhead, making the windows rattle in their frames. The storm is almost here. Just like the threats gathering around us—Johnny Calabrese's sadistic interest, Carmine's barely concealed ambition, the other families watching for any sign of weakness. They'll all be at the funeral, paying respects with one hand while holding daggers in the other. Then they'll attend the wedding, watching Isabella walk down the aisle to me, evaluating every detail for signs of coercion or resistance.

The emerald gleams up at me from its velvet nest, and for a moment, I swear I see Sophia's blood staining the stones again. My hands shake as I snap the box closed. I couldn't protect her. Couldn't save her from the consequences of this world, our choices.

Now Isabella will wear the same ring, face the same dangers. Different circumstances, same curse.

"I'll do better this time," I whisper into the growing darkness. The words could be meant for Gio, for Sophia, for Isabella herself. Or maybe they're just another lie I tell myself, like pretending this marriage is purely about protection. Like pretending I don't feel anything when Isabella looks at me with those artist's eyes that see too much.

The rain finally breaks, lashing against the windows like accusations. Three days. Three days until I make Isabella mine in every way that matters. Three days until I bind her to my darkness forever, all in the name of keeping her safe.

God help us both.

I tuck the ring box into my suit pocket, its weight a constant reminder of what's at stake. Out there, the storm rages, and somewhere in my city, my enemies are moving pieces into place.

But let them come. Let them test my resolve, my protection, my claim.

I've already lost one wife to their games. They'll have to kill me before they take another.

My phone buzzes—another message about the funeral arrangements, the wedding preparations, the thousand details that go into binding one life to another. I ignore it, watching lightning split the sky. In the brief illumination, my reflection stares back at me from the window—a man balancing on the knife's edge between duty and desire, protection and possession.

The monster Isabella fears, and the man who would burn the world to keep her safe.

5

BELLA

The canvas before me bleeds red and black, my brush strokes becoming more violent with each passing minute. Paint spatters across my oldest jeans and favorite oversized sweater, but I don't care. I've been in my studio since dawn, trying to lose myself in my art, but even here—in my sanctuary of turpentine smells and natural light—I can't escape reality.

My father's funeral is tomorrow. My wedding—God, my *wedding*—is the day after that.

A wedding. The word makes my hand shake, sending a streak of crimson across the canvas like a wound. This isn't how it was supposed to be. In my dreams, my father would walk me down the aisle of St. Patrick's Cathedral, beaming with pride in his best suit. The pews would overflow with family and friends, sunlight streaming through stained glass to paint the marble floors in rainbow hues. My faceless groom would wait at the altar, love shining in his eyes as I approached in my perfect white dress.

Instead, I'll walk alone. My father lies cold in his casket, and my groom ... my groom will be Matteo DeLuca. The thought makes my stomach turn. He'll stand there in one of his perfectly tailored black suits, those steel-blue eyes watching me with that mixture of guilt and possession that makes my skin prickle. There will be no love, no joy—just power and politics and protection I never asked for.

Tears blur my vision as memories of my father flood back. His proud smile when I got accepted to Columbia's art program. The way he'd sit in my studio for hours, watching me paint, never once suggesting I should follow in his footsteps instead. "You're an artist, *bella mia*," he'd say, his voice warm with pride. "You create beauty in a world that desperately needs it."

God, I loved him. Worshipped him, really. Even knowing what he was—what he did—I never stopped seeing him as my hero. He tried so hard to keep me away from his world, to give me the normal life he never had.

And now here I am, being dragged right into the heart of everything he tried to protect me from.

My phone chimes for the hundredth time. Elena, my best friend, has been texting nonstop since I told her about the arrangement. Just thinking about that conversation makes my chest tight. The shock on her face when I finally admitted what happened to my father ... She'd gone pale but hadn't run away. Instead, she grabbed my hands and started planning our escape.

You can't marry him! her latest text reads. *We can run. I have contacts, we can disappear.*

My hand trembles as I respond. *They'd find us. They always do.*

Elena's been my touchstone of normalcy since freshman year. The one person who just saw me as Bella, the art student who always had paint under her nails, not Isabella Russo, daughter of one of New York's most powerful men. I tried so hard to keep my two worlds separate, to be just another college student. Now those worlds are colliding in the most violent way possible, and I'm terrified Elena will get caught in the crossfire.

I turn back to my painting, studying the dark twisted thing emerging on the canvas. Professor Martinez would be shocked. Gone are my usual cityscapes and subtle shadows, the careful studies of light and form. This piece screams of cage bars and broken wings, of deals made in blood, and promises that feel like chains. Maybe I'll submit it for my thesis—*Arranged Marriage in Oils*. The thought brings a bitter laugh to my lips.

A knock at my studio door makes me jump, paintbrush clattering to the floor. "We're closed," I call out, even though the gallery hasn't been open since my father's death. The brief moment of dark humor evaporates, replaced by immediate tension.

"Miss Russo." The voice belongs to one of Matteo's men—I recognize him from the hospital. "Mr. DeLuca sent a car. You need to come with me now."

"I'm working," I say firmly, though my heart races. Who does Matteo think he is, sending his men to collect me like I'm some package to be delivered? Just because I agreed to this marriage doesn't mean I'm his possession. Not yet, anyway. I bend down to pick up my paintbrush. "Tell Mr. DeLuca—"

"Johnny Calabrese was spotted in the area." The man's voice drops. "Please, Miss. Don't make this difficult."

My blood runs cold at the name. The paintbrush I'd just retrieved slips from my suddenly numb fingers. Through the studio windows, I catch glimpses of black SUVs lining the street.

Matteo's not taking chances with his investment.

"Let me pack my supplies," I manage, proud that my voice remains steady as I quickly text Elena what's happening. My hands shake as I gather my brushes, trying to focus on the familiar motions instead of the panic clawing at my chest.

My phone buzzes again—Elena.

Bella, no! Don't go with them. I'm five minutes away.

My fingers hover over the keys. Sweet, fierce Elena, always ready to fight my battles. But there's nothing normal about this situation, and I won't drag her into danger. Not when I've seen the casual violence my father's world is capable of.

Not when I know what men like Johnny Calabrese do to people who get in their way.

Stay away, I type back, hoping she'll listen. *It's too dangerous, E. I'll explain later. Just trust me.*

I'm shoving brushes into my bag when movement outside catches my eye. A man stands across the street, watching my studio with predatory intent. He's handsome in a cruel way—expensive suit, perfectly styled dark hair, the kind of face that belongs in boardrooms and charity galas. But his dark eyes ... his eyes remind me of a documentary I once saw about great white sharks. Dead. Soulless. Hungry.

Even without ever having met him, I know it's Johnny Calabrese. Our eyes meet through the window, and his smile makes my skin crawl. It's the smile of a man who enjoys breaking beautiful things.

"Miss Russo." Matteo's man sounds urgent now. "We need to go."

I grab my bag, my hands shaking so badly I almost drop it. The guard—a mountain of a man with close-cropped gray hair and scars on his knuckles—leads me through the back exit. More men in black suits materialize, surrounding me like a moving wall. The autumn air hits my face, carrying the scent of exhaust and rain and fear. Every car horn makes me flinch. Every shadow seems to hide a threat.

They hustle me into a waiting SUV, the leather seats cool against my paint-stained jeans. The interior smells new and expensive—leather and that distinct new car smell mixed with subtle hints of gunmetal that make my stomach turn. Just as the door closes, I hear shouting from the street.

"Drive," the guard orders, and the car peels away from the curb.

Through the tinted windows, I see Johnny Calabrese watching our departure, phone pressed to his ear. The casual menace in his stance, the way he tracks our movement ... bile rises in my throat. This is what I would have been condemned to if I hadn't agreed to marry Matteo. This is what my father died trying to protect me from.

"Where are we going?" I ask, though I already know.

"The compound," the guard answers. "Mr. DeLuca's orders."

Of course. The DeLuca compound—my gilded prison for the foreseeable future. I close my eyes, memories washing over me. I haven't been there since I was twelve, back when I still thought my father's world was normal. The sprawling estate had seemed magical then, with its manicured gardens and marble fountains. I'd spend hours sketching the classical statuary, fascinated by the way the Italian gardens created perfect lines of sight.

Now I wonder how many of those sight lines were designed for security rather than beauty.

The car winds through Manhattan traffic, taking a circuitous route that I recognize as a security measure. Past Madison Avenue's gleaming storefronts, through the Upper East Side where old money hides behind historic facades, across the bridge where the city gives way to old estates and older money. Each mile takes me further from my life, from my dreams, from everything I've worked so hard to build.

My phone buzzes one final time before we leave the city proper. It's my mother.

Really, darling? Matteo DeLuca? Well, I suppose you could do worse. At least he's wealthy. We'll need to get you properly dressed—that paint-splattered look won't do for a donna.

Tears sting my eyes and I refuse to answer. My father's not even buried, and she's already planning my society debut as Matteo's wife. But that's Cher Russo for you—always focusing on appearances, on status, on how to climb higher in our world's twisted social hierarchy.

She never understood why I preferred paint-stained jeans to designer dresses, why I chose art studios over charity committees. "You could be so beautiful," she'd sigh, eyeing my messy hair and practical clothes with disappointment. "If you'd just try."

As if beauty was the only currency that mattered. As if I could paint with perfectly manicured nails or create while constrained in Chanel.

I turn off my phone, watching the city fade away through the window. The skyline retreats behind us—my beloved New York with its endless inspiration, its constant pulse of life and creativity, its promise of freedom. In its place, the old money suburbs rise with their stone walls and security gates. Each property we pass is its own fortress, each mansion its own carefully guarded kingdom.

An hour later, the SUV pulls through imposing iron gates marked with the DeLuca family crest. The compound rises before us, and my breath catches despite myself. It's even more impressive than I remembered—a sprawling Italian villa in pale stone, three stories of old-world elegance backed by thoroughly modern security. Roses climb the walls, their last autumn blooms adding splashes of bloodred to the cream-colored stone. Fountains dance in the circular drive, the water catching late afternoon light like scattered diamonds.

It's beautiful. It's terrifying. It's my prison.

As we pull up to the front steps, I see Matteo waiting, his broad shoulders tense under his suit jacket. The sight of him makes my pulse jump traitorously. Even I can't deny his presence—the way he commands attention simply by existing, the dangerous grace in his movements, the intensity in his steel-blue eyes that makes my skin feel too tight.

Behind him stands a girl who can only be his daughter. Bianca DeLuca is stunning in that particular way that comes from both genetics and expensive maintenance—all glossy dark hair, perfect makeup, and designer clothes that probably cost more than the average New Yorker's annual salary. She has Matteo's eyes, and right now they're filled with pure hatred.

"Welcome home," Matteo says as he opens my car door, offering his hand.

I ignore it, stepping out on my own. "This isn't my home."

"It is now." His voice softens slightly, and something in his tone makes heat curl in my stomach. I hate my body's reaction to him, hate that even now, even knowing what's happening, I can't help but respond to his presence. "Johnny made contact?"

"He was watching my studio."

Something dangerous flashes in Matteo's eyes. He turns to one of his men, giving rapid orders in Italian. The language rolls off his tongue like silk over steel, and I force myself to look away, to not notice how his jaw clenches with controlled rage.

When he looks back at me, his expression is unreadable. "We'll get your things from your apartment tomorrow. For now, Maria will show you to your room." He pauses, and my heart stumbles. "Our room."

"I'd rather stay in a guest room," I say quickly, heat flooding my cheeks.

"Not possible." His tone brooks no argument. "Appearances matter, especially now. The other families will be watching for any sign of weakness."

"Heaven forbid you appear weak," Bianca cuts in, her voice dripping with disdain. "I'm sure Bella understands *all* about appearances. Don't you, future stepmother?"

"Bianca." Matteo's warning is clear.

"What? I'm just welcoming my new mom. Should I call you Mama Bella?" Bianca's smile is razor-sharp, cutting me to the bone. She's everything I'm not—polished, perfect, bred for this world of power and violence. My mother will adore her. "Though you might not want to get too comfortable. Dad's wives tend to have ... unfortunate accidents."

Wait, what? What is that supposed to mean?

"Enough!" Matteo's roar echoes off the marble steps. "Bianca, go to your room. *Now*."

The girl tosses her dark hair and stalks inside, leaving me with more questions than answers. Wives? Accidents?

What exactly had Matteo DeLuca done to earn his daughter's hatred?

"Isabella." Matteo's voice draws my attention back. "We need to talk."

Looking up at him—this man who will be my husband in less than forty-eight hours—I feel a chill that has nothing to do with the autumn air. His eyes hold secrets darker than anything I've painted, promises I'm not sure I want to understand.

"Yes," I say quietly. "I believe we do."

A wind stirs the roses, sending their sweet scent mixing with Matteo's cologne. Behind us, the iron gates close with a sound of finality. There's no going back now. My old life, like my father, is dead. All that remains is to discover what kind of woman I'll become in this new one—and whether I'll survive the transformation.

6

MATTEO

I watch Isabella take in my study with an artist's eye, her gaze lingering on details most people miss. The late afternoon sun streaming through bulletproof windows catches the light in her hair, turning ordinary brown to burnished copper. She moves like a dream through my carefully curated space of dark walnut paneling and leather-bound books, touching nothing but seeing everything.

When she stops before the Rembrandt above the fireplace, something in my chest tightens. I acquired "The Storm on the Sea of Galilee" through less than legal means, though its official provenance is impeccable. The painting was stolen from the Gardner Museum decades ago, and it took considerable resources to track it down.

Worth every penny to see the way her eyes light up now, the way her fingers twitch like she wants to touch the canvas.

"It's beautiful," she breathes, and for a moment I forget she's Giovanni's daughter, forget she's barely twenty-two, forget everything except how the sunlight loves her face. "The way he captured the light breaking through the storm clouds ..."

I make a mental note to have Antonio research her favorite artists. I'll fill this house with masterpieces if it helps ease her transition, helps make this cage feel more like home.

She's still wearing paint-stained jeans and a loose sweater that keeps slipping off one shoulder, revealing a small tattoo I hadn't known existed before the other day. It's a delicate thing—what appears to be a compass rose with an artist's paintbrush as the needle. The urge to trace it with my tongue is so strong I have to clench my fists. She looks entirely out of place among the old-world luxury, yet somehow she belongs here more than any of the polished society women who've tried to claim this space.

God knows they've tried. After Sophia, it seemed every family with an eligible daughter suddenly needed my "counsel." They'd arrive in designer dresses and expensive perfume, these carefully crafted dolls with their practiced smiles and calculated moves. Some were subtle, some were obvious, all were ambitious. I sent them away with varying degrees of politeness, depending on how persistent they proved.

But Isabella ... she's different. Real in a way they never were, with paint under her nails and creativity burning in her eyes. She's not trying to be anything except what she is, and that makes her more dangerous than all the society climbers combined.

"Drink?" I offer, moving to the bar cart before I do something stupid like kiss that tattoo.

"I don't—" She stops herself, squaring those delicate shoulders. "Actually, yes. Make it strong."

I pour two fingers of scotch for each of us, noting how her hands shake slightly as she takes the crystal tumbler. She chooses the leather armchair farthest from my desk, curling into it like she's trying to make herself smaller. Paint smudges her cheekbone—green this time—and my fingers itch to wipe it away.

Control. I need to maintain control. But she makes it nearly impossible, perched in my chair like some wild creature accidentally brought indoors. Everything about her calls to something primitive in me—something that wants to claim, to possess, to mark. The same something I've been fighting since she turned eighteen and stopped being Gio's little girl in my mind.

"Your daughter hates me," she says finally, staring into her drink.

The crystal catches the light, throwing amber shadows across her throat. I force my eyes away.

"Bianca hates everyone." I settle behind my desk, needing the barrier between us. The mahogany expanse feels like my last line of defense against the urge to touch her. "She's been ... difficult since her mother died."

"Died?" Her eyes snap to mine, and Christ, those eyes could bring empires to their knees. Hazel with flecks of gold, artist's eyes that see too much. "Or had an 'unfortunate accident'?"

The bitterness in her voice cuts deep. My grip tightens on my glass as memories surface—memories I've spent a decade trying to bury. "Sophia was murdered," I say flatly. "Ten years ago. The Calabrese family sent her back to me in pieces."

A lie. But Isabella doesn't need to know that.

The color drains from Isabella's face. She's always been pale, even with her olive undertones, but now she goes almost translucent, the green paint smudge on her cheek standing out like a bruise. She downs her scotch in one go, barely wincing at the burn. I'm impressed despite myself—society girls usually sip their drinks, trying to appear delicate. But Isabella drinks like someone who's been to her share of college parties, someone who knows how to handle her liquor.

The thought of her at parties, of other men's eyes on her, makes something dark curl in my gut.

"Why?" she asks, her voice barely above a whisper.

"Because I wouldn't sell them territory in Brooklyn." My knuckles whiten around my glass as the memories flood back. "Because they wanted to prove they could take what was mine. Because they're sadistic bastards who—" I cut myself off, reining in the rage that still burns hot after a decade.

"And now they want me." It's not a question.

"They want to destroy me," I correct, watching her process this. "You're just their chosen method this time."

Isabella stands abruptly, pacing to the window. The sun catches her hair, turning the dark strands to fire. She's beautiful—all wild grace and unconscious sensuality. The paint-stained jeans hug curves that her baggy sweater tries to hide, and that damn tattoo keeps peeking out, taunting me.

"My father knew about Sophia?" The question draws my attention back to her face. In the weak light, shadows play across her features, highlighting the delicate architecture of her cheekbones, the vulnerable line of her throat.

"He helped me hunt down the men responsible." I stand, unable to remain seated with her looking like that—like some tragic heroine in an oil painting, all beauty and sorrow backlit by the sun.

"Did you kill them?"

"Yes." No point lying to her now. She'll need to understand what our world is really like. What *I'm* really like. "Your father helped me track them. Each one died slower than the last."

She's quiet for a long moment, watching the gardens below where security teams patrol the perimeter. Her fingers trace patterns on the glass—artist's fingers, long and elegant, stained with various colors. I imagine those fingers on my skin and have to turn away, pouring myself another drink.

"Will you tell me what really happened to my father?"

I sit, setting down my glass, studying her rigid posture. The sweater has slipped again, revealing the curve of her shoulder, the edge of that damned tattoo. *Control.*

"Are you sure you want to know?"

"No." She turns to face me, and there are tears in her eyes even as she lifts her chin defiantly. The combination of vulnerability and strength hits me like a physical blow. "But I need to."

I gesture to the chair closer to my desk. When she sits, I catch a hint of her scent—jasmine mixed with paint thinner and something uniquely her. It makes my mouth water. Forces me to grip the arms of my chair to stay seated.

"The Calabrese family wanted to expand into your father's territory in Queens. He refused. They made threats." My jaw clenches at the memory. "He thought he could handle it alone. Didn't want to involve me because he knew what they'd done to Sophia. Two days before he died, he came to me, said he needed help. But it was too late. They'd already infiltrated his security detail."

"The shooting wasn't random," she whispers. Her face goes chalk white, fingers clutching the chair arms so hard I expect to hear the leather crack. A tear slips down her cheek, catching the last ray of sunlight like a diamond.

"No. His own driver betrayed him." I lean forward, holding her gaze. Fighting the urge to wipe away that tear. "I found out too late. By the time I got to the scene ..."

"Stop." She wraps her arms around herself, and the protective gesture makes me want to kill someone. Preferably Johnny Calabrese. "Just ... stop."

Silence falls between us, heavy with unspoken grief. Outside, darkness from an impending storm creeps across the grounds like spilled ink. Soon the compound's exterior lights will click on, turning the gardens into a floodlit security zone. But for now, we sit in the growing shadows, and I watch her try to rebuild her composure.

"The funeral is tomorrow," I say finally, hating how inadequate the words feel.

"And our wedding the day after." Her laugh holds no humor, the sound like broken glass. "My professors won't believe my excuse for missing critique week."

"You can continue your studies," I remind her, though the thought of her leaving the compound's protection makes my blood run cold. "That was part of our deal."

"Our deal." She stands again, this time moving to examine the Rembrandt more closely. The last light catches her profile, and for a moment, she could be one of Vermeer's subjects—all quiet grace and contained passion. "Tell me, does this deal include the truth about everything? Or will I have to wait for the next attempt on my life to learn all your secrets?"

The question hangs between us like smoke. I rise, drawn to her like a moth to flame. My feet carry me across the room until I'm standing behind her, close enough to feel her body heat, to breathe in that intoxicating mix of jasmine and paint and woman. She tenses but doesn't step away.

"There are things you don't want to know, Isabella."

"Bella," she corrects automatically, still staring at the painting. Her pulse flutters visibly at her throat. "Everyone calls me Bella except you."

"Bella," I test the name, letting it roll off my tongue like honey. Watching goosebumps rise on her exposed shoulder, I fight the urge to trace them with my fingers, my mouth. She shivers slightly, and the movement draws my attention to the curve of her waist, the slight sway as she shifts her weight.

"Some secrets are better left buried."

She turns suddenly, and we're too close. Much too close. I can see the flecks of gold in her hazel eyes, count each dark eyelash, note how her pupils dilate as she looks up at me. Her lips part slightly, and I swear I can feel her breath on my skin.

"Those secrets got my father killed."

"Those secrets keep you alive." My voice roughens without my permission. Everything about her strips away my control—her scent, her proximity, the way she looks at me like she's trying to solve a puzzle. "Trust that what I do, I do to protect you."

"Like marrying me?" There's a challenge in her tone that makes heat pool in my gut.

"Yes."

"And sharing your bed?" The words come out barely above a whisper, but they hit me like a physical blow.

My control snaps. I catch her chin between my thumb and forefinger, tilting her face up. Her skin is silk under my callused fingers, and I can feel her pulse racing. "That's not about protection," I growl, watching her eyes darken. "That's about making sure every man in New York knows you're mine."

Her breath catches, pupils dilating until only a thin ring of hazel remains. For a moment, the air between us crackles with possibility. I could close this distance, taste those parted lips, finally discover if she's as soft as she looks. My free hand moves to her hip of its own accord, and I feel her tremble.

But then she steps back, putting a safe distance between us. The loss of her warmth is like a physical ache.

"I'm not yours," she says quietly, though her voice shakes. "And I'm not your dead wife. I won't be a replacement for Sophia, or a pawn in your war with the Calabrese family."

"No," I agree, letting my hand fall. The ghost of her skin lingers on my fingers. "You're something far more dangerous."

Before she can ask what I mean—before I can do something unforgivable like pull her back against me—a knock interrupts us. Antonio enters, his expression grim enough to instantly set me on edge.

"Boss, we have a situation. Johnny Calabrese left a message ... at Miss Russo's apartment."

My blood runs cold, desire instantly replaced by rage. "What kind of message?"

"The walls ... they painted them red." Antonio's voice is careful, measured. He glances at Bella, then back to me. "And they left this."

He holds out an envelope. I snatch it, already knowing I'm going to hate whatever's inside. The paper tears under my fingers, and suddenly I'm staring at my past—at everything I've tried to forget, everything I've tried to protect Bella from.

Sophia on our wedding day, radiant in ivory lace and DeLuca emeralds. Her dark hair swept up, blue eyes bright with love and hope. She was beautiful, delicate as a butterfly in my world of violence. That's why they chose her, why they broke her. Because they knew it would break me too.

Written in red across the image: *History repeats.*

The photograph crumples in my grip. I'm vaguely aware of Bella moving closer, of her sharp intake of breath as she sees the image. But all I can focus on is the rage building in my chest, the need to hurt someone—preferably Johnny Calabrese.

"That's her?" Bella's voice is soft. "Sophia?"

I force my fingers to relax, smoothing the photograph. "Yes. Our wedding day. She wore my grandmother's emeralds." The same emeralds sitting in my safe, waiting for another bride. Another potential victim.

"She was beautiful." There's something in Bella's tone I can't quite read. When I look at her, she's staring at the photograph, cataloging details. "She looks ... happy."

"She was. For a while." Until my world destroyed her. Like it might destroy the woman standing before me now, paint-stained and fierce and so goddamn young.

"Boss," Antonio interrupts gently. "There's more. The paint they used on the walls ... it matches Miss Russo's style. They've been watching her studio, studying her work."

Bella makes a small sound, like someone punched her in the gut. Without thinking, I reach for her, but she steps back. Her eyes are huge in her pale face, that damned sweater slipping off her shoulder again like an invitation I can't accept.

"I need to make some calls," I say roughly, turning away before I do something stupid like pull her into my arms. "Antonio, take Miss Russo to Maria. She'll help her get settled."

"Matteo." Her voice stops me halfway to my desk. It's the first time she's used my first name, and it sounds like sin on her lips. "What aren't you telling me? About Sophia, about what they really want?"

I look back at her, this woman who makes me feel things I have no right to feel. Who stands in my study with paint in her hair and defiance in her eyes, demanding truths I can't give her.

"Get some rest, Bella. Tomorrow we bury your father. The day after, you become my wife." I let my voice soften slightly. "Some ghosts are better left undisturbed."

She leaves with Antonio, but her scent lingers—jasmine and turpentine and something uniquely her. I throw back another scotch, staring at the photograph still crimped from my grip. Sophia smiles up at me, forever frozen in that moment of joy before everything went to hell.

"I'll do better this time," I promise her ghost, though we both know it's a lie. Because Bella isn't Sophia—she's stronger, fiercer, more alive. And that makes her infinitely more dangerous.

To the Calabrese family. To my control. To my heart.

The storm that's been threatening all morning finally breaks, rain lashing against the bulletproof glass. Somewhere in my city, Johnny Calabrese is plotting his next move. Somewhere in my house, Bella is probably planning her escape. And here I stand, caught between duty and desire, protection and possession, the ghost of my past and the woman who threatens to become my future.

God help us all.

7

BELLA

The bedroom—*our* bedroom, I guess—is larger than my entire apartment. The late afternoon light filters through floor-to-ceiling windows that overlook the illuminated gardens, casting long shadows across the herringbone hardwood floors. A massive four-poster bed dominates the space, its dark mahogany frame holding what looks like a small fortune in Italian linens. The sheets alone probably cost more than a semester's worth of art supplies.

Everything speaks of old money and masculine taste—from the leather chaise by the fireplace to the abstract paintings that I suspect are original Rothkos. The air itself feels expensive, carrying notes of sandalwood and leather from the candles burning on marble side tables. This is Matteo's domain, his sanctuary, and soon it will be mine too.

The thought makes my stomach flip.

I stand in the center of it all, wrapped in nothing but a towel after my shower, staring at the meager belongings Matteo's men managed to salvage from my vandalized apartment. My throat tightens at the sight. My paintings, my art supplies, most of my clothes—all ruined with red paint. They didn't just destroy my things; they violated my art. Used my own bloodred acrylics to write their message across my canvases: *Welcome to the family.*

The memory of seeing the photos of my studio like that makes bile rise in my throat. Each ruined canvas represented hours of work, pieces of my soul poured onto the surface. My upcoming thesis exhibition pieces, the cityscapes I'd been developing for months, the portrait of my father I'd been working on in secret—all destroyed.

They didn't just take my possessions; they took my voice.

My hands shake as I open the garment bag containing my funeral dress. Black Valentino, the fabric so fine it feels like water between my fingers. The design is elegantly simple—knee-length with long sleeves and a high neck, perfectly appropriate for a Mafia princess burying her father. My mother's choice, of course. Cher had shown up an hour ago with an entire team of stylists and her usual acid tongue.

"Really, darling," she'd said, eyeing me with disdain. "This artistic phase has served its purpose, but it's time to be who you were born to be. The DeLuca name comes with certain expectations."

I'd bit back a retort about what exactly I was born to be. A pawn? A replacement? A pretty puppet in designer clothes?

A knock at the bedroom door makes me jump. "Miss Bella?" It's Maria, the housekeeper. "Mr. DeLuca asked me to bring you these."

The older woman enters, her silver hair neatly coiled at her nape, warm brown eyes crinkling with kindness. She's exactly what a grandmother should look like, from her sensible shoes to her pressed uniform, and something about her gentle presence eases the tension in my shoulders.

She carries a stack of shopping bags—Neiman Marcus, Bergdorf Goodman, La Perla. The signature colors and logos mock me with their luxury. "He said you might need ... everything."

Everything. Because the Calabrese family had destroyed everything I owned. My throat tightens as I think of my ruined supplies—the specialized brushes I'd collected over years, the imported paints I'd saved up for, the sketchbooks filled with ideas and dreams. All gone, replaced with designer labels and price tags that probably equal my yearly tuition.

"Thank you, Maria."

"Do you need help—"

"No," I say quickly, needing to be alone with my grief, my anger, my confusion. "No, I can manage."

Once Maria leaves, I dump the bags onto the massive bed. The contents spill out like a fashion magazine exploded—cashmere sweaters, silk blouses, tailored pants, all in a muted palette of blacks and grays and creams. Everything in exactly my size, because of course Matteo would know my measurements. The thought makes heat rise to my cheeks.

Then I find the La Perla bag.

My breath catches as I pull out piece after piece of barely-there lingerie. Emerald silk and black lace, delicate straps and strategic cutouts. A negligee that would fall like water to my thighs. A bra set that costs more than my monthly rent. Things designed to entice, to seduce, to submit.

The message is clear: I'm to look the part of a Mafia don's wife. Every inch of me, even the parts only he will see, must be perfectly curated.

The bedroom door opens again, this time without a knock. Matteo strides in, and my heart stutters to a stop.

He stops short at the sight of me in just a towel, and the air in the room suddenly feels electric. Even after hours of meetings, he looks devastating in his tailored suit—all controlled power and lethal grace. His jacket stretches across broad shoulders that make me feel delicate in comparison. His hair, usually perfectly styled, is slightly mussed as if he's been running his fingers through it. The silver at his temples catches the lamplight, and something low in my belly tightens at the sight.

"I—I thought you were still in your meeting," I stammer, clutching the towel tighter. That's what I had been told—that Matteo would be busy until late. Water drips from my hair down my back, and I'm acutely aware of how little I'm wearing. The towel suddenly feels too short, too thin. Every drop of water sliding down my skin feels like a caress, and from the way his eyes darken, he's tracking their path.

"It ended early." His voice is rough, deeper than usual. The sound sends shivers down my spine that have nothing to do with being cold. "The Calabrese family sent another message."

Fear slices through my embarrassment, dousing it like cold water. "What kind of message?"

"Nothing you need to worry about." The dismissive tone should infuriate me—and it does—but it's hard to focus on anger when he's looking at me like that. He loosens his tie with one hand, a gesture that shouldn't be erotic but somehow is. The suit jacket comes off next, revealing a crisp white shirt that does nothing to hide the power in his frame.

"The funeral." My knees suddenly feel weak as reality crashes back. I sink onto the edge of the bed, among all the shopping bags. "I don't know if I can ..."

Matteo crosses to me in two long strides, kneeling before me. This close, I can see the faint stubble on his jaw, smell the lingering traces of his cologne mixed with something darker, more masculine. His eyes hold mine—steel blue with hints of gray, like a storm over water—and my breath catches in my throat.

"You can," he says softly, and the gentleness in his voice undoes me more than any show of force could. "You're stronger than you know, Isabella."

"Bella," I correct automatically, then want to laugh at myself for caring about names when he's so close I can feel the heat radiating from his body. A drop of water falls from my hair onto his hand where it rests near my knee, and I watch his fingers twitch.

His lips quirk slightly. "Bella," he concedes, reaching up to brush a wet strand of hair from my cheek. The gesture is surprisingly gentle for hands I know have killed. His callused fingers graze my skin, and my entire body comes alive at the touch.

I should pull away. Should grab my new clothes and retreat to the bathroom. Should maintain some distance between us. But I find myself leaning into his touch instead, my body betraying me as it has since that first moment in his office. He smells like scotch and danger and something uniquely male that makes my head spin.

"Tell me about him?" I whisper, desperate to break this tension before I do something stupid like trace that stubble with my fingers. "My father. Not ... not the Mafia don everyone feared. Tell me about my father, your friend."

Something soft crosses Matteo's face, transforming his features from dangerous to devastating. He rises from his crouch to sit beside me on the bed, close enough that his thigh brushes mine through the towel. The contact sends electricity skittering across my skin.

"He was the best man I knew," Matteo says, his voice warm with memory. "And the worst poker player." His chuckle resonates through me, making my stomach flip. "He'd tell the same terrible jokes at every family dinner, and your mother would pretend to be embarrassed, but she'd laugh every time."

"I remember those dinners." I pull my knees to my chest, careful of the towel even as I'm aware of Matteo's gaze sliding over my bare legs. Water droplets trail down my calves, and I swear I hear his breath catch. "Before ... before everything got complicated."

"You were always covered in paint, even then." His finger traces an old paint stain on my arm, and my skin erupts in goosebumps. The touch is innocent enough, but it feels intimate in a way that makes heat pool low in my belly. "Gio said you got that from his mother—she was an artist too."

"I never knew that." The revelation surprises me, momentarily distracting me from the fire his touch ignites on my skin. My grandmother died before I was born, and my father rarely spoke of her.

"There's a lot you don't know about your family. About this world." His hand stills on my arm, but I can feel each individual finger like brands against my skin. "Things I'll have to teach you."

The words send heat rushing through me. It's the way he says it—dark and promising—that makes my imagination run wild. What else could those hands teach me? What would his stubble feel like against my neck, my breasts, my—

No. Reality crashes back like a bucket of ice water. Tomorrow I'll bury my father. The next day I'll marry this man—this dangerous, captivating man who fills every space he occupies with raw power and barely contained violence.

"I should get dressed," I say abruptly, standing. But my foot catches on an errant shopping bag, and I stumble.

Matteo catches me before I can fall, one hand splaying across my bare back where the towel has slipped. His palm is hot against my damp skin, and I have to bite back a gasp. We're too close again, my nearly naked body pressed against him. His cologne surrounds me, spice and sandalwood and danger, making my head spin. I can feel every hard plane of his chest under my palms where I've braced myself against him.

"Careful, *piccola*," he murmurs, and the Italian endearment in that rough voice sends shivers down my spine. His thumb strokes small circles on my back, each movement making it harder to breathe.

"I'm not little," I protest weakly, but I can't seem to make myself pull away. My body is a traitor, wanting to arch into his touch like a cat.

"No," he agrees, his voice low and rough, his other hand coming up to cup my cheek. His thumb traces my bottom lip, and I swear I can feel my pulse there. "You're not."

For a moment, I think he might kiss me. Part of me—a reckless, hungry part—wants him to. I want to know if his mouth is as dangerous as the rest of him, if he kisses with that same controlled violence that radiates from his every movement. Would he be gentle, treating me like something precious? Or would he devour me, marking me as his in every way?

My lips part involuntarily, and I hear his sharp intake of breath. His eyes darken to midnight, and his hand on my back presses me closer. Just a few inches and I could find out exactly how his mouth tastes, how that stubble would feel against my skin ...

Instead, he steps back, putting a safe distance between us. The loss of his touch leaves me cold, but my skin still burns where his hands were. I watch him struggle to regain control, fascinated by the muscle jumping in his jaw, the way his hands clench at his sides.

"Get dressed," he says, his voice controlled again but rougher than usual. "We have an early morning tomorrow." He turns toward the en suite bathroom, already removing his tie. The simple movement shouldn't be so goddamn erotic, but something about the casual display of masculinity makes heat pool low in my belly.

"And Bella?" He glances back, and the look in his eyes nearly stops my heart. Hunger and possession war with something softer, more dangerous. "The emerald nightgown. Wear that one."

He disappears into the bathroom before I can respond, leaving me trembling in the middle of our bedroom. The shower turns on, and unbidden images flood my mind—water running down his muscled back, those powerful hands sliding over wet skin ...

With shaking fingers, I dig through the La Perla bag until I find it—an emerald silk nightgown that would fall to mid-thigh. The material is impossibly fine, almost sheer, with delicate lace panels at the sides and a neckline that would plunge indecently low. It's the kind of thing designed to seduce, to submit, to surrender.

The same color as the ring I saw him fidgeting with earlier. The ring that belonged to his dead wife.

I sink back onto the bed, surrounded by expensive clothes bought to replace everything I've lost. The sound of the shower seems to echo in my ears, along with the ghost of his touch on my skin. Tomorrow I'll bury my father. The next day I'll marry a man who makes me feel things I shouldn't—desire and fear and a desperate kind of hunger I don't want to examine too closely.

And tonight ... tonight I have to decide if I'll wear his dead wife's color to bed. If I'll play the role he's casting me in—the replacement bride, the perfect donna, the submissive beauty meant to grace his arm and warm his bed.

Steam curls under the bathroom door, carrying his scent with it. I close my eyes, remembering the feel of his hands on my skin, the way he looked at me like he wanted to devour me whole. It would be so easy to give in, to let myself be consumed by him. To wear what he wants and become what he needs.

But that's not who I am.

My fingers find the black silk nightgown instead. The material is just as fine, just as seductive, but it's my choice. Not his. Not his dead wife's. *Mine.*

I may have to marry Matteo DeLuca, may have to share his bed and his name, but I won't be a replacement for his ghosts. I won't let him reshape me into someone else's shadow.

As I slip the black silk over my skin, I hear the shower turn off. My heart races, but I lift my chin defiantly. Let him see that I won't be so easily controlled. Let him learn that while he might own my body after tomorrow, my will remains my own.

The bathroom door opens, releasing a cloud of steam, and I brace myself for his reaction. Whatever comes next, I'll face it on my own terms. In my own colors. In my own skin.

I am not Sophia. I never will be. And it's time Matteo DeLuca learned that.

8

MATTEO

Rain pounds against the study windows, matching my dark mood. The funeral replays in my mind like a film I can't stop watching—the heavy scent of incense mixing with too many lilies, the echo of footsteps on marble, the weight of a thousand calculating eyes watching our every move.

Gio deserved better than the political theater his funeral became. Every family in New York sent representatives, each condolence offered with precise measurement of power and threat. The church had been packed with our world's most dangerous players, all of them watching, assessing how the DeLuca-Russo alliance would reshape the landscape.

But it was Bella who commanded the space, even in her grief. She stood beside me in that elegant black Valentino, her spine straight as steel despite the dark circles under her eyes that even careful makeup couldn't quite hide. Her hand had trembled slightly when I helped her from the car, but no one else would have noticed. By the time she reached the church steps, she was every inch a donna.

The memory of her at the pulpit haunts me. Standing there in profile like a Renaissance painting of a saint, her voice never wavering as she spoke about her father. "He taught me that true strength lies not in power over others, but in remaining true to yourself." Her eyes had met mine then, a clear challenge in their hazel depths.

Even grieving, she fought against the cage I was building around her.

Father Romano's sermon had dragged on, filled with carefully coded messages about family and loyalty. I barely heard it, too focused on the slight tremor in Bella's shoulders, the way she bit her lip to keep from crying. I wanted to reach for her, to offer comfort, but comfort wasn't what she needed from me. Not when I'm the one forcing her into this marriage, this life.

The nauseating sweetness of too many flower arrangements had filled the air, competing with Cher's perfectly theatrical displays of grief. Gio's wife had played her part well—dabbing at carefully smudged mascara, leaning on her brother-in-law Carmine's arm at just the right moments.

But I saw how her eyes kept darting to the other families' representatives, measuring their reactions, calculating her next move.

Now, hours later, the rain matches the heaviness in my chest. Bella hasn't spoken since we returned to the compound, disappearing to our room immediately. I should be with her, but there were too many fires to put out—the thinly veiled threats from the Calabrese family, Carmine's endless machinations, the other families' probing questions about tomorrow's wedding.

I miss Giovanni with an ache that surprises me. He should have been here today, sharing cigars and memories, teasing me about becoming his son-in-law. Instead, I had to watch his daughter stand alone, had to field questions about how quickly I'm claiming her. The politics of it all leave a bitter taste in my mouth.

My phone buzzes. Another message from Johnny Calabrese. I delete it without reading it. Whatever new threat it contains can wait. Right now, I need a drink and silence. The scotch burns going down, but it does nothing to ease the weight of memory, of duty, of the growing need to check on Bella.

The study door opens softly, and my heart stops. Bella slips in like a ghost in black silk, her hair falling loose around her shoulders in dark waves. Tears shine on her cheeks, but there's something else in her eyes—something that makes my blood heat despite the solemnity of the day.

The robe she's wearing clings to curves I shouldn't notice, especially not today. But I'm only human, and she's devastating in her unconscious grace. Her feet are bare beneath the hem, making her look somehow more vulnerable and more dangerous at once.

"I thought you'd be here," she says softly, closing the door behind her. The click of the latch sounds final, intimate.

I set down my scotch, needing my hands empty before I do something unforgivable. "You should be resting. Tomorrow—"

"I don't want to think about tomorrow." She moves to the bar cart with fluid grace, pouring herself a generous measure of scotch. The robe shifts as she moves, revealing glimpses of black lace underneath that make my mouth go dry. "Tell me about the threats. The ones you've been hiding from me."

"Bella—"

"Don't." She turns to face me, and Christ, she's beautiful in her fury. Fire burns in her eyes despite her tears, and her chest rises and falls rapidly with emotion. "Don't treat me like something fragile. My father's dead, I'm marrying you tomorrow, and Johnny Calabrese wants to destroy us both. I deserve to know *everything*."

I study her for a long moment, struggling to maintain control. The silk robe clings to every curve, and a drop of water from her damp hair trails down her neck, disappearing beneath black lace. She looks like every fantasy I've denied having—vulnerable yet fierce, innocent yet knowing. The urge to taste that drop of water, to follow its path with my tongue, is almost overwhelming.

"They've been watching you," I admit finally, forcing myself to focus on the threat rather than how her lips part at my words. "For months. They knew about your art shows, your favorite coffee shop, your morning routine at the gym."

She takes a long swallow of scotch, and I watch her throat work, entranced. Her hand shakes slightly as she lowers the glass. "Before or after they killed my father?"

"Before. They were always going to come for you." I stand, drawn to her like a moth to flame. When I move closer, I can smell her signature jasmine perfume mixed with something uniquely her. It makes my head spin more than the scotch. "Your father knew. That's why he asked me to protect you."

"By marrying me?" Bitterness edges her voice, but I see how her breath quickens as I approach. Her pupils dilate, a flush creeping up her neck.

"By any means necessary."

She sets down her glass with a sharp click. "And what about Sophia? Did you protect her by any means necessary too?"

The question hits like a physical blow, but I barely register the pain. Not when she's looking up at me like that, defiance warring with something darker, hungrier.

"Don't," I warn her, feeling like I'm standing at the precipice.

"Why not?" She steps closer, tilting her head back to meet my eyes. This close, I can see the gold flecks in her hazel irises, count each dark eyelash still damp with tears. "I'm wearing her ring tomorrow, sleeping in her bed. Don't I deserve to know how she died?"

"You know how she died." The words come out sharper than intended, but Bella doesn't flinch. Instead, she steps closer, and the heat of her body tests every ounce of my control.

"I know what you told me. That the Calabrese family killed her. But why? What really happened?"

"Isabella." Her full name comes out as a warning, but even I'm not sure what I'm warning her against—pushing me about Sophia or standing so close I can feel her breath on my skin.

"No more secrets, Matteo." She presses her hand to my chest, directly over my thundering heart, and I can feel her trembling. The touch sears through my shirt like a brand. "If I'm going to be your wife, even in name only—"

My control snaps like a rubber band pulled too tight. I catch her wrist, pulling her against me. Her soft gasp as our bodies collide nearly undoes me. "When are you going to understand?" I growl, my lips inches from hers. "This isn't just about protection or politics. This isn't in name only."

"Then what is it about?" she challenges, not backing down despite our closeness. Her free hand fists in my shirt, and I can't tell if she's trying to push me away or pull me closer.

Instead of answering, I do what I've been dying to do since she walked into my office that first day. I kiss her.

There's nothing gentle about it. All the frustration, the desire, the need I've been holding back pours into this kiss. My hand slides into her hair, silky strands wrapping around my fingers as I angle her head to deepen the contact. She tastes like scotch and tears and defiance, and Christ, she's responding. Her mouth opens under mine with a small sound that shoots straight to my groin.

When my tongue sweeps into her mouth, she moans, the vibration traveling through both our bodies. Her hands move restlessly over my chest, seeking skin, and the feeling of her touching me, wanting me, nearly brings me to my knees.

"Matteo," she gasps when I finally break the kiss to trail my lips down her neck. Her pulse races under my tongue, and the taste of her skin is better than I imagined.

"Tell me to stop," I growl against her throat, even as my hands slide down her sides, memorizing every curve. "Tell me you don't want this."

Instead of stopping me, she pulls my mouth back to hers, this kiss even more desperate than the first. Her tongue meets mine, and the taste of her—scotch and sweetness and sin—makes me groan. Her fingers work at my tie, my shirt buttons, seeking bare skin with an urgency that matches my own. Every brush of her hands feels like fire.

I back her up against my desk, lifting her onto it. Papers scatter to the floor, but I couldn't care less. Not when she's wrapping her legs around my waist, pulling me closer. The silk of her robe is nothing compared to the silk of her skin as I slide my hands up her thighs.

Her head falls back on a gasp when I find the lace edge of whatever she's wearing underneath. Black lace, not the emerald nightgown I'd suggested. My defiant little artist, always challenging me. The thought makes me smile against her throat as I taste the racing pulse there.

"What?" she asks breathlessly, her nails scraping lightly down my now-bare chest.

"Black suits you better anyway," I murmur, sliding the robe off her shoulders. The sight of her in black lace nearly stops my heart. She's a fantasy made real—all creamy skin and dangerous curves, innocence and sensuality combined in a way that makes me want to devour her whole.

She shivers under my gaze, but not from cold. Her nipples peak through the delicate lace, begging for my touch, my mouth. "I won't be her replacement."

"No," I agree, running my hands up her bare thighs, loving how she trembles. "You're nothing like her. You're—"

A knock at the door freezes us both. "Boss?" Antonio's voice carries through the wood. "Johnny Calabrese is at the gates. He's demanding to speak with you."

Bella tenses in my arms, but I don't release her. Can't release her. Not when she's finally in my arms, skin flushed and lips swollen from my kisses. "Handle it," I call back, fighting to keep my voice steady even as my body screams for more of her.

"He says he has more photos. Of Miss Russo. Recent ones."

A low sound escapes Bella—fear or fury, I'm not sure which. I rest my forehead against hers, breathing in the scent of her, memorizing this moment before reality crashes back.

"Go," she whispers against my mouth, but her hands still clutch my shoulders. "Handle it."

I step back reluctantly, physically aching at the loss of her warmth. The sight of her on my desk nearly brings me right back to her—hair mussed from my hands, lips red and swollen from my kisses, black lace askew to reveal the curves I'd barely begun to explore. Her chest rises and falls rapidly, nipples clearly visible through the delicate fabric.

She looks thoroughly kissed, completely tempting, and entirely mine.

My body still thrums with need for her. Every muscle is tensed with the effort not to go back, to finish what we started, to claim her the way I've been dying to since she first challenged me in this very office.

"This isn't over," I tell her, my voice rough with promise and barely contained desire. "What's between us—"

"No," she agrees, sliding off my desk on unsteady legs. The movement makes the robe slip further, revealing more black lace and creamy skin that my hands still burn to touch. "But maybe it shouldn't have started."

She slips out of the study before I can respond, leaving me with the ghost of her taste on my lips, rage building in my chest, and a hard-on that begs to be dealt with. The trace of jasmine in the air mocks me, as does the scattered paperwork on the floor. Every nerve ending in my body screams for her return.

Johnny Calabrese wants to play games? Fine. But he'll learn what happens to men who threaten what belongs to Matteo DeLuca. And Bella, whether she admits it or not, is mine. That kiss proved it. The way she responded to me, melted for me, needed me—that wasn't political. That wasn't about protection or duty or any of the other lies we've been telling ourselves.

That was pure, undeniable desire. The same desire that's still coursing through my veins, making it hard to think about anything except following her upstairs and finishing what we started.

But first, I have a message to deliver to Johnny Calabrese about the consequences of threatening what's mine.

I straighten my clothes and put my shirt back on, but I don't bother trying to erase the evidence of what just happened. Let them see the marks from her nails on my chest, the bruise forming on my neck from her mouth. Let them know that the woman they're threatening belongs to someone who will burn the world down to protect her.

Tomorrow she becomes my wife. Tonight, I'll make sure everyone understands exactly what that means.

Starting with Johnny fucking Calabrese.

9

BELLA

The wedding dress hangs like a ghost in the predawn light, mocking me with its perfection. Yards of Italian silk and French lace cascade from delicate cap sleeves to a cathedral train, the bodice hand beaded with thousands of tiny crystals that catch the gray morning light. It's a Vera Wang masterpiece, the kind of dress I used to sketch in the margins of my notebooks during boring lectures.

But in my dreams, my father was always there to walk me down the aisle.

I curl tighter into the window seat of my studio, pulling the cashmere throw closer around my shoulders. I haven't slept, couldn't sleep, not after what happened in Matteo's study. My lips still tingle from his kisses, my skin burning everywhere his hands touched me. The memory of his mouth on my neck makes heat pool low in my belly even now.

God, the way he'd kissed me. Not gentle or hesitant, but demanding, possessive, like a man starving. The taste of him—scotch and smoke and something darker, more dangerous—haunts me. His groans when I'd touched his chest, the way he'd growled my name against my throat, how his hands had felt sliding up my thighs ... I squeeze my eyes shut, but that only makes the memories more vivid.

My studio, at least, offers some refuge from the madness. Matteo had it prepared before I arrived, setting it up on the third floor with windows facing east to catch the morning light. The space is bigger than my apartment, with pristine white walls, perfect track lighting, and enough room for multiple easels. He even stocked it with better supplies than I've ever owned—imported paints, handmade brushes, canvases of every size.

Another gilded cage, but at least this one speaks my language.

I painted until my arms ached last night, trying to capture the storm inside me. Grief for my father weights every brushstroke—not just that he's gone, but that his death has forced me into exactly the life he tried to protect me from. Rage follows close behind, that the Calabrese family could just decide to destroy our lives, that I have to marry for protection like some medieval princess.

And then there's Matteo.

The canvas before me tells that story too well—dark swirls of midnight blue and crimson, shot through with glints of gold. The colors of desire and danger, of attraction I shouldn't feel and safety I can't trust. How can I want a man who represents everything I've tried to escape? How can my body crave his touch even as my mind rebels against his control?

A knock at the studio door makes me tense. "Go away, Maria. I know it's time."

"It's not Maria." Elena's voice comes through the door, followed by her striking presence. My best friend is everything I'm not—tall, willowy, with the kind of blonde beauty that turns heads. This morning she's perfectly put together in a pale blue dress that makes her eyes look like sapphires, her honey-blonde hair falling in elegant waves past her shoulders. Even at this ungodly hour, she looks like she stepped off a magazine cover.

"Elena." My voice breaks as I launch myself at her. Just having her here makes me feel less alone, less like I'm drowning. "You came."

"Of course I came." She hugs me tight, then holds me at arm's length to examine me. Her perfect features draw into a frown. "You look like hell, B. Did you sleep at all?"

"How did you get past security?" I change the subject, not wanting her to know the truth.

"Please." She rolls her eyes, but there's something tight around her mouth. "I do all the event planning for these families. The guards know me." She pauses, those striking blue eyes turning serious. "There's still time to run."

I shake my head, moving to study my painting. Elena's the best event planner in New York, especially for our world's particular brand of parties. She can make a mob wedding look like a royal celebration, knows exactly how to arrange seating to prevent blood feuds, and can spot an undercover FBI agent at fifty paces.

But even she can't plan an escape from this.

"You know there isn't."

"Then tell me what happened last night. Maria said you never came to bed, and Matteo ..." She trails off meaningfully.

Heat floods my cheeks as the memories rush back—Matteo's hands tangled in my hair, his mouth hot on my neck, the way he'd growled my name like it was something sacred and profane at once. The way his chest felt under my hands, all hard muscle and heated skin ...

"Oh my God." Elena's eyes widen as she takes in what must be a very telling blush. "You slept with him?"

"No! We just ... almost ..." I can't even form coherent thoughts about it. How do I explain that I wanted him so badly it scared me? That part of me wishes Antonio hadn't interrupted? That I'm equal parts relieved and disappointed we didn't finish what we started?

"Details. Now." Elena's demand is cut short as the studio door bursts open. My mother sweeps in like a perfectly coiffed hurricane, her Chanel suit impeccable, her platinum hair styled just so. Even at dawn, Cher Russo looks ready for a society photograph. A team of stylists trails in her wake, laden with bags and equipment, their faces a mix of determination and fear.

"Isabella Marie Russo!" Her voice could cut glass. "What are you doing hiding in here? In your paint clothes, no less! The hair and makeup team has been waiting for an hour."

"Mom—"

"No arguments. You're marrying one of the most powerful men in New York in four hours. You will look perfect." She snaps her fingers at the stylists. "Get her cleaned up. And someone do something about those paint stains under her nails."

Elena squeezes my hand before the whirlwind of preparations sweeps me away. Soon I'm seated in front of my vanity, surrounded by people intent on transforming me into someone I barely recognize. The irony isn't lost on me—this is what I've been doing all my life, trying to paint myself into something I'm not. Only now it's being done for me.

I catch glimpses of myself in the mirror as they work. My dark hair is being curled and pinned in an elaborate style that somehow looks both elegant and effortless. Makeup artists turn my pale skin luminous, define my eyes until they look huge and haunted in my face. My hands—my artist's hands with their telltale stains and calluses—are being scrubbed and buffed into submission.

"The foundation needs to be heavier," my mother critiques, circling like a shark. "Those dark circles are atrocious. And do something about that rebellious curl at her nape."

"She looks beautiful," Elena interjects, earning a glacial stare from Cher.

"Beautiful isn't enough. She needs to be flawless. The other families will be watching her every move, analyzing every detail." My mother's perfectly painted lips twist. "The DeLuca name comes with certain expectations."

I close my eyes, trying to block out her voice, but it only makes everything more intense. This should be a happy day. I should be surrounded by bridesmaids and champagne, giggling about my honeymoon and my future. Instead, I'm being polished like a weapon, prepared for a marriage that feels more like a funeral.

"The dress is Vera Wang," my mother continues, directing the chaos like a general. "The emeralds are from the DeLuca family collection—they belonged to Matteo's grandmother, then his first wife."

My stomach lurches at the mention of Sophia. Another ghost haunting this wedding. "Mom, please—"

"Oh, don't be dramatic, darling. Sophia's been dead for years. Though you might want to avoid emeralds at first, just to be safe. Speaking of safe ..." Her voice drops to a stage whisper, eyes gleaming with gossip. "I hear Johnny Calabrese paid a visit last night."

The makeup artist's hand jerks at the mention of Johnny, smudging eyeliner across my temple. I barely notice, my mind flying back to the interruption in Matteo's study. The way his body had tensed against mine, how quickly passion had turned to rage at the mention of those photos. What happened after I fled? What evidence did Johnny have?

"For God's sake," my mother snaps at the makeup artist, her beautiful features twisting into irritation. "Are you qualified to do anything besides ruin my daughter's wedding photos? Fix it. *Now*."

A commotion in the hallway saves me from my mother's continued criticism. Maria appears in the doorway, her kind face pinched with anxiety. "Miss Bella? Mr. DeLuca sent this for you."

She holds out a large black velvet box. Inside, nestled on white silk, lies a delicate gold chain supporting a stunning oval pendant. My breath catches—it's my painting from last night, perfectly reproduced in miniature enamel and gold, backed by a spiral of tiny diamonds. Every brushstroke I made in my midnight frenzy has been captured with exquisite detail, the dark blues and crimsons swirling around hints of gold.

How did he do this so quickly? More importantly, why? The note accompanying it makes my heart race.

You see the beauty in the darkness. Wear this today instead of Sophia's emeralds. -M

"But the tradition—" my mother begins to protest, gaping at the necklace.

"I'm wearing this," I cut her off, my voice firm for the first time today as Elena helps me put it on. My fingers trace the pendant, remembering how Matteo had looked at my painting when he'd come to the studio last night after dealing with Johnny.

He hadn't said a word when he entered, just studied the canvas for a long moment. I'd tensed, expecting him to try to resume what we'd started in his study. The air had crackled between us with unfinished desire, but he'd maintained his distance.

Still, his presence had filled the room like smoke, making it hard to breathe, hard to think. When he finally left, the ghost of his cologne lingered, reminding me of how his skin had tasted under my lips.

A sharp knock shatters my reverie. Bianca enters, already dressed in her bridesmaid's gown of deep blue silk. She looks exactly like what a Mafia princess should be—all elegant angles and expensive grace. Her dark hair is swept up in a complicated twist, her makeup perfect, her entire demeanor radiating cold disdain. The resemblance to her father is striking, especially in the way she holds herself—like she owns every room she enters.

"Dad wants to know if you're still going through with it," she says bluntly.

The room falls silent. Even my mother stops her fussing to stare at me, waiting for my response.

I meet Bianca's eyes in the mirror—steel blue like Matteo's, yet harder somehow. I touch the pendant as if to ground myself. "Tell him I'll see him at the altar."

She raises a perfectly sculpted eyebrow. "Even after what Johnny revealed last night?"

My hand freezes on the pendant. "What are you talking about?"

"You don't know?" Bianca's smile is cruel, satisfaction gleaming in her eyes. "About how my mother really died? About Dad's part in it?"

"Bianca!" Maria tries to intervene, her voice desperate, twisting her hands in agitation. "This isn't the time—"

"No," Bianca shoots back, "she should know what she's marrying into. Grandfather Giuseppe would have—"

"Don't." Matteo's voice cuts like steel. "Don't ever presume to know what he would have wanted."

I've never heard that tone from him before. It's not anger—it's something deeper, darker. The temperature in the room seems to drop ten degrees.

"That's enough." His voice is still razor-sharp, and my whole body reacts to his presence before I even turn to look at him.

He fills the doorway in his wedding tuxedo, and for a moment I forget how to breathe. The custom Tom Ford fits him like sin, emphasizing broad shoulders and narrow hips. His dark hair is styled just so, the silver at his temples catching the light. But it's his face that undoes me—those steel-blue eyes intense as they lock onto mine, his jaw shadowed with just enough stubble to remind me how it felt against my neck last night.

He looks dangerous and devastating and entirely too attractive for my peace of mind.

"Leave us. Now."

"But it's tradition for the groom to not—" my mother starts to say but Matteo's sharp glare stops her in her tracks.

"I said leave us. *Now.*"

The room clears instantly at his command, leaving me alone with my soon-to-be husband. I rise from the vanity, acutely conscious of being in only a silk robe with my hair half done. His eyes trace over me, and I feel each look like a physical touch.

"What was she talking about?" I demand, proud that my voice doesn't shake despite my racing heart. "What don't I know about Sophia?"

Matteo's jaw clenches as he looks at me. His eyes catch on the pendant around my neck, softening slightly. "Not now, Isabella."

"Yes, now. Before I walk down that aisle, I need the truth." I step closer, drawn to him despite my anger, despite my fear. His cologne wraps around me—that familiar mix of spice and danger that makes my head spin.

He moves closer too, reaching out to touch the pendant where it rests against my collarbone. The brush of his fingers against my skin sends electricity shooting through me. "The truth is complicated."

"Then uncomplicate it." Why does he always talk in riddles? Why does he have to be so infuriatingly controlled when I feel like I'm falling apart?

His hand slides up to cup my cheek, and despite everything—all the secrets, all the lies, all the danger—I lean into his touch. My body is a traitor, craving his contact even as my mind screams for answers.

"The truth is, I'll tell you everything tonight. After you're my wife. After you're safe."

"Safe from what?" My heart thuds against my ribs, though whether from his proximity, his touch, or the warning in his words, I'm not sure.

"From making a decision that will get you killed." His voice roughens as his thumb traces my cheekbone. This close, I can see the flecks of gray in his eyes, count every dark eyelash. "The Calabrese family has people inside the church. If you don't go through with this wedding ..."

The threat hangs in the air between us. I close my eyes, feeling the warmth of his hand on my cheek, the weight of the pendant at my throat. Everything in me wants to lean forward those few inches, to taste his mouth again, to lose myself in the dark pleasure I know he can provide.

Instead, I force myself to focus. "Fine," I whisper. "Tonight then. But I want all of it, Matteo. Every dark truth, every secret. Or this marriage won't last until morning."

His thumb traces my bottom lip, and my breath catches at the intimate gesture. I want him to kiss me so badly it hurts. Want to forget about secrets and lies and just lose myself in the heat that always flares between us.

"Wear your hair down," he murmurs, his voice like gravel. "You look beautiful with it down."

Then he's gone, leaving me alone with my reflection and the haunting certainty that I'm about to marry a man I'm not sure I can trust—but one I'm increasingly sure I want anyway. The worst part?

I'm not sure which scares me more—the secrets he's keeping or how much I want him despite them.

In less than four hours, I'll walk down that aisle alone. No father to give me away, no dreams of true love to sustain me. Just political alliances, death threats, and this maddening attraction to a man who deals in secrets and shadows.

Some wedding day.

10

MATTEO

The cathedral falls silent as the doors open. St. Patrick's soars above us, all Gothic arches and stained glass, the same space where we said goodbye to Giovanni just yesterday. The scent of funeral lilies still lingers beneath today's roses, a reminder that's almost too pointed to bear. My best friend should be here, standing beside me as I marry his daughter. Instead, his ghost haunts every shadow, every whispered prayer.

Yesterday, this church held his casket. Today, it will witness his daughter becoming my wife. The irony isn't lost on me, nor on the hundreds of calculating eyes watching from the pews.

Every major family in New York fills the ancient wooden seats, the women dripping in jewels, the men in custom suits that barely conceal their weapons. The Russo family takes up the first three rows on the bride's side, their red roses marking their territory. The Calabreses sit opposite, white lilies their signature. Behind them, the Marconis with their yellow orchids, the Vitellis with white gardenias. A garden of allegiances and threats, all perfectly arranged.

I catch Johnny Calabrese's smirk from the third row, and it takes everything in me not to order his death right here in God's house. He looks exactly as he did last night, when he showed up at my gates with his threats thinly veiled as congratulations.

"I just wanted to offer my best wishes," he'd said, that snake's smile in place. "After all, we both know how ... fragile brides can be in our world."

My response had been equally coded. "Touch her and I'll send you back to your father in pieces."

Now he sits in my cathedral, wearing that same Brioni suit like armor, his presence a deliberate provocation. But before I can dwell on it, the first notes of Wagner's "Bridal Chorus" fill the space, and everything else fades away.

Bella appears in the doorway, and my heart actually stops. She's a vision in white Vera Wang lace, the dress somehow both elegant and ethereal. The bodice hugs her curves before flowing into a skirt that seems to float with each step. But it's her hair that catches me—she took my suggestion, letting it fall in loose waves down her back, tiny diamonds scattered throughout like stars against dark silk. The style makes her look younger, more vulnerable, yet somehow more powerful too.

A murmur ripples through the crowd. I catch fragments of whispered appreciation, of calculated assessment. "Stunning." "So young." "The DeLuca bride." She's being weighed and measured by every eye in the cathedral, and she knows it.

My pendant rests at her throat instead of Sophia's emeralds, and possessive satisfaction burns in my chest. I'd made the decision last night after seeing her painting—that swirl of midnight blue and crimson, shot through with gold. It spoke to something in me, that blend of darkness and light, danger and beauty. Just like her. I'd paid an obscene amount to have it replicated in precious metals and stones within hours, but seeing it grace her throat instead of Sophia's cursed emeralds makes it worth every penny.

She walks alone, her chin lifted in quiet defiance. She'd refused Carmine's offer to give her away, causing another wave of whispers to sweep through the church. I see Cher's frozen society smile, the muscle working in Carmine's jaw at the public slight. But Bella moves as though she doesn't notice, each step precise and measured, her eyes locked on mine.

When our gazes meet, electricity shoots through me. There's challenge in those hazel depths, but something else too—something that makes my blood heat as I remember her gasps in my study last night, the way she'd melted against me, the taste of her skin.

Soon she'll be mine in every way, and the thought makes it hard to breathe.

My gaze shifts briefly to Bianca, standing stiffly in her deep blue bridesmaid's dress. Her smile is brittle as glass, reminding me of our confrontation after I left Bella's suite earlier.

"You're making a mistake," she'd hissed, catching me in the hallway. "She's not ready for this world. She's not—"

"Enough." I'd kept my voice low, conscious of the bustling preparations around us. "This isn't about readiness. This is about survival."

"Like it was with Mom?" Her eyes—so like mine—had filled with tears she refused to let fall. "How long before history repeats itself?"

Now she stands at the altar, every inch a DeLuca in her perfect posture and controlled expression, but I see the tremor in her hands as she clutches her bouquet. She's so young, still carrying the wounds of her mother's death, and here I am giving her a stepmother barely five years her senior.

But then Bella reaches the altar, close enough that I catch the scent of jasmine and something uniquely her. Her hands tremble slightly as she holds her bouquet of white roses, but her eyes meet mine steadily. Strong. Defiant. Alive in a way Sophia never was.

"Dearly beloved," Father Romano begins, his youthful face solemn beneath his vestments. He's been the family priest for years, and he plays his part well. Too well, perhaps.

I barely hear the words of the ceremony. I'm too focused on Bella's profile, the elegant line of her throat where my pendant rests, the way she holds herself like a queen despite her obvious nervousness. *She'll make a magnificent donna*, I think. *If she survives what's coming.*

The thought of what's coming sobers me. Somewhere in the cathedral, Johnny's men wait for any sign of weakness. One wrong move, one hint that this marriage isn't absolutely real, and Bella's life is forfeit. My hands don't shake as I take the massive diamond ring—not Sophia's, never Sophia's—and prepare to slide it onto her finger.

"I take you, Isabella Marie Russo, to be my wife," I pronounce clearly, letting my voice carry to the back of the cathedral. Making sure every family, every potential threat, hears the possession in my tone. "To have and to hold, to protect and cherish, until death do us part."

She starts slightly at my deviation from the traditional vows—the added "protect" a message to both her and our audience. A faint flush colors her cheeks, and something warm flickers in her eyes. Pride, maybe. Or understanding.

Her voice is steady as she repeats her own vows, though her pulse flutters visibly at her throat where my pendant rests. Each word is clear, deliberate, a performance for our audience but something more too. When she says "to be your wife," her eyes meet mine with such intensity that heat pools in my gut.

"You may kiss the bride."

I cup her face in my hands, gentler than I was last night but no less possessive. Her lips part slightly in surprise at my tenderness, and I take full advantage. The kiss is both a claim and a promise—deep enough to leave no doubt in anyone's mind that this marriage is real, tender enough to make her melt against me despite herself. Her free hand clutches my lapel, and I feel her slight gasp against my mouth.

She tastes of mint and something sweeter, and the small sound she makes when I deepen the kiss nearly breaks my control. I want to devour her right here, show everyone exactly who she belongs to now. Instead, I force myself to end the kiss, though everything in me screams for more.

When we turn to face our guests, I keep my arm firmly around her waist, my hand splayed possessively against her side. The applause is thunderous, political alliances being sealed with each clap. My eyes find Johnny's across the cathedral, and I let every ounce of warning show in my gaze: Mine. Protected. Touch her and die.

His smirk tells me this isn't over.

The reception that follows is a masterclass in Mafia politics. The Plaza's ballroom drips with elegant excess—crystal chandeliers throwing diamonds of light across white roses and silver centerpieces, champagne flowing from a fountain that probably costs more than most cars, an orchestra playing softly in the corner. It's all Elena's work, and she's outdone herself. Every detail screams old money and power, exactly the message we need to send.

I guide Bella through the crowd, watching her handle each interaction with growing pride. She charms old Don Marconi with just the right mix of respect and grace, making the weathered bastard actually smile. When Donna Vitelli makes a thinly veiled comment about "young brides' short lifespans," Bella responds with such elegant brutality that I have to hide my grin in my champagne glass.

"You're doing beautifully," I murmur in her ear as we dance our first waltz. The silk of her dress whispers against my tuxedo, and her scent surrounds me, making it hard to focus on anything but how perfectly she fits in my arms.

"I'm doing what's necessary," she returns quietly, her smile perfectly maintained for our audience. One hand rests on my shoulder while the other is clasped in mine, her new ring catching the light. "But don't think I've forgotten your promise. Tonight, I want the truth."

My hand tightens on her waist, drawing her slightly closer than the waltz requires. "Be careful what you wish for, *piccola*."

"I'm not afraid of the dark, Matteo." Her eyes meet mine, challenging despite our intimate position. The gold flecks in her hazel irises seem to glow in the chandelier light. "I paint with it, remember?"

A new song begins, and Carmine appears at my elbow, wrapped in the scent of expensive cologne and ambition. "May I cut in?" His smile doesn't reach his cold eyes as he holds his hand out to his niece.

Every instinct screams at me not to release her. But this is part of the dance—the political minuet we must perform. I surrender my bride with obvious reluctance, my eyes tracking them as Carmine leads her away. Her back is straight, her movements graceful, but I see the tension in her shoulders.

I make my way to the bar, needing scotch to maintain my composure. Watching another man's hands on her, even her uncle's, sets my teeth on edge. The possessiveness surprises me with its intensity—I've never been a jealous man, but something about Bella brings out the primitive in me.

"Beautiful ceremony," Johnny Calabrese's voice comes from behind me, dripping with false sincerity. "She looks so much like Sophia did on our wedding day. Oh wait ..." He smirks. "That was your wedding day."

I turn slowly, letting him see exactly how close to death he's dancing. "Careful, Johnny."

"Tell me, does she know?" His voice drops to a whisper, though his dark, soulless eyes glitter with malice. "About how Sophia came to me first? About how you—"

"Mr. DeLuca?" Antonio appears at my elbow, a guardian angel in a Zegna suit. "Your wife is asking for you."

The word "wife" pulls at something in my chest. I force myself to walk away from Johnny, though every fiber of my being wants to end him right here, splatter his blood across the elegant parquet floor.

I find Bella surrounded by chattering society wives, their designer dresses and surgical enhancements a sharp contrast to her natural beauty. Her throat works as she swallows repeatedly—a tell I'm learning means she's suppressing anger. Her smile remains perfect, but her knuckles are white around her champagne flute.

"Dance with me," I say, not caring that I'm interrupting their conversation. Relief flashes in her eyes as she takes my hand, letting me lead her back to the dance floor.

"Thank you," she breathes, melting against me more naturally than she has all day. "If I had to hear one more story about their sons who would have been much more suitable ..."

"You're mine now," I remind her, pulling her closer. The possessiveness in my voice surprises even me, but I can't help it. Not with Johnny's threats still ringing in my ears, not with the way she feels in my arms. "No one else's opinion matters."

She looks up at me through dark lashes, and the mix of defiance and desire in her eyes makes my blood heat. "Yours barely matters."

I chuckle despite myself, sliding my hand lower on her back. "Still defiant, even as my wife?"

"*Especially* as your wife." But there's heat in her voice that wasn't there before, and when my fingers trace her spine through the lace of her dress, she shivers. The reaction shoots straight to my groin, making me want to forget this whole reception and take her somewhere private.

The moment shatters at the sound of breaking glass. We turn to see Bianca, face flushed from too much champagne, squaring off with Elena near the fountain. My daughter sways slightly in her bridesmaid dress, all teenage fury and inherited stubbornness. In the background, I see Johnny watching the interaction with interest.

"Tell them!" Bianca shouts, her voice carrying across the ballroom. Heads turn, conversations halt, and I feel Bella tense beside me. "Tell them what kind of man they're celebrating! Tell them what he did to—"

I'm there in an instant, my grip firm but controlled on my daughter's arm. "Enough," I growl, steering her toward the exit. Every eye in the ballroom watches us, and I can practically hear the whispers starting.

"Let me go!" She struggles against me, tears streaking her perfect makeup. "She deserves to know! Bella! Ask him about the video! Ask him what he—"

Two of my security team materialize, escorting her swiftly and discreetly from the ballroom. But the damage is done. Whispers ripple through the crowd like wind through dry leaves. I catch fragments of speculation, see the calculating looks being exchanged.

When I return to Bella's side, her society smile is firmly in place, but her eyes are arctic. "Video?" she asks under her breath as we pose for photographs. The camera flashes highlight the tension in her jaw. "What video, Matteo?"

"Not here," I murmur, pressing my lips to her temple in what appears to be a loving gesture. The scent of jasmine fills my nose, making it hard to focus on anything but how badly I want her.

"Then when?" Her voice is steel wrapped in silk. "Because I'm starting to think tonight's revelations will be more interesting than either of us anticipated."

I turn her to face me, uncaring of the photographers or our watching guests. In this moment, I see everything I could lose—not just my new wife, but any chance of her ever trusting me. The secrets I've kept, the truths I've hidden ... they could destroy whatever is building between us.

"Do you trust me, Bella?"

"No," she answers honestly, and the bluntness of it surprises a laugh out of me. Her lips quirk slightly. "But I'm beginning to think I might want to."

The admission hits me harder than her defiance ever could. Because I'm about to destroy any chance of that trust taking root. Unless ...

"Change of plans," I say suddenly, decisively. "We're leaving now."

"What? We can't—the reception—" Her eyes widen as she sputters, looking more natural than she has all day.

"Antonio will make our excuses." I'm already leading her toward the exit, my mind made up. The warmth of her hand in mine feels right, feels necessary. "If you want the truth, all of it, you'll have it. But not here. Not with Johnny watching and waiting to use it against us."

She allows me to guide her to the waiting Bentley, her wedding dress whispering against the leather seats. In the privacy of the car, I finally let myself really look at her—my bride, my salvation, possibly my destruction. The diamonds in her hair catch the streetlights as we pull away, making her look otherworldly.

"Where are we going?" she asks, and I hear the mix of fear and anticipation in her voice.

"Somewhere safe," I answer, taking her hand. Her new wedding ring catches the light, and I force myself to continue. "Somewhere I can show you exactly who you've married, for better or worse."

As we drive through the gathering darkness, I pray I'm making the right choice. But looking at her now, fierce and beautiful and mine, I know there's no going back. It's time for the truth, whatever the cost.

God help us both.

11

BELLA

The Bentley winds through darkening streets, each turn making me more disoriented. I try to track our path through Manhattan, into what must be Westchester, but the route seems deliberately circuitous. My wedding dress rustles with every movement, the sound impossibly loud in the tense silence, like the whisper of secrets about to be revealed.

Matteo sits beside me, one hand still holding mine while the other types rapid messages on his phone. His rough fingers stroke the back of my knuckles absently, each touch sending electricity up my arm. It's surreal to think that I'm married to him now—my father's best friend, the man whose dangerous reputation kept me awake at night as a teenager.

The man who now makes me lose sleep for entirely different reasons.

The city lights paint shadows across his sharp features, and my artist's eye can't help but analyze the chiaroscuro effect. He's all stark planes and dangerous angles, like something carved from marble by an angry god. The silver at his temples catches the passing lights, and my fingers itch for a pencil to capture the way shadow pools in the hollow of his throat where he's loosened his tie.

I'd paint him in oils, I decide. Dark colors for his power, but with unexpected warmth underneath—burnt umber and deep crimson rather than pure black. Something to capture both the danger and the passion I've glimpsed beneath his control.

"My mother will be furious we left the reception," I say finally, needing to break the silence before I do something stupid like tell him how beautiful he is.

"Your mother," he says, not looking up from his phone, "is currently dealing with a convenient plumbing emergency at the venue. The reception will end early, with our absence blamed on the chaos."

"You arranged a plumbing emergency at my wedding reception?" The words come out strangled. Just when I think I understand how his mind works, he does something like this. Plans within plans, every detail controlled.

He looks at me then, and my heart stammers in my chest. The slight smirk playing at his lips shouldn't be attractive—nothing about him should be attractive, given what he is, what he does. But God help me, in the dim car light he's devastating. The perfectly tailored tuxedo, the barely contained power in his frame, the intensity in his steel-blue eyes ... it's almost too much.

"Would you prefer to still be there," he asks, "listening to Johnny Calabrese make thinly veiled threats while Bianca drinks herself into another scene?"

"I'd prefer the truth." I pull my hand from his, immediately missing his warmth but needing the distance to think clearly. My heart pounds so hard I'm sure he can hear it. "Starting with where we're going."

The smirk fades, and something darker crosses his face. "The lake house. It's secure, private, and ..." He pauses, choosing his words with obvious care. "It's where everything started. With Sophia."

My pulse jumps at her name. All evening I've been demanding answers, insisting on truth, but now that it's coming, fear slides cold fingers down my spine. "Why do I feel like I'm being driven to my execution rather than my honeymoon?" I ask weakly.

"Because you're smart." His voice roughens, becoming something dark and honeyed that makes heat pool low in my belly despite my fear. "And because you know that after tonight, nothing between us will ever be the same."

The car turns onto a private road, trees crowding close on either side like sentinels. Through the branches, I catch glimpses of water, black and mysterious in the gathering dusk. When we finally pull up to the house, my eyes widen in shock.

The lake house is a modernist dream of glass and steel, a structure that looks like it was born from the landscape rather than built upon it. Cantilevered sections stretch out over the water, their clean lines softened by the organic curve of the lake behind them. In the fading light, the glass walls reflect purple-tinged clouds, making the building seem to float between water and sky.

"This is ... not what I expected," I admit as Matteo helps me from the car. His hand is warm at my elbow, and I try not to think about how natural his touch feels. How right. "I thought all Mafia safe houses were stone fortresses."

"That's next door," he says dryly, nodding toward a more traditional mansion visible through the trees. A surprised laugh escapes me before I can stop it, and his answering smile makes my breath catch. Then he adds, "This was my personal project. Sophia hated it."

Just hearing her name sends ice through my veins. Everything always comes back to her—his dead wife, her emeralds I refused to wear, her ghost haunting every moment between us.

Inside, the house comes alive around us, sensors detecting our presence. If the exterior was impressive, the interior steals my breath. I drink in every detail—the way rich walnut paneling softens the industrial elements, how carefully placed lighting creates pools of warmth in the modernist space. One entire wall is windows, offering a stunning view of the lake that makes my fingers itch for paint and canvas.

I can already imagine how it would look in different seasons—autumn leaves creating a fiery frame for the glass, snow transforming the view into a monochromatic study, spring bringing new greens to soften the stark lines. Even at Christmas, the clean architecture would make a perfect backdrop for traditional decorations, the contrast making both more striking.

"Your dress," Matteo says suddenly, his voice cutting through my artistic musings. "There's a closet upstairs with clothes. More appropriate clothes."

"You just happen to have women's clothes here?" The question comes out sharper than intended, a spike of jealousy I have no right to feel. These better not be Sophia's things, preserved like some shrine to his dead wife.

"I had them brought this morning." He moves to a cabinet, pulling out a bottle of scotch. The movement makes his tuxedo stretch across his shoulders, and my mouth goes dry at the play of muscles beneath the fine wool. I shouldn't notice these things, not when he's about to tell me God knows what about his first wife's death. But my body seems to have its own agenda where Matteo is concerned.

Traitor.

"For what?" Even as I ask, heat floods my cheeks. This isn't just about revelations. This is our wedding night, regardless of what truths come between now and then. The thought makes my pulse race, desire and anxiety warring in my stomach.

"Change first," he says, not answering my question and not looking at me. "Then we'll talk."

Upstairs, I find a closet that would make most boutiques jealous. Racks of designer casual wear in exactly my size fill the space—soft sweaters in neutral tones, perfectly cut jeans, silk blouses and cashmere loungewear. Everything is new, tags still attached, and absolutely my style. The attention to detail, to my preferences, makes something warm unfurl in my chest even as it unnerves me.

I choose soft black leggings and an oversized cream sweater that slips off one shoulder, a far cry from the wedding dress I'm wearing. It takes fifteen minutes to extract myself from the layers of silk and lace, another ten to wash away the elaborate makeup. In the bathroom mirror, I look more like myself—except for the massive diamond glinting on my left hand. The ring catches the light like a warning, a reminder that whatever comes next, I'm bound to this man forever.

When I return downstairs, soft jazz plays from hidden speakers, and my breath catches at the sight of Matteo. He's shed his tuxedo jacket and tie, his shirt sleeves rolled to reveal powerful forearms corded with muscle. He stands at the windows, backlit by the last rays of sunset on the lake, looking like something from a Renaissance painting—all power and barely contained violence wrapped in elegant clothing.

"Better?" he asks without turning.

"Depends on what comes next." I move to stand beside him, close enough to smell his cologne—spice and sandalwood and something uniquely him that makes my head spin. Part of me wants to reach out, to trace the strong line of his jaw, to feel if his stubble is as rough as it looks. Instead, I force myself to focus. "You promised me the truth, Matteo. All of it."

The silence stretches so long I think he might have changed his mind. Then, "Sophia wasn't killed by the Calabrese family."

The words hit me like a physical blow. My breath catches, heart stuttering. "But you said—"

"I killed her." His voice is flat, emotionless, but I see how his hands clench at his sides. "Right here in this house. Because she was working with Johnny Calabrese to destroy everything I'd built."

I take an instinctive step back, but Matteo moves faster. His hand catches my wrist, not hurting but restraining. The heat of his skin against mine makes it hard to think straight, even as fear and something darker course through me.

"You wanted the truth, *piccola*. Now you'll hear all of it."

"Let go of me." The words come out breathy rather than firm. I should be terrified—I *am* terrified. I've just married a confirmed murderer.

But beneath the fear is something else, something I'm afraid to examine too closely.

"No." His eyes bore into mine, and I see anguish beneath the steel. "Because you need to understand. Sophia wasn't innocent. She wasn't a victim. She was working with Johnny, plotting to destroy everything. But that's not why I killed her."

"Then why?" I hate how my voice shakes, hate how I'm leaning into his touch even as my mind screams to run.

His laugh is harsh. "She found something. Something that would destroy not just me, but Bianca's future in our world. She was going to use it to force me to step down, to hand everything to Johnny."

"What did she find?" The artist in me can't help but note how beautiful he is in his pain—all sharp angles and raw emotion, like a Caravaggio painting brought to life.

"Documents that could destroy everything I've built to protect my daughter." His voice roughens, and his thumb starts tracing circles on my inner wrist, raising goosebumps. "Some secrets have to stay buried, Bella. For everyone's sake."

"So you killed her to protect those secrets?" God help me, I understand. Family above all—isn't that what my father always taught me?

"No." His grip on my wrist loosens, becomes almost a caress. "I confronted her. Gave her a chance to explain, to choose me instead. She laughed in my face, told me I was a fool to think anyone could love a monster like me. Then she pulled a gun."

"Self-defense." The realization hits me with surprising clarity. The monster isn't the man before me—it was the *woman* who tried to destroy him, who'd have shot him to get what she wanted.

"She got off two shots before I reached her." He gestures to a spot near the windows, and I can almost see it playing out. "One grazed my shoulder. The other ..." His free hand moves to his side, and I remember the scar I glimpsed in his study, silvered with age but still angry looking. The memory of his bare chest under my hands makes heat flood my cheeks.

"And Johnny played along? Why?" I step closer without meaning to, drawn by the raw honesty in his voice.

"Because the truth would have exposed him too." His eyes hold mine, unflinching. "Better to let everyone think he'd ordered her death than admit she'd chosen him in the end." His thumb hasn't stopped its maddening circles on my wrist, each stroke sending sparks through my body. "That's who you've married, Bella. A man who killed his own wife and lied about it for a decade. Still want to stay?"

I should run. Everything I've ever believed about right and wrong tells me to run. But looking at him now—this dangerous, complicated man who had my painting turned into a pendant rather than force his dead wife's emeralds on me—I can't make myself want to.

"You're not a monster," I say softly, watching emotion flicker across his face. "Monsters don't make their wives pendants from their art. They don't protect daughters who hate them. They don't ..." My voice catches as heat pools low in my belly. "They don't kiss like you kissed me last night."

"Don't." But his voice is strained, and his eyes drop to my mouth.

"Don't what? Tell the truth?" I turn my wrist in his grip until our fingers intertwine. His sharp intake of breath emboldens me. "You're not the only one who's been keeping secrets, Matteo."

"Meaning?" The word comes out rough, almost a growl.

"Meaning I've wanted you since that day in your office." The admission makes my cheeks burn, but I force myself to continue. "Even knowing what you are, what you've done ..." I step closer, tilting my face up to his. "I still want you."

His control snaps like a bowstring. One moment he's staring at me with those intense steel-blue eyes, the next his mouth crashes down on mine with devastating force. This isn't like our careful wedding kiss or even the interrupted passion in his study. This is brutal, demanding, a claiming.

I meet his intensity with my own, pouring all my confusion and desire and understanding into it. His hands tangle in my hair, angling my head to deepen the kiss until I'm gasping against his mouth.

He tastes like scotch and danger and something uniquely him that makes me dizzy. When his tongue sweeps into my mouth, demanding and possessive, a moan tears from deep in my chest.

His answering growl vibrates through both our bodies. One hand slides down my back to pull me flush against him, and I gasp at the feeling of hard muscle against my softer curves. Heat pools low in my belly as his other hand finds the bare skin of my shoulder where my sweater has slipped. His fingers trail fire everywhere they touch, and I arch into him helplessly.

"Christ, the sounds you make," he groans against my throat, his stubble scraping deliciously as he trails open-mouthed kisses down my neck. Each brush of his lips sends electricity shooting through my body, making me clutch at his shoulders for support.

His teeth graze my pulse point and my head falls back, giving him better access. The hand in my hair tightens, holding me exactly where he wants me as he finds the sensitive spot behind my ear. When he bites gently, then soothes the sting with his tongue, my entire body shudders.

"Last chance to run," he warns, his voice rough against my skin. But his hands grip me tighter, like he can't bear the thought of letting me go.

I answer by sliding my trembling fingers to his shirt buttons. The first one slips free, revealing more of that tanned skin I've been dreaming about since his study. His chest rises and falls rapidly under my touch, and I feel powerful knowing I affect him as much as he affects me.

"Bella." My name comes out like a prayer and a curse as I work on the next button. "If you start this ..."

"I want this," I breathe, pressing my lips to his thundering pulse. "I want you."

He lets out a sound like I've wounded him, then his mouth is on mine again. This kiss is different—deeper, hungrier, full of dark promises that make heat spiral through me. His tongue strokes against mine in a rhythm that makes me think of other things, makes me ache in places I didn't know could ache.

My hands flatten against his now-bare chest, feeling the rapid beat of his heart under my palms. His skin burns hot, all hard muscle and surprising smoothness except for the raised line of that scar. When my fingers trace it, his whole body shudders.

Whatever comes next, whatever secrets still lie between us, this is my choice. My truth. My monster who's not really a monster at all.

Just a man who would burn the world to protect what's his.

And now, for better or worse, I'm his too.

12

MATTEO

Bella's trembling fingers fumble with my shirt buttons, her rapid breathing the only sound in the quiet room. I catch her hands, stilling them against my chest where my heart pounds beneath her palms. The heat of her touch burns through me, making it hard to maintain control.

"Slow down, *piccola*," I murmur against her mouth, even though every instinct screams to take her right here, right now. "We have all night."

"I don't want slow." She nips at my bottom lip, defiant even now, and Christ, the way she challenges me makes my blood burn. Her hands slide down my chest, leaving fire in their wake. "I want—"

"What you want," I growl, spinning her so her back presses against the window, "and what you need are two different things." The glass must be cold against her skin, but she arches into me instead of away, pressing those perfect curves against my body. "Trust me to know the difference."

Her laugh is breathless, slightly wild. "Trust the man who just confessed to murder?"

I slide one hand into her hair, tugging gently to expose the elegant line of her throat. The way she yields to me, even while maintaining that spark of defiance in her eyes, nearly undoes my control. "Trust the man who's been dreaming of this since that day you walked into his study." My lips trace the path of her pulse, feeling it jump beneath my tongue. "The man who's going to worship every inch of you until you forget everything but my name."

"Matteo," she gasps as my teeth graze her skin, and the sound of my name on her lips sends heat straight to my groin.

"Yes," I approve, my free hand slipping beneath her sweater to find bare skin. She's impossibly soft, warm silk under my calloused fingers. I've been dying to touch her like this since our encounter in my office, imagining how she'd feel, how she'd respond. The reality is better than any fantasy. "Just like that."

She's responsive to every touch, her sensitivity making her hyper-aware of each point of contact between us. When I find a particularly sensitive spot just below her ribs, she makes a sound that shoots straight through me—half moan, half whimper. The urge to take her right here against the window is almost overwhelming, but she deserves better for our first time. For her first time.

I scoop her into my arms, savoring her small gasp of surprise. She weighs nothing, this slip of a girl who's brought the mighty Matteo DeLuca to his knees. I carry her upstairs to the master bedroom, where the lights rise softly as we enter. The massive bed is dressed in crisp white linens—all new, nothing recycled from the past. This room, like everything else, has been prepared just for her.

Setting her down beside the bed, I take a moment to drink in the sight of her. My wife. Mine. Her dark hair is mussed from my hands, tumbling around her shoulders in waves that beg me to bury my fingers in them again. Her lips are swollen from my kisses, her cheeks flushed with desire. That oversized sweater has slipped completely off one shoulder now, revealing the elegant line of her collarbone and the edge of black lace beneath.

"Beautiful," I murmur, reaching for the hem of her sweater. I need to see all of her, need to map every inch of skin with my hands, my mouth.

She raises her arms, letting me pull the sweater over her head, but her hands immediately move to cover herself. The gesture is endearing, speaking to an innocence that makes me want to both protect and corrupt her. The black lace of her bra does little to hide her curves, but it's not shame making her shy—it's the intensity of my gaze.

"Don't," I say softly, drawing her hands away. "Let me look at my wife."

The word sends a visible shiver through her. "Say it again."

"My wife." I press a kiss to her shoulder, tasting her jasmine-scented skin. "My artist." Another kiss along her collarbone, feeling her pulse race beneath my lips. "Mine."

She melts into my touch, her hands coming up to tangle in my hair as I worship every inch of exposed skin. Each gasp, each tremor tells me exactly how to please her. I'm mapping her responses, memorizing what makes her breath catch, what makes her fingers tighten in my hair.

"Please," she whimpers, and the sound nearly breaks my control.

"Please what?" I straighten, enjoying the flush spreading across her chest, the way her eyes have gone dark with desire. "Use your words, *piccola*."

Instead of answering, she reaches for my shirt, pushing it off my shoulders with trembling hands. Her eyes widen at the sight of my scars—the one from Sophia's bullet on my side, others from years of violence. But where I expect hesitation, I find reverence. She traces each mark with gentle fingers, learning my body like she's memorizing it for a painting.

When she reaches the bullet scar, she pauses, her touch featherlight. "Does it still hurt?"

"No." I catch her hand, pressing it flat against my chest where my heart thunders beneath her palm. "But this does."

She understands my meaning—I see it in her eyes, in the way tears gather in those hazel depths even as she tries to smile. No one has ever looked at me like this, with such complete acceptance of both my strength and my vulnerability. Rising on her toes, she presses her lips to the scar on my shoulder, then the one on my side. Her tenderness undoes me more than any seduction could.

The last threads of my control snap. I lift her onto the bed, following her down into the crisp white sheets. Everything feels heightened, more intense—the softness of her skin against mine, the way her breath catches with each touch, the trust in her eyes as she welcomes me into her arms.

Italian endearments fall from my lips between kisses. "*Tesoro mio*," I whisper against her throat. "*Il mio cuore.*" My treasure. My heart. Words I never thought I'd say again, yet they feel right with her.

"Tell me you want this," I demand, needing to hear it. "Tell me you're sure."

"I want this." She meets my eyes without hesitation, and the trust I see there steals my breath. "I want you, Matteo. All of you—the darkness and the light."

I take my time admiring the black lace against her pale skin. The bra is clearly expensive—La Perla if I had to guess—but it's the way she wears it that makes my mouth go dry. Her breasts rise and fall with each quick breath, the lace doing little to hide her peaked nipples.

"You're staring," she whispers, a blush spreading down her neck to her chest.

"How could I not?" My fingers trace the edge of the lace, feeling her shiver. "You're exquisite."

I reach behind her, unhooking the bra with practiced ease. She lets it fall away, and my breath catches. Her breasts are perfect—full but not too large, tipped with dusky pink nipples that beg for my mouth. When I cup them in my palms, testing their weight, she gasps.

"Sensitive," I note, brushing my thumbs across the hardened peaks. Her whole body arches into the touch. "I'll remember that."

Those leggings have to go next. I peel them down slowly, revealing inches of soft skin until she stands before me in only black lace panties that match the discarded bra. My hands span her waist before sliding down to grip her hips.

Her hands tremble as she reaches for my belt, and the slight shake in her fingers makes something protective and primal surge in my chest. When the leather slides free, her breath catches. She's nervous but determined, my brave little artist.

"Let me help you," I murmur, guiding her hands to my zipper. The brush of her knuckles against me, even through layers of fabric, makes my muscles tense. She pushes my trousers down, and I step out of them, leaving me in just black boxer briefs that do nothing to hide how much I want her.

Her eyes widen when they drop to the obvious bulge, and that blush I'm growing addicted to stains her cheeks pink. Christ, her innocence is intoxicating. When her fingers hook hesitantly in the waistband of my underwear, I have to grip her wrists to stop her.

"Together," I tell her, reaching for her panties. "Fair is fair, *piccola*."

The last barriers fall away, and she's finally, gloriously naked before me. She's a masterpiece—all soft curves and elegant lines that would make Renaissance sculptors weep. Her waist nips in before flaring to gently rounded hips, and her legs seem endless.

When she finally sees me completely naked, her blush deepens but she doesn't look away. She takes in every detail—the muscles honed by years of training, the scars that map my violent history, the very obvious evidence of my desire for her. I see the moment her gaze catches on my size, her lips parting slightly as her eyes widen.

"See something you like, *piccola*?" I tease gently, trying to ease her nervousness.

She surprises me by reaching out to trace the muscles of my abdomen, her fingers following the defined lines with an artist's appreciation. "You're beautiful," she whispers, then immediately looks embarrassed. "I mean ... handsome? I don't know the right word ..."

I catch her wandering hand, pressing a kiss to her palm. "From you, I'll take beautiful."

When I pull her against me, we both gasp at the first full skin-to-skin contact. Her breasts press against my chest, soft curves meeting hard muscle, and the feeling of her naked body against mine is almost too much. She fits me perfectly, like she was made for me, and every point of contact burns like fire.

"Matteo," she breathes, and my name has never sounded more like a prayer.

I capture her mouth in a searing kiss as my hand slides between her thighs. She's already wet for me, her body trembling as I explore her most intimate places. When I circle that sensitive bundle of nerves, she breaks the kiss with a gasp, her head falling back against the pillows.

"That's it," I encourage, watching her face as I slip one finger inside her, then another. She's tight, wet heat around my fingers, and the thought of being inside her makes my control fray. "Let me hear you, *piccola*."

Her moans grow louder as I work her body, learning exactly how to touch her, where to press, how to curl my fingers to make her arch off the bed. When my thumb finds her clit again, she cries out my name, her hands fisting in the sheets.

My fingers work her slowly, deliberately. She's so wet, so responsive to every touch, her body telling me exactly what she needs even as she struggles to voice it.

"That's it, *piccola*," I encourage, watching her face as pleasure overtakes her. "Let go for me."

Her release catches her by surprise—one moment she's trembling on the edge, the next she's crying out my name as she clenches around my fingers. She's magnificent in her pleasure, all flushed skin and desperate sounds.

Before she can recover, I slide down her body, pressing kisses to her inner thighs. Her eyes fly wide when she realizes what I'm about to do.

"Matteo, what—" She tries to close her legs, but I hold them open gently.

"Trust me," I murmur against her sensitive skin. At the first taste of her, we both groan. "Christ, you taste perfect."

She writhes beneath my mouth, her hands fisting in the sheets as I discover every spot that makes her gasp my name. When I focus on her clit, alternating between gentle suction and firm strokes of my tongue, her thighs begin to tremble. I slide two fingers back inside her, curling them upward as I work her with my mouth.

"Oh God, Matteo, please ..." Her voice breaks on my name as her second orgasm hits harder than the first. I keep going, drawing out her pleasure until she's pulling at my hair, oversensitive and desperate.

When I finally move back up her body, her eyes are heavy-lidded with pleasure, her lips parted as she tries to catch her breath. I capture her mouth in a deep kiss, letting her taste herself on my tongue. Instead of shying away, she moans, pulling me closer.

"Inside me," she begs between kisses. "I need you inside me."

"Look at me," I demand, positioning myself at her entrance. When those hazel eyes meet mine, I see trust mixed with desperate need. "Tell me if it's too much."

She nods her understanding as I begin entering her slowly, watching her face for any sign of discomfort. The trust she's placing in me is staggering—this beautiful, fierce woman who knows what I am, what I've done, and still gives herself to me completely. When I'm fully seated, I force myself to stay still, letting her adjust to my size. The sensation of her tight heat around me nearly breaks my control, but I force myself to go slow, to let her adjust to my size.

"Okay?" I ask when I'm fully seated. Every muscle in my body trembles with the effort of holding still.

"More than okay," she breathes, rolling her hips experimentally. The movement makes us both gasp. "Move, Matteo. Please."

I begin a slow, deep rhythm that has her arching beneath me, meeting each thrust. Her hands map my back, my shoulders, learning me as thoroughly as I'm learning her. When I shift the angle slightly, she closes her eyes and cries out, her nails scoring my skin.

"Open your eyes, Bella," I command softly. "Look at me."

She does, and what I see there steals my breath. No one has ever looked at me like this—not with fear or calculation or political maneuvering, but with pure acceptance. Not even Sophia, before she betrayed me, looked at me with such complete trust. This slip of a girl, this artist who sees beauty in darkness, who knows the worst of me and still wants me ...

She matches my rhythm instinctively, as if we've done this a thousand times before, as if our bodies were made for each other. When I shift the angle slightly, she cries out, her nails scoring my back. The slight pain only heightens my pleasure, makes me want to mark her in return.

"That's it, *piccola*," I encourage, feeling her begin to tighten around me again. "One more time. Come for me."

Her release takes us both by surprise—one moment she's gasping my name like a prayer, the next she's shuddering beneath me, taking me with her over the edge. I muffle my groan against her throat, holding her close as we both tremble through the aftershocks. Nothing has ever felt like this, so complete, so right.

Later, as we lie tangled in the sheets, she traces patterns on my chest while I play with her hair. The lake reflects moonlight through the windows, casting everything in silver shadows. She looks ethereal in this light, like something I don't deserve but will kill to keep.

Her fingers find a scar near my ribs—old, silvered with time. "Tell me about your childhood," she says softly.

"My father believed in harsh lessons," is all I say, but my body goes rigid beneath her touch. I notice I do what I always do—call him "my father," never Papa or Father. Always formal, always distant. Like proper words can keep the memories at bay.

She seems to sense my tension because she shifts, pressing a gentle kiss over my heart instead. "What happens now?"

"Now we sleep." I kiss her temple, breathing in the scent of jasmine and sex and us. "Tomorrow we face Johnny and whatever else comes."

"Together?" The word holds so much hope, so much trust.

I tighten my arms around her. "Together."

But even as she drifts off against my chest, I stare at the ceiling, remembering Johnny's words at the reception. Because there's one truth I still haven't told her—the real reason Sophia had to die. And when that truth comes out, I might lose this newfound peace forever.

For now though, I have this—my bride in my arms, trusting and warm and mine. Whatever comes tomorrow, tonight I'll hold her close and pretend I deserve the way she looks at me. Pretend I'm the man she believes I am, rather than the monster I know myself to be.

"Sleep, *il mio cuore*," I whisper into her hair. My heart. My salvation. My potential destruction.

God help us both when she learns the rest.

13

BELLA

Sunlight streams through floor-to-ceiling windows, painting the lake in morning gold. For a moment, I forget where I am —then every sensation floods back at once. The delicious ache between my thighs, the slight burn of stubble rash on my neck, the memory of Matteo's hands and mouth mapping every inch of my body. Heat floods my cheeks as I remember how I responded to him, how I begged for more, how he made me fall apart again and again until I couldn't remember my own name.

I stretch languidly, feeling muscles I didn't even know I had protest. The sheets beside me are cold—Matteo must have been up for hours. Typical. Even after sharing something so intimate, he maintains his distance. The thought brings an unexpected ache to my chest.

His dress shirt from last night lies discarded near the bed, a casualty of our passion. I slip it on, inhaling his lingering scent as I button it—spice and sandalwood and something uniquely him that makes my pulse quicken even now. The silk lining still holds his warmth, and memories flash through my mind: how gentle he was at first, then how desperate; the Italian endearments he whispered against my skin; the way he watched me with those intense eyes as he claimed me completely.

In the mirror, I hardly recognize myself. Gone is the scared artist hiding from her family's world. The woman staring back at me looks ... transformed. Dark marks dot my neck and collarbone—Matteo's way of marking his territory, I suppose. My lips are still swollen from his kisses, and my hair is a riot of waves that no amount of brushing will tame. The massive diamond on my finger catches the morning light, a constant reminder of my new reality.

But something nags at me as I study my reflection. Last night, Matteo finally told me the truth about Sophia—or at least, his version of it. Self-defense, he claimed. She pulled a gun.

But why does something about the story feel off? Maybe it's the artist in me, always looking for the shadows beneath the surface, the places where light and dark meet to create something deeper.

Voices drift up from downstairs—Matteo's deep rumble that still makes my body respond even after everything he gave me last night and another I don't recognize. The second voice is sharp, angry, nothing like Matteo's controlled tones. Something about the tension in their exchange makes me creep to the top of the stairs, my bare feet silent on the hardwood.

"—doesn't change anything," Matteo is saying, his voice carrying that edge of danger I'm learning to recognize. "The deal stands."

"The deal," the other voice spits back with barely contained fury, "was based on lies. You think Johnny won't use this? Won't tell her everything?"

My heart stutters at the mention of Johnny. Even here, in what should be the safety of the morning after my wedding night, danger creeps in.

"Let him try, Alessandro." Matteo's tone drops lower, deadlier. "She's mine now. Protected."

That possessive statement should anger me—I'm no one's property—but something in the way he says it makes heat pool in my belly. Until the stranger's next words turn that heat to ice.

"Like Sophia was protected?" A harsh laugh follows. "Face it, Matteo. You're repeating history, and we both know how that ended."

My foot lands on a creaky board, and the conversation cuts off abruptly. By the time I descend the stairs on shaking legs, Matteo is alone in the kitchen, making coffee as if nothing happened. He's shirtless, wearing only black pants that ride low on his hips, and despite my growing unease, my body responds to the sight of all that muscled skin marked by my nails last night. His hair is damp from a shower, and water droplets still cling to his shoulders. He looks devastating, dangerous, and entirely too beautiful for my peace of mind.

"Good morning, *piccola*." His eyes darken appreciatively as they rake over me in his shirt. "Sleep well?"

The tenderness in his voice makes this harder. How can he be so many things at once—gentle lover, dangerous don, keeper of secrets that might destroy us both?

"Who were you talking to?" I try to keep my voice steady, but fear makes it waver. Everything feels fragile this morning—my newfound trust in him, my understanding of our situation, even my own heart that's treacherously falling for a man who keeps too many secrets.

He doesn't insult me by denying it, which I appreciate even as dread pools in my stomach. "Business. Nothing for you to worry about."

"I'm your wife now," I remind him, the word still strange on my tongue as I move to the coffee maker. Last night he claimed every inch of my body, yet this morning he's already shutting me out. "Your secrets are supposed to be my secrets."

His arms snake around my waist, pulling me back against his chest. The heat of his skin through the thin dress shirt makes my breath catch, memories of last night flooding back. "Some secrets protect you," he murmurs, lips brushing my ear in a way that makes me shiver. "Some would destroy you."

"Like the real reason Sophia died?" The words fall out of my mouth before I can stop them.

His body goes rigid against mine, every muscle tensing. Before he can respond, both our phones explode with notifications. My hands shake as I reach for mine first, and my breath catches at the headline that changes everything:

Calabrese Heir Releases Shocking Video: The Truth About Sophia DeLuca's Death.

The security footage shows Sophia in this very house, backing away from someone off camera. Even in the grainy quality, I can see the terror on her face, her hands raised in surrender—not holding a gun like Matteo claimed. She's begging, pleading for her life. My stomach lurches as I realize the implications.

The man I gave myself to last night, the man I'm starting to fall for, lied about killing his wife in self-defense.

"Matteo?" My voice comes out small, broken. "W-what is this?"

"Don't." He releases me, moving to the windows with lethal grace. "Don't look at it. Don't read any of it."

"Why?" I follow him, gripping my phone like a lifeline. Last night I trusted him with my body, my heart beginning to trust him with more, and now this? "What aren't you telling me? You said she pulled a gun, that it was self-defense. But this footage—"

"Shows exactly what Johnny wants it to show." He turns to face me, and something in his eyes—desperation maybe, or fear—makes my heart clench. "Trust me, Bella. Please."

"Trust goes both ways." I hold up my phone, hating how my voice shakes. "The video is *everywhere*. Every family in New York is watching it right now. Whatever truth you're hiding, it's about to come out. Wouldn't you rather I hear it from you?"

For a moment, I see it in his face—the war between truth and protection, between trust and fear. His jaw works as he struggles with something, and I think he might actually tell me everything. Then his phone rings—Antonio's tone cutting through the tension like a knife.

The color drains from his face as he listens, and my world tilts before he even speaks.

"Get dressed," he orders, already moving toward the stairs. "We're leaving. *Now.*"

"Why? What's happened?" I struggle to keep up with his long strides.

"Your mother's dead."

The phone slips from my numb fingers, clattering on the hardwood. The sound seems to come from very far away, like I'm underwater. This can't be happening. Not my mother. Not now. "What?"

"Someone broke into her penthouse last night. Made it look like a robbery gone wrong." His voice softens slightly, and the gentleness in it breaks something in my chest. "I'm sorry, *piccola*."

The room spins violently. I grab the kitchen counter, my knees threatening to give out. Memories assault me—my mother's cutting remarks about my art, yes, but also the way she'd brush my hair when I was little, how she'd sing me Italian lullabies, the pride in her eyes at my first art show even as she criticized my clothes.

Oh God, both my parents are gone. In less than a week, I've become an orphan.

"The Calabrese family?" I manage through the tightness in my throat.

"Most likely." He's already on the phone, barking orders in Italian. "Which means you're next on their list. We need to—"

A window shatters upstairs, the sound like ice breaking in my chest. One moment I'm frozen in grief, the next I'm airborne as Matteo tackles me to the ground. Gunfire erupts through the house, the noise deafening in the modern space. Glass rains down around us like deadly diamonds, catching the morning light before turning lethal.

"Stay down!" Matteo shouts, pulling a gun from somewhere and returning fire.

But my artist's eye, trained to notice details others miss, catches something he doesn't—a red dot appearing on his chest like a deadly brushstroke. Without thinking, just pure instinct, I shove him hard. We roll behind the kitchen island together just as bullets pepper the spot where he'd been standing.

We land with me on top, his gun pressed between us, and for a surreal moment, all I can think about is how we were tangled together so differently just hours ago. Our faces are inches apart as more gunfire sounds outside. The scent of gunpowder mixes with his cologne, with the coffee he was making, with the lingering traces of our lovemaking—the ordinary and extraordinary colliding in this moment of chaos.

"You saved my life," he says roughly, brushing glass from my hair with his free hand. Even now, even after the video, after the lies, he's trying to protect me.

"If I let you die," I manage through chattering teeth, grief and fear and adrenaline making me shake, "who's going to tell me what was really on that video?"

His laugh is more breath than sound, ghosting across my face. "When we get out of this alive, I'll tell you everything. I swear it."

"If," I correct, hearing footsteps crunching on broken glass. Oh God, they're inside now. "If we get out alive."

His free hand cups my cheek, thumb brushing my bottom lip in a gesture so tender it makes my heart ache. Even with death coming for us, he touches me like I'm precious. "When," he insists. "Because now I have something worth surviving for."

The tenderness of the moment contrasts sharply with the violence surrounding us. More windows shatter, and the footsteps are getting closer. I should be terrified—I *am* terrified—but somehow being in Matteo's arms makes me feel safe even as my world falls apart. How can I still trust him, still want him, when he's lied to me? When my mother is dead and I'm probably next?

Before I can sort through my tangled emotions, he rolls us over, shielding my body with his as the kitchen erupts in chaos. His heartbeat thunders against my cheek as bullets fly overhead, and I realize something that terrifies me more than the gunfire—I'm falling in love with a man I'm not sure I can trust, and we might both die before I figure out if that's wonderful or terrible.

Bullets whiz overhead as Matteo keeps his body curved over mine. The kitchen island won't protect us for long—already chunks of marble are flying off as bullets strike. The rich smell of coffee mingles with gunpowder and broken glass, creating a surreal snapshot my brain can't help but catalog even in crisis.

"When I say run," Matteo breathes against my ear, "head for the garage. Don't stop, don't look back."

I want to trust him completely. Last night, when he was inside me, whispering Italian endearments against my skin, trust seemed so easy. Now, with the video of Sophia fresh in my mind and my mother's death a raw wound in my chest, everything feels uncertain. But what choice do I have?

"Three." His arm tightens around me. "Two." A bullet strikes dangerously close, sending marble shards raining over us. "One."

We move as one unit, him firing behind us as we sprint for the garage door. My bare feet barely feel the glass cutting them—adrenaline dulls everything except the awareness of Matteo at my back. The garage is thirty feet away. Twenty. Ten.

A figure steps out from behind a column. Without thinking, I grab a heavy crystal vase from a side table and hurl it at his head. The man drops, gun clattering away. Matteo's approving grunt would make me proud if I weren't so terrified.

"In!" He shoves me toward the waiting Bentley as more shots ring out. I dive into the backseat as he slides behind the wheel. The engine roars to life just as bullets start pinging off the bulletproof glass.

We burst through the garage door in a shower of splintered wood. As we speed down the private drive, I risk a glance back at the house. Smoke curls from broken windows, and dark figures move through the destruction like shadows. My mother is dead, my father's murderers are hunting me, and I'm married to a man who might be lying about everything.

"You promised me the truth," I say as we hit the main road, my voice shaking. "All of it."

"I know." His eyes meet mine in the rearview mirror, and what I see there makes my heart stutter. Fear, yes, but also something deeper. Something that makes me want to believe him despite everything. "And you'll have it. But first, we need to survive."

The Bentley speeds through the morning light, taking us toward an uncertain future. I press my hand against the window, watching the lake house disappear behind us. Last night I gave Matteo my body. This morning, I saved his life even after discovering his lies. And now, as we flee from people trying to kill us, I realize I'm still willing to give him my heart—if he's brave enough to trust me with all his truths.

I just pray we live long enough to find out if that's possible.

14

MATTEO

Blood trickles down my arm as I guide the Bentley through winding back roads, each turn calculated to lose our pursuers. The morning sun flashes through autumn leaves, creating a strobe effect that makes it harder to track the black SUVs in my rearview mirror. My shoulder burns where the bullet grazed me, but I've had worse. What I can't stand is seeing Bella beside me, her bare legs dotted with tiny cuts from the shattered glass.

She clutches my discarded shirt closer, trying to preserve some modesty. We'd had no time to properly dress—the moment there was an opening, I rushed her to the car. The sight of those small wounds on her perfect skin makes rage build in my chest. I'm supposed to protect her, and instead she's bleeding, half dressed, and running for her life less than twenty-four hours after becoming my wife.

"You're bleeding," she says, her voice steadier than I'd expect after our narrow escape. Even now, after everything she's seen, she worries about me. It makes something in my chest twist painfully.

"Graze wound. Nothing serious." I take another sharp turn, the tires protesting as we barely miss a guardrail. The road ahead winds through dense forest, perfect for losing tails if you know the terrain.

And I know every inch of these roads. "Call Antonio. Speed dial three."

She reaches for my phone, but it's already ringing—Elena's name flashing on the screen. Bella answers immediately, putting it on speaker. My jaw clenches. We don't have time for this.

"B, thank God!" Elena's voice is frantic through the speaker. "Are you watching the news? They're saying your mother—"

"I know." Bella's composure cracks slightly, and the sound of pain in her voice makes me want to kill someone. Preferably Johnny Calabrese. "Elena, I need you to be careful. They might come for you too."

"I'm already at the safe house. Your friend Father Romano got me out just in time. Someone tried to break into my apartment an hour ago." There's a pause that makes my blood run cold. "B, the video they released ... you need to see it. All of it."

My hands tighten on the steering wheel until my knuckles go white. Goddamn Elena and her need to protect Bella. Some truths are better left buried. "Elena, hang up. *Now.*"

"Mr. DeLuca, with all due respect, she needs to know what—"

"Hang. Up." I put every ounce of authority into those words, the tone that makes hardened killers obey without question.

But it's too late. Bella's already pulled up the video on her phone, her fingers moving swift and sure across the screen. My wife's stubborn streak is going to get us both killed. The thought would be admirable if it weren't so dangerous.

"Bella, don't—"

"I deserve to know," she cuts me off, pressing play. The determination in her voice reminds me of Sophia, and for a moment my chest feels too tight.

The security footage fills her phone screen, grainy but clear enough to transport me back to that night. Sophia in the lake house, very much alive. She's arguing with someone off camera, her voice thick with tears that I once thought were genuine.

"I won't do it!" Sophia shouts from the tiny screen, her voice bringing back memories I've spent a decade trying to bury. "You can't make me choose."

"Choose what?" Bella whispers beside me, but I keep my mouth shut, taking another sharp turn that sends gravel spraying. The SUVs are falling behind, but my focus splits dangerously between the road and the video that's about to destroy everything.

The footage jumps forward, and my grip on the steering wheel becomes painful. Sophia's at the window now, gun in hand, but she's not pointing it at me like I claimed. She's backing away, terror etched on her face in a way that still haunts my dreams.

"Please," she begs on screen. "The records were buried for a reason. If anyone finds out what really happened—"

The footage cuts out, leaving the car in suffocating silence. I can feel Bella's eyes on me, can practically hear the wheels turning in that quick mind of hers. She's piecing things together, and God help me, she's too smart not to see the truth.

"What records?" She turns to me, face pale in the morning light. The cuts on her legs have stopped bleeding, but seeing them still makes me want to tear someone apart. "What really happened that night, Matteo?"

Before I can answer—before I have to choose between lying to my new wife or destroying my daughter's life—bullets pepper the back of the car. One takes out the rear window, showering us with safety glass. For once, I'm grateful for the interruption. I jerk the wheel hard, taking us down a narrow dirt road that few know exists.

"Hold on," I order, reaching into the center console with my injured arm. Pain shoots through my shoulder, but pain is an old friend. I've learned to use it, to let it sharpen my focus rather than dull it. The small remote feels heavy in my palm as we clear the trees.

I press the button, and the world erupts behind us. The explosion turns the morning sky to fire, a massive fireball blooming like some deadly flower. Both SUVs disappear in the inferno, the blast wave rocking our car. In the rearview mirror, the destruction paints Bella's face in shades of orange and red, making her look like some avenging angel.

"Jesus," she breathes, and I catch the mix of horror and awe in her voice.

"IEDs," I explain shortly, already calculating our next move. "I have them planted on all my escape routes."

"Of course you do." Her voice holds a note of hysteria that makes me want to pull her into my arms. But she's quiet only for a moment before: "You still haven't answered my question. What really happened that night, Matteo?"

I guide the car onto the private airstrip where my jet waits, engines already running. The sun catches the polished metal of the plane, making it gleam like a promise of escape. The pilot stands ready at the stairs, and I can see Antonio's men taking up defensive positions.

"Not here. Once we're in the air—"

"No." The sound of her seatbelt unbuckling makes me tense. She turns to face me fully, and Christ, the sight of her undoes me. Those endless legs bare beneath my shirt, dark hair wild from our escape, tiny drops of blood dotting her skin like rubies.

Even in crisis, she's the most beautiful thing I've ever seen. "I just watched the lake house get shot up. My mother is dead. I'm sitting here in your bloody goddamn shirt with no shoes and about a hundred cuts from broken glass. I think I've earned the fucking truth. Now."

The rising sun catches her wedding ring, and memories of another ring, another woman, another impossible choice flood back. I kill the engine, knowing we have precious little time before someone tracks us here. But she deserves the truth, even if it destroys us both.

"Sophia found something," I force the words out, each one tasting like ash.

Bella's sharp intake of breath cuts through the morning air. Her mind is already connecting dots I've spent years trying to keep separate. "What did she find?"

"Documents that would destroy not just my position, but Bianca's entire future in our world." I make myself meet those hazel eyes that see too much. My daughter's future weighs against my new wife's trust, and for once, I choose honesty. "Sophia was going to use them to force me to step down, to hand everything to Johnny."

"Because Bianca isn't yours?"

Her quick understanding shouldn't surprise me, but it does. My silence stretches as I study her face, wondering how she pieced it together so fast. "The truth about her father ... it's worse than any question of bloodlines."

In the distance, sirens wail—a reminder that our time is running out. Bella's quiet for a long moment, processing. When she speaks, her question reveals why I'm falling for her despite my best intentions. "Does Bianca know? About any of it?"

"No." The word comes out sharp, protective. "And she can never know." I start the car again, pulling up to the jet's stairs. "Now you understand why this video changes everything. Why we need to leave. Now."

"Because once people start investigating ..." Her mind works quickly, filling in blanks I've spent years protecting. "They'll find whatever Sophia discovered."

"They'll tear us apart." I help her from the car, noting how she leans into me despite everything she's just learned. The trust in that small gesture makes my chest ache. "Starting with you."

"Then why tell me at all?" Her eyes search mine, looking for truth in a man who's built his life on lies. "Why not let me believe your original story?"

I catch her chin, making her meet my gaze. Her skin is silk under my calloused fingers, and goddamn, I don't deserve the way she looks at me—like she wants to understand rather than judge. "Because I won't start this marriage with the same lies that ended my last one."

Something soft crosses her face, something that makes me think maybe, just maybe, we have a chance. But before she can respond, gunfire erupts from the tree line. The sound shatters the morning calm like breaking glass.

I shove her toward the jet's stairs as my security team returns fire. The steady rhythm of automatic weapons fills the air, and my body moves on pure instinct, decades of violence making my reactions automatic.

"Go!" I shout, pushing her up the steps. My hands leave bloody prints on the white shirt she wears—my shirt—and the sight of it makes rage burn hot in my chest. "I'm right behind you."

But as I turn to fire at our attackers, movement in the trees catches my eye. A familiar face appears in the scope of a rifle, and my blood runs cold. Not Johnny—someone much worse.

Carmine Russo smiles at me through his gun sight, and in that moment, understanding hits like a physical blow: this was never about Sophia's video at all. This is about power, about control, about a man who would kill his own sister-in-law and niece to claim what he thinks should be his.

The morning sun glints off his scope as I raise my weapon, and I pray Bella is safely inside the jet. Because her uncle is about to learn what happens to men who threaten what's mine.

I take aim at Carmine just as he fires. The bullet whizzes past my ear, close enough that I feel the displacement of air. My return shot catches a tree trunk as he ducks behind it, wood splintering where his head had been. Around us, the air fills with crossfire—my men versus his, bullets painting deadly patterns in the morning light.

"Is this really how you want to play it, Carmine?" I call out, using the jet's landing gear as cover. "Your own niece?"

His laugh carries across the tarmac, cold and calculated. "My brother was weak. His daughter is weaker. The Russo family deserves better than an artist playing at being a donna."

More shots ring out. One catches my already injured arm, tearing through muscle. The pain is immediate, searing, but I force it down. I've fought through worse. Behind me, I hear Bella shouting my name from the jet's doorway. Foolish, brave woman—she should be taking cover.

"Matteo!" The fear in her voice makes something primal rise in my chest. "Behind you!"

I spin just as one of Carmine's men emerges from under the plane. My bullet catches him in the shoulder, sending him sprawling, but more are coming. Too many. They've planned this well, the bastards.

"Your time's over, DeLuca," Carmine calls out. "First you, then your precious daughter. Once everyone knows what Sophia found—"

My roar of rage drowns out his words as I empty my clip in his direction. But he's already moving, and my injury throws off my aim. Fresh blood soaks my sleeve, making my grip slippery on the gun.

"Boss!" One of my men's voices cuts through the chaos. "We need to go! Now!"

He's right. We're too exposed, and I'm losing too much blood. With a final shot toward Carmine's position, I back toward the stairs. The engines roar as I take them two at a time, bullets pinging off the metal around me.

The jet door seals behind me as I collapse into the nearest seat. Bella's hands are immediately on me, pressing something against my wound as the plane lurches into motion. Through the window, I see Carmine emerge from the trees, watching us with cold calculation as we taxi away.

"Hold on," the pilot calls back as we pick up speed. More bullets strike the fuselage, but the reinforced metal holds.

I pull Bella close with my good arm as we lift off, leaving Carmine and his men behind. She's shaking—from adrenaline or fear or rage, I'm not sure. Maybe all three.

"You're hurt," she says, her voice steady despite her trembling hands as she examines my wound.

"I'll live." I press my lips to her temple, breathing in her scent. "But this isn't over."

"I know." She meets my eyes. "But next time, we face it together."

The jet banks sharply west. Somewhere below, Carmine is already planning his next move. But for now, I have my wife in my arms, and we're alive. Sometimes, that has to be enough.

I just pray it stays that way.

15

BELLA

The jet climbs through turbulent air, each bump sending shockwaves of pain through my battered body. Tiny cuts from the shattered glass sting under my borrowed clothes—leggings and a cashmere sweater that probably cost more than my old apartment's monthly rent. The luxury feels surreal against my skin, like everything else about my new life. Was it really just yesterday I was painting in my studio, worried about my thesis exhibition? Now I'm thirty thousand feet in the air, running from someone who wants me dead.

Across from me, Matteo sits perfectly still as the flight attendant—a severe-looking woman with steel-gray hair and hands that move with military precision—cleans and bandages his arm. Blood has already soaked through his new shirt, the crimson stain a stark reminder of how close I came to losing him. His face betrays nothing, but I'm learning to read the subtle signs of his distress—the tension in his jaw, the way his fingers drum against his thigh when he's processing something dangerous.

The attendant works methodically, her practiced movements suggesting this isn't her first time patching up bullet wounds at thirty thousand feet. She removes his shirt with clinical efficiency, revealing the full extent of the damage.

The bullet tore through muscle, leaving an angry furrow that makes my stomach clench. But it's the other scars that catch my eye—old wounds that map his violent history across his skin like some brutal constellation.

"It was Carmine," he says finally, dismissing the attendant with a sharp nod. The words fall between us like stones, heavy with implications. "He orchestrated all of it—your mother's death, the attack at the lake house, Johnny's video release."

"My uncle?" My hands shake so badly I almost drop the scotch Matteo offers. The amber liquid catches the morning light streaming through the jet's windows, creating patterns that remind me of fire. Of explosions. Of everything I'm leaving behind. "Why?"

"Power." Matteo moves to sit beside me, taking the glass back for his own sip before returning it. The casual intimacy of sharing a drink shouldn't affect me so much, not after everything we've shared, but the brush of his fingers against mine sends electricity through my body. "With your father dead and you married to me, he lost his chance at controlling the Russo territory. Unless …"

"Unless I die too." The words taste like ash in my mouth. My uncle—the man who used to bring me gelato after Sunday mass, who taught me to drive in his Mercedes, who cried at my first art show. All of it lies, carefully crafted to hide the monster beneath. "Let me guess—tragic accident on my honeymoon?"

"With evidence pointing to me as your killer." His laugh holds no humor, and the sound makes my skin crawl. "History repeating itself. Johnny releases the video about Sophia, making me look like a man who murders his wives. Carmine swoops in to avenge his beloved niece, taking control of both families in the process."

"And my mother?" The question burns my throat like the scotch. I see her face in my mind—perfectly coiffed even in death, I'm sure. For all our differences, all her criticism of my choices, she was still my mother.

"Knew too much, probably. Or refused to play along." He hesitates, and I see something dark cross his face. "Bella, there's something else you should know about her death."

I turn to face him fully, noting the fresh blood already seeping through his bandage. The sight makes my heart clench. "More secrets?"

"She called me yesterday, before the reception." His words come slowly, carefully, like he's defusing a bomb. "Said she had proof Carmine was working with the Calabrese family. That's why I arranged the plumbing emergency—to get everyone out before—"

He breaks off, jaw clenching, but I finish the thought in my head. Before they could kill her at my wedding reception. The realization hits me like a physical blow. My mother tried to warn us, tried to protect me in her own way. And now she's dead because of it.

Nausea rises in my throat as memories assault me—her critical comments about my art suddenly feeling less like disapproval and more like desperation to keep me away from this world. Her insistence on the perfect wedding dress, perfect hair, perfect everything ... Was she trying to give me one last beautiful day before everything fell apart?

"I should have moved faster," Matteo says, his voice rough. "Protected her better."

"Like you protected Sophia?"

The words slip out before I can stop them, sharp as broken glass. Matteo goes very still beside me, and I feel the temperature in the cabin drop ten degrees.

"I'm sorry," I whisper, reaching for him instinctively. "That wasn't fair."

"No, it was perfectly fair." He takes the scotch glass, finishing it in one swallow. The morning sun catches his profile, highlighting the silver at his temples, the barely contained violence in his frame. "I failed to protect Sophia, failed to protect your mother. You have every right to question whether I can protect you."

"That's not—" I stop, really looking at him. Beyond the dangerous facade, beyond the power and control that radiates from him like heat, I see something that breaks my heart. Guilt. Raw and deep and eating him alive. "You really believe that, don't you? That you failed them?"

"Didn't I?" The vulnerability in his voice makes my chest ache.

"You saved Bianca." I reach for his hand, linking our fingers together. His skin is warm against mine, callused from years of violence but somehow still gentle when he touches me. "You chose to protect your daughter over your wife. Over your own reputation and power. That's not failure, Matteo. That's love."

He stares at our joined hands like they hold some answer he's been seeking. "Love makes you vulnerable. Gets people killed."

"Love makes you human." I shift closer, pressing my free hand to his cheek. The stubble under my palm reminds me of last night, of how it felt against my inner thighs. Heat floods my body at the memory. "And right now, I need you to be both—the ruthless don who can keep us alive, and the human man who'll do anything to protect the people he loves."

His eyes darken as he turns his face into my touch. The man I glimpsed last night emerges, making my breath catch. "And what about you, *piccola*? Where do you fit in all this?"

"I'm your wife." The words come easier now, feeling more true with each passing hour. With each shared danger. With each moment I fall harder for this complicated man. "Which means your fights are my fights. Your enemies are my enemies."

"Even when those enemies include your own blood?" His voice drops lower, sending shivers down my spine.

"Carmine stopped being family the moment he ordered my mother's death." Steel enters my voice, surprising us both. "Just like he stopped being family the moment he conspired to kill me on my honeymoon."

Matteo's hand tightens on mine, almost painful. "I won't let that happen."

"I know." I lean in, resting my forehead against his. His cologne surrounds me, mixed with gunpowder and something uniquely him that makes my head spin. "Because this time, we're in it together. No more secrets, no more lies. Just us against them."

"Us," he echoes, like he's testing the word. His free hand slides into my hair, grip gentle despite the darkness in his eyes. When he kisses me, it's hungry, desperate, full of all the things we can't say. I melt into him, opening for his tongue, letting him claim me all over again.

Somehow we end up stumbling toward the jet's bathroom, need overwhelming common sense. He presses me against the wall, hiking my legs around his waist. The cashmere sweater hits the floor, followed quickly by my borrowed leggings.

"Mine," he growls against my throat, and God help me, I love when he gets possessive like this.

"Yours," I agree, working at his belt. "All yours."

The bathroom is impossibly small, all chrome and luxury finishes, but we make it work. Every touch feels amplified by adrenaline and fear, by the knowledge that we might not get another chance. His hands are everywhere, leaving fire in their wake. When he enters me in one powerful thrust, my head falls back against the wall.

"Look at me," he demands, and I do. In the soft lighting, his eyes are almost black with desire, focused entirely on me, like I'm the only thing grounding him to this moment. His hand braces against the wall for leverage while his other palm digs into my hip, guiding me as he moves, each thrust erasing the shadows of fear and danger that linger around us, leaving only this—us, here, now.

The rhythm between us becomes a frantic, desperate dance, driven by the need to feel something real, something certain. His body is relentless, and mine answers, matching each movement with rising intensity, with a hunger I can't contain. As the tension crests, pleasure sears through me, and I bite down on his shoulder, stifling my cries as I shatter around him. Moments later, he follows, his own release tearing through him as he murmurs my name—a reverent promise that echoes in the stillness.

As we're straightening our clothes, his eyes catch mine in the mirror. "Do you have any idea how dangerous you are to me?"

Before I can ask what he means, the pilot's voice crackles over the intercom: "Sir, we have a problem. Air traffic control is ordering us to turn back. They're saying—"

The rest is lost as the jet suddenly banks hard left, throwing me into Matteo. His arms lock around me protectively as oxygen masks drop from the ceiling like suspended question marks. The luxury cabin transforms instantly into a scene from my worst nightmares.

"Carmine," Matteo growls, reaching for his phone as we head back to our seats. He pulls me into his lap and his body is tense under mine, coiled like a predator ready to strike. "He's got people in the control tower."

My heart hammers against my ribs. Just when I thought we were safe, just when I was letting myself believe in our future ... "Can they force us to land?"

"They can try." He hits a number on speed dial, his other arm still locked around me as the plane shudders through another turn. "Antonio? Plan B. Now."

Through the window, I see something that makes my blood run cold. Two military jets pull alongside us, close enough that I can make out the pilots in their cockpits. The morning sun glints off their wings like knives, and I'm hit with the sudden, terrifying understanding that my uncle's reach extends far beyond what we imagined.

The jet banks again, harder this time. My stomach lurches as we drop altitude, the clouds rushing past our windows at sickening speed. Alarms start blaring through the cabin—high-pitched, urgent sounds that make my pulse spike. The flight attendant straps herself in, her previously unflappable demeanor finally showing cracks of concern.

Matteo's earlier words echo in my mind. *"Love makes you vulnerable. Gets people killed."* But as I feel his heart racing in time with mine, his arms still holding me close despite his injured shoulder, I know it's too late for either of us to protect ourselves from that particular danger.

"Hold on to me," Matteo murmurs in my ear as the jet begins another sharp turn. His voice is steady despite the chaos, an anchor in the storm. "And whatever happens next, remember—we're in this together."

I grip his shirt, breathing in his scent as the plane shudders around us. The military jets are still there, boxing us in like predators herding prey. One tilts its wings—a warning or a threat, I'm not sure which. The gesture makes everything suddenly, terrifyingly real.

My father is dead. My mother is dead. My uncle wants to kill me on my honeymoon. And now we might die in a forced landing, shot down by military jets over New York airspace. The absurdity of it all hits me, and I have to swallow a hysterical laugh.

Warning lights flash red across the cabin as we continue to lose altitude. Through the windows, I watch the clouds thin out, revealing glimpses of the landscape below. We're over water now—the dark expanse of the Atlantic stretching endlessly ahead. Each moment brings us closer to whatever Carmine has planned, each mile marking our countdown to either escape or disaster.

"I won't let them take you," Matteo says against my hair, and even now, even here, I believe him. Whatever happens next, whatever my uncle has planned, we'll face it together.

I just pray we both live long enough to see tomorrow.

The cabin pressure changes suddenly, making my ears pop. More alarms join the chorus, creating a symphony of danger that sets my teeth on edge. The flight attendant's voice comes over the intercom, cool and professional despite the situation: "Please secure your oxygen masks and brace for potential rapid descent."

"Matteo?" I hate how small my voice sounds, but fear claws at my throat as the military jets edge closer. Their missiles are clearly visible now, a deadly promise of what could happen if we don't comply.

"Trust me," he says, but his eyes are on his phone, reading something that makes his jaw clench. His arms tighten around me as the plane banks again, this time so sharply that loose items slide across the cabin floor.

A crackle of static fills the cabin, followed by a voice I recognize. My uncle. "Isabella," Carmine's voice comes through the speakers, dripping with false concern. "Be reasonable. Let the plane land. We just want to talk."

Like he "just wanted to talk" to my mother? Rage burns through my fear, hot and clarifying. This man—this monster wearing my uncle's face—killed my parents, tried to kill my husband, and now thinks he can force me to land and what? Trust him?

"Your father was weak," Carmine continues when we don't respond. "Your mother was foolish. Don't make their mistakes."

Matteo's phone buzzes again. Whatever he reads this time makes his eyes glitter dangerously. "Hold on tight, *piccola*," he murmurs. "And whatever happens, don't let go."

The military jets suddenly break formation, one peeling left while the other drops below us. The move feels choreographed, practiced—like they're executing a plan they've trained for. My eye catches details even through my fear: the way sunlight glints off their weapons, how they mirror each other's movements with deadly precision.

"They're boxing us in," Matteo says, his voice tight. "Forcing us toward Kennedy."

Where Carmine probably waits. Where an "accident" can be arranged. Where I'll disappear like my mother, another tragic casualty in a world of violence I never wanted to join.

16

MATTEO

Military jets flank us on both sides, close enough that I can see the pilots' faces through their cockpit glass. Too close. Dangerously close. Bella remains in my lap, her fingers digging into my shoulders as our pilot executes another evasive maneuver. The wound in my arm throbs with each movement, blood seeping through the fresh bandage, but I barely notice. All my focus is on getting my wife out of this alive.

The morning sun catches on the jets' wings, creating deadly metal angels bracketing our flight path. They're herding us, I realize. Like wolves circling prey, waiting for the kill order. "They're boxing us in," I manage to say. "Forcing us towards Kennedy."

"Sir," the pilot's voice crackles through the intercom, tension evident even through the static. "They're threatening to shoot us down if we don't comply."

"They're bluffing," I respond, though I'm not entirely sure. The fact that Carmine has military backing suggests his reach extends far beyond what I'd anticipated. My uncle-in-law has apparently been planning this coup longer than any of us realized. "Keep on course for the private strip in Montreal."

"The fuel line's been hit," the pilot reports grimly. "Through the window, I catch sight of liquid trailing from our wing like a dark ribbon against the sky. "We won't make it to Montreal."

Bella stiffens in my arms, but her voice remains steady when she asks, "Options?"

I almost smile despite our dire situation. My wife, already thinking like a strategist. Giovanni would be proud. "Antonio," I speak into my phone, calculating distances and possibilities, "how close are we to the backup location?"

"Twenty minutes out, Boss. But there's a problem." Antonio's voice is tight in a way that makes my blood run cold. "Bianca's missing."

The words hit me like a physical blow, worse than any bullet. "What do you mean, missing?"

My heart pounds against my ribs as scenarios flash through my mind—each one worse than the last. Bianca, my daughter, my greatest vulnerability. The one person I've spent seventeen years protecting from the truth about her parentage, about what my father did, about why Sophia really had to die.

"She never made it to the safe house." Antonio's voice carries notes I've never heard from him before—concern, fear, guilt. "Her security detail was found dead ten minutes ago."

Beside me, Bella inhales sharply. She's close enough to hear both sides of the conversation, close enough to feel how my body has gone rigid with tension. The military jets edge closer, but they're suddenly the least of my concerns.

"Johnny or Carmine?" she asks quietly, her mind already connecting dots. Her hand finds mine, squeezing gently. The gesture grounds me, helps me think past the panic trying to cloud my judgment.

"Neither." The pieces click into place with sickening clarity. "She went willingly. Didn't she, Antonio?"

"Security footage shows her meeting someone at a private airstrip three hours ago." Antonio pauses, and I already know what he's going to say. Know it in my bones. "It was Father Romano."

"The priest from our wedding?" Bella's brow furrows, but I see the moment understanding dawns in her eyes. Because of course—who better to manipulate a teenage girl than the priest who's known her since birth? The man who heard her confessions, dried her tears, became the father figure she thought I failed to be.

My jaw clenches so hard I taste copper. "He's been close to our family for years. Close to Bianca." Too close. The priest had known Giuseppe, had heard his confessions, knew exactly what those medical records would prove. What they would do to Bianca if she ever learned the truth.

"Keep your friends close but your enemies closer." Rage burns hot in my veins as pieces of a decade-old puzzle finally align. "Father Romano was my father's confessor. He knows things ... about my father, about Sophia ..."

The knowledge sits like acid in my stomach. All these years, I thought I was protecting Bianca by keeping her close. Instead, I left her vulnerable to the one man who knew every dark secret our family possessed.

"Now they'll use her against you," Bella finishes, her analytical mind cutting straight to the heart of it. Something dark crosses her face, and I know she's thinking of the video, of Sophia's final moments. But what she doesn't understand yet is that the video isn't just about Sophia's death—it's about why she had to die, about what my father did, about secrets that could destroy not just me, but everything I've built to protect Bianca.

The plane lurches suddenly, dropping altitude so fast my stomach rises to my throat.

"Sir," the pilot's voice cuts in again, tight with barely controlled panic. "We're losing altitude. We need to land. Now."

My mind races through scenarios, each worse than the last. If we land at a proper airport, Carmine's people will be waiting. If we crash ... My arms tighten around Bella instinctively. I've already lost my daughter to this mess; I won't lose my wife too.

"The lake," Bella says suddenly. "There." She points out the window where a large body of water glints in the sun like a silver promise. "Can we land on water?"

The pilot's response is immediate: "It's risky, but possible. Better than crashing in the forest."

"Do it," I order, already reaching for the emergency kit under my seat. Years of paranoia—of planning for every contingency—might just save our lives. Inside the waterproof bag are weapons, cash, and documents. Everything we need to disappear, to become ghosts until we can find Bianca.

"You've done this before," Bella observes as she helps me prepare. Her hands are steady despite the fear I see in her eyes. Fear she's trying to hide from me, just like I'm trying to hide my terror about Bianca.

I check my spare gun, then hand her a smaller one. The weight of it looks wrong in her artist's hands, hands meant for creating beauty, not dealing death. "You know how to use this?"

"My father taught me." She handles the weapon with surprising confidence, checking the magazine like she's done it a thousand times. Another secret Gio kept—preparing his daughter for this world while pretending to keep her from it. "Though he probably never imagined I'd need those skills on my honeymoon."

Despite everything—the military jets on our tail, my missing daughter, the fuel hemorrhaging from our wing—I feel my lips twitch. "Not the romantic getaway you imagined?"

"Please." She manages a smirk even as the plane descends sharply, making everything not bolted down slide toward the nose. "Most women get roses and champagne. I get gunfights and water landings."

"When this is over," I promise, cupping her face with my free hand, memorizing every detail in case it's our last moment, "I'll give you any honeymoon you want."

"I just want us both alive." She leans into my touch, and fuck, the trust in her eyes undoes me. "And Bianca safe."

The fact that she includes my daughter—after everything she's learned about Bianca's parentage, about the lies I've told—does something to my chest that I can't afford to examine right now. Not with our death spiraling closer with every passing second.

"Brace for impact!" the pilot shouts.

I pull Bella tight against me, shielding her with my body as the jet hits the water. The impact is brutal, like hitting concrete at speed. The noise is deafening—screaming metal, shattering glass, the roar of water rushing in through the damaged fuselage. My injured arm screams in protest as I hold Bella steady, but I barely feel it through the adrenaline.

"Move!" I order, helping her out of her seat as icy water starts flooding the cabin. The sun streaming through the broken windows turns the rising water pink, like we're drowning in blood. "Through the emergency exit. Now!"

She doesn't argue, doesn't hesitate. We splash through the rising water toward the exit, my body between her and the military jets still circling overhead like vultures. The water is shocking cold as we emerge onto the wing, the metal groaning beneath our feet as the jet starts to sink.

"We need to get clear before it sinks," I shout over the wind and the sound of military engines overhead. Water sprays around us as the jets make another pass. "Can you swim?"

"Better than I can shoot," she returns, already slipping into the water. The sight of her—my bride of less than forty-eight hours—diving into a freezing lake while being shot at makes me want to kill everyone responsible for bringing us to this point.

We strike out for the shore, staying low in the water to avoid being spotted from above. The lake is larger than it looked from the air, each stroke a battle against the cold and our waterlogged clothes. My injured arm feels like it's being torn apart with every movement, but the pain helps me focus. On surviving. On getting Bella to safety. On finding Bianca before it's too late.

Finally, we drag ourselves onto a rocky beach, both gasping for air. In the distance, our jet makes its final descent, slipping beneath the surface like a dying beast. The evidence of our passage disappears with it—exactly as planned.

At least something's going right.

"The pilot and flight attendant?" Bella asks between breaths, water streaming from her hair. Even half drowned and shivering, she thinks of others. It makes me want to kiss her and shake her in equal measure.

"Have their own escape routes." I help her to her feet, noting how she tries to hide her trembling. "They'll meet us at the rendezvous point."

"Which is where?"

Headlights suddenly appear on the road above the beach. I pull Bella behind a large boulder, pressing her between my body and the cold stone. Her heart hammers against my chest, matching my own rapid rhythm as voices carry down to us.

"Find them," Carmine's distinctive voice slices through the morning air. My uncle-in-law sounds different now—gone is the oily charm, replaced by something colder, more calculating. "I want confirmation they're dead before nightfall."

"And if they're not?" Another voice that makes my blood boil—Father Romano. The man who blessed my marriage to Bella less than two days ago, who's heard every confession I've made since I was fourteen, who's been playing us all for fools.

"Then we move to plan B." Carmine's footsteps crunch on the rocky beach. "How's our insurance policy?"

"Sedated, but safe." The priest's response makes my muscles lock with rage. "Bianca's quite upset about her father's ... unfortunate accident."

Bella's hand finds mine, squeezing hard enough to ground me before I do something stupid—like emerge from cover and tear Romano's throat out with my bare hands. They have my daughter. They're *drugging* my daughter.

And they're going to use her to destroy everything.

"Check the shoreline," Carmine orders. "They had to have made it to land somewhere."

We press tighter against the boulder, hardly daring to breathe. Bella's soaking wet body trembles against mine, though whether from cold or fear, I'm not sure. Probably both. Water drips from her hair onto my neck as footsteps crunch closer to our position. One beam of light passes inches from us, and I feel her hold her breath.

My mind races through options, each worse than the last. We're trapped between armed men and deep water, with my injured arm making swimming back out nearly impossible. The guns I managed to keep dry during our swim are professional grade, but we're outnumbered at least five to one based on the footsteps I'm counting.

But it's not the odds that make my blood run cold—it's Carmine's casual mention of Bianca being sedated. My daughter, who's already lost one parent to violence, who doesn't know the truth about her parentage, about why Sophia really died. Now she's drugged and being used as a pawn in Carmine's power play.

The rage that builds in my chest is almost overwhelming. I want to step out from behind this rock and empty both clips into Carmine and Romano. Want to make them suffer for touching my daughter, for threatening my wife, for thinking they could take what's mine.

Bella must sense my tension because she turns her face into my neck, her lips brushing my skin as she mouths silently: "Together?"

I meet her eyes, seeing trust there despite everything she's learned about me, everything she's lost because of me. My free hand cups the back of her neck as I nod once, drawing both guns.

Whatever comes next, we face it as one. Because Carmine and Romano have forgotten something crucial—a wounded animal is most dangerous when protecting its family.

And they've threatened both my wife and my daughter.

God help them all.

17

BELLA

Water drips steadily from my clothes as I crouch behind the boulder with Matteo, his body heat the only thing keeping me from shivering uncontrollably. The lake water has soaked through to my skin, making every breath a battle against chattering teeth. Flashlight beams sweep the beach around us like searching fingers, accompanied by the crunch of boots on gravel. Above us, my uncle's voice continues giving orders, each word a reminder of how completely my world has shattered in the past week.

I risk a glance around the boulder's edge, and my heart clenches at the sight of him. Carmine Russo stands silhouetted against the weak sun, every inch the powerful mafioso in his perfectly tailored suit. Even now, soaked to the bone and hiding for my life, I notice these details with an artist's eye—how the sun catches the silver at his temples, the way his Italian leather shoes seem untouched by the rocky terrain. This is the man who used to play card games with me, who taught me to drive in his Mercedes, who helped me escape punishment whenever I did something I wasn't supposed to.

Now he's trying to kill me.

"Nothing here," one of the searchers calls, his boots crunching closer to our position. "They might have drowned."

"Find the bodies," Carmine snaps, and his voice has changed too—gone is the warmth that used to color his tone when he called me *nipote*. In its place is something cold, calculating, utterly foreign to the uncle I thought I knew. "No assumptions."

Matteo's hand finds mine again, squeezing once. Even through the chaos, his touch grounds me. I know what he's thinking—we're running out of options. The searchers are moving methodically down the beach, their lights drawing closer with each passing second. Soon they'll reach our hiding spot, and then ...

A phone buzzes above us, the sound sharp in the quiet. "Yes?" Carmine answers, and something in his tone makes my skin crawl. This is the real him, I realize. The monster that was always hiding behind the loving uncle mask. "Good. Keep her sedated. DeLuca will be more ... cooperative once he knows we have his precious daughter."

I feel Matteo go rigid beside me, every muscle tensing for violence. His grip on his guns tightens, and through the dim light, I see that look in his eyes—the one that reminds me he's every bit the killer they say he is. He's calculating angles, counting enemies, deciding if he can take them all out before they reach Carmine.

Before they can hurt Bianca.

The beach is exposed, the sun peeking out of the clouds robbing us of shadows. There are at least six armed men that I can count, all with automatic weapons. Even Matteo, deadly as he is, can't take them all before someone gets off a lucky shot. Not with his injured arm already seeping blood through the makeshift bandage.

An idea forms in my mind—reckless, probably suicidal, but possibly our only chance. The artist in me sees the composition of the scene, the angles, the possibilities. My father taught me more than just how to shoot—he taught me how to see opportunities where others see only obstacles.

"Wait," I breathe against Matteo's ear, so softly only he can hear. His skin is fever hot against my lips. "Trust me?"

His eyes meet mine in the dim light, intense and questioning. For a moment, I see everything there—fear for me, rage at them, and something deeper that makes my heart race. After a long moment, he nods once. The trust in that simple gesture gives me courage.

I take a deep breath, trying to still my trembling hands, then step out from behind the boulder. "Uncle Carmine!" I call, raising my hands. "Looking for me?"

Six gun barrels immediately swing in my direction. The sun paints the scene in shades of blue and gold, turning the lake behind me to fire. In this light, I can see Carmine clearly—*really* see him. The expensive suit is Brioni, his signature style. His balding head is perfectly coiffed despite the hour, his Roman nose and strong jaw a mirror of my father's.

But his eyes ... God, how did I never notice how cold his eyes are?

"Bella." His voice drips false concern as he starts down the rocky path. "Thank God you're alive. We've been so worried."

In my peripheral vision, I see Matteo moving silently, using my distraction. Every artist knows about negative space—the places people don't look because something brighter draws their eye.

Right now, I'm the bright distraction.

"Have you?" I take a few steps forward, keeping their attention on me. My bare feet ache on the rocky beach, but I refuse to show weakness. "Like you were worried about my mother?"

Something flashes across his face—annoyance? Or guilt? "Your mother's death was a tragedy. Another of DeLuca's victims, just like his first wife." Carmine reaches the beach, Father Romano close behind him. Four armed men spread out in a semicircle, all focusing their weapons on me. None of them notice the deadly shadow moving into position behind them. "Come with me, *nipote*. Let me protect you before you meet the same fate."

"Protect me?" I force a bitter laugh, channeling every ounce of scorn I can muster. My heart pounds so hard I'm sure they must hear it. "The way you protected my father?"

He reaches the beach, his Italian leather shoes somehow navigating the treacherous rocks with perfect grace. Four armed men create a deadly arc around me, their weapons trained on my heart.

Father Romano hovers at Carmine's shoulder like a dark angel, his priest's collar a mockery of everything it should represent.

"Your father made his choice," Carmine says smoothly, and God, his voice still holds echoes of the man who used to read me bedtime stories in Italian. "Just like your new husband made his. Tell me, did he tell you what his father forced him to do?"

"Giuseppe DeLuca was an interesting man to take confession from." Romano's smile turns cruel in the weak light, transforming his handsome features into something grotesque. "So many ... sins to absolve."

Behind them, I see Matteo's silhouette tense in the shadows, his gun hand trembling—the first time I've ever seen him lose composure. That small tell sends ice through my veins.

What could make Matteo DeLuca, the most controlled man I know, react like that?

I force myself to focus, to keep playing my part. "He told me everything." Another step forward, drawing them further from the path. Every movement is calculated now, a deadly dance. "Which is more than you've done. Does Bianca know why you really took her? What you plan to do with her?"

Something ugly flashes across Father Romano's face, twisting his features into something demonic in the light. "The girl is safe. For now."

"Is she?" I meet his gaze steadily, silently praying Matteo is ready. "Are you sure about that?"

Behind them, a twig snaps. As they turn toward the sound, Matteo explodes into action like some avenging angel. Two shots ring out in perfect synchronization—precise, deadly. Two of Carmine's men drop before anyone can react, their bodies hitting the rocky beach with dull thuds. I dive for cover as chaos erupts around us.

The beach transforms into a war zone. Muzzle flashes light up like deadly fireworks, the sound of gunfire echoing off the lake's surface. I roll behind the boulder, my father's training taking over. When one of the remaining men appears around the edge, I don't hesitate. My shot catches him in the shoulder, the recoil traveling up my arm as he stumbles back with a cry.

"Bella, down!" Matteo's voice cuts through the firefight with commanding urgency.

I drop instantly, bullets pepper the rock where my head had been moments before. Chips of stone rain down on me as I roll to better cover. Through the chaos, I catch glimpses of Matteo in action—he moves like something out of a dream, each motion precise and lethal. His guns bark in concert, every shot finding its mark. He's beautiful in his violence, terrible and magnificent all at once.

But Carmine and Romano are already retreating up the path, using their last remaining man as a human shield. My uncle's face is twisted with rage and something else—fear, maybe. He knows what Matteo is capable of.

"This isn't over!" Carmine shouts as car doors slam above. His voice carries over the lake, full of venom and dark promises. "Ask him about the real truth behind Sophia's death! About Giuseppe's secrets! About what your precious husband has been hiding all these years!"

Engines roar to life, and then they're gone, leaving only the sound of waves lapping at the shore and our harsh breathing. The smell of gunpowder hangs heavy in the air, mixing with the metallic scent of blood and the crisp morning breeze off the lake.

Matteo appears beside me like a ghost, his hands immediately moving over my body, checking for injuries. His touch is gentle despite the deadly grace he displayed moments ago. "That was incredibly stupid," he growls, but I hear the fear beneath his anger, see it in the tight lines around his eyes. "They could have killed you, dammit."

"They could have killed us both if I hadn't created a distraction." I wince as his fingers find a graze on my arm I hadn't noticed in the heat of battle. The adrenaline is wearing off, making everything sharper, more painful. "Besides, now we know Bianca's alive. And sedated, which means she's somewhere nearby. They wouldn't risk moving her far if they're using her as leverage."

His hands still on my arm. The light catches the blood on his knuckles—his or someone else's, I'm not sure. "You did all that ... for Bianca?" There's something in his tone that makes my heart skip a beat.

"I saw your face when Carmine mentioned her being sedated." I meet his gaze steadily, trying to convey everything I can't put into words. How much I understand about protecting family, about the lengths we go to for those we love. "I knew you were about to do something reckless. Besides, she's your daughter, blood or not. Which makes her family. Even if she hates me."

Something flickers in his eyes at the word "blood"—that same haunted look he gets whenever Giuseppe is mentioned. There are still so many secrets between us, still so much I don't understand. But before I can analyze it further, he pulls me close, burying his face in my hair. His heart thunders against my cheek, reminding me that for all his deadly capability, he's still human. Still vulnerable when it comes to those he loves.

Suddenly, headlights appear on the road above, and we both tense. Matteo's body instantly shifts, putting himself between me and potential danger. But a familiar voice calls down, "Boss? Area's secure. But we need to move—local police will be here soon."

Relief floods through me at Antonio's voice. Matteo helps me to my feet, keeping me close as we climb the rocky path. My bare feet are bleeding, I realize distantly, leaving crimson marks on the stones. His security team works with practiced efficiency, already cleaning up any evidence of the firefight. These men are professionals—they know how to make bodies and bullets disappear without a trace.

"We have a safe house thirty minutes from here," Matteo tells me as we reach the waiting SUV. His hand spans my lower back, steadying me. "Medical supplies, dry clothes, everything we need."

I lean into his warmth, exhaustion suddenly hitting me like a wave. The events of the past hour feel surreal—the plane crash, the freezing swim, confronting my uncle, the gunfight. How many lives have I lived since becoming Matteo's wife? Artist, bride, survivor, fighter.

"And then what?" I ask, though I already know the answer.

He pulls me closer, his lips brushing my temple in a gesture that feels both protective and possessive. "Then we find my daughter. And make them regret ever touching our family."

The possessive note in his voice sends a shiver through me that has nothing to do with my wet clothes. Because that's what we are now—family. Complicated, dangerous, possibly doomed, but family nonetheless. Not like Carmine's version of family, built on lies and betrayal, but something stronger. Something forged in blood and bullets and trust.

As the SUV pulls away from the lake, I find myself watching Matteo's profile. The sun paints his features in shades of gold and shadow, highlighting the contradiction of the man himself—deadly yet gentle, controlled yet passionate, hiding secrets yet desperately wanting to trust.

There are still truths to be uncovered about Sophia and Giuseppe DeLuca. Carmine's parting words echo in my mind, hinting at darkness I'm not sure I'm ready to face. But right now, none of that matters as much as finding Bianca. As much as keeping our fragile, newborn family alive.

The only question that haunts me as we speed down the road: what will those secrets cost us when they finally come to light?

Because in our world, truth always demands payment in blood.

18

MATTEO

The safe house is actually a luxury penthouse in downtown Montreal, taking up the top two floors of a building I own through shell corporations. Floor-to-ceiling windows dominate every wall, casting long shadows across Italian marble floors. The sight triggers unwanted memories of my childhood home, where Giuseppe's shadow seemed to stretch endlessly, touching everything, poisoning everyone. I force the memories away, focusing instead on Bella as she takes in the space.

The penthouse is a study in power and luxury—all clean lines and sophisticated minimalism. A floating staircase of glass and steel curves up to the second level, while the main floor opens into a great room dominated by modernist furniture in shades of cream and charcoal. Custom lighting highlights carefully curated art pieces—most of them originals acquired through less than legal means. A Kandinsky here, a small Picasso there. The kind of collection that would make museum curators weep.

But it's Bella's reaction that captivates me. Even soaking wet and shivering, she moves through the space like she belongs here, her artist's eye catching details I've long since stopped seeing. She pauses before the Kandinsky, head tilting in that way that means she's analyzing composition and color. Water drips steadily from her clothes onto the marble floors, each drop echoing in the vast space, but she seems oblivious to her discomfort.

The whole scene feels surreal—my bride of less than forty-eight hours, studying priceless art while we're running for our lives. While my daughter is being held God knows where, drugged and scared. The thought of Bianca makes my chest tighten painfully. I've failed her, just like I failed Sophia.

"The bathroom's through there," I tell her, shrugging off my sodden jacket with a wince. Every movement pulls at my injury, a constant reminder of our narrow escape. "Everything you need should be in the closet."

The master bath is a marvel of marble and chrome, with a freestanding tub that could fit four people and a shower system that cost more than most cars. I had it designed as another show of wealth and power, like everything else in this place. But now, watching Bella nod while water pools at her feet, it feels hollow. Like all the luxury in the world can't make up for the fact that my daughter is missing.

"You're bleeding again." Her voice pulls me from dark thoughts. Those artist's eyes miss nothing—including the fresh blood seeping through my makeshift bandage.

"It's fine." The lie comes automatically. My father's voice echoes in my head: *"DeLuca men don't show weakness."*

"It's not." She steps closer, reaching for my injured arm with gentle hands that belie the strength I've seen her display today. "Let me help."

"Bella—"

"Please." Something vulnerable flashes across her face, something that makes my chest ache. "I need ... I need to do something useful."

I understand then—she needs control over something, anything, in this chaos our lives have become. Just like I need to feel in control when everything's spinning apart. When my daughter is in danger and all my carefully buried secrets are threatening to surface.

"First aid kit's in the kitchen," I concede, watching her move through the space like she's memorizing it. The kitchen is state of the art, all stainless steel and black granite, with views of Mont-Royal through more floor-to-ceiling windows. Like everything else here, it's meant to impress. To intimidate.

She returns with supplies, directing me to sit on one of the Italian leather sofas. The piece probably costs more than most cars, but all I can focus on is her touch as she removes the wet bandage. Her fingers are gentle but sure, artist's hands now turned to healing. The irony isn't lost on me—how many times have these hands tended wounds caused by my world?

"This needs stitches," she observes, cleaning the wound with a steadiness that surprises me.

"You know how?" I study her face in the soft lighting from the recessed fixtures above. Water still drips from her hair, curling around her face in a way that makes me want to reach out and touch. To make sure she's real.

"My father made sure I could handle emergency medical care." Her voice catches slightly on "father," and I hate that I'm the reason she has to say that word in past tense. "Said an art studio could be as dangerous as a gunfight if you weren't careful."

I watch her work, trying to focus on anything except thoughts of Bianca. Of what they might be doing to her.

I'll kill them all.

Bella's fingers move with precision as she stitches the wound, each one neat and even. The lamplight catches the diamond on her finger—not Sophia's ring, never Sophia's—and for a moment, the domesticity of the scene threatens to undo me. My wife, tending my wounds in our safe house, while my daughter ...

"Why did you really create that distraction on the beach?" I ask finally, needing to focus on something besides the gnawing fear about Bianca. The question has been burning in my mind since she stepped out from behind that boulder. Such goddamn bravery. Such fucking recklessness.

Her hands pause for a moment before resuming their work. In the soft light from the Murano glass fixtures, I can see every emotion that crosses her face. She's still learning to hide her feelings—something that both worries and captivates me.

"I told you—for Bianca."

"The truth, Bella." My voice comes out rougher than intended. Too many emotions fighting for control—fear for my daughter, worry for my wife, rage at those who would hurt them.

She secures the last stitch before meeting my eyes. The directness of her gaze reminds me of the girl who first walked into my office, all defiance and hidden strength. "Because I saw your face when Carmine mentioned her being sedated. Because I knew you were about to do something reckless and probably get yourself killed." She swallows hard, and I watch the movement of her throat. "Because I'm not ready to be a widow yet."

That last sentence is said in an almost whisper.

The admission hangs between us, heavy with everything unsaid. With all the secrets I'm still keeping. Secrets about Giuseppe, about what really happened, about why Father Romano's involvement terrifies me more than anything else. I reach up, tucking a damp curl behind her ear. Her skin is still cool from the lake water, but she leans into my touch like she's seeking warmth.

"I thought you hated this marriage." My voice is low.

"I did. I do. I …" She leans into my touch despite herself, a conflict I understand too well. "I don't know anymore. Everything's happening so fast, and I can't tell which feelings are real and which are just adrenaline and survival instinct."

"And what does your instinct tell you now?" Can she hear how loud my heart is pounding?

Instead of answering, she kisses me. It's different from our previous kisses—less desperate, more questioning. My good arm slides around her waist, pulling her closer until she's straddling my lap. She tastes like lake water and gunpowder and something uniquely Bella, and for a moment I let myself forget everything else. Forget about Bianca being drugged. Forget about the Families gathering to vote on my leadership. Forget about all the sins Father Romano knows, all the secrets that could destroy everything.

Her hands find the back of my neck, fingers tangling in my hair, and I can't stop the groan that escapes me as her body presses tighter against mine.

I kiss her again, slower this time, savoring the warmth of her lips, the softness of her skin beneath my hands. I let my fingers slide up her back, brushing over the wet fabric of her shirt before peeling it away from her, tracing the curve of her spine. Bella arches into me, a soft moan escaping her lips, and it sends a jolt of heat straight through me.

I want to give her everything, to show her how much she means to me, how much I need her.

I pull back slightly, my lips brushing against hers as I speak. "Are you sure?"

Her eyes meet mine, and there's no hesitation in her answer. "Yes, Matteo. I'm sure."

That's all I need to hear. I kiss her again, deep and tender, before shifting her gently onto her back, her body stretching out beneath me on the couch. She looks up at me, her lips swollen from our kisses, her cheeks flushed with desire, and she's never looked more beautiful.

My hands move slowly, reverently, as I undress her. I take my time, savoring each new inch of exposed skin, pressing soft kisses to her collarbone, her shoulders, her stomach. Bella shivers beneath my touch, her fingers threading through my hair, guiding me as I kiss my way down her body.

When she's finally bare beneath me, I pause for a moment, just taking her in. The way her chest rises and falls with each breath, the soft curve of her hips, the way her eyes darken with desire.

She's perfect—more perfect than I ever could have imagined.

"You're so beautiful," I whisper, my voice thick with emotion.

Bella's eyes flutter shut, a soft smile playing at her lips. "So are you," she murmurs, and it sends another wave of warmth crashing through me.

I lean down, pressing a kiss to her lips, her neck, her breasts, until I'm completely lost in the feel of her. My hands explore every part of her, my lips following the same path, and Bella's soft moans fill the room, encouraging me, pushing me further.

When I finally slide inside her, it's slow, deliberate, every movement filled with tenderness. Bella gasps, her hands gripping my shoulders, her legs wrapping around my waist, pulling me deeper into her. I can feel her heartbeat against mine, the warmth of her body surrounding me, and it's overwhelming in the best way.

We move together, slowly at first, savoring every touch, every kiss. There's no rush, no need for anything other than this moment, just the two of us, wrapped up in each other. Her nails dig into my back as I thrust deeper, her breathy moans spurring me on.

I bury my face in her neck, inhaling her scent, the softness of her skin beneath my lips. "Bella," I groan, my voice thick with need. "You feel so good."

"So do you," she whispers back, her voice breathless, full of desire. She tightens her legs around me, pulling me impossibly closer, and I can feel the way her body clenches around me, the way she's teetering on the edge.

I move faster, my hand sliding down to where we're joined, my thumb brushing over her clit, and Bella cries out, her body arching off the couch as she comes, her muscles tightening around me, pulling me over the edge with her.

I come with her, burying myself deep inside her, my body trembling as wave after wave of pleasure crashes over me. I collapse against her, my chest pressed to hers, our bodies still joined as we catch our breath.

For a moment, we just lie there, tangled together. I can feel her fingers tracing lazy circles on my back, her breath warm against my neck before she gently presses a kiss to my cheek. "We should get dressed," she whispers, "before someone comes in."

I hate that she's right.

We dress in silence and Bella slips my shirt over her head. Something possessive roars in my chest at the sight. Her skin still glows from sex, and despite everything falling apart around us, she's the most beautiful thing I've ever seen.

"You're thinking too hard," she says softly, catching my reflection in the floor-to-ceiling windows. The Montreal skyline creates a dramatic backdrop behind us, lights twinkling like stars against the darkening sky.

"Force of habit." I move behind her, drawn like gravity. In the glass, we look like something from one of her paintings—light and shadow, softness and steel, artist and killer bound together. My hands find her waist as I breathe her in, memorizing this moment before reality crashes back.

She turns in my arms, reaching up to trace the scar above my eyebrow. "We're going to find her, Matteo. Bianca. We're going to bring her home."

The simple faith in her voice nearly undoes me. After everything she's learned about me, everything she's lost because of me, she still believes in me. Still trusts me.

A throat clearing from the doorway breaks the moment. Antonio stands there, tablet in hand, professional enough not to react to our obviously intimate situation. The massive great room suddenly feels smaller, more confining, despite its twenty-foot ceilings and walls of glass. My body tenses instantly at his expression—he wouldn't interrupt unless it was critical.

"We have a lead on Miss Bianca," he says as Bella steps away from me, smoothing her hair. "Security cameras caught Father Romano's car heading toward Mont-Tremblant."

Ice slides down my spine at the confirmation. "The monastery." The word tastes like ash in my mouth. How many times did I watch my father disappear behind those heavy wooden doors, only to emerge hours later with that look in his eyes? The same look he'd get before the darkness took over, before the lessons about what it meant to be a DeLuca man.

"What monastery?" Bella asks, somehow making my rumpled shirt look elegant.

"Saint Benedict's. It's been tied to the Calabrese family for generations." My mind races through implications, possibilities, threats.

"Remote, defensible ..." I reach for my phone, already calculating. "How many men can we have there in an hour?"

"That's the problem, Boss." Antonio's expression tightens in a way I've rarely seen in fifteen years of service. "We just got word—the Families are meeting tonight. They're voting on whether to recognize your leadership after the video release."

"Let them vote," I growl, rage building in my chest. The Families can go to fucking hell. My daughter is being held in that place, in the same monastery where my father's sins were supposedly forgiven but really just stored away like ammunition. "My daughter—"

"Will die if we move too quickly." Bella's voice cuts through my rage like a blade, sharp and precise. She moves to the windows, her reflection overlaying the city lights. "Think, Matteo. This is exactly what they want—to force you to choose between Bianca and your power base."

"She's right," Antonio agrees, and something in his tone makes me look closer at him. He's worried—not just about Bianca, but about something else. "We go in guns blazing, the other Families will see it as proof you've lost control. They'll back Carmine's play for leadership."

My hands clench into fists. They're right, I know they're right, but the thought of Bianca drugged and alone in that place ... Images flash through my mind—Giuseppe emerging from confession with that cruel smile, Father Romano's knowing looks, the weight of secrets that could destroy everything I've built.

Cool fingers link with mine, and I look down to find Bella watching me with those eyes that see too much. Sometimes I wonder if she can read every dark thought, every buried sin, just by looking at me.

"What if we split up?" she suggests, and something in her voice makes my blood run cold.

"What do you mean?" I ask, though I already know. Already hate where this is going.

"You go to the meeting, maintain control of the Families." Her thumb traces patterns on my palm, somehow both soothing and unsettling. "I'll go to the monastery with Antonio, do reconnaissance only. No engagement without your order."

"Absolutely not." The words come out harsher than intended, but the thought of her anywhere near that place—where Giuseppe's darkness still lingers, where Romano keeps his poisonous secrets—makes something primal rise in my chest.

"It makes sense." She squeezes my hand, and I see Giovanni's tactical mind in her eyes. "They'll expect you to send your best men to find Bianca. They won't expect you to send your wife."

"Which is exactly why it's too dangerous." The windows reflect our image back at us—her still in my shirt, me bare-chested with fresh bandages. We look vulnerable. Human. Everything I can't afford to be right now.

"More dangerous than letting them take everything you've built? Everything you've sacrificed to protect?" She steps closer, her voice dropping to that tone that somehow bypasses all my defenses. "Trust me to do this, Matteo. Trust me to help save our family."

Our family. The words hit me like a truck. This slip of a girl who was forced to marry me less than forty-eight hours ago, who's lost everything because of me, now claims my broken family as her own. Claims Bianca, despite everything. Despite all the secrets still between us.

"Boss," Antonio interrupts quietly, "we need to decide. The meeting's in three hours."

I study my wife's face in the soft lighting—the determination in her hazel eyes, the stubborn set of her jaw. She's not the same girl who walked into my office a week ago. She's become something more, something dangerous and beautiful and mine.

But sending her to that monastery ... The place where Giuseppe's darkness took root, where Romano keeps decades of DeLuca secrets ...

"Two conditions," I say finally, each word feeling like surrender. "First, you take our best team. No arguments."

She nods, relief flooding her features. "And second?"

I cup her face in my hands, uncaring of Antonio's presence. Her skin is warm now, flushed from our earlier activities, alive in a way that makes my chest ache. "Come back to me. No matter what you find there, no matter what secrets come to light. Promise me you'll come back."

Something soft crosses her expression—understanding, maybe, of all the things I'm not saying. Of how much I've already lost in that place, how much more I stand to lose. "I promise."

I kiss her then, hard and quick, pouring everything I can't say into it. My fear for Bianca. My terror of losing her. The weight of secrets that could destroy us all. When we break apart, her eyes are wide with compassion.

"Go," she whispers, smoothing my shoulders with artist's hands that now know how to shoot, how to heal, how to love a monster like me. "Show them why you're the most feared man in New York."

"And you?" My thumb traces her full bottom lip, memorizing the feel of her in case it's the last time. In case Romano's secrets prove too devastating, in case my father's offenses finally come due.

A dangerous smile curves her mouth—one that would make the old Bella unrecognizable. "I'll show them why I'm your wife."

As I watch her leave with Antonio, I try not to think about the last person I sent to that monastery. Try not to remember my father's words about family and sacrifice and the price of power. Try not to imagine what secrets Romano might whisper in my wife's ear.

Because some sins can never be forgiven, no matter how many confessions you make.

19

BELLA

Saint Benedict's Monastery looms against the darkening sky like something from a Gothic nightmare. Through my binoculars, I study every detail with an artist's eye—the weathered stone walls that seem to absorb what's left of the daylight, the spires that pierce the purple-tinged clouds like accusing fingers, the ancient windows that hold who knows how many dark secrets.

Something about the place feels wrong, like the very stones are soaked in decades of sins and confessions.

The monastery grounds spread out below our observation point like something from a medieval painting. Stone walls, weathered by centuries of harsh Canadian winters, rise at least thirty feet high. Gargoyles perch at regular intervals, their grotesque faces seeming to watch our every move. The courtyard is paved with ancient cobblestones, uneven and treacherous, creating shadows perfect for concealment.

As I watch the guards make their rounds, I can't help but think of all the art history classes I've taken. How many times have I studied buildings like this in textbooks? Analyzed their architecture, their purpose? But this place feels different.

I crouch beside Antonio in our observation point, surrounded by pine needles and early autumn chill. The forest provides good cover, but there's something oppressive about the air here. Like we're being watched not just by the guards, but by something older. Something darker.

"Two men at the main gate," I murmur, counting defensive positions just as my father taught me. The memory hits unexpectedly—afternoons I thought were just father-daughter time at the shooting range, now revealed as careful preparation for exactly this kind of situation.

My father's voice echoes in my head as I count defensive positions: *"Always note your exits, bella mia. Pattern their movements. Find their weaknesses."* At the time, I thought he was just being paranoid. Now I wonder how long he knew this day would come.

"Three patrolling the walls. Security cameras covering the courtyard."

"Good eye." Antonio sounds impressed despite himself. "The Boss taught you well."

"My father did." I shift position, pine needles crunching under my boots as I get a better angle on the east wing. Something bitter rises in my throat. "Though I'm starting to think they were both preparing me for this life, whether I wanted it or not."

Movement at an upper window catches my attention. My heart jumps as a figure in priest's robes crosses past the glass, followed by another man carrying what appears to be medical equipment. The sight sends a chill down my spine—what kind of monastery needs *medical* supplies?

"There," I whisper, passing the binoculars to Antonio. "Third floor, east wing. That has to be where they're keeping her."

The window is large, Gothic-arched, its stained glass partially broken out as if someone wanted a clearer view inside. Or outside. The thought makes my skin crawl.

He studies the window for a long moment, his weathered face grim. "Agreed. But getting in there ..."

"We don't need to get in." I pull out my phone, quickly sketching the monastery's layout. My artist's training comes in handy as I mark entry points and guard positions. Years of studying perspective and composition now being used to plan a potential rescue mission.

Is this what my father saw in me? A tactical mind hidden behind an artist's eye?

My phone buzzes—Matteo. His message is brief.

Meeting starting. Stay safe.

I send back a quick acknowledgment, trying not to think about what he's facing. The other Families voting on his leadership, Carmine's political maneuvering, the video of Sophia still circulating ... And beneath it all, these whispers about Giuseppe DeLuca. What could his father have possibly done that's worth all this?

"Movement," Antonio's voice pulls me back to the present. "North side."

I redirect my attention as a black SUV pulls through the iron gates, its headlights cutting through the gathering dusk. Father Romano steps out, along with another priest I recognize from my wedding. Their black robes seem to absorb what's left of the daylight as they move, heads bent together in conspiratorial closeness.

"Can we get closer?" I ask, frustration building in my chest. More secrets, more whispered conversations that seem to hold the key to everything. "Maybe hear what they're saying?"

Antonio shakes his head. "Too risky. But ..." He pulls out a small device. "We might be able to pick up their phone calls. The Boss had their frequencies tracked after the wedding."

As if on cue, Romano's voice crackles through the device: "—getting restless. The sedatives are wearing off."

"Keep her under," Carmine's voice responds, and hatred burns hot in my chest at the sound of my uncle. "DeLuca should be at the meeting by now. Once the Families vote him out, we move to phase two."

"And what of Giuseppe's records? The DNA tests?" Romano asks impatiently.

That damned name again. Giuseppe DeLuca. Every time someone mentions Matteo's father, it's like a shadow falls across the room. What kind of monster was he? What could he possibly have done that's worth all this?

"Those files could destroy everything the DeLucas built," Carmine continues, his voice turning cold. "Once we prove what he did ..." He pauses, and I can hear the smile in his voice. "Matteo's precious family will crumble."

"And the girl? His wife?"

"Bella's proved more resourceful than expected," I hear Carmine say. "But some truths even she won't be able to forgive."

My hands clench around the binoculars, rage and frustration burning hot in my chest. Always more secrets, more lies. Every answer seems to lead to ten more questions, and at the center of it all is Giuseppe DeLuca, a man whose shadow seems to poison everything it touches.

Movement in the courtyard catches my eye. A medical team wheels a gurney through the stone archway, heading toward the east wing. The sight that greets me makes my blood run cold. Bianca lies unconscious, her dark hair spilling over the white sheets like ink. Even at this distance, I can see Matteo's features in her face. She's pale but breathing, an IV drip attached to her arm like some macabre lifeline.

I quickly photograph the scene, my hands shaking slightly as I send it to Matteo with our location coordinates. His response is immediate: *Coming. Don't engage.*

"We should go," Antonio says quietly. "We have what we need."

But I can't look away from my stepdaughter's unconscious form. The medical equipment they're bringing in looks far more sophisticated than what you'd need for simple sedation. Through my binoculars, I can make out specific pieces—not just monitoring equipment but blood testing supplies, genetic testing kits. The kind of equipment you'd need to run DNA analysis.

"What are they doing to her?"

"Mrs. DeLuca—"

"Look." I point to where the medical team has stopped, consulting with Father Romano under the Gothic archway. Modern medical equipment looks out of place against the ancient stones, like two worlds colliding. "That's not just sedatives they're giving her. Those are serious medical supplies."

Antonio tenses beside me. "You think they're—"

"Testing her for something specific." The pieces start clicking together, but not completely. Like looking at an abstract painting where you can see the shapes but not quite grasp the meaning. "Why go to all this trouble? What kind of tests would be worth this risk?"

"The kind that could destroy a family legacy." Antonio's voice is careful, measured. "There are certain things even Matteo doesn't talk about."

Something in his tone makes me look closer at him. He knows something—something he's not sharing.

I think about how Matteo reacts whenever Giuseppe is mentioned—the way his whole body goes rigid, like he's bracing for a blow. How he keeps that old family photo turned away in his office. The way Father Romano smiled when he mentioned Giuseppe's confessions.

Something dark lives in those memories, something that makes even the most feared man in New York flinch.

The medical team wheels more equipment through the courtyard—centrifuges, PCR machines, advanced testing equipment that seems wildly out of place in a monastery. My mind races as I catalog each piece, trying to understand what could possibly require this level of sophisticated technology in a place meant for prayer.

A branch snaps behind us. We whirl around to find Father Romano's second priest, gun aimed steadily at my head. In the dying light, his collar seems to glow against his black robes, a mockery of everything it's supposed to represent.

"Clever girl," he says softly, and his voice carries none of the gentleness he used during my wedding ceremony. "Too clever for your own good. Hands where I can see them, both of you."

The priest's gun doesn't waver as he steps closer. In the dying light, I notice details my eye can't help but catalog—the expensive cut of his cassock, the gold cross at his throat that probably costs more than most parish priests make in a year.

This is no simple man of God. This is someone who's comfortable with power.

Antonio moves to step in front of me, but another gun cocks from the shadows. They've surrounded us while we were focused on the monastery. Amateur mistake.

"You're very like your father," he observes, head tilting slightly. "Giovanni had that same look when he figured things out. That same inability to leave well enough alone."

"My father is dead," I say coldly, "because of secrets like the ones you're keeping."

"You know," the priest continues conversationally, as if I hadn't even spoken, "this could work out better than planned. Instead of just the girl, now we have DeLuca's wife too." He smiles, and the expression turns my blood cold. "Giuseppe DeLuca left quite a legacy of secrets. Come quietly, and you'll learn just how deep they run."

I think of Matteo's words: *"Come back to me."* Of his kiss before we parted, desperate and claiming. Of Bianca lying unconscious on that gurney, being tested for God knows what. Of all the secrets that seem to be circling us like wolves, waiting to strike.

I make my decision in a heartbeat.

"Antonio," I say quietly, "tell my husband I'm sorry."

Then I step forward, hands raised in surrender. Because sometimes the only way to protect your family is to break their trust.

And sometimes the only way to uncover the truth is to walk straight into the devil's den.

20

MATTEO

The private dining room at Le Saint-Martin hums with tension, the kind that makes lesser men's hands shake. Crystal chandeliers cast strategic shadows across the massive mahogany table, their light reflecting off cut crystal glasses filled with wine worth more than most people make in a month. Every surface screams old money, old power—from the hand-painted silk wallpaper to the antique Aubusson carpet beneath our feet.

I sit at the head of the table, a position earned through blood and cunning. My external calm is a mask I've perfected over decades, hiding the rage burning in my chest. Around me, New York's most powerful families have gathered—twelve dons whose combined influence could reshape the city's underworld. Every one of them has watched the video of Sophia. Every calculating eye weighs my worth, my control, my right to lead.

Don Vitelli sits to my immediate right—old guard, traditional, dangerous in his rigid adherence to the old ways. His silver hair gleams under the chandelier light as he swirls his Bordeaux, the ruby liquid catching the light like blood. To my left, Alberto Marconi—younger, hungrier, already calculating how my potential fall might benefit him. He's here on behalf of his father, whom Bella charmed at our wedding.

As I survey the table, Johnny Calabrese's absence is conspicuous. He always represents the family at these meetings—his sadistic nature perfectly suited for our world's political games. But neither he nor Don Calabrese sits in their usual place. Instead, a younger man occupies the Calabrese seat—Anthony, Johnny's nephew, probably no older than Bella.

He has his uncle's classic good looks—the sharp jaw, the aristocratic nose—but none of the cruelty that makes Johnny so dangerous. His Zegna suit still has that fresh-pressed look of someone not used to wearing one daily, his signet ring too bright and new on his finger. He keeps glancing at other dons for guidance. The Calabrese family is clearly making moves, but sending this wet-behind-the-ears boy to represent them?

"Interesting choice of representation," I observe coolly, watching Anthony try not to squirm under my gaze. "The Calabrese family must be ... distracted."

Don Rosetti—always eager to curry favor with stronger allies—jumps in with a sneer. "Perhaps they're too busy playing with drugs and whores to attend to real business."

Anthony's face flushes red as he half rises from his chair. "You'll explain yourself, old man."

"I don't explain anything to children playing at being made men," Rosetti snorts, swirling his wine with deliberate casualness. "Come back when your balls have dropped."

The temperature in the room drops ten degrees. Anthony's hand twitches toward his jacket as his bodyguards step forward. Around the table, other guards mirror the movement, hands disappearing beneath tailored suits. The click of multiple safeties being released echoes off the silk wallpaper.

I sit back, sipping my scotch, enjoying the spectacle. Let them posture and threaten—every moment they spend snapping at each other is one less focused on questioning my control. Besides, there's something almost entertaining about watching the next generation fumble through our deadly dances.

"Gentlemen." Don Vitelli's aged voice finally cuts through the tension as he sets down his wine with precise movement. "While I find this display of testosterone amusing, we have more urgent matters to discuss." His pale eyes fix on me. "Specifically, the video that's been circulating through our circles. The one showing Sophia DeLuca's final moments."

The entertainment I'd been feeling at the younger men's posturing evaporates. Around the table, the atmosphere shifts from potentially violent to deliberately calculating.

"And how is this the Families' problem?" I ask carefully, my voice measured.

"The problem," Vitelli continues, running his finger along the rim of his wine glass, "isn't just the video. It's the pattern of deception."

"Pattern?" I keep my voice controlled, arctic. The temperature in the room seems to drop an additional ten degrees.

"First Sophia's death. Now your new wife's mother. And your daughter missing ..." Vitelli spreads his manicured hands across the white tablecloth. His signet ring catches the light—a reminder of his family's centuries of power. "It doesn't look good, Matteo."

"Careful, old friend." I infuse the last two words with enough venom to make several of the younger dons shift uncomfortably in their leather chairs. Vitelli might be old guard, but he's forgetting who made him rich enough to afford that ring.

"He's right though." A minor don—Salvatore, one of Carmine's recent acquisitions—chimes in from further down the table. He's sweating slightly, despite the room's perfect temperature. Amateur. "The Families need stability. If you've lost control—"

"Lost control?" My laugh makes several dons flinch, wine sloshing in their glasses. Through the floor-to-ceiling windows, the city's lights spread out below us like a carpet of stars, reminding me of everything I've built. Everything at stake. "Let me be clear about what's happening here. Carmine Russo orchestrated his own sister-in-law's murder. He's holding my daughter hostage. And you sit here, questioning my control?"

"Bold accusations," Carmine says smoothly. "Where's your proof?"

He stands near the ornate double doors, playing his part perfectly. His Brioni suit probably cost more than Salvatore makes in a year—blood money bought with my mother-in-law's death. With my best friend's murder. With my daughter's freedom.

My phone vibrates against my chest, and something in me knows before I even look. Antonio's message makes my blood turn to ice: *They have her. I'm sorry, Boss.*

A photo follows—Bella being led into the monastery at gunpoint. Even in captivity, she carries herself with that quiet dignity that first caught my attention. Chin lifted defiantly, spine straight despite the gun at her back. My beautiful, stubborn, *foolish* wife, walking straight into their trap. Into the same monastery where darkness takes root, where secrets I've spent seventeen years burying lie waiting like coiled snakes.

The rage that floods me is unlike anything I've felt since Sophia's death. It takes every ounce of control not to put a bullet through Carmine's skull right here, consequences be damned. But control is what separates men like me from common killers.

Control is what will keep my family alive.

"No proof?" I let my voice turn silky dangerous as I rise from my chair. Around the table, I note who tenses, who reaches subtly for weapons. Old Vitelli's hand disappears beneath the tablecloth. Marconi shifts his weight, ready to dive for cover. Good. Let them remember why they fear me. "Tell me, Carmine, how's my wife enjoying the monastery?"

Color drains from his face so fast it's almost satisfying. The other dons shift uncomfortably in their chairs, sensing the change in atmosphere. The game has shifted, pieces moving into their final positions.

"That's right." I stalk toward my wife's uncle, each step measured and deliberate. The carpet muffles my footsteps, but the tension in the room amplifies every movement. "I know where you're keeping them both. I know about the medical tests you're running on my daughter. I know everything."

Like a cornered animal, Carmine shows his teeth. The polished mask of the society don slips, revealing the desperation beneath. "You know nothing," he snarls, and I see the same madness that consumed Giuseppe starting to eat at his edges. "You don't even understand what your father did. What you helped cover up."

"Enlighten me." Around the table, the other dons are frozen, watching our deadly dance. Vitelli's hand hasn't left his weapon. Marconi's eyes dart between us like he's watching a tennis match. But with deadlier stakes.

"You still don't understand what Sophia found, do you? What those records proved?" Carmine's smile turns cruel, and for a moment I see my father in his face. The same twisted pleasure in holding power over others. "About that night. About why Giuseppe insisted on that marriage so quickly."

The words land like physical blows, each one threatening to crack the control I've spent a lifetime perfecting. Seventeen years of secrets, of protecting Bianca from the truth, all balanced on a knife's edge. But I don't flinch. Can't flinch. Not with twelve of the most powerful men in our world watching for any sign of weakness.

"Interesting theory." I muse as I continue my advance, noting how the other dons lean forward in their chairs, scenting blood in the water. The crystal chandeliers cast shifting shadows across faces that have ordered countless deaths, made and broken countless fortunes.

"Medical records can be altered. DNA tests can be manipulated. The only question is what exactly you think you'll prove about my daughter."

"You understand nothing," Carmine snarls, backing up until he hits the hand-painted wallpaper. Sweat beads on his forehead despite the room's perfect temperature. "About Sophia. About the—" He shuts up abruptly, realizing he's said too much.

I press harder, using his slip to my advantage. "Why wait ten years to use Sophia's death against me? Why do you need both Bianca and

Bella under your control?" Each question drives him further into the corner, both literally and figuratively. "You can run all the tests you want. You'll never find what you're looking for."

The other dons lean forward, the scrape of their chairs against hardwood almost deafening in the tense silence. This is what they came for—the truth behind the power plays, the real stakes in our deadly game.

"You're still protecting him," Carmine's voice comes out wet, desperate. His fingers inch toward his jacket. "Even now, you're protecting Giuseppe's legacy of lies. About Sophia. About who Bianca really—"

"Bianca," Don Vitelli breathes from his seat, his aged voice cutting through the tension. "She's not your daughter at all, is she, Matteo? She's Carmine's. With Sophia."

The accusation hangs in the air for one heartbeat, two. I can almost taste the anticipation as the other dons hold their breath, waiting for my reaction. So many theories over the years, each one wrong but dangerous in their own way. Each one threatening everything I've built to protect her.

Carmine moves suddenly, reaching for his gun with the desperation of a man who knows he's already dead. But I'm faster. I've always been faster.

The first shot echoes through the dining room, the sound magnified by the elegant acoustics. Carmine stumbles back, red blooming across his suit like a macabre rose. His blood stains the hand-painted wallpaper—some designer in Milan's masterpiece ruined forever.

Good.

"That was for my wife's mother," I say coldly, watching the life drain from his face. Another shot—this one higher. "That was for Giovanni." The final shot, center mass. "And that was for involving *my* daughter in your games."

He slides down the wall, leaving a crimson trail in his wake. His last words come out as a wet chuckle, blood staining his teeth: "You think this ends with me? Giuseppe's secrets will come out. Ask

Matteo ... ask him why his father insisted on that marriage. Why Sophia had to die ..."

Then he's gone, taking his secrets with him. Or so he thinks.

I turn to face the shocked dons, noting who looks afraid and who looks calculating. Power abhors a vacuum, and Carmine's death will create ripples. But that's a problem for another day.

"Any other questions about my control?"

Silence greets me. One by one, they shake their heads. Even Vitelli keeps his mouth shut about Bianca's parentage. Smart man.

"Good." I straighten my cuffs, already moving toward the door. Carmine's blood has splattered my sleeve—Italian wool ruined, but worth it. "Then this meeting is adjourned. I have a family to rescue."

Vitelli's voice stops me at the threshold: "The girl—Bianca. If she's not yours ..."

"She's mine in every way that matters." I don't turn around, but my words carry enough threat to make the crystal vibrate. "Anyone who suggests otherwise won't live to repeat the mistake."

My phone buzzes again as I reach my car. Another photo from the monastery—Bella being led into the east wing where they're keeping Bianca. But something about her posture catches my eye. I zoom in, and a slight smile curves my lips despite everything.

My brilliant wife has managed to slip a note into view of the camera. In her elegant hand, two words: *Third floor.*

She's giving me exactly what I need to find them. Even in captivity, she's thinking three moves ahead.

My dangerous, beautiful wife, turning her capture into an advantage.

"Hold on, *piccola*," I murmur, calling in my strike team as I drive. The Montreal skyline spreads out before me, lights twinkling like fallen stars. Somewhere in those lights, a monastery holds my family. Holds secrets that could destroy everything.

They've forgotten the first rule of our world: never threaten a man's family unless you're prepared for war.

And I've been fighting wars since before they were born.

21

BELLA

They keep me in what was once a monk's quarters—a stone cell barely ten feet square, with walls that seem to breathe centuries of prayers and secrets. A narrow window, more arrow slit than proper opening, lets in thin ribbons of moonlight that paint silver stripes across the rough floor. I pace the space, counting steps—eight long strides one way, six the other—trying to keep my mind off what might be happening to Bianca in the medical wing.

The image of my stepdaughter's unconscious face haunts me, so like Matteo's in repose that it makes my chest ache. Strange how quickly she's become family, despite her initial hatred of me. Or maybe not so strange. After all, we're both products of this violent world, both pawns in games played by powerful men.

My mind is still racing through the path they took to bring me here. Even with a gun at my back, I had cataloged every turn, every doorway, every possible escape route—just as my father taught me.

"Move." The guard's grip is bruising on my arm as he marches me through ancient stone corridors. But while they expect fear or submission, I do what I've been trained to do since childhood—I observe. I paint the layout in my mind like I'm composing a canvas.

First floor: A massive wooden door marks the main entrance, its hinges ancient but well-oiled. Three guards posted there, all with automatic weapons. The entrance hall splits two ways—east wing to the right, where modern medical equipment is being unloaded, west wing to the left, where the original monastery kitchens must be, judging by the faint scent of old smoke and herbs that still lingers in the stone.

Second floor: They take me up a spiraling staircase, the steps worn smooth by centuries of use. More medical equipment here, being installed in what were once prayer rooms. A modern security door stands out garishly against medieval stone—that must be the lab. Two key card readers, retinal scanner. Expensive. Important.

Through a window, I glimpse the courtyard below, mentally mapping the patrol patterns. Four guards, probably rotating every fifteen minutes. Predictable. Exploitable.

Third floor: Where they're keeping Bianca, judging by the concentration of guards and medical personnel. They pause outside a heavy door, and I catch a glimpse of my stepdaughter through the reinforced window. The sight makes my blood boil, but I force myself to focus. Count the turns. Note the cameras. Find the blind spots.

They finally shove me into the monk's cell, but I'm already building the map in my head, adding details like brushstrokes to a canvas. Because that's what my father really taught me all those years ago—not just how to shoot or fight, but how to *see*. How to turn observation into survival.

But now, those mental brushstrokes could mean the difference between life and death.

An ancient wooden crucifix hangs crooked on one wall, its shadow wavering in the weak light like a dark guardian. I wonder about the monk who once lived here, who sought peace and salvation in this austere space. Did he find it? Or did he too lie awake at night, haunted by the weight of the secrets these walls have absorbed?

The heavy iron lock clicks, and Father Romano enters. He's traded his priest's robes for an expensive suit that probably costs more than most parish priests make in a year. The black Brioni fits him perfectly, but something about seeing him in civilian clothes makes him more threatening. The pretense of holiness has been abandoned, revealing the predator beneath.

"Comfortable?" His voice carries none of the warmth it held during my wedding ceremony but more of what I heard on the beach after the jet crash. His eyes—pale blue and cold as arctic ice—study me with clinical detachment.

"Lovely space." I lean against the rough wall, channeling my mother's social grace. The thought sends an unexpected pang through my chest—has she even been buried yet? Have I been so caught up in survival that I haven't properly mourned? "Though the hospitality could use work. How's Bianca?"

"Awake." His smile reminds me of documentaries I've watched about great white sharks—all teeth and soulless eyes. "And asking for her father. She's quite confused about why he hasn't come for her yet."

The taunt is meant to hurt, to make me doubt Matteo. Instead, it gives me hope. If Bianca's awake and asking questions, she's stronger than they expected. Like her father—whether by blood or choice—she won't break easily.

"What are you testing her for?" I move to the window, keeping my movements casual despite my racing heart. Through the narrow opening, I can see the monastery's courtyard three stories below. Guards patrol in regular patterns, their weapons visible even from this height. "It must be important if you're willing to risk Matteo's wrath."

"Clever girl." Romano steps closer, and something about his movement reminds me of a serpent preparing to strike. The expensive cologne he wears can't quite mask an underlying smell—something medicinal and sharp that turns my stomach. "You've figured out some of it, haven't you? About Sophia?"

"I have theories." I turn to face him, noting how the moonlight catches the silver at his temples, highlighting features that might be handsome if they weren't twisted by cruelty. A small scar bisects his left eyebrow—old, with a story I probably don't want to know. "But I think you want to tell me. Isn't that why you had them bring me here? So you could gloat about finally destroying Matteo DeLuca?"

He studies me for a long moment, head tilted like a bird of prey assessing its next meal. "You're nothing like Sophia was. She was ... fragile. Easily manipulated. But you ..." His hand reaches out as if to touch my face, and it takes everything in me not to flinch away. His fingers are manicured, soft—hands that have never known real work, only the administration of other people's pain.

I hold my ground, though every instinct screams to back away. "Tell me what you found in those medical records. What was worth killing for?"

"Giuseppe DeLuca's sins run deeper than anyone knows." His voice drops to a whisper, but in the stone cell it seems to echo endlessly. "Ask yourself why he forced his son to marry a pregnant teenager."

The words hit me hard, making my knees weak. "What are you saying?"

"That some secrets are written in blood." He circles me slowly, like a shark tightening its hunting pattern. His shoes make no sound on the stone floor—expensive Italian leather, the same brand Matteo favors. "But Carmine ... he saw an opportunity. A way to protect Sophia, to give her child legitimacy. A secret marriage, performed right here in this monastery."

My mind races, trying to process the implications. "You're saying Carmine married Sophia first? Before Matteo?"

"Which makes their marriage invalid. And Bianca's claim to the DeLuca empire void." His smile widens, showing too many teeth. "Though her claim to the Russo family remains intact. Funny how these things work out."

Wait, what the *hell*? Bianca is—she's my *cousin*?

But something doesn't add up. The way Matteo reacts to any mention of his father. The timing of it all. The look in Sophia's eyes in that security footage ... There's more here, something darker that makes Romano's revelation about Carmine feel like misdirection.

"That's what this is about? Succession?"

"Power, my dear. It's always about power." He moves to the door, his movements smooth and practiced. "I'll let you think about what that means for your own position. After all, if Matteo's marriage to Sophia was invalid, what does that make his marriage to you?"

The door closes behind him with a heavy thud, the lock's click echoing in the stone cell. I wait until his footsteps fade completely before moving into action. The bobby pin Elena insisted I always hide in my sleeve (another memory that makes my chest tight—my best friend, probably sick with worry) comes free easily. Her voice echoes in my head as I work the lock: *"Every society girl needs an escape plan, B. Especially in this world."*

The lock yields after two minutes of careful manipulation. My hands shake slightly, but years of controlling brushes for detailed work helps me maintain the precision needed. The ancient mechanism finally gives with a soft click that sounds deafening in the quiet cell.

The hallway stretches before me like something from a Gothic nightmare—all worn stone and shadows, lit intermittently by modern LED fixtures that seem obscene against the medieval architecture. The contrast makes my artist's eye twitch—clinical white light harsh against ancient stone, like the past and present are at war. The air smells of incense and antiseptic, another jarring juxtaposition.

I move silently toward the medical wing, remembering the path they'd taken me past earlier. Every shadow could hide a guard, but I push forward, driven by the need to reach Bianca. My boots make no sound on the stone floor. Through narrow windows, moonlight creates patterns that my mind automatically tries to capture—how would I paint this? What colors would convey this mixture of ancient holiness and modern corruption?

The medical wing's security focuses outward—guards at external doors, cameras covering approaches from outside. But they're overconfident about their internal security, another sign of Romano's arrogance. I slip through a service door, following the steady beeping of medical monitors.

The sound leads me to a private room that makes my blood run cold. The space might once have been another monk's cell, but now it's been transformed into something out of a nightmare. Modern medical equipment crowds the small space—heart monitors, IV stands, and more sinister-looking machines whose purposes I don't want to contemplate. The harsh fluorescent lighting makes everything look sickly and unreal.

Bianca lies amid this technological invasion like a broken doll. They've dressed her in a hospital gown that makes her look younger than her seventeen years. Tubes and wires connect her to various machines, their steady beeping a mockery of lullabies. Dark bruises mark the crooks of her arms where they've drawn blood—too many times, judging by the rainbow of colors that speaks to different healing stages.

"Bianca?" I whisper, moving to her side. Up close, the resemblance to Matteo is even more striking—the same sharp cheekbones, the same dark hair. Even unconscious, she has that DeLuca grace.

Blood or not, she's her father's daughter.

Her eyes flutter open, revealing those steel-blue eyes that match Matteo's exactly. "Bella?" Her voice comes out rough, like she's been screaming. The thought makes rage burn hot in my chest. "What ... what are you doing here?"

"Breaking you out." I start removing monitoring leads with trembling fingers. Each one seems determined to mock me with its steady rhythm. "Can you walk?"

"I think so." She tries to sit up, wincing. New bruises peek out from under her gown—they've been none too gentle with their "tests." "They've been ... taking samples. Blood, tissue ... They keep asking about my mother."

"I know." I help her stand, supporting her weight against my side. She feels too light, like they haven't been feeding her properly. Another sin to add to Romano's growing list. "But right now we need to move. Your father's coming, but we need to help ourselves first."

"My father ..." Her voice breaks slightly, vulnerability showing through her usual ice princess facade. "Is it true? What they said about him not being ..."

"Hey." I turn her to face me, one hand cupping her chin like Matteo does when he's trying to make a point. "Listen to me. Family isn't about blood. It's about who stays, who fights for you, who loves you no matter what. Your father has fought for you since the day you were born. That's what matters."

Tears slip down her cheeks, cutting through the pallor of her skin. "Why are you helping me? After how I treated you ..."

"Because you're family. And I protect my family." The words come easily, naturally, surprising us both with their truth. I check the hallway—still clear. "Now, can you run?"

A shadow of Matteo's dangerous smile crosses her face, transforming her from victim to survivor in an instant. "Try to stop me."

We make it three corridors and a flight of stairs before the alarms start wailing—high-pitched electronic screams that seem to pierce the ancient stone like daggers. The sound echoes off the vaulted ceilings, making it impossible to tell where pursuit might come from. I guide us toward the monastery's old kitchen, following the mental map I'd created during my earlier captivity. My father's voice echoes in my head: *Always know your exits, bella mia. Always have a plan.*

"Wait." Bianca pulls me to a stop near a modern security door that looks obscene against the medieval stonework. Despite her weakness, her grip is strong—DeLuca strength showing through. "The lab. We need to destroy the samples."

"Bianca—"

"Please." Steel enters her voice, transforming her from scared teenager to Mafia princess in an instant. "I won't let them use me against my father. Against our family."

Our family. The words echo my own from earlier, and something warm unfurls in my chest despite the danger. I nod once, changing course. The lab isn't far—I noted its location earlier, my artist's eye automatically mapping the incongruous modern additions to the ancient space.

The laboratory itself is a jarring intrusion of chrome and fluorescent lighting into the monastery's sacred space. Banks of sophisticated equipment line the walls—centrifuges, PCR machines, genetic sequencers that probably cost more than most hospitals can afford. The air smells sharp with chemicals, burning my nose and making my eyes water.

While Bianca moves through the space with surprising purpose, destroying samples and hard drives, I stand guard. Her hands shake slightly as she works, but her movements are precise, deliberate. Another thing she gets from Matteo—that ability to focus through fear, to turn terror into fuel for action.

The sound of running feet echoes through the stone corridors, growing closer. "Time to go," I urge, already calculating escape routes.

But as we turn to leave, Father Romano appears in the doorway like a demon manifesting from shadow. The gun in his manicured hand looks wrong—too modern, too brutal for hands that were meant to offer blessings. His expensive suit is slightly disheveled now, his mask of civility slipping to reveal the monster beneath.

"Going somewhere?" His voice still carries that false gentleness that makes my skin crawl.

"Actually," a familiar voice growls from behind him, "they are."

The priest's eyes widen as Matteo's gun presses against his skull. Relief floods through me at the sight of my husband—dangerous and beautiful in his rage.

"How—" Romano starts, but Matteo cuts him off with a harder press of the gun.

"You really should update your security." My husband's voice carries that deadly calm that makes smarter men tremble. His eyes find mine across the lab, and the intensity of his gaze steals my breath. Pride and possession and relief war in those steel-blue depths. "Bella's note was very helpful."

"Dad," Bianca whispers, and the vulnerability in that one word speaks volumes. She still sees him as her father, blood or not. Still trusts him despite whatever poison Romano has tried to pour in her ear.

But before any of us can move, Romano laughs—a horrible, knowing sound that seems to corrupt the very air. "Kill me if you want, DeLuca. The truth is already out there. About Sophia, about your father, about what really happened that night in the monastery. About what you've been hiding about your precious daughter—"

"My *real* father," Bianca cuts in, her chin lifting in that defiant way she gets from Matteo, "is right here." She moves to his side, and even in her hospital gown, she radiates that DeLuca strength. "The rest is just DNA."

Something in Romano's face twists—rage and madness and decades of secrets all warring for control. He moves suddenly, spinning toward Matteo with inhuman speed. Two shots ring out simultaneously, the sound deafening in the enclosed space.

Both men fall.

22

BELLA

"Dad!" Bianca's scream echoes off the stone walls as Matteo crumples to the ground. I'm moving before conscious thought kicks in, muscle memory from years of first aid training taking over as I drop to my knees beside my husband. The lab's harsh fluorescent lights turn his blood almost black against his white shirt, but his eyes are clear and focused as they lock onto mine.

"I'm fine," he growls, though the pallor of his skin betrays him. "Check Romano."

"He's dead." Bianca's voice trembles as she kneels on Matteo's other side. Even in the harsh lighting, I see how she unconsciously mirrors his mannerisms, that DeLuca grace present in every movement. "Your shot ... right through the heart."

"Excellent." Matteo tries to sit up, a hiss of pain escaping through clenched teeth. "You're getting good at saving my life, *piccola*."

My hands shake as I tear open his shirt, finding the wound high in his shoulder. The sight of his blood makes something primal rise in my chest—rage and fear warring for control. "Stop talking. You're lucky—through and through, missed anything vital." I snatch gauze from the lab's first aid kit, pressing it against both entry and exit wounds. "Bianca, find me something to bind this with."

She moves with that innate DeLuca grace, returning moments later with strips torn from Romano's expensive suit jacket. Together, we work to stabilize the bleeding, our shared concern for Matteo temporarily erasing any tension between us. Her hands are steady as she helps me bind the wounds, and I see steel beneath her teenage facade—the same steel I've come to recognize in her father.

"Security team's sweeping the building," Matteo reports, his free hand covering mine where it presses against his wound. The heat of his skin grounds me, reminds me he's alive despite the blood staining my hands. "But we need to move. The Calabrese family won't be far behind."

"You need a hospital," I argue, though I already know it's futile.

"What I need is to get my family somewhere safe." His eyes move between Bianca and me, carrying that intensity that still makes my breath catch. "Both of you."

The word "family" catches us all off guard. After everything that's been revealed about parentage and succession, it should feel hollow. Instead, it feels more real than ever—like steel forged in fire, stronger for the tempering.

"Both of us?" Bianca's voice sounds younger than her seventeen years, vulnerability bleeding through her usual ice princess facade. "Even though I'm not ..."

"You *are* my daughter." Matteo's voice carries that tone that makes hardened killers obey without question. "Some bonds matter more than blood. Some choices define us more than the ones made for us."

Tears spill down Bianca's cheeks as she throws herself into his arms, uncaring of the blood. He holds her with his good arm, pressing a kiss to her dark hair. The gesture is so tender, so paternal, it makes my chest ache. For a moment, her profile against the fluorescent lights is pure DeLuca—the same commanding presence he has in that turned-away photo frame in his office.

The moment shatters as footsteps approach. Antonio appears in the doorway, gun ready. "Building's secure, Boss. But we've got incoming—multiple vehicles approaching from the south."

"Time to go." Matteo starts to stand, but his legs buckle. Blood loss is taking its toll, though he'd never admit it.

I catch him before he can fall, pulling his good arm across my shoulders. To my surprise, Bianca mirrors me on his other side, careful of his injury. The trust in the gesture—both of them letting me help, letting me in—makes something warm unfurl in my chest.

"Together," I say firmly, meeting both their eyes. "We move together."

Before we leave, I pause by Romano's body. His dead eyes stare at nothing, expensive suit now ruined with blood. The gun in his manicured hand still looks wrong, but I take it anyway.

In our world, you never know when you might need another weapon.

We make our way through the monastery's winding corridors, Antonio's team providing cover. The sound of gunfire erupts outside—staccato bursts that echo off ancient stone, announcing the Calabrese family's arrival in bullets and blood. Each shot makes me flinch, memories of my father's death still too fresh.

"Exit route?" I ask as we reach the ground floor, adjusting my grip on Matteo. His skin burns with fever against mine, though he'd never admit weakness.

"Underground tunnel system," he manages through gritted teeth. Sweat beads on his forehead, and I can feel tremors running through his body. "Connects to the old wine cellars. Transportation waiting on the other side."

"Of course there are secret tunnels," Bianca mutters, but her grip on her father remains steady. Her hospital gown is spattered with his blood now, making her look even younger, more vulnerable. "What else don't I know about this place?"

"Later," I cut in as more gunfire sounds closer, close enough to shower us with stone dust from the ancient walls. "Stories later, survival now."

We find the tunnel entrance hidden behind a false wall in the chapel's confessional—because of course the Catholic Church would have escape routes built into their houses of worship. The passage is narrow, medieval stone giving way to packed earth. Emergency strips along the floor cast everything in sickly green light that makes Matteo's pallor look worse.

Our progress is slow with his injury, but no one suggests splitting up. We've all learned the hard way what happens when family separates. The tunnel air is thick with centuries of secrets, heavy with the weight of earth above us. Water drips somewhere in the darkness beyond the emergency lights, a steady rhythm like a dying man's heartbeat.

"Wait." Bianca stops suddenly, her body tensing. "Listen."

Footsteps echo behind us, followed by voices—Johnny Calabrese's distinct tone carrying through the tunnel like poisoned honey. The sound makes my skin crawl, remembering how he looked at me through my studio window, like I was something to be broken.

"Keep moving," Matteo orders, though his voice is weaker now. "Antonio's team will hold them—"

"No." I help him lean against the rough wall, my decision already made. "They'll follow us straight to the exit." I pull out Romano's gun, checking the magazine. Six shots left. It'll have to be enough. "Bianca, get your father to the cars. I'll delay them."

"Bella, don't—" Matteo reaches for me with his good hand, blood seeping through his makeshift bandages. The sight steels my resolve.

"Trust me," I whisper, echoing his words from our wedding night, from every moment he's asked me to believe in him. "Like I trusted you."

Before he can argue, I kiss him hard and fast, pouring everything I can't say into it—how quickly I've come to need him, how afraid I am of losing him, how much I might just love him despite everything. When I pull away, I find Bianca watching us with an unreadable expression.

"Take care of him," I tell my stepdaughter, this girl who's become family in the strangest way.

To my surprise, she nods, something like respect flickering in those DeLuca eyes. "Take care of them." She presses something into my hand—a small explosive device, clearly lifted from one of Antonio's men. A smile curves her lips, and for a moment I see the woman she'll become. "Make it count."

The footsteps grow closer as Bianca helps Matteo deeper into the tunnel. I wait until they turn a corner, then set the charge where the passage narrows. The timer gives me two minutes—more than enough time to create a distraction that will either save my family or get me killed.

"I can smell your perfume, little artist," Johnny's voice echoes off stone walls, turning my blood to ice. "Jasmine, isn't it? Like Sophia used to wear. Like all DeLuca women wear before they die."

I back away from the charge, deliberately letting my footsteps be heard. My heart pounds so hard I'm sure it must echo off the walls, but my hands are steady on Romano's gun. "Come find out."

I make it thirty feet before they appear—Johnny and three of his men, their shadows stretching grotesque and massive in the emergency lighting. His smile reminds me of a shark scenting blood, all teeth and soulless eyes. The sight makes my finger tighten on the trigger, but I force myself to wait. Timing is everything.

He emerges from the shadows like a nightmare given form, three of his men flanking him. The emergency lighting casts his features in sickly green, highlighting the cruelty in his perfect smile. He moves with a predator's grace, every step measured and deliberate.

"The artist princess," he mocks, spreading his arms wide. "Giovanni's precious daughter, who thought she could escape her birthright by hiding behind easels and paint." His laugh echoes off the stone walls. "How's that working out for you, sweetheart?"

My finger tightens on the trigger. "Better than being your puppet, Johnny. How's it feel, being Carmine's attack dog?"

Something ugly flashes across his handsome features. "You think you know so much, little girl. But you don't even know how your father died, do you?"

The words are like a knife through me, but I force myself to stay focused. Keep him talking. Buy time. "Why don't you tell me?"

"He begged at the end." Johnny's voice drops lower, silkier. "Not for his life—no, Giovanni was too proud for that. He begged for yours." He takes another step closer, and I have to fight the urge to back away. "Want to know what his last words were?"

Forty seconds. My blood roars in my ears, but I make myself stand my ground. "You're lying."

"'Not my *bella mia*,'" Johnny mimics my father's accent perfectly, twisting the endearment into something obscene. "'Not my little artist.' Such a disappointment you must have been to him—the heir to his empire, running away to play with paintbrushes."

"Shut up." The words tear from my throat before I can stop them. Thirty seconds.

"He died thinking he'd failed you." Johnny's smile widens, showing too many teeth. "Thinking his only child was too weak to carry on his legacy. And he was right, wasn't he? Look at you now—Matteo's pet artist, playing at being donna when we both know you're just a scared little girl with paint under her nails."

I think of my father's proud smile at my first art show. Of his hands steady on mine as he taught me to shoot. Of all the lessons he gave me that I never understood until now.

"You want to know what my father really taught me, Johnny?" My voice comes out steady, cold. Fifteen seconds. "He taught me to see the whole canvas. To look for weaknesses. To understand that sometimes the most dangerous player is the one you underestimate."

Johnny laughs loudly at that. "And you think that's *you*?"

Thirteen seconds.

"Trying to delay us while they escape?" He tsks, the sound obscene in the ancient tunnel as he notices me checking my watch. "Brave, but ultimately pointless. There's only one exit, and my men are already there."

I check my watch. Ten seconds. "Sure about that?" Adrenaline makes everything sharper, clearer. I catalog details like I would for a painting—the way his suit is perfectly pressed even now, how his signet ring catches the dim light, the slight tremor in his gun hand that betrays his cocaine habit. "You people never learn, do you? Always underestimating what we'll do to protect our family."

"Family?" Johnny laughs, the sound bouncing off stone walls like broken glass. "You've been married two days. What do you know about family?"

"I know that real family chooses each other." Five seconds. I shift my weight, preparing to move. "Blood is just genetics. Love? That's a choice."

Understanding dawns on Johnny's face just as the timer hits zero. I dive around the corner as the explosion rocks the tunnel, the concussion stealing my breath even as I roll away from falling debris. Centuries-old stone and earth cascade down, cutting off half of Johnny's scream.

Through the settling dust, I hear him coughing, raging. "You fucking bitch! I'll find you! I'll make you watch while I kill them both—your precious husband and his bastard daughter!"

"No." My voice carries over the sound of shifting rubble. "You won't. Because my father taught me one more thing, Johnny." I pause, thinking of Papa's last lesson—the one he taught me without words. "He taught me that real power isn't about violence or territory or blood. It's about love. About family. About what we'll do to protect the people who choose us."

His answer is lost in another crash of falling stone, but I'm already running, following the emergency lights toward the exit. My lungs burn with every breath, stone dust coating my throat, but I don't slow down. Not with Matteo bleeding, not with Bianca still weak from drugs, not with everything we've fought for hanging by a thread.

I emerge into predawn darkness to find Matteo's security team waiting, guns trained on bodies that used to be Calabrese's men. The sight should horrify me—these men I'd probably served drinks to at my wedding, now cooling in the dirt. Instead, I feel nothing but relief.

"Mrs. DeLuca." Antonio helps me into the waiting SUV where Matteo and Bianca occupy the back seat. "All clear?"

"Johnny's trapped on the other side of about ten tons of rock." I slide in beside my husband, immediately checking his bandages. "He'll dig out eventually, but ..."

"But we'll be long gone." Matteo pulls me close with his good arm, pressing his lips to my temple. His skin still burns with fever, but his eyes are clear as they meet mine. "You impossible, brilliant woman."

"I learned from the best." My voice falters as the events of the night catch up with me. The monastery, Romano's death, Johnny's trap, Matteo's blood still staining my hands. "Both of you."

From her place on Matteo's other side, Bianca reaches across to squeeze my hand. No words are needed—we've forged something stronger than blood in that tunnel, something that can't be broken by secrets or lies or DNA tests.

"Where to?" Antonio asks from the front seat as we speed into the lightening sky.

Matteo's good hand finds mine, his wedding ring pressing against my palm like a promise. "Home," he says simply. "Take us home."

As dawn light paints the sky in shades of gold and crimson, I think about how many meanings that word can have. Home isn't just a place—it's people, it's trust, it's love despite darkness. Or maybe because of it.

The SUV speeds toward safety as the sun rises behind us, turning the monastery into a dark silhouette against the morning sky. We may have escaped its ancient walls, but I know the secrets buried there will follow us. Some truths refuse to stay buried, no matter how much stone you pile on top of them.

But that's tomorrow's battle. For now, I have my husband's blood on my hands, my stepdaughter's trust in my heart, and a future that's terrifying and beautiful and ours.

For now, that's enough.

23

MATTEO

The mansion's medical suite fills my senses with sharp antiseptic and the metallic tang of blood as the doctor finishes redressing my shoulder. I barely register the sting of new stitches, too captivated by the scene through the observation window.

Bella and Bianca sit in the adjacent room, dark heads bent together over steaming cups of tea, talking quietly. My daughter still looks too pale, shadows under her eyes from whatever drugs Romano pumped into her system, but color is finally returning to her cheeks. And Bella ... my impossible wife maintains a casual posture while her eyes constantly scan the room, checking exits, monitoring movements outside. She's become a protector as fierce as any of my trained guards.

The sight of them together does something to my chest that has nothing to do with my injury. They mirror each other unconsciously —the same slight tilt of the head, the same way of cradling their cups.

Artist and ice princess, forced together by circumstance, now finding common ground in survival.

"The wound will heal clean," Dr. Marcus says, securing the

bandage with practiced hands. He's been the family's private physician since Giuseppe's time, which means he knows better than to sugarcoat things. "But you need rest, Boss. No shooting anyone for at least a week."

"No promises," I mutter, already shrugging my shirt back on one-handed. The movement pulls at fresh stitches, but I've had worse. Much worse.

Through the window, I watch Bianca say something that makes Bella laugh—not the polished society smile she's perfected this past week, but something real and bright that transforms her entire face. The sound carries through the glass, hitting me like a physical blow.

When was the last time I heard such genuine joy in this house?

"They're quite remarkable," Antonio observes from his post by the door. My most trusted captain has seen enough to know when something extraordinary is happening. "Both of them."

"They are." I button my shirt carefully, each movement a reminder of how close I came to losing everything in that monastery. How close I still might come, with Johnny still out there and so many secrets still buried. "Status report?"

"Johnny Calabrese survived the tunnel collapse. He's in the wind, but we have teams tracking him." Antonio consults his tablet with military precision. "The other Families have officially recognized your leadership after Carmine's ... removal. And Miss Bianca's blood work came back clean—whatever they were testing for, they didn't find it."

"They were testing for specific genetic markers," I say quietly, watching my daughter's profile through the glass, seeing shadows of the past in her features, but more importantly seeing the strength she's developed despite everything—or maybe because of it.

Seventeen years I've spent protecting her, making sure she grew up knowing she was loved, wanted, protected. Making sure she never felt the kind of fear I knew as a child.

"Boss?"

"I had those tests done years ago." I turn to face him, choosing words carefully. Antonio's been with me long enough to understand the weight of what I'm about to reveal. "The results were ... conclusive. But not in the way anyone expected."

Understanding dawns on his weathered face. He was there during Giuseppe's reign, saw how things played out with Sophia. "That's why you let everyone believe the official story. To protect her."

"From the truth." My jaw clenches as memories surface—Sophia's tears, Giuseppe's rage, the weight of choices that would echo through decades. "Sophia knew what those medical records would prove. That's why she tried to use them against me, thinking she could force my hand."

"But you chose Bianca." It's not a question.

"I'll always choose her." The words come out rougher than intended, raw with seventeen years of protection and sacrifice. "She's been mine since the day she was born. The rest is just details."

Antonio, who's served the family long enough to recognize when not to press for details, simply nods. Through the glass, Bianca laughs again at something Bella says, and my chest tightens at the sound. For so long, this house has been filled with shadows and silence. Now, somehow, these two women have brought light back into it.

"Sir?" Antonio clears his throat. "There's one more thing. We found this in Father Romano's office at the monastery."

He hands over a thick manila envelope that feels like it contains secrets and gunpowder. Inside, I find photos that make my blood run cold—surveillance shots of Bella. Her at art shows, dark hair wild as she gestures at her paintings. At college, head bent over sketchbooks in the campus coffee shop. With Elena at their favorite bistro, both of them laughing at something now lost to time. All dated before Giovanni's death.

"They've been watching her for years," Antonio explains quietly. "Planning to use her against you even before her father died. Romano's notes suggest they knew you'd been keeping tabs on her too."

I thank Antonio with a nod as he leaves. My hands clench around the photos, crinkling their edges. I had been watching her, though I'd never admitted it to anyone. Monthly reports on her progress at college, her art showings, her life. Telling myself it was for Giovanni's sake, to protect my friend's daughter. But the truth was far more dangerous, far more selfish.

"You loved her then, didn't you?"

My head snaps up at my daughter's voice. Bianca stands in the doorway, Bella a few steps behind her. Both women watch me with eerily similar expressions—part challenge, part understanding. When did they start moving in sync like that?

"Bianca—" I don't want a fight. Not now.

"It's okay." My daughter moves closer, taking the photos from my hands. Her fingers trace Bella's face in one shot—carefree, paint splattered, beautiful. "You were waiting for her. To finish college."

"I wasn't—" But the denial dies on my lips as Bella enters the room. Because my daughter's right. I'd been waiting, watching, protecting from afar. Never intending to act, but unable to look away. Like a moth drawn to flame, knowing it would burn me but flying closer anyway.

"That's why you agreed to the marriage so quickly," Bella says softly, and something in her voice makes my heart stutter. "Not just because of your promise to my father."

"Your father knew." The admission costs me, but they deserve the truth. Everything in me wants to reach for her, to pull her close, to make her understand. "He knew how I felt about you. It's why he asked me specifically to protect you if anything happened to him."

The memory hits me with sudden clarity—that last evening with Giovanni on my terrace, just days before everything changed.

"If anything happens to me, Matteo," he'd said, staring into the gathering darkness, "protect her. Isabella ... she's everything good I ever did in this life. Don't let our world destroy that."

"You know I will," I promised, the words automatic after years of protecting her from afar. But Gio had turned to me then, something knowing in his dark eyes that made my breath catch.

"I've seen how you watch her," he'd said quietly. My heart had stopped, fingers tightening on my glass until I thought it might shatter. But his voice held no accusation, no rage—only a strange sort of understanding. "At her art shows. At family functions. When you think no one's looking."

"Giovanni, I would never—" Panic had clawed at my throat, decades of friendship suddenly balanced on a knife's edge.

But he'd just smiled, that peculiar peace still radiating from him. "You think I don't know you've had men watching over her at college? That you've been protecting her all these years?" He'd taken another sip of scotch, the amber liquid gleaming like fire in the dying light. "A father knows these things, my friend."

"I've never—"

"Of course you haven't. You're too honorable for that." He'd turned to face me fully then. "That's why I'm trusting you with her future. Because you love her enough to protect her, but respect her enough to let her choose her own path."

I remember staring at him, this man who'd been my best friend for twenty years, wondering if the scotch had gone to his head. "You're not angry?"

"Angry?" He'd actually laughed. "Matteo, you're the only man I've ever trusted with my daughter's safety. Why wouldn't I trust you with her heart?" His expression had grown serious then. "Just promise me one thing."

"Anything."

"Let her paint. Let her create. Don't try to turn her into something she's not." His eyes had held mine. "She's not Sophia, my friend. She's stronger than any of us know."

Now, looking at Bella's face as I admit this truth, I see exactly what Giovanni meant. She's not Sophia—she's fire where Sophia was ice, strength where Sophia was calculation. She's everything I never deserved but somehow found anyway.

"He knew how I felt about you," I continue softly, watching emotions play across her face. "It's why he asked me specifically to protect you if anything happened to him."

"And how do you feel about me?" She steps closer, fearless as ever. The sunlight streaming through the windows catches the gold in her hazel eyes, making them almost glow. "Now that you're not watching from a distance?"

The air between us crackles with tension. From the corner of my eye, I see Bianca slip out, closing the door behind her. Smart girl. She's learning when to fight and when to retreat—another thing she gets from me.

"You know how I feel," I say roughly, fighting the urge to pull her into my arms. The stitches in my shoulder burn, but it's nothing compared to the ache in my chest.

"Do I?" She moves closer still, close enough that her jasmine perfume wraps around me like a spell. "Because a lot has happened in the past week. Forced marriage, murder attempts, family secrets ..." Her voice catches slightly. "I'm not sure what's real anymore."

I catch her chin with my good hand, tilting her face up to mine. Her skin is silk under my callused fingers, and the trust in her eyes nearly undoes me. "This is real. You, saving my life multiple times. Fighting for our family. Looking at me like you're looking at me right now ..."

"And how am I looking at you?" A whisper.

"Like you might love me too," I admit.

The words hang between us for a heartbeat, heavy with possibility and fear and hope. Then Bella rises on her toes, pressing her lips to mine. The kiss is different from our others—softer, questioning, full of promise. No violence driving it, no desperate need to prove anything. Just us, here, choosing each other.

"I might," she whispers against my mouth, her hands coming up to frame my face. "God help me, I think I do."

I kiss her properly then, pouring everything I can't say into it. My good arm bands around her waist, pulling her onto my lap as her hands fist in my shirt. She tastes like tea and hope and something uniquely her that makes my head spin. Everything I've ever wanted, everything I never thought I deserved, right here in my arms.

Her hands move over my chest and every touch is electric,

sending sparks of warmth cutting through the cold dread that's been wrapping around my heart for so many years.

I deepen the kiss, my tongue exploring hers with a hunger that makes Bella moan. My good hand moves lower, skimming over her waist, her hips, and she arches into me, clearly craving more. Our breaths mingle, our movements frantic as we lose ourselves in each other. My lips trail down her neck, nipping at her skin, and the moan she releases drives me fucking crazy. It only spurs me on.

"Matteo," Bella gasps, tilting her head to give me better access. "I want you."

I pull back to look at her. Christ, she's so beautiful. "Want or need, *piccola*?"

"Need," she gasps again, her artist's hands already unbuttoning my shirt. "Definitely *need*."

That's all the encouragement I need. Her mouth opens slightly, and I take the invitation, deepening the kiss. Our tongues meet, and the sensation sends a shiver down my spine. I can taste her, sweet and intoxicating, and it makes me crave her even more. My heart pounds in my chest, every beat echoing the desire that courses through me.

Bella's body molds against mine, fitting perfectly as if we were made for each other. I feel the curve of her waist, the rise and fall of her chest against mine, and it drives me wild. My hands move lower, gripping her hips, pulling her even closer until there's no space left between us.

I break the kiss only for a moment, our foreheads touching as we both gasp for breath. Her eyes are dark with passion, mirroring the fire I feel within. "Bella," I murmur, my voice rough with desire. "I love you."

She answers me with another kiss, just as fervent and desperate as the first. My hands find the hem of her shirt, tugging it upwards, and she lifts her arms to help me remove it.

Our clothes come off in a frenzy, each layer discarded without a second thought, but my shirt stays on to protect my stitches. Her skin is warm and inviting, her touch electric.

I slide my hand between us, fingers seeking, finding, and she gasps against my mouth, her hips bucking in response as I curl my fingers inside her. Fuck, she's so *wet*.

"You're always so wet for me, Bella," I whisper into her ear.

"Matteo," she breathes before she bites down, muffing a cry. "Oh, please, *don't stop*."

The electricity of our bodies ignites. We are two ravenous beasts, consumed by the desire to please one another.

Her hands search their way down my body as I finger her, caressing my abdomen before finally resting around my hardened cock.

I reciprocate her passion with fervor. Both of us are in the same rhythm of pleasing each other, relentless as we build each other with pleasure higher and higher until a chorus of soft moans rips through the medical suite.

I push my fingers harder and she claws at my back while I thrust my hand into her depths, each motion propelling us toward the apex of climax.

"I want to be inside you," I whisper into her ear before I remove my hand from her slick pussy, drawing out a whimper from her.

Without warning, I enter her, and it's like coming home, her warmth enveloping me, drawing me deeper into her.

The sensation is overwhelming—her tightness around me, the way she clenches and relaxes, the slick heat that surrounds me. Every thrust feels like heaven, each movement drawing us closer together. Her moans are muffled against my lips, but I can feel them vibrating through me, a testament to the pleasure I'm giving her. She's lost in it, her eyes closed, her body arching against mine, and it drives me wild knowing I'm the one bringing her to this level of ecstasy.

"I love you," I whisper, my voice thick with emotion.

Bella's eyes flutter shut, a soft smile playing at her lips. "I love you, too," she murmurs again, and it sends another wave of warmth crashing through me.

We move together, a rhythm as old as time, our bodies locked in a dance of passion and desperation. It's different this time. Sweeter, slower. As if we're savoring every second, every touch, every heartbeat. I look down at her, at her flushed cheeks, her parted lips, the way her eyes are fixed on mine, and I can't help but think that this—this moment, this woman—is everything I've ever wanted.

And when I finally reach the edge, when the pleasure crests and I fall apart, it's her name that's on my lips, her face that fills my vision.

I collapse against her, my face buried in between her breasts, the room filled with the sounds of our pants as we try to steady our breathing. My arm is burning and screaming but I don't care.

The intensity of what we've just shared leaves me feeling both exhilarated and vulnerable. Everything in this past week—the fear, the violence, the desperate need to protect what's mine—has culminated in this moment. Her body trembles against mine, both of us catching our breath in the aftermath of passion that was somehow both fiercer and more tender than anything we've shared before.

I pull back just enough to look at her, drinking in the sight of her on my lap. Her dark hair spills around her like ink, and the afternoon sun paints her skin gold. She's the most beautiful thing I've ever seen —not because she's perfect, but because she's real. Because she knows exactly what I am, what I've done, and still looks at me like this.

Tears glisten in her eyes as she whispers, "I love you."

It's the most beautiful sound I've ever heard. Three words I never thought I'd hear again after Sophia, never thought I'd want to hear. But this is different. Everything about Bella is different.

Where Sophia was arranged, a marriage made of duty and manipulation and coercion, Bella crashed into my life like a force of nature. Where Sophia played the perfect Mafia wife, all calculated moves and hidden agendas, Bella challenges me at every turn. Fights me. Saves me. Forces me to be better even as she accepts my darkness.

A fierce need burns inside me to take her again, to hear her scream my name until it's the only word she knows. But I need to have more control than that. We both need to dress, to face whatever crisis Johnny's latest move will bring.

I help her up, both of us moving slowly, reluctantly. Her skin is marked with evidence of my passion—small marks blooming on her throat. Possessive satisfaction wars with tenderness as I watch her dress, each piece of clothing hiding the proof of what we've shared.

"What are you thinking?" she asks softly as she slips on her blouse. There's a new intimacy in her voice that makes my chest ache.

"That I never thought I'd have this again." I pull on my own clothes, wincing slightly as the movement pulls at my stitches. "After Sophia ... I locked everything away. Convinced myself I was better off alone."

"And now?" She moves to help me with my buttons, her artist's hands gentle against my chest.

"Now I know I was wrong. What I felt for Sophia ..." I catch her hands, pressing them against my heart. "It wasn't this. It was *never* this."

A knock at the door interrupts whatever she might have said. We pull apart slowly, reluctantly, to find Bianca standing there. My daughter's expression is a mix of amusement and concern that reminds me eerily of her mother.

"Sorry to interrupt," she says, not sounding sorry at all, "but Antonio says we have a problem. Johnny's been spotted ... at Elena's apartment."

The words land like a bucket of ice water. Because suddenly I remember—Elena had caught Johnny's eye at the wedding reception when Elena had squared off with a drunk Bianca. And Johnny Calabrese has a very specific way of dealing with his fascination with women.

"Call in everyone," I order Antonio, already reaching for my jacket. "I want—"

"No." Bella's voice cuts through the room like a blade. "You're injured, and Bianca's still recovering from whatever drugs they pumped into her. This one's mine."

"Bella—"

"He's using my best friend to draw me out?" Her smile is all danger now, all Russo steel wrapped in artist grace. "Fine. Let's give him what he wants."

Looking at her now—my artist, my warrior, my salvation—I realize I've never loved her more. And I've never been more afraid of losing her.

Because some choices, once made, can never be unmade. And some loves, once admitted, can never be denied.

Even if they destroy us both.

24

BELLA

"Absolutely not." Matteo's voice fills his study like a thundercloud, dark and threatening. He's been arguing against this for the past hour and a half, ever since I declared my intention to rescue Elena. The protest would carry more weight if he weren't still pale from blood loss, his shoulder heavily bandaged beneath his perfectly tailored shirt.

I check my gun—my own now, not Romano's. The weight of it feels different, like it was made for my hand. Is this how my father felt before going into battle? Did he too find strange comfort in the cold steel, in knowing he had the means to protect what's his?

"I'm not going alone." I tuck the weapon into my shoulder holster, the movement already feeling natural. Another change this week has brought—artist's hands now equally comfortable with brushes or bullets. "Antonio's team will be in position. But I need to be the one to make contact."

"Because you're bait." His good hand clenches on his desk, knuckles going white. I see the muscle jumping in his jaw, the telltale sign of barely contained emotion. "He wants to use you to hurt me."

"No." I move to him, resting my hands on his chest. The steady thud of his heart beneath my palms grounds me, reminds me what

I'm fighting for. I almost smile at his protectiveness—this dangerous man who makes hardened killers tremble, reduced to worry by one small artist. "He wants to use Elena to hurt me. There's a difference."

"I don't see one." The words come out like gravel, rough with fear he'd never admit to feeling.

"The difference," I say softly, smoothing the lapels of his jacket, "is that he doesn't know what I'm capable of. He still sees Giovanni Russo's sheltered daughter. The artist playing at being a Mafia wife."

Understanding dawns in his steel-blue eyes, turning them to storm clouds. He sees it now—the advantage of being underestimated, of letting Johnny think I'm still that scared girl who walked into this office a week ago.

"But that's not who you are anymore."

"It's not who I've been since the moment I said yes in your office." I rise on my toes to kiss him briefly, tasting scotch and worry on his lips. "You taught me that. You and Bianca both—showing me that we choose who we become, regardless of blood or background."

"Let me come with you." His free hand cups my face, and the near pleading in his voice tells me exactly how much this costs him. Matteo DeLuca doesn't beg. Ever. "Please, *piccola*."

"You can barely lift your arm." I turn to kiss his palm, breathing in the familiar scent of his skin. Gun oil and sandalwood and something uniquely him that still makes my pulse race. "Besides, I need you here. Keeping Bianca safe in case this is another distraction."

"I hate that you're right." The words come out like they're being dragged from him.

"I know." I step back, checking my appearance in the study's gilt-framed mirror. My mother would be proud—gone are the paint-stained jeans and messy hair of a week ago. In their place stands a donna in a black Armani suit that costs more than my old apartment's monthly rent.

The jacket's cut is precise enough to hide my shoulder holster while highlighting every curve. My hair falls in careful waves past my shoulders, and subtle makeup makes my hazel eyes look huge in my pale face. Even the Louboutins are deadly—four-inch stilettos that could double as weapons in a pinch.

"How do I look?"

"Like a donna." Pride and fear war in his expression as he drinks me in. "Like my wife."

A knock interrupts whatever else he might have said. Bianca enters, carrying something wrapped in black silk. My stepdaughter moves with that innate DeLuca grace, but there's tension in her shoulders that wasn't there before the monastery.

"I want you to take this," she tells me, unwrapping the package to reveal an ornate dagger. The blade gleams wickedly in the afternoon light, its handle inlaid with mother-of-pearl and what look like actual emeralds. The craftsmanship is exquisite—this is no mere weapon, but a work of art designed for killing.

"It was my mother's. Dad gave it to her for protection, but ..." She swallows hard. "She never used it. Maybe you'll be braver than she was."

The gift carries weight beyond the physical—it's acceptance, acknowledgment, family. I take it carefully, securing the sheath at my ankle beneath my tailored pants. The blade settles against my skin like a promise.

"I'll bring it back," I promise.

"Bring yourself back," Bianca corrects, surprising us both with a fierce hug. Her arms are strong around me despite the lingering effects of Romano's drugs. "I just got used to having a stepmom. I'm not breaking in a new one."

I hug her back, meeting Matteo's eyes over his daughter's shoulder. The love I see there nearly steals my breath. How did we get here? A week ago, I was just a college student trying to escape this world.

Now I'm walking willingly into danger, armed with his and my father's training and his daughter's trust.

"Time to go," Antonio says from the doorway. "Elena's neighbor reported movement in her apartment."

One final kiss for Matteo, one last hug for Bianca, and I follow

Antonio out. The Mercedes glides through Manhattan traffic like a shark through dark water. I review the plan as we drive, noting how the city I've lived in my whole life looks different now. Every shadow could hide a threat, every glittering window could conceal a sniper's scope.

Is this how my father saw the world? How Matteo sees it?

Elena's building rises before us, a gleaming tower of steel and glass that has always represented safety to me. How many nights have I spent in her apartment, drinking wine and dreaming of gallery openings? Now only one window shows light on the tenth floor, a beacon or a trap, I'm not sure which.

"Remember," Antonio says as we take position, "the Boss's orders are to extract Elena and get out. No unnecessary risks."

I check my weapons one last time—gun at my shoulder, knife at my ankle, backup piece strapped to my thigh. "Define unnecessary."

His laugh is grim. "Just try to come back in one piece. He's impossible when you're in danger."

"Speaking from experience?" I tease.

"Speaking as someone who's never seen him like this." Antonio's voice softens. "Not even with Sophia."

The comparison should bother me, but it doesn't. Because I understand now—Sophia was his past, his lesson in trust and betrayal. But me? I'm his future. The one he chose, just as I chose him.

My phone buzzes with a text from an unknown number. The video attachment makes my blood run cold—Elena tied to one of her designer dining chairs, mascara streaking her face. Her bottom lip is split, a bruise darkening her left cheek. But her eyes ... her eyes are fierce despite her fear.

Come alone, the message reads. *Or she dies like your mother.*

My hands don't shake as I respond: *Coming up. Touch her and I'll show you exactly what I learned from Matteo DeLuca.*

"Ready?" Antonio asks as I step out of the car.

I think of Matteo's lessons in strategy, of Bianca's fierce acceptance, of my father's voice teaching me to shoot. Of Elena, who's only in danger because she loved me enough to stay when she learned the truth about my world. "Ready."

The lobby is eerily silent—no doorman at his usual post, no residents coming and going. My heels click against marble floors that have been polished to mirror shine, the sound echoing off walls that usually buzz with Manhattan's elite. The emptiness raises the hair on my neck. How many of Johnny's men are watching? How many guns are trained on me right now?

The elevator ride gives me time to center myself, to become who I need to be. Not the artist, not the scared girl forced into marriage. But Matteo's wife. A donna in her own right.

I catch my reflection in the mirrored walls—black suit, perfect makeup, eyes that have seen too much in too little time.

My mother would be proud of how I look.

My father would be proud of why I'm here.

Elena's door stands slightly open when I reach it. The scent of her signature perfume—Chanel No. 5—mingles with something metallic that makes my stomach turn. Blood. Taking a deep breath, I step into the apartment that's been my second home for years.

The space has been transformed into something from my nightmares. Elena's carefully curated furniture has been shoved aside to create sight lines to every entrance. Her collection of fashion photographs—all originals, all signed—hang crookedly on walls now marred by bullet holes. And in the center of it all, Johnny Calabrese lounges in her favorite armchair, gun trained lazily on my best friend's head.

He's not as polished as he was at my wedding. The tunnel collapse left its mark—a nasty cut above his eye, the way he favors his left side. But his smile is still razor-sharp, still promising beautiful violence.

"Bella," Elena manages through split lips. Even bound and bleeding, she maintains that society poise. "I'm sorry. He said he just wanted to talk, and I—"

"Shut up." Johnny presses the gun harder against her temple.

"Well, well. The artist becomes the warrior. Love the suit, by the way. Very donna."

"Let her go, Johnny." I keep my voice even, the way I've heard Matteo do countless times. Like I'm discussing the weather rather than life and death. "She's not part of this."

"Oh, but she is." His smile widens, showing too many teeth. "See, I've learned something about you, Bella DeLuca. You're not like Sophia—weak, easily manipulated. No, you're much more interesting." He circles Elena's chair like a shark scenting blood. "You actually love him."

"This isn't about Matteo."

"It's always about Matteo." Johnny moves behind Elena's chair, using her as a shield. Smart. He knows I won't risk hitting her. "He took everything from me. My family's territory, my chance at true power, even Sophia. Now? Now I take everything from him. Starting with you."

"You already tried that." I take a careful step forward, cataloging details with an artist's eye and a killer's intent. The distance to Elena's chair. The angle of Johnny's gun. The way his injuries affect his balance. "How's that tunnel collapse treating you?"

His handsome face darkens with rage. A bead of sweat rolls down his temple despite the apartment's perfect temperature. Withdrawal, maybe. The Calabrese family's cocaine habit is no secret. "Brave little artist. But you made one mistake." The gun shifts from Elena to me, and I see his hand trembling slightly. "You came alone."

I meet Elena's eye. She nods subtly.

"Did I?" I ask.

The words are barely out before I move. Sophia's knife slides into my hand like it was made for me, the emeralds catching light as it flies. Johnny's eyes widen a fraction of a second before the blade buries itself in his shoulder—not a killing blow, but enough to make him stumble back, cursing.

"Now!" I scream, and everything happens at once.

Elena throws herself sideways—exactly as we'd planned when I caught her eye—just as Matteo's men burst through windows and doors. The sound of shattering glass rains down like lethal music, but I'm already moving.

Johnny's men materialize from doorways and behind furniture, their automatic weapons filling Elena's pristine apartment with deafening thunder. I dive behind her overturned marble dining table just as bullets chip away at its edge. The Italian stone that she was so proud of now becomes my shield.

"Kill them all!" Johnny's voice rises above the gunfire, tight with pain and rage. "But leave DeLuca's bitch for me!"

I risk a glance around the table's edge. Through gun smoke and flying debris, I count positions—two men by the kitchen, another near the bathroom, Johnny himself using Elena's designer bookcase for cover. My father's voice echoes in my head: *"See the whole battlefield, bella mia. Find their weaknesses."*

A man appears to my left, thinking he has the drop on me. But I was taught better than that. I roll as he fires, my Louboutins finding purchase on Elena's blood-spattered marble floor. My gun seems to lift itself, muscle memory taking over. Two shots—one to the knee, one to the shoulder. Nonlethal, but effective. Just like Papa taught me.

"Bella, down!" Antonio's voice carries over the chaos.

I drop instantly as one of Johnny's men sprays bullets where my head had been. A vase that probably cost more than my old car explodes above me, raining crystal and roses. The scent of Elena's favorite flowers mingles with cordite and blood.

"The girl!" Johnny shouts, and I see two of his men moving toward Elena where she's still bound to the overturned chair.

"Not happening." I come up firing, catching one in the thigh. The other drops as Antonio's shot takes him in the chest. But the distraction costs me—Johnny uses the moment to close the distance.

His fist catches my jaw, sending me stumbling back. The gun flies from my hand, skittering under Elena's imported Swedish couch. But my father didn't just teach me to shoot—he taught me to fight. I turn the stumble into momentum, using Johnny's own weight against him. My elbow finds his throat as I spin, driving the air from his lungs.

"Not bad, little artist," he wheezes, blood from his shoulder wound staining his custom suit. "But not good enough."

He comes at me again, but his injuries slow him. I see him favor his left side—damage from the tunnel collapse that didn't properly heal. My next kick finds that weakness, making him double over. But Johnny Calabrese hasn't survived this long by being easy to kill. His hand locks around my ankle, pulling me off balance.

We go down together, rolling across Elena's ruined floor as Matteo's men engage the last of Johnny's backup. My head cracks against something hard—probably the same marble table that saved my life earlier. Stars explode behind my eyes as Johnny's hands find my throat.

"I'm going to enjoy this," he snarls, his handsome face twisted with hate. "Making him watch as the life drains from your pretty eyes. Just like Sophia—"

The name of Matteo's dead wife becomes a gurgle. Because Johnny made the same mistake so many others have—he underestimated me. The backup gun strapped to my thigh slides into my hand like it belongs there. The barrel presses under his chin as his eyes widen in surprise.

"I'm not Sophia," I say clearly, making sure he hears every word. "I was *never* Sophia."

The shot echoes through the suddenly quiet apartment. Johnny's body slumps forward, but I'm already rolling away. My hands shake slightly as I push to my feet, taking in the carnage around us. Elena's beautiful home looks like a war zone—bullet holes in imported wallpaper, blood on Swedish furniture, her carefully curated life turned to chaos.

But Elena herself is alive. That's all that matters. I scramble towards her.

"I've got you," I soothe as I work at her bonds, my fingers steady despite everything. The zip ties have cut into her wrists, leaving angry red marks that make rage burn hot in my chest. "You're safe now, E. I've got you."

"Boss wants confirmation," Antonio says, his voice cutting

through the silent aftermath. The gunfire has stopped, leaving only the crystalline sound of broken glass settling and Elena's quiet sobs. The acrid scent of cordite hangs heavy in the air, mixing with spilled perfume from Elena's shattered collection and the copper tang of blood.

I look up at him from where I kneel beside Elena, my designer suit ruined with blood and gunpowder residue. Johnny's body lies a few feet away, his handsome features forever frozen in that final moment of surprise. My hands should shake after taking a life, but they remain steady as I hold my best friend. "Tell my husband the threat's been eliminated. Permanently."

"And you?" A careful question.

I touch the graze on my arm where his last bullet found home. The wound stings, but the adrenaline still coursing through my system dulls the pain to background noise. "Tell him I'm bringing his wife and our friend home. Where we belong."

Rising carefully, I take in the full scope of destruction around us as Antonio relays the message. Blood—some Johnny's, some his men's, some mine—stains the Swedish furniture and Italian marble. This was her sanctuary, her escape from our world, and now it's just another casualty of the life I was born into. The life I finally stopped running from.

"I'm so sorry," I whisper into her hair as I help her stand. My body aches from the fight, but I push the pain aside. "This is all my fault."

She pulls back enough to look at me, and despite her split lip and mascara-stained cheeks, despite having watched me kill a man in her living room, I see resolve in her eyes. "Don't you dare apologize. You came for me. You *saved* me."

"Always." My voice breaks slightly as I steady her on shaky legs. "That's what family does."

Because that's what this was always about—belonging. Finding my place not just in Matteo's world, but in myself. Becoming not who I was forced to be, but who I chose to be. Learning that sometimes the most beautiful art comes from destruction. Sometimes the most important choices are made in moments of violence.

Sirens wail in the distance as Antonio's team begins cleanup. By the time the police arrive, they'll find nothing but an unfortunate break-in, no suspects to be found. Elena will be safely hidden away at the compound until we're sure no other threats remain. And I ...

I choose this. This family, this life, this love. The weight of the gun at my shoulder, the knife retrieved from Johnny's corpse, the wedding ring that means more now than it did a week ago.

I choose to be both artist and donna, creator and destroyer, wife and warrior.

For better or worse, till death do us part.

As we leave Elena's ruined apartment, I send one text to my husband: *Coming home. All of us.*

His response is immediate: *Hurry. Some of us are terrible at waiting.*

I smile despite everything, because I hear what he's not saying. He loves me. He trusts me. He's proud of me.

And that's worth every drop of blood, every hard choice, every step into this dangerous new life we're building together.

One bullet at a time.

25

MATTEO

I pace my study like a caged predator, each step sending fresh waves of pain through my injured shoulder. The security feed shows three black SUVs approaching the mansion's gates, but I won't breathe properly until I see her. Until I can touch her, hold her, make sure she's real and whole and alive.

"She did it," Bianca says from her perch on my desk, watching the feed with forced casualness. But I see how her fingers grip the edge, betraying her own tension. "Of course she did it."

"Of course," I echo, but my hands clench as memories assault me—Sophia's broken body, Giovanni's closed casket, Cher Russo's crime scene photos. I've lost too much, buried too many, to trust in certainty. The thought of Bella facing Johnny alone, even with Antonio's team in position, makes something primal rage in my chest.

The study door opens and suddenly she's there, alive and fierce and mine. But the sight of her makes my blood boil—her elegant suit is spattered with blood and gunpowder residue, her jaw darkening with what will become an impressive bruise. A cut above her eyebrow still seeps blood, and the way she holds herself speaks of other injuries she's trying to hide.

She's helped Elena to the mansion's medical suite, briefed security, handled the cleanup—every inch a donna. But when her eyes meet mine, she's simply my wife, my salvation, my heart walking around outside my body.

"Johnny?" I ask, though Antonio's already reported. I need to hear it from her.

"Dead." She moves to me, and I pull her close with my good arm, breathing in her scent beneath the gunpowder and blood. Jasmine and paint and life. "He won't threaten our family again."

Our family. The words still send something warm through my chest, especially when Bianca slides off my desk to join our embrace. My daughter, who once hated the idea of this marriage, now fits perfectly into our unlikely circle.

"Elena's resting," Bella continues, one arm around each of us. Her voice is steady, but I feel fine tremors running through her body—adrenaline crash setting in. "The doctor says she'll be fine—mostly bruises and shock. She wants to help with the other Families, prove her loyalty."

"She already did," Bianca points out, and I hear admiration in my daughter's voice. "By surviving. By not breaking under Johnny's torture."

I feel Bella tense at the word "torture," but she merely nods. "She'll need protection. The Calabrese family won't take Johnny's death lightly."

"Let them try something." Bianca's smile is pure DeLuca danger, and for a moment my chest tightens at how much she looks like me. "We protect our own."

"Speaking of protection." I guide Bella to my desk chair, ignoring her protests as I examine her injuries. Each mark on her perfect skin makes rage build in my chest. That anyone would dare touch her, hurt her ... "You're hurt."

"Barely a scratch." But she doesn't stop me from gently touching her jaw, her temple where blood has matted in her hair. Her own hand comes up to my chest. "Your shoulder's bleeding again."

I glance down to find red seeping through my shirt. "Worth it."

"Worth what?"

"Getting to hold you." I cup her face with my good hand, careful of her bruises. My thumb traces her bottom lip, and I feel her breath catch. "Watching you come back to me."

"Always," she whispers, leaning into my touch. Her eyes hold mine, full of things we're still learning to say. "I'll always come back to you."

Bianca makes an exaggerated gagging sound. "And that's my cue to check on Elena. Try not to conceive any siblings while I'm gone."

She slips out before either of us can respond, but her teasing carries no bite. If anything, there's affection in it—acceptance of how much has changed in just a week.

Once we're alone, I pull Bella to her feet, needing her closer. The sight of her injuries makes something primal rise in my chest. "You could have died today."

"So could you, at the monastery." Her fingers work at my shirt buttons with practiced grace, checking my wound with careful hands. The brush of her skin against mine sends electricity through my body despite my anger, despite my fear. "So could Bianca. It's who we are, what this life is."

"And you're okay with that? This life you were forced into?"

"I wasn't forced." She meets my eyes steadily, and the conviction in her gaze steals my breath. "You gave me a choice that day in your office, remember? I chose this. Chose you."

"Because of your father's wishes—"

"Because something in me recognized something in you." Her fingers trace my chest above my heart, leaving fire in their wake. "The same something that made you watch over me, that made you choose Bianca over everything, that made you trust me today to handle Johnny myself."

I catch her hand, pressing it more firmly against my chest so she can feel my heartbeat—the rhythm that exists only for her now. "When did you get so wise, *piccola*?"

"Somewhere between saying 'I do' and throwing your dead wife's knife into Johnny Calabrese's shoulder." Her smile turns wicked, though it pulls at her split lip. "Speaking of which, your daughter gave me *quite* a wedding gift."

"Our daughter," I correct, watching pleasure flash across her face at the words. Despite her injuries, despite the blood still staining her clothes, she's the most beautiful thing I've ever seen. "And you've more than earned your place in this family."

"Have I?" She rises on her toes, lips brushing mine with exquisite softness. "Maybe you should show me exactly what that place is."

A growl escapes me as I pull her flush against me, ignoring the protest from my shoulder. Having her in my arms, alive and fierce and mine, makes every injury worth it. "Careful what you wish for, wife."

"Why?" Her hands slide into my hair, nails scraping lightly against my scalp in a way that makes heat pool in my gut. "Afraid you can't handle me?"

Instead of answering, I capture her mouth with mine. The kiss is different from our others—deep and thorough but achingly tender. She matches me emotion for emotion, her teeth catching my bottom lip in a way that makes me groan. The taste of her—tea and copper and something uniquely Bella—makes my head spin.

"We should check your shoulder," she gasps when we break for air, but her hands continue mapping my chest.

"Later." I'm already backing her toward the door that connects my study to our private rooms. Every step feels like coming home. "Right now, I need to show my wife exactly where she belongs."

"And where's that?"

I pause, studying her face—flushed with desire but still watching me with those artist's eyes that see too much, understand too well. Even with her bruised jaw and blood-matted hair, she's the most beautiful thing I've ever seen.

"Here," I say simply. "With me. With our family. For as long as you'll have us."

Her smile is radiant despite her split lip. "Till death do us part?"

"Even longer than that, *piccola*." My voice is raw, the words roughened by all the feelings I can't fully express. I kiss her again, pouring everything I can't say into it. All the fear of almost losing her, all the pride in her strength, all the love I never thought I'd feel again. My thumb brushes the soft curve of her jaw, careful not to press too hard where her skin is bruised.

She kisses me back just as fiercely, her hands fisting the front of my shirt like she's afraid I'll disappear if she lets go. When we part, she leans her forehead against mine, her breath warm against my lips.

"Come on," I murmur, slipping an arm around her waist to guide her to our bedroom. Step by step, we make our way inside, where the afternoon sun streams through the floor-to-ceiling windows. The golden light bathes everything in warmth, catching on the edges of her hair and skin, making her look like something divine. I want to worship every inch of her, but first ...

"Let me clean these," I murmur, retrieving the first aid kit we now keep in every room. Her eyes follow me as I tend to her wounds—the cut above her eyebrow, her split lip, the bruise darkening her jaw. Each mark makes rage build in my chest, but I keep my touch gentle.

Her eyes never leave me, watching every move I make with a mix of trust and quiet intensity. I work my way to her split lip, dabbing at it with a damp cloth. Her breath hitches when I touch the corner of her mouth, and I freeze, afraid I've hurt her.

"I'm fine," she whispers, her voice hoarse but firm.

I nod, resuming my work, but each bruise and scrape I uncover sends a sharp pang of rage through my chest. When I reach the deep purple bruise darkening her jaw, I pause, my fingers trembling. She places her hand over mine, grounding me.

"It's okay," she says softly. "I'm here."

"Your turn," she says when I finish, helping me remove my shirt. Her fingers trace the edges of my bandage with an artist's precision. "We're quite a pair."

"We are." I catch her hand, pressing it against my heart. "My brave, beautiful, impossible wife."

"Your wife," she echoes, her voice thick with emotion, pulling me down for a kiss that steals my breath. "Show me."

I don't rush. My hands find the buttons of her jacket, undoing them one by one. The designer fabric is stained with blood, a grim reminder of everything we've endured. And as it falls away, I focus only on her—on the soft curves of her body, the golden glow of her skin in the sunlight. Her blouse follows, slipping off her shoulders to reveal more bruises, more signs of the fight she survived. Each injury is a reminder of how close I came to losing her, but each breath, each heartbeat proves she's here, alive, *mine*. When she's finally bare beneath me, I worship her with lips and hands and whispered devotion in Italian.

"Every mark," I murmur, brushing my lips over the dark bruise blooming on her collarbone, "is proof of how strong you are."

Her breath hitches, and her hands move to my belt, fingers deftly working the buckle. There's no hesitation in her movements, only quiet determination as she tugs the leather free and sets it aside. When she looks up at me, her eyes are steady.

"Your turn," she says again, this time with a hint of a challenge.

I let her push my pants down, the fabric pooling at my feet as she sits back to take me in. Her own hands aren't idle, mapping my skin like she's memorizing me for a painting. Each touch leaves fire in its wake, building something between us that's both tender and devastating.

When she leans back against the pillows, I move to join her. My hands slide down her sides, fingers catching the waistband of her pants. I ease them down, piece by piece, until she's bare beneath me. Her beauty steals my breath.

I trail kisses along her body, starting at her collarbone and working my way lower. My hands map every curve, every hollow, learning her anew. Her skin is soft under my palms, warm and alive, and I can't stop murmuring soft words in Italian—praises, prayers, confessions of love.

"*Ti amo,*" I whisper against her throat, tasting her pulse. "*Ti amo, tesoro mio.*"

Her hands tangle in my hair, her nails grazing my scalp as she arches beneath me. Her body responds to every kiss, every touch, her breaths coming faster. When her voice breaks on a whisper, "Show me," it's all I can do to hold on to the last threads of control.

I slide back up her body, capturing her lips in a kiss that's deep and unhurried. When I finally join our bodies, the connection feels like coming home. We move together slowly, savoring each sensation, each shared breath. It's different from our other times—less desperate, more tender. A celebration of life and love and belonging. Her hands tangle in my hair as I worship her with lips and tongue, learning every sound she makes, every way she moves.

Her release builds slowly, beautifully, until she comes apart beneath me whispering my name like a prayer. The sight of her—flushed and perfect, trusting me with her pleasure—sends me over the edge after her. My forehead rests against hers as we both tremble through the aftershocks. For a moment, the world narrows to just us, just this, just love.

After, I hold her close as our heartbeats slow. The setting sun paints our room in shades of gold and crimson, but all I see is her—my salvation, my future, my heart.

A knock interrupts us—Antonio with updates about the Calabrese family's reaction to Johnny's death, about Elena's statement, about a thousand things that need our attention.

But for now, I just hold my wife close, feeling her heartbeat against my chest. Because we have time now. Time to love, to heal, to build something stronger than blood or duty or arranged marriages.

We have forever.

And forever, I'm learning, is just the beginning.

26

BELLA

Four weeks after Johnny's death, I stand in my studio at the mansion, studying my latest piece. The canvas towers over me, six feet of emotion poured onto linen in oils. In the center, three figures emerge from a maelstrom of darkness and light —a man, a woman, and a girl, their features suggested rather than defined. I've used every shade of blue and black in my collection, building layers of shadow that seem to breathe. Gold leaf catches light where it breaks through the darkness, like hope emerging from chaos. The man's protective stance, the woman's outstretched hand, the girl's lifted chin—family, protection, belonging, all the themes that have consumed me since that day in Matteo's office.

The brush slips from my paint-stained fingers as a wave of dizziness hits. I've been working too long without eating, lost in the flow of creation. I steady myself against my worktable, breathing deeply. The familiar scent of turpentine and oils that usually comforts me now seems overwhelming.

"It's different from your other work."

I turn to find Elena in the doorway, looking better though still carrying shadows in her eyes. The bruises on her face have faded to yellowed memory, but I catch how she still flinches at sudden movements. Her designer dress is perfect as always—black Chanel that makes her look even more willowy than usual—but she holds herself differently now. More carefully. More aware.

Like a survivor rather than a victim.

"Good different or bad different?" I ask, wiping paint from my hands with a stained rag. Some habits are too hard to break, even as a donna.

"Powerful different." She moves closer, studying the painting with a curator's eye. Her hand traces the air near the canvas, following the sweeping lines of gold through darkness. "Less hiding, more truth. Like you."

I smile, remembering our conversation just weeks ago about running away from this life. Now here we both are—deeper in than ever. Elena has taken over all event planning for the Families, her near-death experience earning her respect among even the most traditional dons. Her talent for managing egos and arranging seating charts that won't start blood feuds has proven invaluable.

"Mrs. DeLuca?" Maria appears in the doorway, her silver hair neatly coiled at her nape, her crisp uniform a sharp contrast to my paint-splattered appearance. The housekeeper's warm eyes hold a mixture of affection and concern as she takes in my disheveled state. "Mr. DeLuca needs you in his study. The Calabrese family's representatives have arrived."

I exchange a look with Elena. This meeting will determine whether Johnny's death leads to war or peace. Whether his family accepts the evidence of his crimes or seeks revenge.

"I should change," I say, looking down at my clothes. Paint stains my favorite jeans and oversized sweater—Matteo's actually, stolen from his closet this morning.

"No." Elena's voice carries an edge I've never heard before. "Let them see you exactly as you are. The artist who became a donna. The woman who killed their heir to protect her family."

Understanding flows between us as I nod. Following Maria through the mansion's corridors, I breathe in the familiar scents—

leather and wood polish, fresh flowers from the conservatory, the lingering traces of Matteo's cologne. His study door stands open, and my heart still skips when I see him behind his desk.

My husband looks every inch the don today in a charcoal Brioni suit that emphasizes his broad shoulders. His hair is perfectly styled despite the hand he occasionally runs through it when stressed, and the silver at his temples catches the afternoon light. He's finally stopped favoring his injured shoulder, though I know it still pains him more than he admits.

Bianca stands at his right hand, every inch his daughter despite what blood might say. She's traded her usual casual style for a navy sheath dress that makes her look older than her seventeen years. Her dark hair is swept up elegantly, highlighting cheekbones that mirror her father's. The past four weeks have changed her too—she stands straighter, more confident in her place in our family.

They both look up as I enter, twin expressions of pride crossing their faces at my appearance. Because Elena's right—there's power in this, in being exactly who I am. Let the Calabrese family see the paint under my nails, the creativity that makes me different from their polished society wives.

"Don Calabrese," Matteo greets the elderly man seated across from him. "You remember my wife."

The don's eyes narrow at my paint-stained appearance, but he rises with proper respect. He's elegantly dressed in an Italian suit that probably costs more than most cars, his silver hair perfectly coiffed despite the humidity. But there's something predatory in his dark eyes that reminds me too much of Johnny.

"Mrs. DeLuca." His voice carries decades of power and threat wrapped in courtesy. "My condolences on your mother's loss."

"And mine on your son's," I return smoothly, moving to stand at Matteo's left. My eyes catch movement behind the don—Anthony Calabrese, Johnny's nephew, stands quietly observing. He's younger than I expected, maybe twenty-five, with clean-cut good looks and an air of sophistication his uncle lacked. "Though we both know Johnny's actions left no other choice."

"Did they not?" The don's smile is cold, reptilian. "A son dead, a family heir lost ... some might say that demands response." The threat hangs in the air like smoke, making the familiar scent of Matteo's study—leather and sandalwood and power—feel suddenly oppressive.

"Some might," Matteo agrees, his tone carrying that deadly calm that makes smarter men tremble. "Others might consider the evidence we gathered at the monastery. The medical records showing your son's ... proclivities with his previous wives. The video footage of his attack on an innocent event planner."

I feel Bianca tense beside me as Elena enters quietly, taking her place near the door. The don's eyes track her movement like a snake watching prey, noting the fading bruises on her face. But it's Anthony's reaction that catches my eye—the slight softening of his expression, the way his hands clench at his sides as if fighting the urge to reach for her.

"Johnny was ... troubled," Don Calabrese admits finally. His manicured fingers tap a rhythm on the arm of his chair. "But he was my blood."

"Blood isn't everything," Bianca speaks up, chin lifted in that defiant way she gets from Matteo. "Family is who we choose. Who chooses us."

Something shifts in the don's expression as he studies us—this unlikely family unit forged in fire and choice rather than genetics. His gaze lingers on Bianca, and I know he's heard the confirmation about her parentage. The sunlight streaming through Matteo's windows catches on his signet ring as he strokes his chin thoughtfully.

"Perhaps," he says slowly, "it's time for new alliances. My grandson, Anthony, will take Johnny's place as heir. He's a bit older than your daughter, but in a few years ..."

"No." Matteo's voice brooks no argument. The muscle in his jaw jumps—the only sign of how close he is to violence. "Bianca will choose her own path. Her own family."

The don inclines his head, but I catch the calculation in his eyes.

They remind me of a shark's—cold, ancient, patient. "Of course. Then perhaps we can discuss other arrangements. Territory agreements, business partnerships ..."

The negotiations continue, subtle threats wrapped in politeness as expensive as their suits. I observe it all—the power plays, the careful words, the way Matteo manages to secure peace while giving up nothing of real value. Every movement in this room is choreographed, a deadly dance where one misstep could start a war.

A movement near the door catches my attention. Elena slips out, but not before I see her exchange a look with Anthony Calabrese. The heat in that glance, the barely concealed longing, makes my stomach clench with familiar worry. How many times will history try to repeat itself?

"We have an understanding then," Don Calabrese says, rising with that predatory grace that makes my skin crawl. His eyes sweep our family unit one last time, lingering just a moment too long on Bianca. "Though remember, the Calabrese family has a long memory. And even longer reach."

"As do we," Matteo responds, his voice carrying that lethal softness that makes even hardened killers pause. "I trust you'll remember that when considering future ... arrangements."

The threat hangs in the air between them like smoke. Anthony steps forward, offering his hand to his grandfather. In that moment, the family resemblance is striking—the same aristocratic features, the same calculated charm. But where Johnny's eyes held cruelty, Anthony's hold something else.

"Tell me, Mrs. DeLuca," the don says suddenly, his smile cold. "Do you still paint? I heard you were quite ... talented. It would be a shame if anything happened to interfere with such a ... delicate pursuit."

The words send ice through my veins. He's reminding us that they've been watching, gathering intelligence, learning our routines and vulnerabilities. Matteo's hand finds mine, squeezing once as Antonio escorts our guests out.

Once they're gone, the tension bleeds from the room like a physical thing. Bianca collapses onto the leather sofa, kicking off her heels. "Well, that was suitably terrifying."

"You did well," Matteo tells her, pride evident in his voice as he moves to the bar cart. The crystal decanter catches late afternoon light as he pours three fingers of scotch. "Standing your ground about choosing your own path."

"Yes, well." She shoots me a look that's half grateful, half mischievous. "I learned from the best. Knowing Bella killed Johnny rather than be forced into anything tends to clarify one's priorities."

I move to Matteo's desk, needing the familiar comfort of this space. The room still carries traces of his cologne, mixed with leather and aged wood. That turned-away photo frame catches my eye again —young Matteo with his father's hand on his shoulder, a gesture that had always struck me as wrong somehow.

Now I understand why he keeps it faced away, why Giuseppe's shadow still darkens even our brightest moments.

"They're watching us," I say, perching on the desk's edge. "Have been for a while, judging by his comment about my painting."

"Let them watch." Bianca's voice carries that DeLuca steel. "We protect our own now."

"Speaking of protection." Matteo hands me a glass of water instead of scotch—he's noticed I haven't been drinking lately. The gesture makes my heart flutter. "That look between Elena and Anthony ..."

"Elena's stronger than Mom was," Bianca points out, twisting a strand of dark hair around her finger—a gesture so like her father it makes my chest ache. "And Anthony seems ... different from Johnny."

"Still." Matteo's jaw clenches. "We watch. We wait. We protect."

"Always." Bianca stands, smoothing her dress. "And now, if you'll excuse me, I have a FaceTime date with Sophie Martinez." At our raised eyebrows, she adds, "What? A girl needs normal friends too. Even Mafia princesses."

She kisses both our cheeks before leaving, her designer heels clicking against hardwood floors. The sound fades, leaving us alone in the gathering dusk.

The setting sun paints his study in shades of gold and crimson, turning the space into something from a Renaissance painting. The light catches on his signet ring as he moves to stand behind his desk, every inch the powerful don—except for how his eyes soften when they meet mine.

"You saw it too?" he asks, pulling me into his lap. His cologne wraps around me, and for a moment I have to fight a wave of nausea that has nothing to do with stress.

"Elena and Anthony?" I trace the scar on his shoulder through his shirt, remembering how close I came to losing him. "Yes. History repeating?"

"No." He catches my hand, pressing a kiss to my palm that sends electricity through my body. "Because this time we know better. This time we protect our own."

"Speaking of our own ..." I take a deep breath, gathering my courage as I place his hand on my still-flat stomach. "We might need to clear out that room next to Bianca's."

I feel him go absolutely still beneath me. "Bella?" He barely breathes.

"I'm late." I meet his eyes, seeing my own mix of fear and hope reflected there. "And the doctor confirmed it this morning. Six weeks."

"Since our wedding night," he breathes, hand spreading possessively across my stomach. For a moment, something dark crosses his face—old fears, old wounds—I'm only beginning to understand. I see him glance at that turned-away photo of his father, then back to me. His hand trembles slightly when it rests against me.

"Talk to me," I whisper, cupping his face. "What are you thinking?"

"I'm thinking ..." His voice is rough with emotion. "I'm thinking about how terrified I am of becoming him. Of failing this child like he failed me."

"You won't." I press my forehead to his. "You're nothing like Giuseppe. Look at how you are with Bianca—how you protect her, support her, let her choose her own path."

"A baby," he whispers against my lips, wonder breaking through the fear. "Our baby." His other hand slides into my hair, cradling my head like I'm something precious. "You're sure?"

I nod, watching joy finally overtake the shadows in his eyes. "I know it's fast, and with everything that's happened—"

He cuts me off with a kiss that steals my breath. When we break apart, I see everything in his face—the lingering fear of his father's legacy, the fierce protective instinct already building, and underneath it all, a deep, staggering love that makes my heart ache.

"You know what this means?" he murmurs, both hands now cradling my stomach. "No more rushing into gunfights. No more facing down killers alone."

I laugh despite the tears gathering in my eyes. "I wasn't planning on making that a habit anyway."

"Good." He kisses me again, softer this time. "Because I need you both safe. Need you *all* safe."

"You're happy?" My stomach flips but it has nothing to do with morning sickness.

"Terrified," he corrects, holding me closer. "But yes, *piccola*. So damn happy."

We stay like that for a long moment, his hand protective over our child, my head tucked under his chin. Outside, the sun sets over our empire—an empire built on blood and sacrifice, but sustained by choice and love.

"We should tell Bianca first," I say finally. "Before anyone else knows."

"Together?"

I smile, remembering all the times that word has saved us. All the times it's meant the difference between survival and destruction. Between fear and hope. Between duty and love.

"Together."

Because that's what we are now—this unlikely family built from violence but bound by choice. Artist and don, daughter and heir, mother and father. Creators and destroyers, lovers and fighters, protectors and protected.

Together. *Always* together.

And in eight months, our family will grow by one more choice, one more love, one more chance to prove that blood isn't what makes a family.

Love is.

27

MATTEO

I can't stop touching my wife. Even now, hours after her revelation, my hand keeps finding its way to her still-flat stomach as we lie in our bed. Bella's curled against my chest, her breathing even but not quite asleep—I can tell by the way her fingers trace absent patterns on my skin, the slight tension in her shoulders that says her mind is still racing.

A baby. The thought hits me again like a physical blow, equal parts terror and joy. My hand spreads wider across her abdomen, as if I could already feel the tiny life we created. Six weeks. Since our wedding night. Since everything changed.

Memories of another pregnancy surface—Sophia, barely seventeen and terrified when she came to me. The circumstances of Bianca's conception remain a dark shadow in my mind, but from the moment I agreed to marry Sophia, to claim the child as mine, nothing else mattered. Blood, biology, the whispers of others—none of it compared to the fierce love that seized my heart the moment I first held my daughter.

I remember every detail of that day—the weight of her tiny body in my arms, how her fingers wrapped around mine with surprising strength, the way she stopped crying the moment I held her. Sophia had been too drugged to hold her, but I stood guard over that hospital bassinet for three days straight, daring anyone to question my claim on this perfect creature who somehow became my whole world.

Now, seventeen years later, I'll get to experience it all again. But this time with a woman I truly love, with a marriage built on choice rather than obligation. This time everything is different.

Unless ...

The darker thoughts creep in, unbidden. Giuseppe's voice echoes in my head: *"Children are weakness, boy. Something for enemies to use against you."* I remember watching him pace the hospital corridor when Bianca was born, his cold calculation as he studied her features, searching for something I refused to see.

My arm tightens around Bella instinctively. No. This child will never know that kind of fear, that kind of manipulation. This baby will be born into love, into protection, into a family that chooses each other every day.

But still ... the image of Bella pregnant and vulnerable makes something cold settle in my gut. A pregnant donna is a prime target—something to be used against a don, a way to bring the mighty to their knees. I'll need to increase security, maybe move up the timeline on the Tuscany villa. Somewhere safe, somewhere far from New York's politics and vendettas.

"She'll be happy," I murmur against Bella's temple, breathing in her familiar scent. "Once the shock wears off."

"Will she?" Bella shifts to look at me, and even in the dim light she takes my breath away. Her dark hair spills across my chest like ink, and those artist's eyes search my face with their usual perception. "Everything's changed so fast. Her whole world's been turned upside down in seven weeks. And now this ..."

"Now this is something good." My hand splays possessively over her stomach again, hoping somehow our child can feel how much I already love them. The emotion catches me off guard—this fierce protectiveness, this overwhelming need to keep them both safe. "Something that's just ours."

She covers my hand with hers, our wedding rings catching the moonlight. The simple gesture makes my chest tight. "I'm scared," she admits quietly. "Not of the baby, but of bringing a child into this world. Our world."

I understand her fear because I share it. Our world is built on violence and vendettas, where a pregnant donna becomes a prime target. The thought of anyone using my child—*either* of my children—as leverage makes something dark and deadly rise in my chest. I'll need to be careful though, to find the balance between protection and suffocation. Bella's too strong, too independent to be locked away in a gilded cage.

I've also seen what this life can do to children, how it can twist them into something hard and cold. But Bianca somehow escaped that fate—her heart remained open, loving, despite everything. Maybe because she had what I never did: a father who chose her, who loved her without conditions or expectations.

But fear plagues me. Not about biology or bloodlines—those concerns died the day I chose Bianca as mine—but about the kind of father I can be. The weight of legacy sits heavy on my chest.

Every choice I've made since taking control of the DeLuca empire has been calculated, measured against potential consequences. But this? This tiny life Bella and I created? There's nothing calculated about the way my heart races every time I think about it. About tiny fingers and first steps and the chance to do everything differently this time.

With Bianca, I was barely more than a boy myself, thrust into fatherhood by circumstances I couldn't control. I made mistakes—too protective sometimes, too distant others, always terrified of becoming the monster who raised me. But Bianca's love, her unwavering trust even when I didn't deserve it, somehow made me better. Made me want to be better.

Now I have a second chance. A child created in love rather than obligation. But the old fears whisper in Giuseppe's voice: *Can a man like me, with blood on his hands and darkness in his soul, really be the father this baby deserves?*

Can I protect them from the violence of our world without becoming the very thing I fear?

I press my hand more firmly against Bella's stomach, trying to convey through touch alone how much I already love this child. How I'll die before I let anyone hurt them. How I'll spend every day making sure they know they're loved, wanted, chosen—everything I never had growing up.

My own childhood rises like a specter—Giuseppe's "lessons" about power and control, the weight of expectations crushing any hint of weakness. I was never a son to him, only an heir to be molded. But Bianca changed everything. Holding her that first time, I finally understood what a father should be. What love without conditions felt like.

This baby will never know that kind of fear. Will never question their worth or their place in our family. I'll make sure they grow up surrounded by art and love and possibility—just like their mother. They'll inherit my name, my protection, but not my sins. Not my father's legacy of pain.

"What are you thinking?" she asks softly, her fingers tracing the scar on my chest. "You've gone somewhere dark."

"Just thinking about protection." I press a kiss to her hair. "And how much has changed since Bianca was born."

"Tell me?" Her request is gentle, understanding. "What was it like, becoming a father then?"

The memories flood back—not all of them dark. "I was terrified," I admit. "Not because she wasn't mine by blood, but because suddenly this tiny perfect being depended on me completely. Me, who'd only ever known how to destroy things."

"But you learned to protect instead."

"She taught me." My voice roughens with emotion. "That first night in the hospital, when she wrapped her whole hand around my finger ... I knew I'd burn the world down to keep her safe."

Bella's quiet for a moment, processing. Then, "Do you want this one to be a boy?" The question holds a note of insecurity that makes my heart ache. "To carry on the DeLuca name?"

"No." The firmness of my response surprises us both. The truth is, the thought of a son terrifies me in ways I can't fully express. Would I see Giuseppe's features in his face? Would I hear my father's voice every time I tried to guide him? "I mean, I'll love this baby regardless, but ..." I cup her face, needing her to understand. "I'd love another daughter. One with your eyes and fierce heart."

Her laugh is watery. "The great Matteo DeLuca, brought to his knees by his daughters?"

"Gladly." I kiss her softly, tasting salt from tears she's trying to hide. Having two daughters to love, to protect, to watch grow into strong women who know their worth—it would be everything I never knew I needed. Everything Giuseppe was wrong about. "Though if it is a boy ..." I hesitate, suddenly nervous. "I'd like to name him Giovanni."

"Your father was the best man I knew." My voice catches as memories of my best friend surface. All the times he showed me what a real father should be, how he loved his daughter unconditionally, supported her dreams, chose art supplies over weapons. Everything Giuseppe wasn't. "He'd have loved being a grandfather."

"He'd have spoiled them rotten," she whispers, and I feel her tears against my chest. "Taking them to art museums, teaching them to shoot ..."

"Just like he did with you." I hold her closer as she cries, understanding this mixture of joy and grief. My mind drifts to Giovanni, to how he would have handled today's news. He'd have been overjoyed, probably already planning how to turn my security room into an art studio for his grandchild.

"He knew, you know." I find myself saying, lost in memories of my best friend. "That this baby would be a possibility."

She stills in my arms. "What do you mean?"

"That last night we shared cigars, before everything went wrong ... he talked about grandchildren." The memory is still fresh, still painful. "Said he hoped that when the time came, our families would be joined by love rather than arrangement. That any child of yours would be ..." My voice catches. "Would be something good in this dark world."

"You never told me that," she whispers, clutching onto me.

"There's still so much I haven't told you. So much I want to share ..."

A knock interrupts whatever else I might have confessed. "Dad?" Bianca's voice carries through the door, tension evident even muffled. "Antonio needs you. Both of you."

We dress quickly, years of midnight emergencies making the process efficient. My eyes follow Bella as she pulls one of my sweaters over her silk nightgown. The sight of her drowning in my clothes, her hair tumbling loose around her shoulders, makes my chest ache. Even like this—or maybe especially like this—she's the most beautiful thing I've ever seen.

We find Bianca and Antonio in the security room, the space lit only by the blue glow of multiple monitors. The technological heart of our protection system hums with quiet efficiency—dozens of screens showing every angle of our territory. Elena's apartment building features prominently on the main display.

"What happened?" Bella demands, instantly alert. Her hand finds mine in the dim light.

"Anthony Calabrese paid her a visit," Antonio reports, his weathered face illuminated by the screens. His tie is loosened, sleeves rolled up—signs he's been monitoring this situation for hours. "Brought flowers, apologized for his uncle's actions. Asked her to dinner."

"And?" I study the footage, noting how Elena's body language shifts from defensive to interested. Years of reading people let me catalog every tell, every micro-expression.

"She said yes." Bianca's voice holds worry. Like this—perched on the edge of a desk, brow furrowed in concentration—she looks so much like me it hurts. "Dad, we can't let her—"

"We can't stop her," Bella cuts in gently. "She's an adult, and after what Johnny did ... she needs to feel in control of her own choices."

"But we can protect her," I add, seeing both women relax slightly.

My hand finds Bella's stomach unconsciously, needing to touch our child. Our future. "Antonio, full surveillance on Anthony Calabrese. I want to know everything—his movements, his contacts, his true position in the family."

"Already on it, Boss." Antonio brings up more screens showing Anthony's recent activities. "He seems genuinely at odds with his grandfather's old-school methods. Been pushing for legitimate business ventures, modernization."

"People can seem like a lot of things." I pull Bella closer, remembering how Sophia had seemed. How she'd played us all. The weight of that deception still haunts me, makes me fear history repeating.

Bianca catches the protective gesture, sharp as ever. Her eyes narrow, tracking between us before settling on where my hand rests on Bella's stomach. In the monitor light, I see the exact moment understanding dawns in her expression—she's always been too perceptive for her own good, my girl.

"There's something you're not telling me," she says suddenly, straightening to her full height. In her silk pajamas and messy ponytail, she looks younger than her seventeen years, but those eyes—so like mine in their intensity—miss nothing. Her voice holds a mixture of hope and uncertainty that makes my chest ache. "What's going on?"

I meet Bella's gaze, seeing my own mix of joy and nervousness reflected there. This isn't how we planned to tell our daughter, but when has anything in our lives gone according to plan? I remember holding Bianca for the first time, promising to always protect her heart. Now I pray she has room in that heart for one more.

"Bianca," I say softly, "how do you feel about being a big sister?"

She freezes, processing the words. For a long moment, no one breathes. Even Antonio, usually unflappable, looks stunned. I watch emotions play across my daughter's face—shock, wonder, and something else that makes my throat tight. Something that looks like pure joy.

Then Bianca launches herself at us both, wrapping us in a fierce hug that makes my heart clench. Because this—this is what I've always wanted. What I never thought I'd have. A family bound by choice and love, growing stronger with each challenge.

"A baby," she breathes against my chest, and I hear tears in her voice. Joy radiates from her like light. "Really?"

"Six weeks along," Bella confirms, her own voice thick with emotion. "I just found out this morning."

I watch my daughter's hand join mine over Bella's stomach, generations of love and protection already surrounding this new life. The sight nearly undoes me. Whatever darkness lurks in my past, whatever sins stain my soul, I must have done something right to deserve this moment.

This is my redemption—not in blood or violence or power, but in love. In the way Bianca looks at Bella with pure sisterly affection, in how they both lean into my embrace like they know they're safe there. In the tiny life growing beneath our joined hands, already so loved, so wanted, so protected.

This is my legacy. Not the DeLuca empire, not Giuseppe's lessons in cruelty, but this. This love. This family. This choice we make every day to be better, to love harder, to protect what matters most.

"Perfect timing," Antonio observes with a slight smile. "The villa in Tuscany is ready. A few weeks away might be good for all of you."

I shoot my captain a look for spoiling the surprise, but the joy on both women's faces is worth it. Still, as I hold my family close, I catch movement on the security screens—Anthony Calabrese's car pulling away from Elena's building. A reminder that danger never truly leaves our world.

But for now, in this moment, I let myself feel only gratitude. For my fierce daughter who loves without reservation. For my brave wife who carries our future beneath her heart. For this new life we've created together.

Whatever comes next, we'll face it as one.

As a family.

28

BELLA

Morning sickness, I decide, is cruelly misnamed. It should be called all-day-and-night-endless-torture sickness. I rinse my mouth in the marble sink of our en suite bathroom, trying to steady myself before the meeting with Matteo's captains. Six weeks of pregnancy have turned my body into a battlefield—every smell is an assault, every movement a potential trigger. Even the scent of my favorite perfume now makes my stomach roll.

"Here." Bianca appears in the doorway, offering a cup of peppermint tea. She's already dressed for the day in a navy blazer and silk blouse, looking every inch the Mafia princess. The concern in her eyes—so like her father's—makes my heart squeeze. "Maria says it helps."

"You told Maria?" I accept the tea gratefully, letting the warmth seep into my trembling hands.

"Please," Bianca snorts. "She knew before any of us." She perches on the counter, one leg swinging casually. "She says she can always tell. Something about the way expectant mothers glow."

"I'm not glowing. I'm green." But I manage a small smile, touched by my stepdaughter's concern. We've gone from barely tolerating each other to this fierce protectiveness that catches me off guard. Like now, as she hovers anxiously, so like her father in her need to fix things.

"Dad's waiting in his office. The captains are arriving." Bianca slides off the counter, her Louboutins clicking against marble tile. A shadow crosses her face. "Something about trouble in Brooklyn."

My stomach clenches, and not from morning sickness. Brooklyn means Mario DeLuca's old territory—the territory he lost when Matteo exiled him five years ago. My husband rarely speaks of his half brother. In fact, everything I know about Mario DeLuca comes from overheard conversations between my father and his captains. Stories that always ended with lowered voices and worried glances.

"I'll be right there." I straighten, examining my reflection. The woman in the mirror looks pale despite careful makeup, dark circles visible beneath my eyes that even Laura Mercier can't fully conceal. The black Altuzarra dress I've chosen skims my figure, hiding any hint of my condition—we're not ready to announce it beyond family yet. Not with so many threats still lurking.

I find Matteo in his study, seven captains arranged around the massive mahogany table that dominates one end. The scent of expensive coffee mingles with leather and gun oil, an oddly comforting mixture that thankfully doesn't turn my stomach. Each captain brings their own energy to the room—Salvatore with his battle-scarred face and suspicious eyes, Alberto whose youth belies his tactical genius, Vicente who served under Giuseppe and still carries that old-world menace.

The men's quiet conversations cease when I enter, respect and wariness mingling in their expressions. They've learned to fear the donna who took down Johnny Calabrese. But there's something else in their faces today—a tension that speaks of past loyalties and divided hearts.

My husband stands at the head of the table, every inch the powerful don in his perfectly tailored Tom Ford suit. But I see what others might miss—the slight tremor in his hand as he adjusts his cuffs, the muscle jumping in his jaw, the way his eyes keep drifting to the turned-away photo on his desk.

Whatever this is about Mario, it's bad.

"Problem?" I ask, taking my place at Matteo's right hand. Bianca stands just behind us, absorbing everything as she always does. I notice how the older captains avoid looking at her directly. Whatever happened five years ago with Mario clearly involved more than just an exile.

"Mario's been spotted in the old territories in Brooklyn. Particularly around the properties Giuseppe left him." Antonio pulls up surveillance photos on his tablet, broadcasting them onto the study's screens. The images make my artist's eye immediately start cataloging details.

Mario DeLuca shares his brother's height and build, but there's a rougher edge to him, like an expensive painting left out in harsh weather. His dark hair falls messily across his forehead, and scars mark his jaw and left eyebrow—badges of violence worn like honors. But it's his eyes that catch my attention. Dark where Matteo's are blue gray, intense in a way that speaks of barely contained chaos.

"Meeting with some of the old guard who were loyal to him before the exile." Antonio's weathered face betrays concern as he swipes through more photos. I notice how Vicente and two other older captains exchange glances, their loyalty to Matteo warring with old allegiances.

"Left him to manage, you mean," Matteo corrects, an edge to his voice that makes even Salvatore flinch. Something passes between them—some shared knowledge that makes the air feel suddenly heavy. "Nothing was ever truly given."

The next image makes my blood freeze in my veins. Mario stands outside Elena's office building, leaning against her car with calculated casualness. He's smiling—that devastating DeLuca smile that seems genetic—and though Elena's expression is wary, I can see her guard lowering slightly as she listens. Unlike Matteo's controlled intensity, Mario radiates a wild charm that draws people in despite themselves.

The sight terrifies me more than any interaction with Johnny Calabrese.

"When was this taken?" I fight to keep my voice steady despite my racing heart. Elena's been through enough with Johnny. The last thing she needs is another DeLuca complication.

"Yesterday." Antonio swipes to another image that makes several captains mutter darkly. Mario exits a café with Anthony Calabrese, both men in sharp suits that probably cost more than most people make in a month. They're laughing about something, heads bent close in conspiracy. The casual camaraderie sends chills down my spine—this is no chance meeting.

"He's building alliances," Salvatore growls, his scarred hand clenching on the table. "First Carmine's betrayal, then Johnny's death ... he sees weakness in the family structure."

"Mario always did know how to exploit chaos," Vicente adds, his accent thickening with emotion. "Like a shark smelling blood in the water."

"There is no weakness," Matteo says quietly, but his hand finds mine under the table. The gentle pressure grounds me even as fear claws at my throat. "My brother made his choice five years ago. He chose wrong."

"What did he do?" The words slip out before I can stop them. The reaction in the room is immediate and visceral. Alberto actually crosses himself, while Vicente's face drains of color. Even Antonio, usually unflappable, looks unsettled. "Why was he exiled?"

Silence falls like a blade. Even the usual city sounds beyond the windows seem muted, as if nature itself holds its breath. Finally, Matteo squeezes my hand once before releasing it.

"He broke our most sacred rule," he says, and his voice—that deadly soft tone that usually precedes violence—makes several captains shift in their chairs. One actually loosens his collar. "Family first. Always family first."

"He tried to kill Dad," Bianca says from behind us, and when I turn, the look on her face steals my breath. Gone is my confident stepdaughter, replaced by the child who lived through whatever horror Mario inflicted. Her hands tremble as she continues, "Used me as bait when I was twelve. Would have succeeded if ..." She trails off, but the implications are clear.

If Matteo hadn't chosen his daughter over his brother.

"And now he's back." I look at the photos again, seeing them with new understanding. Mario with Elena, with Anthony—not just building a network, but choosing his targets carefully. People we care about. People we have fraught relationships with. "Using our people against us again."

"Not this time." Matteo rises, authority radiating from him like heat. Even the oldest captains straighten instinctively. His voice carries that tone that brooks no argument, that reminds everyone why he's the most feared man in New York. "Antonio, increase security on all family members. I want Elena brought to the compound until we assess the threat. And get me everything on my brother's movements since he left New York."

The captains snap into action, each with their assigned tasks. Soon only the four of us remain—Matteo, Bianca, Antonio, and me. The sudden quiet feels oppressive, like the air before a storm.

"The villa in Tuscany," Matteo says softly, and something in his tone makes my heart stutter. "It's not just a vacation. It's a secure location, off Mario's radar. Somewhere they'd never think to look."

"You want us to run?" Bianca's voice cracks with hurt. She sounds young again, vulnerable in a way that makes my maternal instincts flare despite myself.

"I want you safe." He turns to his daughter, cupping her face in that gentle way that always makes my chest ache. "Both of you. All of you." His eyes flick meaningfully to my stomach, where our child grows beneath Italian silk. Three lives to protect now. Three potential targets.

"We're stronger together," I argue, moving closer to them both. The morning sickness seems distant now, replaced by a clarity born of fear. "The moment we separate, we give him opportunities."

"She's right," Antonio adds, ignoring the thunderous look Matteo shoots him. "Mario will expect you to send them away. He'll be watching the airports, the usual routes. And if he has people inside our organization already ..." He lets the implication hang heavy in the air.

Matteo's jaw clenches, but before he can respond, Maria appears in the doorway. The housekeeper's usual calm demeanor seems shaken, her hands trembling slightly. "Sir? There's a delivery for Mrs. DeLuca."

She holds out a small box wrapped in black silk paper, tied with a bloodred ribbon. No card, no marking to indicate its sender. The elegance of it makes my skin crawl—like a beautiful snake coiled to strike.

I reach for it instinctively, but Matteo moves faster. "Don't," he orders, taking the package himself. His voice carries that edge of command that usually makes everyone obey without question. "Antonio ..."

But it's too late. A high-pitched whine fills the air, mechanical and wrong, like the sound death might make if it had a voice. Matteo's eyes meet mine for one frozen moment—fear and love and rage all warring in those steel-blue depths. Then he's moving, hurling the box through the study's windows.

The explosion rocks the room, shattering glass and spewing flames. Matteo tackles both Bianca and me behind his desk as security swarms in. The chaos is deafening—shouted orders, breaking glass, the wail of distant sirens. The acrid smell of smoke mingles with gunpowder and fear.

Then all our phones chime simultaneously.

The message that appears makes my blood turn to ice:

Welcome to the family, little artist. Time to play a game.

29

MATTEO

Smoke curls through the shattered study windows, acrid and sharp in my lungs as security sweeps the grounds. Radio chatter and tactical movements create a familiar symphony of controlled chaos, but I barely register it. All I can focus on is the precious weight of my wife and daughter in my arms, their bodies still protected by mine even though the immediate danger has passed. I won't release them—can't release them—while Mario's message burns in my mind: *"Time to play a game."*

My brother always did love games. Dangerous ones that left scars both visible and hidden. The product of Giuseppe's affair with his secretary, Mario came into our world already fighting for a place. His mother fled shortly after his birth, leaving him to be raised alongside me in a household where competition meant survival. He grew up in my shadow, forever trying to earn our father's approval, to prove he was worthy of the DeLuca name despite being the "bastard son."

"I'm fine," Bella insists, trying to step away from my protection. But I can't let go—not when the memory of another explosion, another threat to my family, still haunts my dreams. "We both are."

Her hand rests protectively over her stomach where our child grows, and the gesture ignites fresh rage in my chest. Mario's timing is too perfect, too precise. He knows about the pregnancy—which means someone close to us has betrayed us. Someone with access to medical records, to security protocols, to our most intimate moments.

Another game, another test of loyalty.

I will find the traitor. And when I do, their death will serve as a message to anyone else considering betrayal.

"The compound's clear," Antonio reports, holstering his weapon. Through his earpiece, I hear the coordinated movements of our security teams sweeping the grounds. His weathered face shows the strain—he was there five years ago too, when Mario first turned on us. "No signs of other devices. But Boss ... we've got movement at the old Brooklyn territory. Mario's been seen meeting with some of your former captains."

Bella goes rigid beside me. "The ones who were loyal to him before the exile?"

"Not just them." Antonio pulls up surveillance photos on his tablet. The images flood the room's screens—crystal clear shots that make my blood boil. "He's been watching the wedding reception. These were taken right before all hell broke loose."

The photos show Mario lurking in the shadows of the gardens at the reception, observing the chaos after Bianca's outburst. He looks exactly as I remember—that same calculated cruelty in his eyes that I first saw when we were children. Even then, he watched from shadows, waiting for moments of weakness. I remember finding him in Giuseppe's study once, going through private files, searching for something to use against me. When I confronted him, he just smiled that cold smile and said, "Knowledge is power, brother. And in this family, we take what power we can get."

"He's planning something," Bianca says quietly. Her voice trembles slightly—the first crack in her armor I've seen since the explosion. "Using the chaos in our family to find weak points."

"Like he did before." Ice coats my words as memories assault me. Five years ago, that warehouse in Red Hook where my brother chose to make his stand. I can still smell the rotting fish and diesel fuel, still hear water lapping against the pier. The call had come at midnight—

Mario's voice carrying that edge of madness I'd always feared would surface:

"Remember how Father always made us compete, brother? How you always won? Well, now we play my game. Your empire or your daughter. Choose quickly—she's running out of air."

I'd found Bianca in a shipping container at a warehouse, curled into herself like a broken bird. Twelve years old, wearing the navy school uniform she'd been taken in, her wrists raw from fighting the restraints. The sight of her—my fierce, proud daughter reduced to that—broke something in me that's never fully healed.

"Daddy?" Her voice had been barely a whisper, hoarse from screaming. "I tried to fight. Like you taught me. But Uncle Mario ... he said it was just a game ..."

The memory of her tears soaking my shirt, of her body trembling against mine as I cut her free, feeds the rage building in my chest now. Mario had wanted me to choose between my power and my child, never understanding that there was no choice. Never comprehending that real power comes from what we protect, not what we destroy.

My phone buzzes with another message from Mario, and the image that fills the screen makes my blood freeze. It's us leaving Elena's apartment yesterday—Bella's hand resting protectively over her stomach, Bianca laughing at something, all of us unaware we were being watched.

New life brings new possibilities, brother. But can you protect them all? -M

The threat ignites something primal in my chest. Five years ago, I'd found my daughter terrorized by a man who shared my blood. I remember lifting Bianca from that container, how light she felt in my arms, like all her usual spark had been drained away. The days that followed were worse—nightmares, panic attacks, her voice breaking as she told me what Mario had whispered to her: "Your father always thinks he can save everyone. Let's see who he chooses to save this time."

Now he threatens not just my daughter, but my wife and unborn child. The parallel makes me pull them both closer, breathing in Bella's jasmine scent, feeling Bianca's strength as she stands tall despite her fear. I won't let history repeat. Won't let Mario play his sick games with another generation of our family.

"Let me see," Bella demands, reaching for my phone. Her face hardens as she reads the message, understanding its implications. "He's threatening the baby. Our family."

"He's threatening everything," I correct, pulling her closer. This is what Mario never understood—that real power comes from protecting what matters, not destroying it. "Mario wants what he's always wanted—total control. And he knows the best way to get it is to strike when we're vulnerable."

"We're not vulnerable," Bianca says fiercely, joining our huddle. "We're stronger together. He doesn't understand that."

Pride and fear war in my chest as I look at my girls—my fierce daughter who survived Mario's games once before, my brilliant wife carrying our child, both of them ready to fight rather than run. The memory of Bianca in that warehouse haunts me still—how she'd clung to me afterward, whispering "Don't let him take me again, Daddy. Please." I'd promised her then that Mario would never touch her again.

A promise I intend to keep.

"Antonio," I bark, decision made. "Full lockdown of the compound. I want every possible entry point covered. And get me everything on Mario's movements since he arrived back in New York. *Now*."

"Already on it. But Boss ..." Antonio hesitates, his hand tightening on his weapon in a way that speaks of old loyalties and older fears. "He's not working alone. The explosives used in that package? They're military grade. Someone with serious connections is backing him."

"The Irish." The pieces click together—the weapons, the timing, the precision of the surveillance. "That's where he went after the exile. Built connections with the O'Connor family in Boston."

"Which means we're not just fighting Mario," Bella realizes, her analytical mind already mapping the implications. "We're fighting an entire organization that wants to take New York."

"Let them try." I move to my desk, pulling up building plans for all our key properties. The blue light from the screens casts shadows across the room, turning the smoke still curling through broken windows into ghostly figures. "Antonio, get the war room ready. Full briefing in one hour. We need to know exactly what we're dealing with."

"And Elena?" Bella asks quietly. The worry in her voice makes my chest ache. "She could be in danger if Mario's watching us all."

"I'll increase her security detail," I assure her, though my heart clenches at how pale Bella looks, how one hand stays protectively over our child. "But right now, we focus on the immediate threat. Mario won't wait long to make his next move."

I pull both women close, breathing in their strength, their trust, their love. "We plan together," I tell them, meeting Bella's eyes, silently begging her to understand, "but when we move ..." I can't finish the thought. The idea of her in danger, of our child at risk, makes something primitive rise in my chest.

"We plan together, you execute," she finishes for me. Her hand finds mine, squeezing once. "But Matteo?" Her voice hardens. "End this. Before he can hurt anyone else we love."

"Oh, he'll pay." The promise of violence coats my words. "Mario wants to play games? Fine. But this time, we make the rules."

I lose myself in building plans and security protocols, marking vulnerable points and potential threats. Time blurs as I study evacuation routes and safe houses, my mind racing through scenarios. Every detail must be perfect—I won't risk my family's safety because I overlooked something.

"Boss," Antonio's quiet voice breaks through my focus. "Mrs. DeLuca left about ten minutes ago. She seemed ... unsettled."

My head snaps up, guilt flooding my chest. With everything happening, I'd forgotten how this must be affecting her—newly pregnant, just finding happiness with our family, and now this threat hanging over us.

I find her in our bedroom, staring out the windows with her arms wrapped around herself. Her shoulders shake with silent sobs, and the sight breaks something in my chest. My fierce, strong wife finally letting her guard down.

"Come here," I murmur, my voice low but steady as I hold out my hand. She hesitates for a moment before crossing the space between us, letting me pull her into my arms. She melts against me, her soft curves fitting perfectly against the hard planes of my body, as if she was made to be here.

"I won't let him hurt you," I promise, my lips brushing against her temple. "Or Bianca. Or anyone. I'll protect you all. Always."

Her hands clutch at my shirt, her fingers twisting the fabric as if anchoring herself. "I know," she whispers, her voice trembling. "But we just found this happiness, Matteo. Found each other, this family we're building. And now ..."

Her voice breaks, and I can't stand to hear the pain in it. I cup her face, tilting her chin up to meet my gaze, before silencing her with a kiss. It starts soft, a gentle reassurance, but the fear and need bubbling between us quickly turn it into something fiercer.

Her lips part beneath mine, and I deepen the kiss, pouring every ounce of my love and desperation into it. She meets me with equal intensity, her fingers sliding into my hair, tugging just enough to make me groan. Her mouth is warm and demanding, all teeth and tongue and promises, and I lose myself in her.

"I choose you," I breathe against her mouth. "I choose this family. Like I did five years ago with Bianca, like I do every day since you walked into my office." My hand splays over her stomach, where our miracle grows. "Mario never understood that real power comes from protecting what matters, not destroying it. I'll protect you and this baby with my life."

Her lips crash into mine again, stealing the rest of my words. Her hands slide down my chest, tugging at my shirt until she pulls it free. Her touch is urgent but tender, her nails raking lightly over my skin as if she can't bear to leave any part of me unexplored.

I lift her into my arms, her legs wrapping around my waist as I carry her to the bed. Her breath hitches when I lower her onto the soft sheets, and I pause, taking a moment to admire her. The golden light catches in her hair, her flushed cheeks, her swollen lips, and she's breathtaking.

"Bella," I whisper, my voice thick with emotion.

She doesn't respond with words, just reaches for me, her hands sliding up my chest and curling around the back of my neck. With a gentle pull, she brings me down until I'm hovering above her, our bodies separated by the frustrating barrier of clothing. Her breath is warm against my face, her lips parted, her eyes heavy with longing.

Her hands trail down my chest, her fingertips brushing over every ridge of muscle, until they find each button of my shirt. Slowly, deliberately, she unbuttons them, her fingers grazing my skin as she helps pull it off my shoulders. The moment it's gone, her hands are back on me, exploring every inch like she's memorizing me anew.

"Yours," I murmur, capturing her lips in a kiss that's deep and consuming.

She answers with a quiet moan, her nails lightly scraping down my chest as she moves to the waistband of my pants. Her fingers work the buttons with surprising steadiness, even as her breaths grow quicker. The slight scrape of metal against fabric fills the space between us as she slides the pants over my hips, letting them fall to the floor. Her gaze dips, a flicker of heat in her eyes as she takes in the sight of me.

But I can't wait any longer. My hands move to her dress, my fingers trembling slightly as I undo the zipper. The soft fabric parts under my touch, revealing the smooth expanse of her skin inch by inch. I press a kiss to her sternum, then another just below her collarbone, tasting the faint hint of salt and the warmth of her.

"Matteo ..." she breathes, her voice barely audible, filled with need.

"Patience, *piccola*," I murmur against her skin, letting my lips linger there before continuing my journey downward.

I slip the dress off her body, letting it fall in a silken heap beside us. My hands trail over the soft curve of her arms as I reach for the clasp of her bra. It takes only a moment to undo it, and the straps slide down her arms with a whisper. Her bare skin is radiant in the golden light, and for a moment, I can only stare, awestruck by her beauty.

"Perfect," I murmur, brushing a kiss over the swell of her breast.

She shivers beneath me, her hands finding their way to my underwear. With a determined tug, she pushes them down, her touch leaving a trail of heat in its wake. I rid myself of the last barrier quickly, then turn my attention back to her. My hands slide to the waistband of her panties, fingers curling around the fabric. I draw them down her hips, my knuckles grazing her thighs as I strip them away.

When she's finally bare before me, her breath quickens, her chest rising and falling as I let my gaze roam. The sunlight streaming through the window catches on her curves, painting her in gold, and I feel my pulse stutter.

"You're so beautiful," I whisper, my voice rough with need and adoration.

I lower myself back to her, letting our bare skin brush for the first time. The heat of her against me sends a shiver down my spine, but I don't rush. Instead, I press my lips to her throat, just beneath her jaw, where her pulse flutters wildly.

My kisses are slow and deliberate, a path of reverence down the column of her neck. I pause at the hollow of her throat, sucking lightly, leaving a faint mark of possession. Her head tilts back, granting me more access, and I take it greedily, trailing lower to her collarbone. I alternate between soft kisses and the light graze of my teeth, enough to make her shiver.

Her hands tangle in my hair, her nails scraping against my scalp as I continue my descent. I brush my lips over her sternum, then trace the curve of her breast with the tip of my tongue, savoring the way her breath catches. Her body arches into me, her back leaving the mattress as she silently begs for more.

"You're mine," I murmur against her skin, my voice barely above a whisper.

Her response is a soft moan, her fingers tightening in my hair as I worship every inch of her. My hands slide over her sides, memorizing the dip of her waist, the swell of her hips, the strength hidden beneath her softness. She's all fire and vulnerability, and I'm utterly consumed by her.

"Matteo," she gasps, her voice a mix of plea and demand.

"I've got you," I murmur, pressing a kiss to the swell of her stomach before moving back up to capture her lips.

When I finally rise to kiss her again, her lips are already parted, waiting for me. The kiss is deeper this time, hungrier, our bodies pressing together as if we can't get close enough. Every touch, every brush of skin, every whispered word is a declaration: she is mine, and I am hers. Forever.

When I finally join us, it's with a slowness that feels reverent, every movement deliberate and filled with meaning. I pause, savoring the exquisite sensation of us coming together, her warmth enveloping me completely. The world around us fades away until there's nothing but her—her soft gasps, her trembling body, the way her eyes lock onto mine, full of trust and desire.

We move together in a rhythm that feels like it was written just for us, a language only we understand. Her body rises to meet mine, her hips arching in perfect harmony with my thrusts. Each connection is deliberate, a silent promise exchanged with every shift and press of our bodies. I'm acutely aware of every sensation—her nails tracing the ridges of muscle along my back, the way her thighs tighten around me, the soft, breathless sounds that escape her lips.

Her hands roam my body, as though she's memorizing every inch of me. Her fingertips press into my shoulders, trailing fire as they slide down to grip my sides, pulling me even closer. The way she moves beneath me, the way her body yields to mine, drives me to the edge of control.

"Matteo," she whispers, her voice breathless and raw, and the sound of my name on her lips sends a shiver through me.

Her release builds slowly, her body trembling as she climbs higher and higher. I watch her face, captivated by the way her brows draw together, her lips parting as soft cries spill from them. I feel her nails dig into my skin, the bite of them grounding me even as I'm lost in her.

When she finally lets go, it's breathtaking. Her head falls back, her throat arching beautifully as a broken moan escapes her. The sheer trust and vulnerability in her gaze, the way her body quivers against mine, is more than I can bear.

I follow her over the edge, my own release crashing through me like a wave. My body tenses, my movements faltering as pleasure consumes me. I press my forehead to hers, our breaths mingling as I let out a deep groan, her name slipping from my lips like a prayer.

For a moment, we remain locked together, our bodies trembling, our hearts pounding in unison. The world feels distant, unreal, as we bask in the aftershocks of the connection we've just shared. I lower myself carefully, wrapping her in my arms, and press a kiss to her damp temple.

"You're everything," I murmur against her skin, my voice hoarse.

She responds with a soft hum, her fingers lazily tracing patterns along my back as we come down from the high together. The intimacy lingers in the air, wrapping around us like a protective cocoon. In this moment, nothing else matters but her.

"I love you," she whispers. Her head rests on my chest, her fingers drawing idle patterns over my skin. "All of you. Our whole complicated, dangerous, beautiful family."

I hold her closer, one hand still protectively covering our child. Outside, security teams patrol the grounds, ready for Mario's next move. But here, in this moment, I let myself feel only gratitude. For my fierce daughter who survived his games once. For my brave wife who fights beside me. For this new life we've created together.

Whatever comes next, we face it as one.

As a family.

30

BELLA

The war room buzzes with carefully controlled chaos as Matteo's captains gather to plan our response to Mario's threat. From my place at my husband's right hand, I catalog details with an artist's eye—the way shadows from tactical screens paint faces in shifting blues, how each captain arranges themselves around the massive table with practiced precision. They move like dancers in a deadly ballet, everyone knowing their exact position.

Except for one chair that remains conspicuously empty. At the head of the table opposite Matteo—Giuseppe's old place. No one acknowledges it, but no one sits there either. The vacuum it creates feels like a haunting, the ghost of Matteo's father still presiding over every decision. I notice how the older captains' eyes occasionally drift to that empty seat, decades of conditioning still governing their movements.

My father taught me to read these subtle power plays, these unspoken traditions that govern our world. *"Watch how they arrange themselves, bella mia,"* he'd say during family gatherings. *"Every empty space tells a story."*

"The Irish connection changes everything," Antonio explains, drawing my attention to the map dominating the main screen. Red markers dot the Brooklyn waterfront like bloodstains, each one representing property acquisitions we've only just discovered. The pattern makes my stomach clench—not from morning sickness this time, but from growing dread.

"Using Mario's old network," Matteo adds, his voice carrying that edge that makes younger captains flinch. "The captains who stayed loyal to him, the businesses that never fully accepted my leadership..."

I study the map, my father's lessons about territory and influence surfacing in my mind. *"Every stronghold needs a supply line, bella mia. Find that, and you find their weakness."* The markers form a clear pattern, creating a corridor from the docks inland like a river of blood flowing through our city.

"These properties form a pattern," I say, moving closer to the display. "They're creating a corridor from the docks inland."

Several captains look at me with surprise—these strategy sessions have always been male territory. But Matteo smiles grimly, pride mixing with concern in his eyes. "For weapons shipments. The Irish are well-connected with European arms dealers."

"But that's not Mario's endgame," Bianca speaks up from her position near the door. Even though she's changed into torn jeans and a T-shirt she looks every inch the Mafia princess, her spine straight despite the tension in the room. "He doesn't care about weapons or territory. This is personal."

"Very personal." My hand moves unconsciously to my stomach. "He's targeting the future of the family. Especially with threats against the baby."

Matteo's hand finds mine under the table, squeezing gently. Before he can respond, a guard enters with a package—another delivery, this one marked specifically for Bianca. The box is wrapped in expensive black paper with a bloodred ribbon, an echo of the one that exploded in Matteo's study.

The room erupts into controlled chaos. Vicente crosses himself, muttering in Italian. Two younger captains reach for weapons. Matteo moves with lethal grace, putting himself between the package and us. But it's the older captains' reactions that catch my eye—the way they look at that empty chair at the head of the table, as if seeking guidance from Giuseppe's ghost.

"Clear the room," he orders, his voice carrying that tone that brooks no argument. "Now."

"Dad—" Bianca starts to protest, but Matteo cuts her off.

"Antonio, get them to the panic room." His eyes never leave the package as he pulls out his phone. "Full containment protocol. No one in or out until we're sure."

Antonio appears at my elbow, trying to guide us toward the door, but I resist. "Matteo—"

"Please, *piccola*." The rare plea in his voice makes me pause. "I can't think if you're in danger. Let me handle this."

I let Antonio lead us to the reinforced room down the hall, designed specifically for situations like this. Through the security feeds, we watch Matteo coordinate with precision born of experience. The bomb squad arrives within minutes—they've been on standby since the first explosion—in full protective gear. The package is moved to a containment unit, scanned with equipment that looks military grade.

Only after they confirm it's clean does Matteo allow us back in. But those ten minutes of waiting, of watching him handle another threat to our family with such lethal efficiency, remind me exactly who I married.

Not just the don who commands respect, but the man who would die to protect what's his.

The bomb squad's equipment confirms what their initial scan suggested—no explosives, no chemical agents, nothing overtly dangerous. Just a single photograph that makes my blood run cold when they finally clear us to open it.

A preteen Bianca tied to a chair in what appears to be a warehouse, Mario standing behind her with a gun to her head. The image is dated five years ago—the night that led to his exile. The harsh fluorescent lighting catches every detail my artist's eye wishes it couldn't see—Bianca's slumped over body, the rope burns on her small wrists, the casual way Mario's finger rests on the trigger.

But it's his expression that haunts me most—that DeLuca smile twisted into something cruel, something that speaks of carefully planned revenge rather than spontaneous violence.

"I never saw ..." Bianca's voice catches beside me, her face draining of color. Her hand finds mine, squeezing hard enough to hurt. "He knocked me out before taking that picture. I didn't know ..."

I watch Matteo's reaction, see the muscle jumping in his jaw as he studies the photo. His hands clench at his sides—the only visible sign of how close he is to violence. The older captains exchange knowing looks, and once again their eyes drift to Giuseppe's empty chair.

"He's playing mind games," Vicente growls, his scarred hand clenching on the table. "Trying to destabilize us with old wounds."

"No." I embrace my stepdaughter. She feels fragile in my arms despite her fierce facade, trembling slightly as she leans into me. Unlike the confident young woman of moments ago, she suddenly feels like that twelve-year-old girl again. She can't hide how she shakes, how the past reaches out with cruel fingers to grab her all over again.

"He's showing his hand," I continue, holding her closer. "This isn't about territory or power—it's about family. About what he lost when Matteo chose Bianca over him."

"And now there's another child coming." Matteo's voice carries that deadly quiet that usually precedes violence. His eyes meet mine across the room, dropping briefly to where our baby grows beneath my heart. "Another choice he thinks he can force me to make."

A new message appears on the screens: *Remember the warehouse, brother? History has a way of repeating. But this time, you have so much more to lose.*

I feel Bianca stiffen in my arms as Salvatore breaks the tense silence. "The O'Connors won't just provide weapons. They're worse than any of us—no code, no honor. Just chaos and blood."

"Tell me," I say, keeping my arms around Bianca. "What makes them so dangerous?"

The older captains exchange loaded glances before Vicente speaks, his voice heavy with old memories. "The O'Connors make the worst of our world look civilized. They started in Boston during the Troubles, running guns to the IRA. But it wasn't just weapons—they specialized in making people disappear. Politicians, witnesses, entire families. No bodies ever found."

"Seamus O'Connor runs things now," Antonio adds, pulling up surveillance photos. A man with steel-gray hair and cold eyes fills the screen. Despite his expensive suit, there's something feral about him—like a wolf in designer clothing. The kind of predator that plays with its food before killing it. "He modernized their operation, made it global. But they still prefer the old ways when it comes to handling problems."

"What old ways?" I ask, though something in my gut tells me I don't want to know. Beneath my arms, I feel Bianca's slight tremor at the question.

"They believe in sending messages," Matteo says quietly. His eyes never leave the photo of young Bianca. I hear the strain in his voice, the effort it takes to maintain control. "Five years ago, when a rival family challenged them in Boston, the O'Connors didn't just kill the don. They took his entire family—wife, children, even his elderly mother. Made him watch as they ..." He glances at Bianca and stops, but the unfinished sentence hangs heavy in the air.

"That's why Mario chose them," Salvatore adds, his scarred face grim. "They share his taste for psychological warfare. For making it personal."

"There's more," Vicente says, looking uncomfortable. His eyes dart to Giuseppe's empty chair before returning to me. "The O'Connors have a particular interest in pregnant women. They believe taking a family's future is the ultimate power play." His eyes meet mine briefly before darting away. "That's why Mario told them about the baby. He knows they can't resist that kind of target."

My hand moves protectively to my stomach as the implications sink in. The warehouse photo suddenly takes on new meaning—not just a reminder of past trauma, but a blueprint for future violence.

"The photo," I say suddenly, my tactical mind racing. "Antonio, can you pull up property records from five years ago? Find out who owned that warehouse?"

Minutes tick by as Antonio's fingers fly over keyboards. Screens fill with property deeds, shell companies, offshore accounts—a complicated web designed to obscure ownership. But there, buried in the paperwork, a connection appears. O'Connor Holdings LLC, registered in the Cayman Islands.

"The same warehouse where Mario held Bianca," Vicente breathes, crossing himself again. "It belonged to the O'Connors even then."

"Which means this whole thing—Mario's exile, the five years away ..." I look at Matteo, seeing understanding dawn in his eyes. "He wasn't just running. He was planning. Building connections. Waiting for the perfect moment to strike."

"Like now," Bianca says softly. She's moved away from me to study the warehouse photo, her spine straight despite her pallor. "With a new baby coming. A chance to recreate that night, but with higher stakes."

"He's going to try to make me choose," Matteo's voice carries that lethal edge. "Between my empire and my family. Again."

"No." I move to stand beside him, letting my strength flow into him through our joined hands. "There will be no choice this time. No games. Mario wants to use the past against us? Fine. But he's forgotten something important."

"What's that?" Bianca asks, moving to join us. Despite everything, she looks more like her father than ever—that same dangerous grace, that same ability to transform fear into tactical advantage.

"The warehouse is still there," Antonio reports, bringing up recent satellite images. "Recently purchased through another shell company linked to O'Connor's Dublin office."

"Then we know where he'll make his move." My mind races through possibilities, through angles and approaches like I would with a complex painting. Every detail matters. Every shadow holds potential. "He'll expect you to send us away, to try to protect us. That's when he'll strike."

"Which is exactly why you're staying in the compound," Matteo starts, but I cut him off.

"No. We make him think we're separated. Make him think his plan is working." I meet my husband's eyes steadily, seeing the war between love and strategy play out in their steel-blue depths. "Let him think he's recreating the past. But this time, we control the game."

Understanding dawns on Matteo's face as the pieces align. Because this is what Mario never understood about me—I'm not just an artist playing at being a donna. I'm Giovanni Russo's daughter, raised on strategy and survival even when I tried to escape it. And now, with everything I love at stake, those lessons surface like muscle memory.

"Together," Matteo says finally, and it's both a promise and a battle cry. His hand finds mine, then Bianca's, forming an unbreakable circle.

"Together," I agree, one hand still protective over our child, the other holding Bianca close.

Because Mario and the O'Connors have made a fatal mistake. They think love makes us vulnerable, that family ties can be used as weapons. But they don't understand that real strength comes from what we choose to protect. What we choose to fight for.

And I choose this—this complicated, dangerous, beautiful family we've built. This future growing beneath my heart. This love that transforms fear into power.

Let them come with their games and threats. Let them think they understand family bonds and blood debts.

We'll show them what real family means.

Together.

31

MATTEO

Rain pounds against the bulletproof glass of my SUV, each drop a staccato reminder of another night like this five years ago. The rhythmic sound mingles with the low rumble of the V8 engine and the squelch of tires on wet asphalt, creating a symphony of tension that sets my teeth on edge. Even the familiar scent of leather and gun oil can't calm my racing thoughts.

Phase one of our plan is in motion. The media—those vultures who've been circling our family since Johnny's death—have been carefully fed stories about Bella and Bianca's departure to a "safe location." Page Six couldn't resist the scandal: "DeLuca Women Flee New York—Trouble in Criminal Paradise?" While the *Daily News* went with "Mafia Princess and New Bride Seek Italian Sanctuary." The kind of headlines that would make Mario think his psychological warfare is working.

In reality, both of my women are secure in the panic room beneath the compound, surrounded by guards I've known since childhood. The thought of Bella there, probably driving the security team crazy with her tactical suggestions while protecting our unborn child, almost makes me smile.

Almost.

"Mario's people took the bait," Antonio reports from the passenger seat, his weathered face illuminated by the glow of his tablet. "They're tracking the decoy convoy heading to the airport."

I nod, my knuckles white on the steering wheel as we approach the warehouse district. The industrial wasteland rises around us like a graveyard of broken dreams—abandoned buildings with shattered windows, graffiti-covered walls that hold too many secrets. Five years of memories flood back, turning the rain-slicked streets into a battlefield of ghosts.

Every shadow, every corner of this district holds echoes of that night. Finding Bianca tied to a chair, her school uniform torn and bloody, tears cutting tracks through the grime on her face. The way she'd whimpered "Daddy" when I cut her free, how light she felt in my arms—my stubborn daughter reduced to something small and broken by a man who shared my blood.

"You never told me what really happened that night," Antonio says quietly, his voice barely audible over the rain. "Why you let him live."

"Because killing him would have proved him right." My jaw clenches as memories assault me—Mario's voice on the phone, taunting me about choices and worthiness. Giuseppe's lessons about family and power playing out in real time through his sons. "That I was exactly what our father always said—ruthless, unfeeling, incapable of mercy."

"And now?"

"Now he's threatening my wife. My children." Ice coats my words as my phone buzzes with a message from Bella: *Security feed shows movement at the warehouse. He's there.*

Of course he is. Mario always did have a flair for dramatic symbolism. The warehouse where he lost everything—where he forced a choice that was never really a choice at all—would be the perfect stage for his revenge.

Another text follows quickly: *Be careful. Come back to us.*

I allow myself a moment to picture her, safe in the panic room with Bianca. My beautiful artist, probably pacing like a caged tiger, one hand protective over our child while the other gestures as she argues strategy with the security team. The image brings both comfort and fear—everything I have to protect, everything Mario threatens to destroy.

"Boss." Antonio's voice draws my attention to the warehouse looming ahead of us like some Gothic monster in the rain. The old brick structure seems to absorb the darkness, its broken windows like hungry eyes watching our approach. Water cascades down its walls in sheets, creating a curtain that seems designed to hide secrets.

Three black SUVs emerge from the shadows, boxing us in with practiced precision. Even their driving style screams Irish training—aggressive but controlled, leaving no room for escape. Through the rain-streaked windshield, I watch a familiar figure step out of the center vehicle.

Mario.

Five years haven't changed his core essence, though new scars mark his face—one particularly nasty one bisecting his left eyebrow, another along his jaw. He moves with that same predatory grace we both inherited from Giuseppe, but there's something wilder about him now. Where I learned to contain my darkness, to channel it into protection, his burns openly in eyes that mirror my own.

"Brother," he calls, his voice carrying that distinctive DeLuca timbre despite the rain. He's dressed like me—black suit, tactical gear underneath—but where mine is precisely tailored, his has a deliberate dishevelment. A calculated display of chaos. "Expecting me?"

"Considering you practically sent an engraved invitation?" I keep my tone casual despite the dozen guns trained on me from his Irish backup. I count eight men, all with that hard-eyed look of O'Connor's personal guard. "Subtle was never your strong suit."

We face each other in the rain, neither mentioning how we've unconsciously taken the same stance—shoulders squared, chin lifted, hands relaxed at our sides ready to reach for weapons. Giuseppe's stance, though acknowledging that would give Mario too much power. Water drips from his dark hair, plastering it to his forehead in a way that makes him look younger, more like the brother I failed to protect from our father's games.

His laugh holds no humor, just decades of bitterness crystallized into sound. "Says the man who sent his pregnant wife to Italy. Tell me, how does it feel? Knowing you have to choose again? Family or power, brother. It always comes down to that."

"You still don't understand." I study him, truly seeing how the years of exile have carved new lines around his eyes, hardened the set of his jaw. The boy I once protected, who would crawl into my bed during thunderstorms, is gone. This man, this creature of vengeance wearing my brother's face, is someone else entirely. "There is no choice. Family is power."

"Family?" He spits the word like poison, but I catch the flash of raw pain in his eyes—that same wounded look he'd get when Giuseppe would compare us, always finding him wanting. "You've become just like him, choosing who's worthy of the DeLuca name. Who deserves to be called family."

"I chose an innocent child over a man who would hurt her to prove a point." My voice hardens, though something in me flinches at his comparison to our father. Because isn't that what I fear most? Becoming the monster who raised us? "Just like I'll choose my wife, my children, every time."

"Your children?" Mario's smile turns cruel, rain dripping from his jaw like tears—or blood. "Bianca isn't even yours. And this new baby ... well, accidents happen. Especially to women in our world. Just ask Sophia. Though I suppose protecting daughters isn't a DeLuca strong suit, is it, brother?"

The words hit like a physical blow, carrying weight beyond their surface meaning. We both know what he's really saying—about fathers and daughters and sins that echo through generations. About Giuseppe's legacy of pain that we can never quite escape.

"Always the golden son," he sneers, taking a step closer. His men tense, fingers tightening on triggers. The rain seems to fall harder, turning the space between us into a curtain of silver needles. "The worthy heir."

Something flashes through me—an old pain I usually keep buried beneath layers of control. The memory of Giuseppe's hand heavy on my shoulder in that photograph I keep turned away, his voice a constant whisper of expectations and threats. I mask it quickly, but Mario sees. He always could read me better than anyone.

"No?" His bitter laugh carries over the storm. "Tell me, brother, do you still keep his photo turned away? Or have you finally made peace with what we came from?"

I ignore that particular knife thrust, though the question burrows deep. Truth is, I'm not sure why I keep that photo out at all. Maybe as a reminder of what not to become. Maybe as penance.

"Five years," I say instead, watching him for tells, for weakness. "Five years with the Irish, building connections, planning your revenge. And for what? To recreate a moment you already lost?"

"To take everything you love." Mario steps closer, and his men shift like shadows in the rain, following their choreographed dance of death. Water streams down his face, but his eyes burn with a fever that makes him look almost possessed. "To make you feel what I felt when you cast me out. When you chose that little bitch over your own brother. Just like he taught us, didn't he? Always choosing who's worthy of the DeLuca name?"

Lightning flashes, illuminating the warehouse behind him. For a moment, I see Bianca's small form tied to that chair, hear her crying for me. The memory feeds something dark in my chest, something that wants to tear my brother apart with bare hands.

"You don't get to use his methods against me." Steel enters my voice as thunder rolls overhead. "I protect what's mine. Blood or not, Bianca is my daughter. Just like Bella is my wife. Just like this family is my legacy—not his."

"Legacy?" Mario's laugh sounds like breaking glass. Rain plasters his expensive suit to his frame, highlighting how exile has hardened him, turned him lean and dangerous as a street dog. "Look at you, standing in judgment like he used to. Deciding who belongs and who doesn't. For now."

He raises his gun with that fluid grace we both learned too young.

The barrel looks black as night against the rain. "But after tonight? After I finish what I started five years ago? Everything you love will be gone. And you'll finally understand what it feels like to lose everything that matters."

I allow myself a small smile, watching understanding slowly dawn in my brother's eyes. Because he's so focused on recreating Giuseppe's patterns, on forcing those same impossible choices, that he's missed the most important detail. He's still playing our father's game while I've learned to write new rules.

"You're right about one thing," I say softly, my voice carrying under the storm's fury. "Family is everything. But we choose what that means now. Not him. Not anymore. Which is why you've already lost."

Before Mario can process my meaning, shots ring out from the warehouse roof. His men drop one by one—precision shots from Antonio's team, already in position. Because while Mario was watching the convoy to Italy, watching me, he forgot about the most dangerous player in this game.

Bella's voice comes through my earpiece, cold and clear: "Target acquired. End this, husband."

My brilliant, dangerous wife. The memory of our argument about her participation floods back—her standing in our bedroom this morning, eyes blazing as she loaded her rifle. "I was Giovanni Russo's daughter before I was your wife," she'd said, chambering a round with practiced ease. "I know how to protect what's mine too."

Now she's perched on a neighboring roof with that same rifle, having refused to stay in the panic room despite my protests. Like her father, she understands that some battles require personal involvement. Bianca monitors the security feeds from below, coordinating our teams with a precision that makes pride war with fear in my chest.

Together, just as we promised.

Mario's eyes widen as he realizes his mistake. As he finally understands that this time, this choice, was never his to make. Rain streams down his face, mixing with sweat as he watches his carefully orchestrated plan crumble. His Irish backup lies still in growing puddles, their blood turning the rainwater pink.

"You really think she'll pull the trigger?" he sneers, but I hear the tremor beneath his bravado. His gun hasn't wavered from my chest, but his other hand shakes slightly—that same tell he had as a child when he knew he'd miscalculated. "Your artist wife? The mother of your child? She's soft, brother. Like you've become soft. Like—"

"Yes." I don't flinch, don't move. Through my earpiece, I hear Bella's steady breathing, so like her father's when he lined up a shot. "Because she understands what you never did. Real family protects its own."

The shot echoes through the rain like thunder. Mario falls, clutching his shoulder where blood blooms across his expensive suit—not a kill shot, but precise. Deliberate. Just like everything else about my wife.

I approach my fallen brother slowly, my own gun raised. Water pools around his body, but his eyes—my eyes, Giuseppe's eyes—still burn with defiance. With decades of pain and rejection neither of us has ever fully escaped.

"Last chance, Mario." My voice carries over the storm. "Surrender, leave New York, never contact us again. Or—"

"Or what?" Blood stains his teeth as he grins up at me, and for a moment I see that little boy again, always trying to prove himself worthy of the DeLuca name. "You'll kill me? Prove Father right about what kind of man you really are?"

"No." My voice softens, remembering other rainy nights, other choices that shaped us both. "I'll let my wife decide your fate. After all ..." I smile coldly as another crack of thunder punctuates my words. "Family is everything."

32

BELLA

The compound's medical wing reeks of antiseptic and copper as doctors treat Mario's shoulder wound. Through the observation window, I watch them work with clinical efficiency, the fluorescent lights turning everyone's skin a sickly shade of blue white. My hands still feel the phantom weight of the sniper rifle—the cold metal, the precise mechanics, the shocking recoil when I pulled the trigger.

I've never fired a weapon like that before tonight. Target practice with my father was one thing—neat paper targets in controlled environments. But this? Watching the red bloom across Mario's expensive suit through my scope, knowing I could have easily shifted two inches left and ended his life? The power of that choice sits heavy in my chest.

"You didn't kill him," Matteo says softly, appearing beside me. He's shed his wet jacket, but rain still darkens his hair, making it curl slightly at his temples. Even after everything, the sight of him affects me—power and danger wrapped in elegant violence. "You could have."

"He's your brother." I meet his eyes in the glass reflection, seeing the war of emotions he tries to hide. Through the window, Mario stirs on the hospital bed, already fighting the sedation. "And I wanted him to live with his failure. Death would be too easy."

His arm slides around my waist, hand protective over our child. The warmth of him against my back steadies something in me that's been shaking since I pulled that trigger. He smells of rain and gunpowder and something uniquely him that still makes my pulse race despite everything.

"You're a better person than I am, *piccola*." His breath stirs my hair, and I lean back into his strength.

"No." I turn in his embrace, placing my hands on his chest where his heart thunders beneath Italian cotton. Even his shirt is still damp from the rain. "Just different. You would have killed him to protect us. I chose to wound him to protect you."

Understanding floods his expression—that rare softness few ever see beneath his dangerous facade. Because he knows I'm right—killing Mario would have changed him, would have proved Giuseppe's poisonous lessons about violence and worthiness. This way, the choice and the mercy come from me.

"The Irish won't be happy," Antonio reports, joining us at the window. His lined face reflects in the glass, lined with decades of loyalty and violence. "O'Connor's already making threats about what happens to people who betray Irish hospitality."

I turn back around in Matteo's arms to face the window, watching Mario fight against the doctor's ministrations. Even wounded, even sedated, he radiates that dangerous DeLuca charisma. His eyes find us through the glass, and something dark crosses his face as he takes in our embrace, Matteo's hand curved protectively over where our child grows.

"He's still dangerous," I observe, noting how Mario's fingers twitch toward phantom weapons even as nurses bind his shoulder. Every movement, every glance carries calculation. "Even wounded, even failed ... he'll try again."

"Yes." Matteo doesn't sugarcoat it, his chest solid against my back. "But not here. Not now."

"What will you do with him?" I ask.

Before Matteo can answer, Bianca appears in the corridor. She's traded her tactical gear for leggings and an oversized sweater, looking every bit the teenager she is rather than the Mafia princess who helped coordinate tonight's operation. But her spine is straight, her chin lifted in that distinctly DeLuca way that speaks of steel beneath silk.

"Send him back to Boston," she says, joining our vigil at the window. In the harsh medical lighting, I see how much she looks like her father—that same intensity in her eyes, that same ability to mask emotion beneath control. "Let him live with the Irish he chose over family. But make it clear—if he ever comes near us again ..."

"Then I won't aim for the shoulder," I finish quietly, the words tasting like copper in my mouth.

Mario's laugh carries through the glass, harsh and knowing. He pushes himself up on his uninjured arm, ignoring the doctor's protests. "Sweet family reunion," he calls out. "But tell me, nephew or niece? What kind of child will the artist and the monster create?"

Matteo tenses against me, but I press my hand over his where it rests on my stomach. His heartbeat thunders against my back, rage barely contained. "He's trying to provoke you. Don't let him."

"Listen to your wife, brother." Mario's smile is all teeth and old wounds. "She's smarter than Sophia ever was. Though just as dangerous to love, I'd wager."

"Enough." Bianca's voice cracks like a whip. "You lost the right to speak about our family the moment you put a gun to my head."

"Your family?" Mario barks out another laugh, but there's something calculating in his gaze as it lands on Bianca. "Such a DeLuca trait, isn't it? The way we reshape truth to protect what's ours. The way we build families on carefully constructed lies. Some things really do run in the blood, don't they, brother?"

His words carry weight I don't quite understand—some hidden meaning that makes Matteo go perfectly still against me. Like all of Mario's taunts, they seem designed to cut deep beneath surface wounds.

"Blood doesn't make family," I say, meeting Mario's gaze through the glass. His eyes—so like Matteo's but somehow colder—lock onto mine with predatory interest. "The lengths we go to protect each other, the secrets we keep, the love we have, the choices we make—that's what builds a family. Something you threw away the moment you decided revenge was more important than loyalty."

"Love?" Mario snorts, his eyes fixed on where my hand covers Matteo's over our child. "Love makes us blind in our world. Makes us ignore the signs, bury the truth. Just ask my brother about Sophia—about what a father will do to protect his secrets."

"I'm not Sophia." I'm so fucking tired of her ghost haunting every corner of our lives. "And Matteo hasn't failed anyone. You did that all on your own."

Something shifts in Mario's expression—not quite respect, but recognition perhaps. Like a predator acknowledging another hunter's skills. "You're right about one thing, artist. You're nothing like Sophia." His smile turns cryptic, almost amused. "You're *much* more interesting."

The way he says it sends chills down my spine. Because it's not a threat, not exactly. It's something worse—interest. The kind that suggests this isn't over, that he's seen something in me worth studying. Worth using.

"Boston," Matteo says, decision made. His voice holds that tone that brooks no argument. "Tonight. Antonio, make the arrangements."

"Running me out of town again, brother?" Mario's voice drips with mockery, but something vulnerable flashes beneath the bravado. For a moment, I see the younger brother Matteo must have once protected, before Giuseppe's games turned them against each other.

"No." Matteo's voice is pure ice. "Giving you one last chance to live. Bella's mercy, not mine. Remember that the next time you think about coming near my family."

Mario's laugh follows us as we leave the medical wing, Matteo's men entering to secure him for transport. But it's his last words that echo in my mind: "Family is such a fragile thing, isn't it? So easily … broken."

In the elevator, Matteo pulls me close. His clothes are still damp from the rain, but his body radiates heat against mine. "He's trying to get in your head. Don't let him."

"I know." I rest my head on his chest, listening to his heartbeat. The steady rhythm grounds me, reminds me what we're fighting for. "But he's right about one thing—family is fragile. Precious."

"Which is why we protect it." He kisses my temple, his lips warm against my skin. "Together."

The elevator opens to reveal Elena waiting in the foyer. She starts toward me but freezes as commotion erupts behind us—Mario being escorted out, flanked by guards. Despite his bound shoulder and disheveled appearance, he moves with that lethal DeLuca grace.

Recognition flashes across Elena's face as she realizes this is the charming stranger who'd stopped her outside her office building last week. His eyes meet hers, and a slow, knowing smile spreads across his face—the kind of smile that has probably charmed countless women to their doom.

"What the hell?" Elena's voice shakes as she looks between us. "How do you know him? Why is he here?" Her eyes fix on Mario's bound shoulder, the blood staining his expensive suit.

"Surprised to see me?" Mario's voice carries that dangerous charm that clearly had made her stop and talk to him that day, despite her better judgment. "I suppose I should have introduced myself properly outside your office. Mario DeLuca, at your service." His smile widens as understanding dawns in her expression. "But then, the DeLuca name tends to complicate simple conversations."

The color drains from Elena's face as she looks between the brothers. "DeLuca? You're ..." Her voice trails off as she finally sees what I've been noticing all night—the similar profiles, the shared mannerisms, the way they unconsciously mirror each other's stance.

"My brother," Matteo says flatly, and something in his tone makes Elena take a step back. But there's something else in her expression that makes my blood run cold—not just fear, but fascination. She's always been drawn to power, to danger—it's what makes her so good at navigating our world. But this? This pull toward Mario? It could destroy everything.

"Beauty and danger," Mario continues, his gaze caressing her like a physical touch. "A DeLuca weakness, wouldn't you say, brother?"

Matteo's eyes are cold. "Get him out of here."

As Matteo's men lead Mario away, he pauses at the threshold. Both brothers' gazes are drawn to the same spot—where Giuseppe DeLuca's portrait once hung, now conspicuously empty. In the glass reflection of the frame, I catch how similar their profiles are, how they unconsciously mirror each other's stance. That same proud lift of the chin, that same coiled tension ready to explode into violence. Bianca stands just in front of Matteo, and the resemblance between all three of them makes something click in my mind—some puzzle piece I can't quite place.

"Some things never change," Mario says softly, his voice carrying decades of pain beneath its smooth surface. "The chosen son, the cast-off son. Though I suppose some choices were made long before either of us understood what they meant."

"We make our own choices now," Matteo responds, his hand protective on Bianca's shoulder.

"Do we?" Mario's smile is knowing, almost pitying. "Or are we still playing the roles he assigned us? Still protecting secrets that aren't even ours to keep?"

Mario is shoved out into the rain, but his words linger like smoke in the air. Once he's gone, Elena lets out a breath. "I don't understand. He seemed so ... when he stopped me outside my office, he was ..." Her voice carries a note of wonder that makes Matteo's head snap toward her with lethal precision.

"He seemed charming? Trustworthy?" Matteo's voice could cut glass. The sudden shift from protective husband to dangerous don makes Elena step back. "That's how he works. How he destroys people. First Sophia. Then using my twelve-year-old daughter as bait. Now trying to draw you in?" His eyes go cold in a way I've rarely seen directed at family. "Let me be very clear. Mario DeLuca is more dangerous than Johnny Calabrese ever dreamed of being. If I see you within fifty feet of him again, you'll be on the first plane out of New York. Permanently. Are we clear?"

The dismissal in his tone makes Elena flinch. I catch the flash of hurt in her eyes, quickly replaced by something harder—almost defiant. But before she can respond, Matteo dismisses her and Bianca with a curt nod that brooks no argument.

His hand finds my lower back as he guides me toward our rooms, but I can't shake the image of Elena's expression. Or the way Mario looked at her—like a man who'd just found another piece to play in his game.

Matteo's hand steady at my lower back as we climb the stairs towards our room. The familiar scent of our bedroom—sandalwood and leather and us—helps ease some of the tension from my shoulders, but I can't stop thinking about Elena's face. About how quickly fascination can turn to obsession in our world. About how Mario seemed to recognize that weakness instantly.

The adrenaline finally starts to fade, leaving me shaky. I can still feel the rifle's weight in my hands, still see Mario's blood blooming across his suit through my scope. Still hear the calculation in his voice when he spoke about family secrets. When he looked at Elena like she was a gift he hadn't expected.

Matteo's arms circle me before the spiral can pull me deeper. I fall into his embrace, my body sagging against his solid frame. His lips find mine, the kiss frantic, demanding, all teeth and tongue and the unspoken need to remind each other that we're alive, that we're here, that we're together.

"I could have killed him," I whisper against his mouth, the words trembling between us. "If I'd moved the scope two inches left ..."

"But you didn't." His hands frame my face, thumbs brushing away tears I didn't realize I was shedding. "You chose mercy. Chose to protect this family without becoming like him. Like Giuseppe."

I nod, but the words don't settle the ache in my chest. Matteo must see it in my eyes because his expression softens, his thumb tracing the curve of my cheek. "Let me take care of you," he murmurs, his voice low, almost pleading.

I nod again, and he kisses me once more, slower this time, but no less intense. His hands slip under my blouse, his fingers grazing the bare skin of my waist. The touch sends a shiver through me, and I gasp against his mouth. Matteo takes his time, peeling away my blouse and then my bra, exposing me to the light spilling through the windows.

He steps back, his gaze sweeping over me. "Beautiful," he breathes, his voice rough.

Before I can respond, he lowers himself, his lips finding the hollow of my throat, trailing soft, open-mouthed kisses down to my collarbone. His hands slide over my hips, deftly unfastening my pants and tugging them down along with my underwear. I step out of them, the cool air brushing over my bare skin as he stands and looks at me like I'm something sacred.

"You're perfect," he murmurs, his hands skimming up my sides before settling on my waist.

He guides me to the bed, sitting me down before he kneels between my thighs. My breath catches as his hands part my legs, his fingers trailing along the sensitive skin of my inner thighs. His eyes flick up to meet mine, holding my gaze as he presses a soft kiss just above my knee.

"Matteo ..." I whisper, my voice trembling with anticipation.

"Trust me, *piccola*," he says, his voice dark and commanding.

He doesn't wait for a reply. His lips blaze a trail up my thigh, each kiss growing closer to where I ache for him. When his mouth finally finds me, a strangled cry escapes my lips. The first touch of his tongue is electric, sending a jolt of pleasure straight through me.

Matteo takes his time, his mouth exploring me with an intensity that leaves me trembling. His hands hold my thighs apart, his grip firm but gentle as he devours me. He alternates between long, languid strokes of his tongue and gentle, focused pressure, drawing soft moans and gasps from me with every movement.

My hands find their way to his hair, tangling in the dark strands as my hips lift instinctively to meet him. "Please," I gasp, my voice breaking as the pleasure coils tighter and tighter inside me.

He hums against me, the vibration sending another wave of heat through my body. "Let go for me, Bella," he murmurs against my skin, his voice rough and full of promise.

It's all I need. My release crashes over me like a tidal wave, my back arching off the bed as a cry tears from my throat. Matteo doesn't stop, his mouth and hands guiding me through every pulse of pleasure until I'm trembling and breathless beneath him.

When I finally come down, he presses one last kiss to my inner thigh before rising. His lips are swollen, his eyes dark with desire as he leans over me. I pull him down, kissing him deeply, tasting myself on his lips. My hands work quickly, stripping him of his clothes until he's bare above me.

He presses himself against me, the heat of his body reigniting the fire that had barely begun to fade. "I need you," he whispers, his voice raw.

"You have me," I reply, my voice a breathless promise, my legs wrapping around his waist to draw him closer.

Matteo's gaze locks with mine as he aligns himself, the intensity in his eyes sending a shiver through me. When he finally pushes into me, it's slow and deliberate, every inch a careful, measured claim. The sensation is overwhelming—the stretch, the fullness—sending a ripple of pleasure through me that makes my breath hitch. A soft gasp escapes my lips as my body adjusts to him, the deep, perfect fit a testament to how we belong together.

He stills, his forehead pressing against mine, his breath warm and unsteady against my lips. For a moment, we stay like that, our bodies connected, our breathing synchronized as we absorb the depth of the moment. I can feel the rapid beat of his heart against my chest, mirroring my own, and it grounds me, filling the space between us with something raw and unspoken.

"You're mine," he murmurs, his voice low, rough, and possessive, but there's a tenderness in the way his lips brush over mine as he speaks, as though he's asking for something deeper.

"Always," I whisper back, my voice trembling with the weight of the truth in that word. My hands grip his shoulders, feeling the taut strength beneath my fingertips as he begins to move.

The first thrust is slow, deliberate, sending a wave of sensation through me that pulls a soft moan from my lips. He sets a steady rhythm, each motion unhurried but intense, his hips rolling into mine with a precision that leaves no space between us. Heat coils low in my belly, spreading outward as the friction builds, each movement lighting me up from the inside out.

I feel every inch of him, the warmth of his skin pressed against mine, the powerful muscles of his back shifting beneath my hands as he moves. His hands roam my body with purpose—gripping my hips to pull me closer, sliding up my sides to cup my face, his thumbs brushing over my cheeks with a gentleness that makes my chest ache.

The way he looks at me steals the air from my lungs. His eyes burn with an intensity that lays me bare, making me feel seen, cherished, and utterly his. My body responds instinctively, arching into him, meeting each thrust with a hunger that matches his.

The pleasure builds with a relentless intensity, every nerve ending alive with the sensation of him—his heat, his strength, the way his body molds to mine as though we were made for this. The coil in my belly tightens, my breath coming in shallow gasps as the pressure becomes almost too much to bear.

"Matteo," I gasp, his name a plea, a prayer, as my hands slide up to tangle in his hair, holding him close.

"I've got you," he whispers, his voice hoarse, his lips brushing against my ear. His movements quicken, his thrusts deeper, the angle sending sparks of pleasure through me that push me closer to the edge.

When my release finally crashes over me, it's like an unrelenting wave, pulling me under and leaving me trembling in its wake. My back arches, my body clenching around him as a broken cry of his name spills from my lips. The pleasure is overwhelming, consuming, and I cling to him as though he's the only thing keeping me from unraveling completely.

The sight of me coming undone pushes him over the edge. His

movements grow erratic, his hips pressing hard against mine as he groans against my neck, his body shuddering with the force of his release. I feel the heat of him spill into me, his breath ragged and uneven as he collapses against me, his weight grounding me in the aftermath of everything.

For a moment, the world fades away, leaving only the sound of our breathing and the steady thrum of his heartbeat against my chest. He doesn't pull away; instead, he wraps me in his arms, holding me close as though afraid to let go. His hand rests protectively over our growing child.

But Mario's words echo in my head—about choices and secrets, about the roles we play. About things that run in blood.

"Stop thinking so loud," Matteo murmurs, pulling me closer.

But I can't shake the feeling that some secrets run deeper than blood, some choices echo through generations. And this—Mario, Elena, the web of lies and family bonds we're all tangled in—is just the beginning.

33

MATTEO

Dawn breaks over Manhattan like spilled blood, painting the skyline in shades of crimson and gold. From my study window, I watch the city awaken—delivery trucks rumbling down empty streets, early commuters hurrying with coffee cups clutched like lifelines, the steady pulse of a world unaware that power shifted last night. Every shadow seems deeper this morning, every light somehow harsher.

Or maybe that's just what happens when you exile your brother. Again.

The Irish have already sent confirmation of Mario's arrival in Boston, their message carrying thinly veiled threats about consequences and broken alliances. The words sit heavy in my inbox: *Your brother's reception will match the hospitality he was shown in New York.*

The photo they attached shows Mario being escorted into O'Connor's compound, his shoulder bandaged but his spine straight. Even wounded, even defeated, he carries himself like a DeLuca.

Let them fucking threaten. Right now, my focus is entirely on the sleeping woman in our bed upstairs.

My wife. My miracle. My match in every way that matters. Bella's aim last night was perfect—precise enough to stop Mario without killing him. Just like her heart is strong enough to love me without fearing me.

Memories of last night assault me—Mario's blood blooming across his suit, Bella's steady hand with the rifle, the way Elena looked at my brother like he was something fascinating rather than lethal. The same way Sophia once looked at him, before everything went to hell. Before choices were made that still echo through generations.

I touch the turned-away photo on my desk, Giuseppe's face hidden but his presence still haunting every decision. Like father, like sons—always choosing who to cast out, who to protect, who to love.

"The Families are waiting for your statement," Antonio says from the doorway. His weathered face shows the strain of a sleepless night, his usually pristine suit slightly rumpled. Dark circles rim his eyes—he's been up all night coordinating with our Boston contacts, monitoring Mario's transport. "They want assurance that the threat is contained."

"The threat is never contained," I respond, turning from the window. The taste of copper lingers in my mouth, though I haven't eaten since yesterday. "We just change how we fight it."

"And how do we fight this one?" Antonio's voice carries a note of caution I've rarely heard from him. After thirty years of service, very little rattles my consigliere. But Mario has always been different—a snake we can't quite kill, a threat we can't fully eliminate. A brother I can't quite bring myself to destroy.

"By being stronger than they expect." I move to my desk, pulling up property records on multiple screens. Maps of Brooklyn glow blue in the dim morning light, each marker representing a piece of Mario's old territory. "I want it completely restructured. New businesses, new management, new everything. Leave the Irish nothing to work with."

"Already in progress." Antonio's tablet lights up with plans, his fingers moving swiftly across the surface. He pauses, something like concern flickering across his features. "But Boss ... there's something else. Elena's been asking questions. About Mario."

My jaw clenches as I remember the way my brother looked at

Bella's best friend yesterday, that calculating interest I recognized too well. I'd once looked at Bella the same way—like a fascinating puzzle to solve, a weakness to exploit. But where my interest grew into love, Mario only knows how to destroy what he desires.

The anger in Elena's eyes when I ordered her away concerns me more than her fascination. That kind of defiance in our world usually ends one of two ways—submission or destruction. And Elena has never been one to submit.

She's like Bella in that way—danger hidden behind beauty.

"Increase her security detail," I order. "Quietly. And get me everything on her contact with the Calabrese family. Especially Anthony." His interest in Elena takes on new significance now. One more thread in this web of alliances and betrayals we're all tangled in.

"You think they're connected?" Surprise colors Antonio's tone.

"I think nothing in our world happens by coincidence." Mario's words echo in my head—about Bella being "more interesting" than Sophia. The comparison makes something dark curl in my gut. Sophia was a pawn, a means to an end. But Bella? She's a queen on this chessboard, powerful in her own right. If Mario sees similar potential in Elena ... "And I think my brother's already planning his next move."

A soft knock interrupts us. Bianca enters, already dressed in leggings and an oversized NYU sweatshirt that makes her look more college student than high school student. I hate it.

But there's tension in her shoulders, worry in her eyes that makes my pulse spike.

"Dad? Bella's asking for you. She's ..." My daughter hesitates, and that small pause sends ice through my veins. Bianca never hesitates. Not unless something's truly wrong. "She's not feeling well."

I'm moving before she finishes speaking, taking the stairs two at a time. Every worst-case scenario plays through my mind—complications from the pregnancy, delayed reaction to last night's stress, Mario's final act of revenge. My security training catalogs the minutes until my private doctor can arrive, the distance to the nearest hospital, the safest routes through morning traffic.

Each step feels too slow, memories of other losses threatening to overwhelm me. Not again. I can't lose the woman I love. Can't watch another family shatter like glass.

I find Bella in our bathroom, huddled over the toilet. Her dark hair spills around her shoulders, and her skin has taken on a sickly pallor that makes my heart clench. One of my shirts drowns her small frame.

"I'm fine," she manages between waves of nausea, but I see the shadows under her eyes, the slight tremor in her hands. Yesterday took more from her than she'll admit—the weight of the sniper rifle, the burden of choice, the constant strain of protecting our family. Our child.

"Come here, *piccola*." I sit on the bathroom floor, pulling her between my legs so her back rests against my chest as relief pours through me. The marble is cold beneath us, but her body burns hot against mine. One hand splays protectively over her stomach while the other holds back her hair. Every breath she takes helps calm my racing heart. She's here. She's safe. They both are.

"Some donna I am," she mutters, leaning back into me. Her body trembles slightly, though whether from sickness or exhaustion, I'm not sure. "Can't even keep breakfast down."

"You're exactly the donna I need." I press my lips to her temple, tasting salt on her skin. My heart still hasn't quite settled from the panic of moments ago. The fear of losing her—of losing them both—sits like ice in my chest. "Strong enough to wound my brother, wise enough not to kill him, brave enough to carry our child in this dangerous world."

She relaxes slightly against me, her body molding to mine like she was made to fit there. The persistent shaking begins to ease as I run my hand up and down her arm. But even through her exhaustion, her mind never stops working. Never stops protecting.

"Speaking of dangerous ... I can't stop thinking about Elena's face when she watched Mario leave. The way she looked at him ..."

"I know." My arms tighten around her instinctively. The memory of Elena's fascinated expression, so like Sophia's once was, makes something cold settle in my chest. How many times will I watch this pattern repeat? How many women will my brother destroy before he's satisfied? "Antonio's handling it."

"Like you handled me?" There's a smile in her voice despite her discomfort. "Watching from afar, protecting without revealing yourself?"

"That was different." How can she compare us?

"Was it?" She turns in my embrace, and even pale and shaking, she takes my breath away. Those artist's eyes see too much, understand too well. "Or did you recognize something in me that you needed? Like Elena might see something in Mario?"

The parallel makes my blood run cold. Because she's right—I'd watched her for years, drawn to her strength and artistry, her ability to straddle both worlds even as she tried her best to reject this world. If Mario sees similar qualities in Elena ...

"He's dangerous," I say finally, the words tasting like ash. "More dangerous than I ever was."

"Because he has nothing left to lose?" Her fingers trace my jaw with an artist's precision. "Or because he finally sees something worth fighting for?"

Before I can respond, her body jerks as another wave of nausea hits. She pushes away from me, turning back to the toilet. I hold her through it, murmuring soft Italian endearments against her hair. Each heave feels like a knife in my chest—this fierce woman reduced to vulnerability because she carries our child.

When it passes, she says quietly, "We can't control who they choose to love. Elena or Bianca or this little one." Her hand covers mine over our child. "We can only be there when they need us. Like my father was for me."

"Your father led you straight to me," I remind her with a slight smile.

"No." She kisses me softly, and I taste the truth in her words. "He just made sure I was strong enough to choose my own path. And it led me here anyway."

The bathroom door creaks open to reveal Bianca with a cup of peppermint tea. The sharp, clean scent cuts through the sour air of sickness. She takes in our position on the floor without comment, simply sliding down to sit beside us. In this moment, she looks so much like me it hurts—that same protective instinct, that same ability to mask emotion.

"The Families are demanding a meeting," Bianca reports, handing Bella the tea. Steam curls up between them, fragrant and soothing. "They want to know what happens next."

I study my unlikely family—my daughter who carries my heart, my brave wife growing our child beneath her heart, both of them stronger than anyone could have predicted. Both of them worth everything I've sacrificed, everything I'll still have to sacrifice.

"What happens next," I say softly, "is we protect what matters. Everything else is just details."

Bella's hand finds mine as Bianca leans against us both. The weight of both my girls grounds me, reminds me what I'm fighting for. Outside, the city awakens to a new reality—one where the DeLuca family is stronger than ever, bound by choice rather than blood.

But in the back of my mind, Mario's words echo like a warning: *"Family is such a fragile thing, isn't it? So easily ... broken."* The way he looked at Elena, the secrets still buried in our past, the baby growing beneath my hand—so many vulnerabilities, so many ways this happiness could shatter.

The Irish will move against us eventually. Elena's fascination with Mario could lead to complications. And somewhere in Boston, my brother plans his next move, patient as a snake waiting to strike.

I press a kiss to Bella's temple, breathing in her jasmine scent beneath the lingering traces of sickness. "You should rest today. Both of you." My hand spreads wider over where our child grows, still amazed that something so precious could come from my darkness.

"We're fine," Bella insists, rolling her eyes, but she doesn't resist when I help her stand. "Just normal pregnancy stuff."

"Nothing about this pregnancy will be normal," Bianca says, her voice carrying that DeLuca steel. "Not with the Irish making threats,

Elena asking dangerous questions, and Mario ..." She trails off, but we all hear the unspoken concerns.

"Which is why we adapt," I say, guiding Bella back to our bed. "We strengthen our defenses, watch our vulnerabilities, protect what matters most."

"And Elena?" Bella asks as I tuck her under the covers. "She won't just let this go, Matteo. I know her."

"Then we make sure she understands the stakes." But even as I say it, I remember how fascination can override self-preservation. How love—or what we think is love—can blind us to danger. "Like I said, Antonio's increasing her security. Beyond that ..."

"Beyond that, she makes her own choices," Bella finishes. "Like I did."

"And look how well that turned out," Bianca quips, but there's real affection in her voice now when she looks at her stepmother.

A different kind of family, built from broken pieces and careful choices. Not what Giuseppe would have wanted, but stronger for it. Better.

Let the Irish plot. Let Elena chase dangerous fascinations. Let the Families demand their answers.

Right now, I almost believe we're invincible. That love really can conquer blood feuds and old wounds. That choice matters more than genetics.

But Mario's last words echo in my mind, a shadow across the morning light: *"Family is such a fragile thing, isn't it? So easily ... broken."*

EPILOGUE: BELLA

One month after Mario's exile, I stand in my studio examining my latest piece—a triptych commissioned by the Families as a show of support for Matteo's leadership. Early morning light streams through the floor-to-ceiling windows, catching on still-wet oils and making the gold leaf glimmer like fire. Three panels depicting power, protection, and family, rendered in my signature style but with new depth. The shadows are darker now, the lights brighter—every brushstroke reflecting the complexity of the world I've chosen.

In the first panel, a don stands before his empire, face turned away but power radiating from every line. Matteo's stance, though I've obscured his features. The second shows a mother shielding her child, the gesture both protective and fierce. The third, and most complex, depicts a family emerging from darkness into light. Three figures that could be us—father, mother, daughter—but could also represent any family choosing love over blood.

My hand drifts to my slight baby bump as I study the work. At ten weeks, it's barely visible to others, but I feel the changes in how I move, how I see, how I create. Every piece I paint now carries the weight of legacy.

"It's not like your thesis work at all."

I turn to find Elena studying the paintings, dressed impeccably in a Chanel suit. There's something different about her—not just the designer clothes or the perfect makeup, but a new edge to her presence. A hardness that wasn't there before Mario.

Her heels click against the hardwood as she moves closer, each step precise and measured. She's thrown herself into work since that night, taking on even more responsibility within the Family structure. Getting deeper into the life she once helped me try to escape.

But now I wonder if she's getting deeper into it for the wrong reasons.

"Everything's different now," I respond, watching how the morning light plays across the still-wet paint. I watch how she studies the central figure. Her gaze lingers too long on the shadows I've painted around him, like she's searching for something. Or someone.

The slight swell of my stomach beneath my paint-stained smock reminds me just how much has changed in such a short time. "We're different."

"Are we?" Elena moves closer, her perfectly manicured finger tracing the air near the panel. Her designer perfume—Clive Christian this time, replacing her usual Chanel—mingles with the scent of oils and turpentine. There's something almost accusatory in her tone when she adds, "Or are we just finally becoming who we were always meant to be? Who we're allowed to be?"

The slight emphasis on "allowed" makes my skin prickle. As does the way she's been studying my paintings—not with her usual appreciation for art, but with calculation. Like she's looking for hidden meanings. Messages.

The question holds weight beyond the obvious. I study my best friend's face, remembering how she looked watching Mario leave. That dangerous pull toward power that seems to run in DeLuca blood. "And who are you meant to be, E?"

"I don't know yet." Elena's smile doesn't quite reach her eyes, though her lipstick is perfect MAC Russian Red. The same shade she wore at my wedding, now stained with new meaning. "But I'm tired of being the scared little event planner everyone underestimates."

"Being underestimated can be useful." I set down my brush, the silver ring Matteo gave me catching the light. Not Sophia's emeralds—never those—but something new, something ours. "It's how I got close enough to shoot Mario."

"About that ..." Elena hesitates, her fingers playing with her Cartier bracelet—a nervous tell I've known since college. "People are talking. About why you didn't kill him."

"Let them talk." I turn back to my painting, adding another layer of shadow to the central figure. Every brushstroke feels weighted with meaning now.

"They say it was weakness. Mercy where there should have been justice." Elena's voice carries an edge I've never heard before—something almost like disappointment.

"No." Matteo's voice carries from the doorway, making us both turn. He stands there like something from a Renaissance painting, power and danger wrapped in an expertly tailored Tom Ford suit. Bianca's at his side, looking more like him than ever in her dark blazer and confident stance. "They say it was strength. The kind of strength our world rarely sees."

He moves to me with that lethal grace that still makes my heart skip, his hand automatically finding my stomach. The warmth of his palm through my smock grounds me, reminds me what we're fighting for. What we've built from broken pieces and careful choices.

"The Families have accepted your leadership completely," Elena reports, all business now though her eyes linger on my paintings. "The show of mercy, followed by absolute control of Mario's territory ... it sent the right message."

"And what message is that?" Bianca asks, studying Elena with those steel-blue eyes that mirror her father's. She's positioned herself slightly between Elena and us—protective even now, even here.

"That the DeLuca family is stronger than blood. That choice and loyalty matter more than genetics or tradition." Elena's voice carries something like longing that makes my stomach clench. "That love doesn't make you weak."

The words hang in the air between us, heavy with implication.

We all hear what she's not saying—how closely she's been following Mario's movements in Boston, how many questions she's asked about his exile. How hunger for power can disguise itself as love.

"Speaking of messages," Bianca interjects, moving to examine the central panel. Morning light catches her profile, highlighting how much she looks like Matteo when she's analyzing a threat. "Anthony Calabrese has been asking about you."

Elena's expression shutters faster than a camera flash. "He's not my type."

"No," I say quietly. "He's not dangerous enough, is he?"

Her sharp look confirms everything. Matteo's hand tightens on my waist—he sees it too. The fascination brewing, the potential for history to repeat itself in the worst possible way. The same pattern of beauty drawn to danger, of power masquerading as love.

"The Families are gathering tonight," he says, changing the subject though tension still ripples beneath his controlled tone. "Time to present your work, *piccola*."

"Time to show them the new face of our world," Bianca adds with pride, but her eyes never leave Elena. Bianca's seen too much, lost too much, to trust easily anymore.

I look at my paintings—at the family I've depicted emerging from darkness into light. At the strength I've captured in every brushstroke, every layer of meaning. "Not new," I correct, understanding settling into my bones. "Just finally seen clearly."

As we prepare to leave, Elena holds me back for a moment. Something in her expression sets off warning bells—that same look she had when watching Mario leave. "They say Mario asks about you. About the baby."

My blood turns cold at her casual mention of him. At the implication that she's hearing things she shouldn't be hearing. "And how would you know what Mario says?" My voice carries an edge that makes her flinch slightly.

Elena's perfect composure slips for just a second—long enough for me to catch a flash of defiance. Of resentment. "People talk, B. Especially when Matteo gives orders like he did that night."

The reference to how Matteo dismissed her makes my spine stiffen. This is my husband she's criticizing—the father of my child, the man who's protected us all. "He was right to say what he said. Mario is dangerous, E. More dangerous than Johnny ever was."

"Of course," she says smoothly, but something in her tone suggests she doesn't agree. That perhaps she sees Matteo as the dangerous one. "Family first, right? Isn't that what we're all supposed to believe?"

"No." I step back, creating distance between us for the first time in our friendship. "Love first. Truth first. Loyalty first." *Not betrayal*, I think but don't say. *Not secrets and whispered conversations about Mario.*

We join Matteo and Bianca and prepare to face the Families, show our unity. My hand finds my husband's. He's right to be wary of Elena's fascination. Right to protect us from Mario's influence.

My hand drifts to where our child grows. Still too small to make its presence known, but already changing everything. Already teaching me what really matters.

Family. Choice. Love.

Everything else is just details.

EXTENDED EPILOGUE

Mario

Boston's winter wind cuts across the harbor, but I don't feel the cold. Pain is an old friend by now—like the constant ache in my shoulder where my sister-in-law's bullet struck two months ago. My fingers trace the scar through Italian silk. Such precision in her aim. Such mercy. Such a fascinating combination of strength and weakness.

So like my brother, to find a woman who matches him in both power and foolish compassion.

The surveillance photos spread across my mahogany desk tell their own story, each one a piece in my growing collection: Here's Bella at her art show, playing donna like she was born to it—but I see the paint still staining her fingers, the artist trying to become what Matteo needs. Another photo shows my brother's hand possessive on her slight baby bump—always so protective, dear Matteo. Always so sure he can keep what's his.

As if our father failed to teach us that nothing is truly ours forever.

Bianca stands tall beside them, and oh, if she only knew the truth about her parentage. The delicious irony of her DeLuca bearing, carrying secrets in her very blood that would destroy everything my brother has built.

But it's the fourth figure that holds my attention. Elena Santiago—always slightly apart, always watching. Such hunger in her eyes, such barely contained rage. The photo captures her perfectly: designer suit armor-like in its precision, spine straight with suppressed defiance.

She reminds me of myself at that age, watching Matteo inherit everything while I got nothing. The perfect son. The worthy heir. If only they knew what that perfection cost.

"O'Connor's getting impatient," my lieutenant reports, shuffling like a nervous dog. The Irish—so predictable in their blunt ambitions. So limited in their vision. "He wants to know when we move on Brooklyn."

"We don't." I keep my voice soft, the way our father taught us. The quieter the voice, the more dangerous the threat. Another lesson Matteo learned too well. "Not yet."

"But the territory—"

"Was never the point." I pick up a particular photo—Elena watching them load me into the transport, something like recognition in her eyes. The same look I used to see in mirrors, watching Matteo play the perfect son. I recognize that hunger, that need to prove oneself more than what others see. "The point is family. Always has been."

My phone buzzes with a message from an unknown number, though I've memorized it by now: *Your brother increased my security. Again.*

Worried about you, little planner? I text back, already knowing how she'll respond. Elena is so wonderfully predictable in her defiance. So perfectly positioned to be both sword and shield in what's to come.

Her response is immediate: *Worried about what I know.*

A smile curves my lips. Of course she's been digging—into my past, into Sophia's death, into all the carefully buried secrets the DeLuca family would rather forget. She's smart, my brother's wife's best friend. Smart enough to be dangerous. Hungry enough to be useful.

Beautiful enough to be believable as just another society girl with more ambition than sense.

"The Irish want assurances," my lieutenant pushes, like a child demanding attention. "About your commitment to—"

"To what?" I cut him off, bored already with his limited vision. "To being their attack dog? Their tool for taking New York?" I stand, moving to the window overlooking the harbor. Gray waves match gray skies—a perfect canvas for the chaos to come. "I have my own plans."

My phone buzzes again—another photo from my network in New York. This one shows Bella leaving her doctor's appointment, Matteo hovering like an anxious shadow. Always protecting, always controlling. Just like with Bianca, just like with Sophia. My brother never learned that the tighter you hold something, the more likely it is to shatter.

The next shot makes my blood sing: Elena trailing them at a distance, watching, learning. Such a good student, this one. So eager to prove herself more than just the event planner, the best friend, the girl on the sidelines. She moves through their world like a ghost, seeing everything while being seen as nothing. Perfect.

Careful, little planner, I text her. ***Curiosity can be dangerous.***

So can underestimating me, comes her reply.

I laugh softly, the sound echoing in my empty office. She's right, of course. Everyone underestimates Elena Santiago—just like they underestimated me. The spare son, the exile, the brother who wasn't good enough. Matteo's greatest weakness has always been his arrogance, his certainty that he knows best. That he can control everything and everyone around him. He sees Elena as just another potential threat to neutralize, never considering she might be the weapon that finally brings him down.

"Sir?" My lieutenant shifts uncomfortably, reminding me of his presence. "O'Connor's calling a meeting. He wants to discuss the Brooklyn situation."

"Tell him I'll be there." I don't look away from the harbor, from the city that was almost mine. Will be mine. "And get me everything on the Santiago family. All of it."

"The event planner? But she's not—"

"She's more important than any of them realize." I pick up the photo of Elena again, studying how she watched me that day. Such recognition in her eyes, such hunger. "She's the key to everything."

My phone lights up with another message: *Your brother talks about you sometimes. About who you were before. Who you could have been.*

I trace my fingers over her words, imagining her typing them in secret, probably from some dark corner of the DeLuca compound. Like a viper in their garden, beautiful and deadly. My response is careful, measured: *And what do you think, Elena? About who I could be?*

Her answer makes something dark unfurl in my chest: *I think you're exactly who you're meant to be. The question is ... am I?*

I save the message, adding the photos to my growing collection. Each one a piece in the game Matteo doesn't even know he's playing yet.

Elena's right—we're both becoming exactly who we're meant to be. She'll be my sword, just as Sophia was once my shield. But where Sophia was weak, Elena burns with that same fire that consumes me. That need to prove ourselves more than what others see.

Looking out over the harbor toward New York, I allow myself to imagine it: Elena by my side, as sharp and dangerous as I am. The way she'll slip past Matteo's defenses, turn their trust into weakness. The look on Matteo's face when he realizes his closest allies have become his greatest threats. The way everything he loves will crumble, piece by carefully orchestrated piece.

"Family first," I murmur to the darkness, touching the scar Bella's bullet left. A reminder of mercy that will prove to be their greatest mistake. "Isn't that right, brother?"

My phone buzzes one last time. Elena again: *They're celebrating tonight. The baby, the art show, their perfect little family. Wish you could see it.*

My smile turns cruel as I respond: *Oh, little planner. I see everything. And soon, so will you.*

Because that's the thing about family—it's not about blood or loyalty or choice. It's about power. About who's willing to take it, to wield it, to burn everything down to claim it.

And I've always been very, very good at playing with fire.

Ready to dive into Mario and Elena's story? Get your copy here.

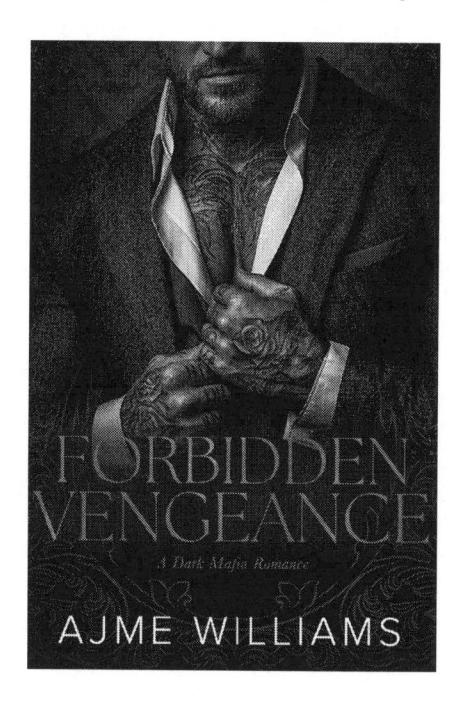

WANT MORE AJME WILLIAMS?

Join my no spam mailing list here.

You'll only be sent emails about my new releases, extended epilogues, deleted scenes and occasional FREE books.

Printed in Great Britain
by Amazon